WHO DARES?

"This is exhilarating," the king said. "Exhilarating." He pulled off his gloves and shrugged his shoulders, adjusting the cloak of the Guard.

"I am gratified to h——————————————d. "I trust you are hold——————————

"It's like a hunt," ———————————————at there is no quarry."

Richelieu didn't a———————————————*re is a quarry, my king*, he though——————————*es.*

"Do you think she has given birth yet?"

"It is difficult to say, Majesty. If she began her labor early in the morning, it would be close now. I directed Léonore d'Étampes de Valençay, my lord bishop of Chartres, to attend the queen. If there is any trouble at Baronville, he will be a good one to have on hand."

"Trouble? What sort of trouble?"

"I expect none . . . but I am inclined to be careful, Sire."

"That is most wise, my friend. I—"

Somewhere nearby in the foggy gloom there was the sound of a high-pitched whistle.

"What was that?"

"I am not sure," Richelieu said. He turned away from the king and signaled to the captain of his guard.

And then, as if it were a passage from a costumed drama, a score of mounted men, hooded and weapons drawn, burst from the wood on either side. The scene erupted into chaos. Those Guards who had not dismounted urged their horses into the fight, moving to form a protective ring around Richelieu and the king.

"Who dares to attack thus?" Richelieu shouted. He stretched out his hand and drew a flintlock pistol from his saddlebags.

"Don't worry," Louis said. "There is not a bandit alive whom I cannot best in combat." He ran a half-dozen steps and swung himself up onto his horse, drawing a sabre and placing himself in the path of a handful of oncoming attackers.

ERIC FLINT'S BEST-SELLING RING OF FIRE SERIES

1632 by Eric Flint

1633 with David Weber

1634: The Baltic War with David Weber

1634: The Galileo Affair with Andrew Dennis

1634: The Bavarian Crisis with Virginia DeMarce

1634: The Ram Rebellion with Virginia DeMarce et al

1635: The Cannon Law with Andrew Dennis

1635: The Dreeson Incident with Virginia DeMarce

1635: The Eastern Front

1635: The Papal Stakes with Charles E. Gannon

1636: The Saxon Uprising

1636: The Kremlin Games with
Gorg Huff & Paula Goodlett

1636: The Devil's Opera with David Carrico

1636: Commander Cantrell in the West Indies with
Charles E. Gannon

1636: The Viennese Waltz with
Gorg Huff & Paula Goodlett

1636: The Cardinal Virtues with Walter Hunt

1635: A Parcel of Rogues with Andrew Dennis

Grantville Gazette I–V, ed. Eric Flint

Grantville Gazette VI–VII, ed. Eric Flint & Paula Goodlett

Ring of Fire I–IV, ed. Eric Flint

1635: The Tangled Web by Virginia DeMarce

1636: Seas of Fortune by Iver P. Cooper

1636: The Chronicles of Doctor Gribbleflotz by
Kerryn Offord & Rick Boatright (forthcoming)

Time Spike with Marilyn Kosmatka

**To order these and other Baen titles in e-book
form, go to www.baen.com**

1636
THE CARDINAL
VIRTUES

ERIC FLINT
WALTER H. HUNT

1636: THE CARDINAL VIRTUES

A Baen Books Original

Baen Publishing Enterprises
P.O. Box 1403, Riverdale, NY 10471
www.baen.com

ISBN: 978-1-4767-8169-3

Cover art by Tom Kidd
Maps by Michael Knopp

First Baen paperback printing, August 2016.

Library of Congress Cataloging-in-Publication Data

Flint, Eric.
  1636 : the Cardinal virtues / Eric Flint and Walter H. Hunt.
      pages ; cm. — (Ring of fire ; 19)
  ISBN 978-1-4767-8061-0 (hardcover : acid-free paper) 1.
Louis XIII, King of France, 1601-1643—Fiction. 2. Richelieu,
Armand Jean du Plessis, duc de, 1585-1642—Fiction. 3. Time
travel—Fiction. 4. France—History—17th century—Fiction. 5.
West Virginia—History—17th century—Fiction. I. Hunt, Walter
H. II. Title. III. Title: Cardinal virtues.
  PS3556.L548A618669 2015
  813'.54—dc23
                                                    2015009697

Distributed by Simon & Schuster
1230 Avenue of the Americas
New York, NY 10020

Pages by Joy Freeman (www.pagesbyjoy.com)
Printed in the United States of America

To Lisa

I hope you like my first venture
beyond the Ring of Fire

Contents

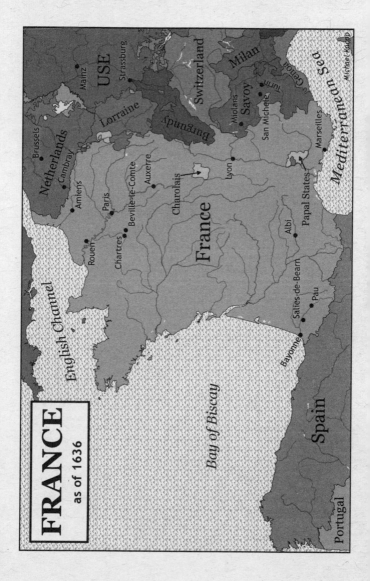

FRANCE
as of 1636

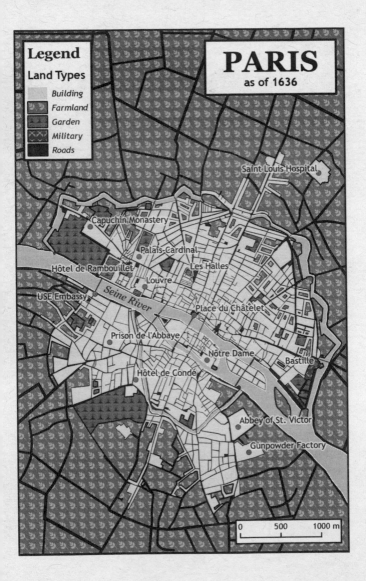

Legend

Land Types

- Building
- Farmland
- Garden
- Military
- Roads

PARIS
as of 1636

Saint Louis Hospital

Capuchin Monastery

Palais-Cardinal

Les Halles

Hôtel de Rambouillet

Louvre

USE Embassy

Seine River

Place du Châtelet

Prison de l'Abbaye

Nôtre Dame

Bastille

Hôtel de Condé

Abbey of St. Victor

Gunpowder Factory

0   500   1000 m

Prologue

Chapter 1

Late July, 1635
Outside of Paris, France

The need for secrecy was constant. No one believed that more strongly than Armand-Jean du Plessis, Cardinal-Duke de Richelieu, Principal Minister to His Most Christian Majesty Louis XIII, king of France. Within the palace of the Louvre as well as at his own residence, the *Palais-Cardinal*, secrets were guarded most jealously. They were a valuable commodity, esteemed by the cardinal and protected by those who surrounded him—those particular to the crown and those plucked from other nations.

However, the secret now contemplated was too sensitive even for those protected within the halls of king and cardinal; an even more private venue was required. Thus it was that when the king of France rode to the hunt on a sultry, humid July morning, his entourage included his minister astride a fine horse, riding at his side.

3

The courtiers and servants gossiped about it among themselves—quietly, of course, out of the sight and hearing of their betters. Whenever the searching glance of Cardinal Richelieu settled upon them they fell silent and avoided his eyes.

For his part, King Louis—always at greater ease on the hunt than at court—was pleased to have his minister by his side. Those usually accorded the privilege of taking up the position had to remain at a respectful distance.

The morning was not productive, the hounds and beaters flushing only inferior prey: a few rabbits and foxes, nothing worthy of His Majesty's attention. But it was the hunt itself and not the results that pleased the king. Toward midday Louis called a halt. The royal stewards began the process of laying out a repast for the gently-born in a beautiful clearing, while grooms attended to their mounts.

Minister and king walked away from the crowd, seeming to enjoy the scenery. But far from the court and away from prying ears, their conversation turned to more serious manners.

"I trust all is in—in readiness," the king said.

"I am pleased to say that it is, Majesty. We have secured the Château de Baronville in Beville-le-Comte for the queen's use during her seclusion; and I have engaged the services of an up-timer physician."

"Is he anyone I know?"

"*She*, Majesty. And no, I do not believe that you are acquainted with her. She is a distant relative of the Masaniello family."

"The Steam Engine people."

"Exactly, Sire. She has put certain up-timer protocols

into practice that have caused marked improvement in the health of the technical center employees. The queen will be in good hands."

"Their midwives qualify as physicians also?"

"Up-timers," Richelieu said in response, as if that was sufficient explanation.

"Is my lady wife prepared?"

Richelieu permitted himself the slightest smile. "I daresay that her work does not come until somewhat later. The other participant in the event is ready to do his duty, however. He will be at the Château Fontainebleau, where you and Queen Anne will be making a progress."

"When?"

"Whenever you are ready, Sire, but if I may suggest that the Feast of Saint Louis—the twenty-fifth of August—might be a propitious occasion."

"Our noble ancestor and namesake. We can hear Mass and wave royally. At least it's less unpleasant than Saint Denis. The sight of some peasant dressed as the saint, carrying a plaster head under his arm, always disturbed me."

"As Your Majesty says," Richelieu said. "The people will enjoy being reminded of the divinity of kingship."

Louis shrugged. "As *you* say. So—the Feast of Saint Louis it is. You will inform Queen Anne that we shall progress to Fontainebleau. But . . . why not, why not simply complete the matter at Baronville?"

"Ah." Richelieu removed a speck of dust from his soutane. "I would think, Sire, that we would prefer the location to remain secret, to be used when Her Majesty is more advanced in her pregnancy. There is no reason to reveal it sooner."

"Yes. Quite—quite correct. You have been most thorough, Monseigneur."

"I thank you, Sire." Richelieu inclined his head. "I seek only to serve; and in this instance I wish to leave nothing to chance."

"Nothing . . . other than the occasion itself. And that is in the hands of God." He crossed himself and looked upward.

Richelieu followed the gesture, but refrained to mention to the king the many methods the up-timers knew about to help assure success.

"God will smile upon France, I am certain," he said after a moment.

Chapter 2

August, 1635
Paris

On the morning of the Feast of Saint Louis, the king of France awoke in the darkness. He was unable to sleep any longer. By the time he rose and shrugged into his robe, his ever-attentive valet Beringhien was already in his bedchamber, building up the fire to help his master ward off the unexpected late summer chill.

Beringhien knew better than to ask Louis why he was up and about at this hour. The king had long since ceased to observe the hours an adult man would normally keep. The *lever* and the *coucher* took place at the appointed times, so that the gentlemen who had the honor of assisting with the royal robing and disrobing could be present as needed. But what took place behind the door of the king's cabinet was entirely different.

This was a special morning. Beringhien had laid out some of the king's wardrobe when he retired just before Matins, and as soon as he dealt with the fireplace he retired without a word to complete the task, leaving Louis to attend to his duty with the chamber pot.

In his dressing chamber, the king yawned, removing his robe and dropping it on the ground so that he could stand in his small-clothes. As he noted the attire that his valet had chosen he favored Beringhien with a slight smile. Even in the chilly predawn dark it warmed the valet's heart to see it. So little brought his royal master to smile these days, with the press of duty and the swirl of intrigues and the weight of the crown upon Louis' brow.

"Send word to Father Caussin that I desire to have him hear my confession," the king said when he was done. "And present my respects to my lady, my lady the queen and inform her that I wish to call upon her when she is ready to receive me."

"Majesty—" Beringhien began to reply, and then saw the expression on his master's face: excitement, tinged perhaps with impatience. "Sire. It is two hours before dawn."

"You do not think that my confessor will be ready to serve me at this hour?"

"No, Sire . . . but the queen . . ."

"When my spiritual duty is done she shall receive me. See to it, see to it," he said, waving the valet off.

"As you wish, Your Majesty," Beringhien answered, and bowed himself out of the king's presence.

The stern voice of Père Nicolas Caussin, the king's Jesuit confessor, pronounced the absolution upon the king as he knelt in the confessional. After a few polite words thanking His Majesty for his piety and his goodness in setting an example, Caussin withdrew from his side of the screen, leaving the king alone.

The king offered up a private prayer and rose, stepping back into his private chapel, and then made his way along a corridor, just beginning to brighten with the first rays of sunlight. Three of his gentlemen-in-waiting kept a respectful distance from the king as they followed. In the distance, the first lauds-bells were chiming across the city, calling the faithful to prayer.

Presently he came to the apartments in the Louvre set aside for the queen. The outer door was already open. As he walked through, he received a low bow from François de Crussol, the duke of Uzès, gentleman-in-ordinary to the queen. He was of an age with the king and had been in Anne's service for a dozen years, attending her before and at the *lever*—when she rose from bed and emerged to greet her courtiers. He had received word from Beringhien, and though he appeared to have scarcely performed his morning toilet, was alert and ready to receive the king.

"Sire," Uzès said. "Her Majesty humbly begs her pardon as she is not yet ready to receive you, but asked that I present you in just a few minutes."

"Very well, very well. It is—it is quite early."

"Indeed so, my lord. I trust you rested well, Sire?"

"I could hardly sleep. A great day, a great day, Uzès." The king shifted from foot to foot, then turned suddenly to his entourage. "My good *gentilhommes*, your service is not required—I shall call for you at once if you are needed."

The three young noblemen offered deep bows and withdrew, scarcely concealing their delight in being released from the royal presence. They knew not to stray far, since the king's mood might suddenly change, but they were clearly eager to be away from his sight.

The king turned again. "And how do you, Monsieur le duc? Are you well this fine day?"

"I thank Your Majesty for asking. I am quite well."

"And the queen?"

"I believe she does well also. I—"

His reply was interrupted by the opening of the inner door of the chamber and the appearance of Marie-Aimée de Rohan, the duchess of Chevreuse, the principal lady-in-waiting for the queen. The king disliked the duchess. At one time they had been very close, when she was married to Charles d'Albert, duc de Luynes—the king's falconer and favorite, who had died fifteen years before. Since then she had descended into various intrigues, primarily aimed at Cardinal Richelieu. She had even been dismissed and exiled at one point, only to be reinstated earlier this year at the request of his queen.

As in so many things, Louis felt that circumstances had trapped him into such a decision—but it would soon be of no matter.

"Madame," the king said, removing his hat. "Is Her Majesty ready to receive me?"

"Yes, Sire," the duchess answered. "She has just risen from her bed and made her morning prayer. She begs to receive you in her cabinet."

"Splendid, splendid," Louis said. "I would speak with her alone."

The duchess de Chevreuse let one eyebrow drift upward, as if it were the strangest thing in the world for husband and wife—king and queen—to be alone together. But she had no inclination to gainsay her sovereign, and merely stood aside as the king entered the chamber. Uzès remained without, and the duchess closed the door behind her and looked at him.

"Do you have any idea—" she began.

"I have found that it is best not to ask, madame," the duke answered. "I am sure that if it is intended that I know, that I shall learn in due time."

"Aren't you the least bit curious?"

"Do you wish the polite answer or the truth?"

"The truth, of course."

"I am insanely curious. The king here, at dawn? I have no idea why he might come, and then seek private audience with our mistress. But it is his right. Perhaps they want to—"

"On a feast-day? Really, François—"

The duke shrugged, with a slight smile at her shocked look. He thought she was being quite disingenuous. When they were much younger they had both seen the loose morality of the court when Louis' father was king. There had been eight *légitimés*, the recognized offspring of Henry IV with his various mistresses, and God only knew how many other by-blows that had never been brought to court.

"The calendar is stuffed with feast-days, Marie. I rather think the saints turn a blind eye to it all."

She gave him another shocked look, which he continued to disregard. She reached for the door handle as if preparing to stalk back into the queen's inner chambers, then, realizing the order for privacy, let her hand drop to her side, and settled with as much dignity as she could manage into a chair.

❖   ❖   ❖

Louis stood just inside the doorway for several seconds. Anne—who at court was called *Anne of Austria* though she was a Spanish princess—his wife of more than twenty years, sat at her toilet-table, her back to him; her long tresses lay loosely on her shoulders rather than being bundled up in a *chignon* or elaborately pinned in a coiffure, as she preferred and as court style demanded. She was dressed in a long plain underdress, and was examining herself in the mirrors at the back of the table.

She had seen him there; but it was some sort of game for her to pretend she had not. At another time, with an audience, this was something she might have prolonged to keep him waiting—to make sure he understood that he moved in *her* realm, that in these rooms he followed an orbit around her rather than she about him. But the time for such artifice and entertainment was past, if indeed it had ever been the true course she had wished to follow.

"Madame, I—"

"Sire." She turned on her backless chair, affecting to see him for the first time, and allowed herself to fall to one knee. "I beg your pardon. I did not hear you come in."

"It is nothing. A few moments." In a few steps he was before her and extended his hand, which she took. He assisted her to rise.

"I do not wish Your Majesty to think me discourteous or ill-bred." She smiled.

"I could not imagine such an accusation. You are my queen, my betrothed, and . . ." It was his turn to smile. "A true daughter of Hapsburg. I am pleased that you would receive me so early."

"I am at Your Majesty's service, as he knows."

"Yes. I know." He let go of her hand and walked slowly toward the patio doors, closed against late summer chill. Beyond, a beautiful day beckoned, the leaves on the trees in the enclosed garden just beginning to turn.

She followed, stopping at a respectful distance.

"We have not spoken for some time," Louis said. "Not like—like this. The two of us. No courtiers, no cardinal. No confessors or—or—others."

"As you wish."

"Not as I wish: not, not just as *I* wish, Anne. I would have wished otherwise, I think, if things had been different." He turned to face her. "I have reached the conclusion after many years that—that you have been ill-used. Perhaps I have been as well. When we married...when we were first together...we were not ready. Neither of us."

Anne looked down at her hands, folded in front of her. She wanted to say, *I was ready: I was trained to be ready. You were...*

You were your mother's son, she thought to herself. Marie de Medici, the domineering, controlling, manipulative queen mother who was Regent of France during Louis' minority had done everything in her power to make sure she maintained that situation, even as she stunted the maturity of the king of France. Indeed, they fought two wars in the space of a year, his partisans on one side and hers on the other. But it took a personal, direct conflict to make him decide between mother and minister.

And to many, she thought, *you simply became the cardinal's creature. Weak, indecisive, tongue-tied... and even now without an heir of your body, or mine.*

I was ready, she thought. But she did not say it.

"Things have not gone as planned, Sire," she said at last.

"Louis."

"Louis," she repeated, and though she spoke French very well it still sounded like *Luis*. "My king. I consented to this arrangement so that there might be a future for the royal house, but it would not have been my decision if it had not been decided for me. The...cardinal, your servant, saw it as a practical solution, and I allow that it is so."

"It was his arrangement, Anne," he said. "But it is—it is my will."

She looked down again at her folded hands. "I know it is your will, Sire. But you asked my consent—or, rather, your...servant...asked it, and I gave it. It is my choice to participate."

"My servant loves France, and so do I."

"And so do *I*, Louis. I am its queen. Though you sometimes doubted it, though there have been times that my actions and words have not truly convinced you that it is true, I love France." She was not looking down now: she was looking directly into his eyes. She had not meant to be so emotional, but she felt that it was time for truth. After all of the intrigue, all of the scheming, all of the failed pregnancies and petty jealousies and court rivalries—after all of that—it was time for truth.

"I want—I want to believe you."

"Do you not?" She continued to stare at him. "I cannot imagine what I must do to convince you that I speak the truth. Words fail me. Only deeds will do." She reached forward and took his hand in both of hers. He did not pull away: there was no one to see the gesture, no one to titter at her sentimentality or at his discomfort. Perhaps Madame de Chevreuse or one of the other ladies of her chamber was watching the scene—or perhaps one of the cardinal's spies, for that matter: they said that his eyes and ears were everywhere. She had already decided that she did not care. "We will undertake this and we will do it for France. For you, Sire, and even for . . . for your servant."

"It is not for him."

"Then it is for France, my lord."

"I can accept that. We do this for France, my lady. For the France that will be—not what the up-timers speak of in their mysterious future past, but for our, for our France of the near future. I ask for a son, Anne, who will be king after me—another Louis. Louis the Fourteenth, when I am in my tomb."

"I pray that is far from now, Sire. After all of this time you deserve to see that son, and perhaps many more."

He smiled slightly, wistfully. "The nation has not always done well when there are many sons."

She lifted the hand she still held between her own, and softly kissed it. His lip trembled as she did so, but he did not pull it away.

"For France," she repeated, and let go of his hand, offering him a deep curtsey that would have made the sternest instructor in Madrid beam with delight.

"Inde vero, morte suae matris audita, reversus in Franciam, sic sanctitatis insistebat operibus quod ut ipsius jejunia vigilias et disciplinas multimodas pretereamus.

"Plura monseria et pauperum hospitalia constuxit, infirmos et decumbentos inibi visitando personalieter, et minibus propriis ac flexo genu eis cibaria ministrando...."

Cardinal Gondi, archbishop of Paris, droned on, reciting Joinville's account of the great deeds of the king's blessed namesake: of his crusades against the infidel and of piety and devotion to works of humility, particularly after the death of his mother. The ceremony was held in the great church of Paris' patron saint and his great church. When the *oriflamme* went abroad with King Louis IX—and others—the French knights had rallied to the cry of *"Montjoie! Saint-Denis!"* Montjoie meant "showing the way," and Saint Denis was the bishop and martyr who had so alarmed the pagan priests of the Parisii that they beheaded him on the highest hill nearby, the *mons martyrius*—thus *Montmartre.*

The story didn't end there, much to the delight of the hagiographers. After the deed was done, Denis picked up his head and walked several miles, preaching a sermon all the way. Where he stopped walking was consecrated with a shrine. Now the holy relics of both Saint Louis and Saint Denis lay beneath the altar of the great church on Montmartre that the blessed Sainte-Geneviève had originally begun fourteen centuries ago.

The king and queen rose to join in the Collect and attended closely to the words of the archbishop as he recited from the second letter to the Corinthians and the Gospel of Matthew:

You are the salt of the earth; but if salt has lost its taste, how shall its saltiness be restored? It is no longer good for anything except to be thrown out and trodden under foot by men. You are the light of the world. A city set on a hill cannot be hid. Nor do men light a lamp and put it under a bushel, but on a stand, and it gives light to all in the house. Let your light so shine before men, that they may see your good works and give glory to your Father who is in heaven.

When they rose for the responsory—

> *Although they go forth weeping*
> *Carrying the seed to be sown,*
> *They shall come back rejoicing,*
> *Carrying their sheaves.*
> *Those who sow in tears shall reap*
>   *rejoicing.*

Louis thought he saw the hint of those tears in the eyes of his queen: and in that moment, with cloudy morning light filtering through the stained-glass of the great church, she had never seemed more beautiful.

Chapter 3

Before the sun reached its height, the royal party was on the king's road to Fontainebleau. The queen and king rode in a luxuriously appointed carriage, escorted by two dozen members of the King's Musketeers, and followed by carriages bearing gentlemen and ladies of the royal courts. The fresh air of late summer was a welcome change from the smoke and stink of Paris.

Anne had a complex work of needlepoint in her lap to which she gave scarce attention. Louis' breviary lay beside him on the seat.

"This is very pleasant," Anne said. "Just the two of us..."

"Yes," Louis answered. He stretched his legs out, almost touching the hem of his queen's long skirts, then hastily pulled them back. "I feel as if a weight is gradually lifting from my shoulders. And you?"

"I'm not sure that's what I meant."

18

"Is there some other meaning I should divine?"

"I . . . no," she said. "No. But we have rarely been in so quiet a setting. Alone."

He narrowed his eyes. "This—this sounds like an amorous advance."

Anne looked down at the needlepoint: a half-finished depiction of the blessed Saint Clotilde, the mother of King Clovis, who helped bring the light of the Gospel to the Franks. She was just starting to pick out the little church she held in her hands.

Queen, she thought. *And soon, if God wills it, queen mother.*

"I meant nothing of the sort. And if you are offended, I most humbly beg pardon—but this is no circumstance for me to bow low and curtsey."

"It is not necessary."

"I thank Your Majesty for his magnanimity."

"Are you mocking me, my lady? Is this—is this another jest, another opportunity to remind me of what kind of husband I am?"

"No. Of course not."

He was armed with a severe reply, but hesitated. Anne's face was a mask of civility, but somewhere in her expression he could see the face of the young princess he had taken as his wife more than twenty years ago.

"I think it is I who should beg your pardon," he said, and laid his hand on his breviary, but did not take it up. "During my time on the throne I have had many hands turn against me: nobles and churchmen, high and low, men and, and women. It is like being strapped to a Catherine's wheel." He drew out a lace handkerchief and coughed delicately into it.

"It is as I read in a play," Anne answered. *"La*

tête couronnée dort à l'œil ouvert . . . 'the crowned head sleeps with one eye open.' In English it reads, 'Uneasy lies the head that wears a crown.'"

"The English are clever with words, madame. Not as clever as the French by half, but still clever. And in this case they are on point."

"I was given a translation of this play by the cardinal. He took quite a fancy to it. He is deficient in many things, but he is clever beyond doubt. Look at what he has arranged for us." She smiled, and then laughed briefly: not the sharp, cruel laughter that had so often troubled Louis, but a soft, musical sound.

"The four of us . . ." Louis began, and trailed off. Anne knew who the fourth one was: Giulio Mazarini, the one who now styled himself *Jules Mazarin*, just as he had done in the up-time world, her ally in the future when she became regent for the young king upon the death of this one.

And in this world—her lover? At least for now, with royal sanction he was her partner by this arrangement.

"Yes, my king?"

"The four of us will always have a bond," he said at last. "We do this for France. I tell myself that, that it must be done. It makes you more of a queen, rather than less. It is just as we discussed months ago; and yet, and yet now we stand on the precipice of this event and I confess myself somewhat faint."

"I remain your queen, Sire. As long as you wish it."

"I have never wished otherwise."

"Never?"

"You have my word as your king and your husband. Is that sufficient?"

She knew that he was not telling the truth—or, to

be generous, that he deceived himself that it was true. After she miscarried the first time; after the intrigues that had associated themselves with her, the lonely and neglected queen of France; at the Day of Dupes, when she was certain she would be sent back to Spain—yes, she was sure that he might have put her aside as his father had put aside his first wife because *Paris is well worth a mass*. In the course of twenty-one years she believed the opposite: that he had wished often and most fervently that she was *not* his queen, that she had never *become* his queen, that there were a hundred other diversions more interesting and less threatening.

And now, at this *precipice* as he put it, he found himself faint, and spoke gallant words? Her Hapsburg temper made her want to throw the words back in his face.

That was not a choice.

"Quite sufficient," she said.

In the needlepoint, Anne thought she recognized a faint smile on Saint Clotilde's face.

Château de Saluce

The royal party halted just before dark at the Château de Saluce, deep in the Forest of Senârt south and east of Paris. They had followed the king's high road across the Meuse over the bridge that Louis' father Henry IV had fortified early in his reign; from there the land gave way to rolling hills and a deep forest, its greens showing the first hint of browns and oranges, a sign of the coming change of seasons.

Senârt was a royal preserve, managed by foresters in service to the king and, lately, watched by troops loyal to the cardinal. Highwaymen and robbers had long since found more fruitful hunting grounds, but the veteran musketeers made sure that no one even approached. The chateau was a hunting lodge enhanced with creature comforts: it was hardly the Louvre—or Fontainebleau, for that matter—but it was a long way from rustic either. The troops dismounted first and made the place secure; servants and courtiers entered next, so that when the king and queen alighted from their carriage all was ready.

Louis and Anne parted in the entrance hall to refresh themselves from the trip, and reunited at a dinner laid on by the staff. After the first few courses, the poet Corneille—one of Richelieu's *cinq auteurs*, patronized by the court—appeared to declaim verses in praise of truth and love and virtue.

The queen, placed to the king's right, whispered, "will the gentleman be accompanying us to Fontainebleau?"

"I had thought to send him back to Paris tomorrow," Louis replied. "Is he to your liking?"

"He preaches like a Calvinist and prances like a fine horse," Anne said. "I would rather be purged than hear him in the palace."

"My physician could—could certainly oblige you, madame," Louis said. "But I shall dispense you from the obligation. Monsieur Corneille will part from us tomorrow."

"I shall say additional prayers for you, Sire."

"Thank you."

Corneille completed his current verse and offered a deep bow to the royals. Louis made an indulgent gesture with his hand, making the poet beam. Anne merely gave Corneille a frozen smile.

❖   ❖   ❖

The queen retired first by the king's leave, her ladies escorting her from the dining hall. As this progress was intended to portray a romantic retreat by king and queen, Louis made a great show of kissing Anne's hand and presenting her with a beautiful, perfect rose before she departed. Those of the court on hand for the scene gossiped to themselves, which made the king smile.

Louis went to his own chamber not long after. While he was preparing for his rest, there was a tentative knock at the door. Beringhien went to the door; after a moment he returned, bearing a folded sheet of foolscap which he carried to the king.

The faint perfume told Louis immediately who had sent it. His hands trembled slightly as he opened it and read the short note.

"Beringhien," Louis said. "Who brought this note?"

"Madame de Chevreuse, Sire," he answered. "She was most furtive."

"Indeed." He took the letter and tucked it into his doublet. "I can imagine."

"Is there anything amiss, Majesty?"

"The queen requests my presence. She—she wishes me to visit her cabinet." He stood in the middle of the room, arms hanging loosely at his sides. His valet was hesitant to speak; in the candlelight he could see a faint sweat on his master's brow.

Finally Louis walked to the sideboard, where a crystal decanter and two goblets were laid. Beringhien moved to serve the king, but Louis waved him away. He poured wine into a glass, spilling some onto the table. He took a long drink.

"Shall I send word that you are not available, Majesty?"

"No—no. I shall go." He walked slowly past, holding out the glass. Beringhien took it from him and watched as he went through the door and into the hall.

As the king stood outside the queen's chamber, he wondered to himself what Anne intended. There had been so many ploys, so many embarrassments, so many times that his discomfort and awkwardness had made him an object of ridicule among her ladies. He had thought that this progress was evidence that in the end Anne was truly what she had said—the queen of *France*: not his tormentor, not an estranged, bitter, childless Spaniard. He couldn't be wrong—could he? Not after all this?

He knocked at the door. Madame de Chevreuse opened it, a candle in her hand.

"Majesty," she said, bowing. "The queen will be so happy to see you." She beckoned him within.

He hesitated, then crossed the threshold. The duchess closed the door behind him and gestured toward the bedroom. There were no ladies in sight; the sitting-room was empty. Madame de Chevreuse handed him the candle, bowed again, and withdrew into the shadows.

He knew what was intended as he took the candle-holder in his hand. He felt like walking away; he felt like running. He was sweating and shivering: and even if there was no one watching while he stood there.

Then he realized that this was a test as well. If he walked away from this, everyone would know and the deception they'd planned at Fontainebleau would be seen as a transparent lie.

If this was one last act of spite by his queen, then he would have to accept it and play it to the end.

He walked slowly toward the bedroom. In the dim light, he could see the queen of France alone on her bed, waiting.

Paris

The cardinal was not amused.

Pierre Corneille was a thorough courtier and accustomed to swings in a patron's mood, whether king or cardinal; he kept his eyes averted and did not speak.

Richelieu paced back and forth, leaving the poet to stand uncomfortably before him.

"You're quite sure?"

"It is without doubt, Eminence. The king left his chambers and made his way to those of the queen."

"Unattended."

"He was only accompanied by the duchess, Eminence. She brought him the note."

Richelieu extended his hand. Corneille reached within his doublet and drew out the scented page. It had been a trifling thing to slip in and purloin it. The distracted king and his dullard valet would probably not even notice it was gone.

Corneille handed it to the cardinal, a slight odor of the queen's scent wafting up from it. Richelieu did not seem to take notice other than a slight wrinkling of his patrician nose. He opened it and scanned its contents.

When he was done he flourished it in front of the poet. "Do you know what this means?"

"I am not sure, Eminence."

"It means—ah." Richelieu made as if to toss it aside, thought better of it and lowered his hand. "It means that our lady queen continues to be the same devious soul she has always been. She seeks to seduce him. Seduce him! Mother of God. I cannot imagine."

"Eminence, the king went willingly to her chamber—"

Richelieu held his hand up.

"Do you question our sovereign?"

"No, of course not, but . . ."

"But?"

Corneille's experience as a courtier gave him the intuition to know when his tongue had outrun his good sense. He realized that this was one of those times. One false word, one improper inclination and . . .

"Nothing, Eminence. Nothing at all. I ask your indulgence if I have spoken out of turn."

Richelieu did not answer; he made him stand there at least a minute longer than was necessary. Corneille enjoyed being one of the favored poets at court—but as always, there was no doubt that it was as easy to lose that position as it was hard to gain it in the first place.

"You have a mission, Monsieur Corneille. You will ride to Fontainebleau and present yourself to Monseigneur Mazarin and with my compliments deliver a note which I shall compose. You will be sure to do this right away, before the royal party arrives."

"But—Eminence—they are due to arrive there this night."

"Then you should undertake to find a fast horse, monsieur. And you should depart at once to fulfill this mission."

Fontainebleau

From the window overlooking the courtyard, Jules Mazarin watched for the approach of the royal procession.

By the late afternoon light he opened and reread the letter from Cardinal Richelieu that the foppish poet Corneille had delivered a few hours earlier. The poet had ridden all night from Paris to Fontainebleau to bring it. Exhausted, Corneille had come into the palace looking for him: he made sure to be found in the chapel, assuming the proper air of sanctity and humility. He didn't know how much Corneille knew about the reason for Mazarin's presence here at the palace, but there was no reason to cause further idle gossip. Now, he assumed, the poet was in some tavern in Melun recovering from the stress that the cardinal had imposed on him.

Richelieu's letter was considerate. Ruthless, but considerate.

There is some possibility that the king lay with his queen last night. There is also some possibility that our monarch will have become so discomfited by her approach that he may be unwilling to proceed. I will not pretend that it makes our task and your position any easier. Indeed, it may make it quite perilous.

It only slightly reassured him to think that Richelieu was concerned for his welfare. But His Eminence was two days' ride away, and wouldn't be subject to summary prosecution should the king's mood turn against their plan.

And what a plan! To bring an heir to the kingdom

of France they had decided—the four of them: king and queen, cardinal and...*tool of the state*, he supposed...to allow the tool to lie with the queen in the hope that this union would be more successful than the ones King Louis himself had attempted.

Was there something wrong with the royal seed? The cardinal had suggested that up-timer science considered it a distinct possibility: not that Louis did not *want* to father a child, but that he did not have the *capability* to do so. There were some at the court who said, behind their hands or in private gossip, that the king...walked on the other side of the avenue. Women seemed to make him nervous, especially the queen.

Mazarin looked back down at the cardinal's letter.

I rely upon your discretion and your judgment to complete the task that is so crucial to the realm. Even more, I rely on the blessing of the Almighty to guide our counsels and vouchsafe our success.

Corneille had his stresses. But Mazarin himself had some stress coming. Assuming he wasn't clapped in irons as soon as the royal party arrived, he would have to ask the queen the crucial question: *did she sleep with her king?*

It was a question that he would rather not ask.

In the distance he could see the dust rising off the road, caught by the slanting rays of late afternoon light—the horsemen and carriages carrying the king and queen and entourage.

All Mazarin could think of was an up-timer expression.

Showtime.

Part One

The Virtue of Temperance

A due restraint upon affections and passions

Chapter 4

November, 1635
Castello del Valentino, near Turin in Savoy

Terrye Jo Tillman had spent at least an hour sitting at the writing desk, leaning back in the chair and looking out across the beautiful mountain view outside her window. The blank letter paper lay stacked, the quill sharpened and the ink mixed, ready for her to start the letter; but it was hard to find the right way to begin.

Uncle Frank's letter was nearby. She still wasn't sure how he'd found out where to send it, but it had arrived that morning and was delivered to her apartment by a liveried footman on a silver platter as if she were royalty, or at least nobility. She'd managed a gracious thank you. Her French and Italian was much improved from when she'd arrived a year ago with the team hired to build Duke Victor Amadeus' radio tower. It *had* to improve; the rest of the group had gone home or elsewhere, turning down the duke's invitation to stay, but she'd remained to operate the shiny new up-time technology for Victor Amadeus.

For her part, Terrye Jo didn't want to go back to Grantville, and didn't really have anyplace else to go.

The letter's not going to write itself, girl, she thought. *Mooning out the window doesn't help.*

She hated it when she was right.

She sat up straight in the chair and pulled back her sleeves. It was a new blouse and it wouldn't do to get ink-stains all over it. Then, with a sigh, she pulled a sheet of paper off the stack, took the quill and dipped it in the ink, and began to write.

> *Dear Dad,*
>
> *I'm sorry that it's taken me so long to write to you. I want to say it's because it's been so busy here, setting up the radio tower and getting everything settled, but you know it's not a good enough excuse. I was angry when I left, and so were you, and maybe it's time for that to end. I left you to take care of Mom without me—but you'd had to do that when I was in the army, and she didn't recognize me anymore. There was nothing left to do but kiss you goodbye. Uncle Frank's letter told me that she died in the spring. When I come home I'll visit the grave with you, if you want.*

She paused and put the quill down. For a moment she thought about crumpling up the paper and tossing it out the window. That was a terrible way to begin. It was worse than just being unable to find the words—it was as if there *weren't* any right words.

Her mother was dead. Her doctor had called it *Huntington's chorea*—the same thing that had taken her Aunt Gloria two years after the Ring of Fire. Both Mom and Gloria had been messed up even before the Ring, but there were medications and treatments. Dad and Uncle Jim took turns driving them up to Wheeling and they were both better for a while afterward.

Then Wheeling disappeared, along with the rest of the twenty-first century. They did the best they could after that, which wasn't very good. Her aunt was already gone by the time Terrye Jo graduated. Dad came alone to see it, because Mom was having a bad week. He'd only gotten to eighth grade, and had been so proud of his daughter who made it through even though it happened back here in the seventeenth century.

By the time she came home to work for VOA, her mother didn't even know her own daughter. That was when she knew it was time to leave. The invitation from the duke of Savoy came at just the right time.

Just a year or two, she'd thought. Then she'd come home with enough to live well. But she didn't go home.

> *I'm living in the Castello del Valentino, which is the ducal palace. I have a room about the size of our old house and a workshop downstairs. The duke and duchess have been very kind to me. Duke Victor Amadeus is about your age and very handsome—he's got one of those pointed beards and turned-up moustaches, and has a huge wardrobe.*

Every day I see him wearing something new.

His wife Christine—the duchess—is much younger. She's the sister of the king of France, and has a temper worse than Gramma Dorothy. She mostly uses it on the servants—I think the duke told her not to scare the up-timer away. She did come to me before a ball and told me that my jeans and flannel shirts were quite unsuitable, and had her dressmaker fit me for a beautiful pale blue gown. The court artist did sketches of all the ladies. You wouldn't be able to tell I was an infantry grunt in disguise.

A few weeks ago the court took a trip to a monastery, Hautemont Abbey, which is on a tall hill overlooking a lake. It's a gorgeous place, like something out of a fairytale movie. A few dozen of the duke's ancestors are buried there, and he and his wife expect that they'll go there too, but hopefully not any time soon. They took all of their children along. They have three and the duchess is pregnant with another. She's already lost two others—one stillborn, another when he was just six. They want to bring in an up-time doctor, and they hoped I was trained for that too. Even with nothing more than field medic training they're glad to have me nearby.

She almost threw this sheet out the window too. *Nice going. Focus on death—the place where the* dukes of Savoy get buried and the number of kids the duchess has lost.

She set that thought aside and plowed ahead.

> I want you to know that this is a great situation for me, even though it's far from home. I miss you, and Uncle Frank and Aunt Lana and Uncle Jim and my grandmothers and Grampa Fogle too. But I can't come home now, even though you want me to. I need—

She stopped and scratched out *I need*. She didn't need anything. It was her Dad who needed what she was going to ask. She was almost to the bottom of a page, so she set the current one aside and started with a new sheet.

> When Aunt Gloria died, you cursed the Ring of Fire, and you cursed fate, and a whole lot of other things. There was no medicine, no up-time clinic, nothing to help her get better. I'm pretty sure you did the same when Mom died. It's all true, but even up-time neither of them were getting better—they were mostly staying the same, and not a lot of that. You can blame God and curse fate all you want, but not the Ring of Fire. They didn't die because we're back here. They died because there was something that killed them. In the Guard we lost people—up-timers—who survived coming back to this time only to be killed.

It didn't make sense, it wasn't fair, but it happened all the same. I don't know why we're here in this time, but we're here and we're not going back.

Because of that, I need to ask you something important. I need to ask you to move on: from Mom, from the Ring of Fire, from wanting me to be in reach to lean on. Even Uncle Frank told me that I have to find my own way in this world and that I'll be a better daughter because of it.

I hope you will love me anyway and that you'll write back

With love, your daughter

Terrye Jo

She set the last sheet aside, making a neat stack, and laid the quill next to it. The window was still there, and she could throw it all away and start again. Or not.

After some dithering she sealed the letter, with no further corrections, and passed it to a courier. Dad would have it in a few weeks, and maybe it would make him feel better. In any case writing back to Grantville had lightened her mood.

The Castello del Valentino had been under constant construction since 1630, long before the radio team arrived. It had been the private home of the duchess of Savoy—Christina Maria, the sister of King Louis of France—and she kept carpenters, stonemasons and other craftsmen continually occupied with renovations. The Castello was an impressive building: square and roughly horseshoe-shaped, with four towers along the central edge and two each on each of the legs; an interior courtyard ended in a rounded arch with a gate tower in the center, taller than all the rest. Tree-lined avenues framed gardens beyond, leading off into the countryside, while the long side of the building faced the Po River. A river-gate in the middle of a palisaded wall led down a few steps to a dock.

Despite the noise, Her Grace seemed very comfortable there. Whenever she was with child—which, as far as Terrye Jo could tell, was just about always—she had left Turin and come out into the country. A Grantville-trained doctor—really a down-timer with a few months' education in up-time nursing techniques—had been hired out by the duke to attend her, and he had a permanent apartment in the north wing. His expertise was the first up-time knowledge that Duke Victor Amadeus had imported into his lands, and it was better than a chirurgeon who knew nothing other than bleeding and purging.

Late in 1634, the duke had decided that Savoy needed a radio transmission facility, and had paid handsomely to have it built, along with the spider-work of antenna wires that now draped it, stretching between the many parapets and towers of the Castello. Naturally, that meant more renovation and construction. It also meant that the duke himself spent more time in residence.

The duchess might have resented it, except that she considered Terrye Jo herself a *project*. Her Grace had one daughter, Luisa Christina, six years old but already court-wise and self-assured, but hardly someone who could be *dressed* and *groomed* quite yet. Terrye

Jo was twenty-one, and gave no indication of interest in marrying or child-rearing. It was a challenge for both noblewoman and country girl, but it was a nice interruption from the workshop.

This morning, with her letter sent off, Terrye Jo made her way from her apartment in an upper floor of the south wing to the workshop, located in one of the towers that overlooked the Po. It was a big, airy place, originally designed for something else—a ballroom, maybe—but had been cleared out for work. The framework of the radio tower had been built above, and the hardware installed in the room. Long tables of planed timber had been placed there to hold equipment and parts and tools.

"Ah, Donna Teresa." Artemisio Logiani, a local *Torino* who had graduated from castle handyman to junior radio tech, looked up from his work and offered her a bow she didn't deserve. "You brighten up the morning."

It would have been all too serious but for the wink and the grin.

"I doubt it."

"Forgive me, Donna," he answered. "I cannot help myself." He smiled, showing not enough teeth. "I can scarcely focus my eyes in your presence."

She ignored the compliment. It was a little dance she did with the down-timer every morning. She knew what he had in mind—there was really no question—but of the crew of radio operators she'd trained, he was the best. He could send almost as fast as she could. "How are you doing with the long-range antenna adjustment?"

"It goes slowly," he said. "The materials are poor,

especially now that there is war." He gestured to a stretch of wire on the table behind him, painstakingly hand-twisted and mounted on an antenna strut. "I try to follow the book, but it is difficult." He tapped the open book, a manuscript copy of a radio operator's manual from the 1930s that the team had brought with them.

"I'm sure we'll get it. We can reach Lyon now, but the duke said that he needed to get a further reach—someplace like..."

"Paris."

They both looked across at the voice. Terrye Jo sighed. Artemisio made a face, but not so the new-comer could see it. The young assistant was no fan of *Dottore* Umberto Baldaccio—and to be honest neither was she.

"Might be," Terrye Jo said. She put her hands on her hips. "Do you know something we don't, Umberto?"

He scowled: he preferred his title to his Christian name, which was why Terrye Jo didn't use it.

"I know nothing that you do not," he said, walking across to his part of the workshop. He occupied roughly a quarter of the usable area with books and crates and jars full of who know what, and glassware and powders and strips of metal and all kinds of unidentifiable crap.

When they'd installed and tested the equipment for the radio facility, most of the team had declined Duke Victor Amadeus' offer to remain in Turin on retainer. There wasn't anything wrong with Turin—it just wasn't Rome or Paris or London or Magdeburg. Only Terrye Jo had stayed behind, as much an expert radio operator as down-time Turin had ever seen. The duke had assigned her this workshop but Baldaccio had already moved in, taking up from a third to a half of the available space. She'd gone to the duke herself and complained. He was a fraud, he was an *alchemist*, for Christ's sake—but it turned out he was a well-established and well-connected fraud with the full confidence of the duke, who brushed off her protests. She'd gone away dissatisfied.

Then she'd gone to the duchess.

Christina Maria had been in Savoy for twenty years as the wife of the prince of Piedmont, who had come into his inheritance as Duke of Savoy in 1630. She was still thought of a foreigner even so. After her first son had died stillborn and her second had died young, during her third pregnancy (when she was lying-in here at Castello del Valentino) the duke had sent Umberto Baldaccio to her. He was a loyal retainer who had saved the duke's life in some fashion that was never discussed, and he used all of the standard practices available to a seventeenth-century physician: purging and bleeding and hocus pocus and astrology. The baby turned out to be a girl (apparently Baldaccio's prediction that it was a boy was conveniently forgotten) and the experience was enough for her to want to keep him as far away as possible. Thus, she warmed to the task of helping the young up-timer against the old charlatan.

One morning, Baldaccio ambled into the workshop to find that Terrye Jo and a group of retainers had gotten there far earlier and had moved his equipment and tools and dusty books full of Latin gibberish into neat stacks in the draftiest corner of the big room, close enough to a window that he could point his telescope but far enough to keep from being underfoot. He had been furious—but when Terrye Jo had smiled sweetly and invoked the name of the duchess, he had gone quiet and set to work disorganizing his work area to his own satisfaction. A large metal crate part way down on the two closest work benches served as an effective barrier, preventing him from taking over any more territory.

"At least in regard to politics," Terrye Jo said.

"Yes. Of course. As for the rest . . ." he settled himself in a creaky armchair and flipped a page in the book in front of him. "There is much I could teach you, signorina, if you would merely open your mind to science."

It was an old argument, and she bit back a reply. Him chiding her about science was . . . typical, if absurd.

"Why do you think that the duke wants to contact Paris?"

"Haven't you heard?"

"Heard what? I didn't take breakfast this morning. Wasn't hungry."

"We have a guest. His Highness Gaston Jean-Baptiste de France, and his lovely wife Marguerite de Lorraine. Come to pay his sister a visit."

"Gaston." Terrye Jo knew the name, but wasn't up on the politics. "Prince Gaston, except they always call him *Monsieur* Gaston. The king's younger brother."

"Estranged brother, I daresay," Baldaccio said. "He is in exile from France for his intrigues. Yet, for all that, he is the heir to the throne, since the king appears . . . disinclined to produce one of his own."

"So he's the next king of France? What's he doing here?"

"I would not venture to say. But I suspect that your—instruments—" he gestured toward the disassembled antenna strut in front of Artemisio. "They might have something to do with it. The prince is here to make use of them."

"Huh. But...you said he was in exile."

Baldaccio sighed. He leaned back, making the chair complain. "Foolish girl. *Monsieur* is in exile, but not all of his friends are so disadvantaged. He is here—but his friends are *there*." He folded his hands over his ample belly, looking satisfied—like a snake that has just enjoyed a particularly filling meal.

She ignored the *foolish girl*, though she had an image in her mind of stuffing the words one letter at a time down his throat. "I got the impression that Duke Victor Amadeus is a friend of the king of France. You're suggesting that he's part of some intrigue with Monsieur Gaston."

"I am not suggesting anything, signorina, and will deny any imputation of the sort. I am merely employing logic, which is a key to science, as—"

"As you'd teach me if I'd only listen. I understand." She sat on the bench next to the antenna. Artemisio, who had remained silent through the entire exchange, joined her at once. "I've got work to do. Maybe later."

Monsieur Gaston's reasons for visiting his sister were made clear to Terrye Jo a few days later. She was in the operator's room, a cubicle below the tower that was built into the ceiling above the workshop; it was accessible by a staircase made of new, unfinished wood.

It was dusk, the shadows from the mountains lengthening across the valley. She was trying to pick up a broadcast signal from Magdeburg when she felt, rather than heard, the tramp of boots. When they came into the cubicle, she had taken off her headphones and stood up to see who had come to visit.

"Mademoiselle Tillman."

The man who addressed her was young—about Terrye Jo's age—and richly dressed in the latest fashion. He had a piercing gaze with deep blue eyes and a smooth, clear voice. The four men with him were also well dressed, but were clearly no more than ornaments for the one who had spoken.

"Monsieur," she said, standing. Her Italian was better than her French, and this man was a native speaker.

"No, please sit. I am Louis de Vendôme, at your service." He offered a courtier's bow. "And you are the most distinguished up-time . . . er, *radio* operator."

"Yes. My lord," she added, realizing it was appropriate and he'd be expecting it.

A tiny smile appeared on Louis de Vendôme's face. "My father is César de Vendôme, mademoiselle. I am in Monsieur Gaston's company, and at his direction I have come to . . . inspect your facility. With the permission of His Grace the duke, we will require some extra work from you."

"I'm not sure I understand," Terrye Jo said. She had decided to remain standing, rather than sit in the presence of this nobleman. "Extra work?"

"Yes. Some communications. Do not worry, you will be paid well for your trouble."

On vous paiera bien de vos travaux. It sounded very nice in French.

"I am always happy to hear that," she said. "I would like assurance that it is with the permission of the duke."

Louis looked over his shoulder at his companions,

then back at her. "Do you have any doubts, mademoiselle?"

"The . . . no, monsieur. My lord, I do not doubt your intentions, but this equipment is in my care, and I am obligated to the duke as an employee. If anything were to happen it would be my responsibility, no matter who is operating it."

"It would be you, surely?"

"Not necessarily. There are a dozen people qualified to run it at the moment," she said. "But it's me in charge regardless of who—"

"You are quite right to be cautious, mademoiselle, but it would be His Highness's wish that for *his* communications that it would be you, and *only* you, at the instrument." He held up one hand, the lace cuff hanging limply at the wrist, as if to forestall any response. "Your ability at teaching the skills is not in question. I can assure you—"

"I am sure you can."

"What do you want? Exactly?"

"I think written permission would be helpful. A note with Duke Victor Amadeus' signature and seal would do, indicating that I should be selected to do what a dozen people at the Castello del Valentino can competently handle."

The little smile disappeared. For a moment, Terrye Jo wasn't sure whether she'd stepped across some line with the man. Then she decided that she didn't care—this *was* her gear, and she *was* responsible. Getting bullied by some French prince, or duke, or whatever he was, wasn't going to work.

"I assume that there won't be any problem with that."

"You are a very determined young woman, made-moiselle. Is this a characteristic of all up-time females, like . . . trousers?"

She smiled. Her working clothes weren't exactly what someone like Louis de Vendôme was used to.

"Only the tough ones." She smiled, and Louis' expression softened slightly. "I don't know about the others."

"In the instance that I obtain this permission I will expect that you will provide the service that Monsieur Gaston requires, and that you will keep all that you see—and send over your radio—in confidence. This is most important, mademoiselle. Many things, and many people, depend on your care in this matter."

"I know how to keep secrets, my lord," Terrye Jo said. "You can ask the duke and duchess."

"Yes," he answered. "I already did. You are highly regarded. Particularly by the duchess." He looked her up and down, from the fierce smile to the trousers and work boots. "Otherwise we would not be having this conversation."

Chapter 5

Turin

"You look fine, my dear. For Heaven's sake, stop fussing."

Terrye Jo twisted, trying to settle the fall of her very full skirts, draped over pleated pads at the hips and ending in a small train. There were petticoats and underclothes, more than she knew existed. The front of the gown was a single piece, while the back was separated at the uncomfortably high waistline. The bodice had a wide neck, with the side seams running into the full sleeves, which puffed out like a pair of frilly balloon animals. And she wasn't even able to describe the boning at the waist.

"Your Grace must realize how uncomfortable this all is."

"Mademoiselle, I am perhaps two months from term. If you think that *you* are uncomfortable, consider my position." Duchess Christina Maria smiled and reached out a hand, clad in a delicate, white lace glove. "Really, Teresa. It will be all right. Now put on your gloves and your smile."

Terrye Jo drew on her own gloves, of thin doeskin leather. At least they covered up her hands, which showed ample evidence of hard manual work—but even though they were comfortable and beautiful, they seemed alien on her.

As for the smile, it came much more easily.

"That's better," Christina said. "Now you have no need to be nervous. You have attended to your bows and curtseys with *military* attention—you will do fine."

"That's not what worries me, Your Grace."

"Then what is it, dear?"

"I've . . . never met royalty before."

"You've met a *duke*. And a *duchess*," Christina added, smiling again. "Whose father was a king. That's almost the same."

"I suppose it is, but not quite. I mean no offense, Your Grace, but an heir to a throne is a different thing."

"Gaston is just a man, my dear. He's my unrepentant, dissolute brother. He sits at table and squats in the privy like every other man. There is nothing to be afraid of."

"I'm not *afraid* of him."

"Then . . ."

"I—nothing. I don't know." Terrye Jo walked away from Christina, turning her back on her—which was probably bad protocol, but she didn't know if she cared. Honestly, she wanted to run away, even though she wasn't exactly wearing shoes for running.

Christina had a temper and was a little thin skinned, but she was very fond of Terrye Jo. Rather than follow her first instinct, she waited for her up-timer friend to gather herself.

"I'm sorry," Terrye Jo said at last. She came back to stand before the duchess. "I beg your pardon, madame."

"Oh, nonsense." The duchess extended her hands to Terrye Jo, who took them and held them for several moments. "Let me tell you something. The world of the court—this one, any one, really—is a man's world. There are kings and princes and dukes and ministers and archbishops, and any number of courtiers. The best of them include and honor their ladies, but many do not. We are no more than ornaments, decorations. Brood mares."

She placed her hand on her womb. "And we are otherwise ignored. But that does not make *us* less: it makes *them* weaker for ignoring us. Teresa, when we walk out into court and are presented, we should hold our heads high and look each man in the eye. Even if the man is the heir to a mighty throne."

"I still have to bow."

"Unless it is your up-time custom not to do so. I'm told that there aren't many princes there."

"I've never met one, Your Grace. Not even here down-time. You and the duke are the first great lords I've ever met."

"And we're not so bad, are we?"

"No, you're—" Terrye Jo folded her hands in front of her and blushed. "You've been so nice to me."

"We don't do that for everyone, my dear." When Terrye Jo didn't answer, she turned to a mirror and adjusted the fit of her bodice and continued, "All right, then. Let's go in."

When she was growing up, Terrye Jo's dad was a big fan of graphic novels—what some folks in Grantville called *grown-up comic books*. That came to mind when she first saw Monsieur Gaston. One of the ones her father liked was a sort of scary dystopian future in which the government was brought down by a freedom-fighting terrorist in a mask—a "Guy Fawkes" mask with a pointy beard and moustache and painted-on smile. That was the face she saw on the heir to the throne of France: a permanent charming grin and deep brown eyes.

When she was finally presented to the prince, he took her hand in his and afforded her a first-class royal smile. Terrye Jo could hardly take her eyes off him; he seemed to draw attention to himself from every corner of the room. She managed the curtsey that the duchess had made her practice. Just as Gaston was taking her hand, she glanced aside at the duchess of Orléans, Marguerite, who didn't look at all pleased. But, even with the tightness of her dress, she breathed much easier.

As she stood a little while later on the side of the room watching the festivities, she saw Monsieur Gaston extricate himself from a small knot of people and make his way toward her, the crowd of people parting to let him through. His wife seemed to be watching him carefully, and Terrye Jo noticed that the duchess had taken note as well. For a few seconds she thought he might be headed toward someone else, but it seemed as if anyone within ten feet of her moved away until she stood alone beside a small alcove.

"Mademoiselle," he said, offering her a courtly bow. "If you would indulge me with a few moments of your time?"

She gave him a curtsey. "Of course, Your Royal Highness." All of a sudden she felt as if her French wasn't up to the task.

"Excellent," he said, steering her gently by the elbow

into the alcove. They were still completely visible from the hall, but were afforded a small bit of privacy.

Terrye Jo composed herself, hoping she didn't look as alarmed as she felt. *Head high*, she thought.

"Mademoiselle Tillman," Monsieur Gaston said. "I am honored to have the chance to speak with you. I have met so few up-timers. I know that my associate has already visited you to discuss my need for your specific services."

"He was . . . pretty direct, Highness."

"I apologize most humbly, mademoiselle. He has spent far more time in the saddle than at a court."

"It's all right." She absently tugged on the sleeve of her right glove. "I'm used to it."

"Ah, but you should not have to be. I think that you put the fear of God into him."

"I'm used to that, too."

Gaston smiled. "I expect you are. Tell me, young lady, what do you think of France?"

She wasn't quite ready for the question. "I . . . I don't know, Highness. France used to be our enemy, the USE's enemy. I guess it isn't anymore."

"No. Our countries are now at peace. And tell me, Mademoiselle Tillman . . . what do you think of Cardinal Richelieu?"

"I'm not sure. He's—well, I guess we don't trust him."

"As well you should not." Gaston ran a finger along his cheek. He wore the carefully-trimmed chin beard and flowing moustaches, but his jaw was clean-shaven. "Richelieu is a spider in the middle of a web, mademoiselle. He keeps secrets and makes plots and intrigues, and holds lives and souls in the palm of his hand. All of his secrets are, as his says, 'beneath his red robe.'

"But he is not *France*, young lady. What he does places my country in peril and twists the commands and endangers the rule of my royal brother."

"Didn't he also exile you?"

Gaston's face hardened. "His Majesty exiled me at Richelieu's direction. You are correct . . . but even that cannot stand forever."

Terrye Jo didn't answer.

"It is my desire to reconcile with the king," he said. "I know that if I have a chance I can do so. But Richelieu must go."

"As you say, Highness."

"I am sure . . ." Gaston's voice, which had become harsh and angry, softened and warmed. "I am sure, madame, that the relations between my country and yours could become much more cordial in the absence of the cardinal."

"Your Royal Highness," Terrye Jo said carefully, "That sort of thing is *way* above my pay grade."

Gaston frowned for a moment; she thought perhaps she'd messed up the translation into French. Then he smiled again, like the sun breaking through clouds. "Yes. Of course. That is something that would have to be negotiated. I am sure that I could find common ground with your emperor."

"I . . . imagine the king and Emperor Gustav could find a way."

Gaston did not answer for a moment, then said, "Yes, of course. If God wills it I may someday be king of France, but in the meanwhile my royal brother might be able to make progress toward friendship and peace, free of the malign influence of the cardinal."

"Peace is better than war, for sure."

"Yes. Of course it is." The beatific Guy Fawkes smile came back. "Now, I do not wish to keep you much longer from all the young men who wait to dance with you, mademoiselle. I wish only to confirm for my own satisfaction that your radio equipment has been brought to the standard I require, and that you can personally handle the task."

"I've been able to pick up traffic all the way from Magdeburg and Venice. I expect that if the other station is transmitting, the equipment here can communicate with it."

"I'm counting on it."

"I am at your service, Your Royal Highness, with the permission of His Grace the Duke."

"Excellent." He made a very formal leg. "I shall call upon you personally when the time comes."

"I look forward to it, Your Highness."

"Yes," he said as he turned away, smiling. "I am sure you do."

As Monsieur Gaston walked back among the many visitors to the Castello del Valentino, Terrye Jo Tillman wondered to herself just what that had been about.

"So." The duke of Savoy gestured with his wine glass, which caught the firelight and sparkled. "You seem impressed with our resident up-timer."

They were sitting in the dimly lit library. Victor Amadeus had dismissed the servant, choosing to serve personally as cupbearer for his brother-in-law.

"What makes you think that?"

"You paid court to her, Highness," he said.

Gaston leaned back in his armchair and stretched like a hunting cat. "Is *that* what you call it?"

"You were very charming."

"I am always very charming. She is a comely one, though to be honest, she knows very little about how to enhance it. A wig might have been in order to cover that man's haircut, and—I don't know, some face powder or some such. I can imagine that under her gloves there are a pair of laborer's hands."

"She was a soldier, Gaston."

"Ah. That explains it, I suppose, but it does not excuse it. Still, she is no Helen."

"My wife rather likes her."

Gaston shook his head. "My dear sister, the duchess, sees a rose under every thorn. Has she taken this up-timer as a pet?"

"That's a bit disparaging."

"Gentle birth—*royal* birth—has its privileges, Victor." He patted his stomach. "But in all earnest: doesn't she have something else more important to think about?"

"I don't think it's ever far from her mind."

"Then she should stick to it," Gaston said, shrugging off all pretense of conviviality. "Christina is neither qualified to involve herself in ducal—or *royal*—affairs, nor aware of the pitfalls of befriending these up-timers. She should stick to the affairs of women, Victor, and nothing else."

The duke of Savoy did not answer. Perhaps Gaston expected him to agree, or object, but Victor Amadeus said nothing.

"I suspect that you have not given much thought to up-timers, Brother-in-law," he continued. "I know what I think of them. Holy Mother Church has been very cautious about the Ring of Fire: what it is, why it happened, and what we should think about it. But as for the up-timers themselves, they are not to be trusted."

Victor Amadeus drank his wine and set the goblet on a sideboard. "I will vouch for Mademoiselle Tillman. She is trustworthy, honest, hard-working and reliable."

"And you stand behind her."

"I do."

"Then, my dear Victor Amadeus, you are gullible. The up-timers are a tightly knit society: three thousand men and women who speak the same language."

"Many people speak English or—what is it they call it?—Amideutsch."

"That's not what I mean." Gaston leaned forward and jabbed the air with his finger toward his brother-in-law. "I'm talking about their common culture, their context. They are all a part of the same world and not our world. They think differently than we do."

"Of course they do. They're from the *future*, Gaston."

"But not our future."

"I don't even know what that means."

"Oh, don't you." Gaston stood up and walked across the library to a table, where a map of Europe was spread. "Look at this, Victor. Our world, from the Pillars of Hercules to the mountains of Russia. And right in the middle of it, squatting like a big, fat toad, is the United States of Europe. For the last four and a half years it has been growing and growing, sending its agents and its . . . *ideas* in every direction. The future that the up-timers come from, the one in which France becomes the greatest power in the world, is never going to happen.

"Have you read the up-time histories, Victor? Have you? In *their* world—what do they call it? Time line? In *their* time line, France allies with the king of Sweden, and he is killed at a battle at Lützen in 1632. It continues in alliance with Sweden against the Imperial forces for years afterward and ultimately wins a great battle." He poked at the map, at a place in the Netherlands. "A place called Rocroi, about seven years from now—if *now* hadn't been destroyed by the Ring. Of. Fire." The last three words were punctuated by raps of his knuckles.

"But it's not going to happen. It is never going to happen. Instead, we have the fat toad squatting in the middle of the Germanies, spreading their ideas of *democracy* and *freedom.*"

He fell silent for a moment. "I cannot change the past," Gaston said at last. "But I can help mold the present. The up-timers can help with that task—even this soldier and telegrapher that you favor so much. But they will never be allies. They cannot be trusted, Victor. I trust that you will never, *ever* forget it."

"Is that a royal command?"

"I am not your king."

"No," the duke said. "You are my brother-in-law, and heir to the French throne." He walked back to the sideboard and poured another glass of wine. He took a moment to contemplate it, then drank it down like water.

Chapter 6

Turin

If it hadn't previously been obvious to Terrye Jo, it became quite clear what it was about a few nights later.

It had been a cold, blustery day, rather like late fall in West Virginia. The kind of day that Ms. Maddox, when she was in a particularly cruel mood—which happened a lot—would make the girls in her P.E. class run outside, to be blown around by the wind or be forced to stand and do exercises and wait for the rain to pelt down on them. It was a part of West Virginia she didn't miss. Ms. Maddox had joined up with Harry Lefferts, Terrye Jo had heard, and instead of operating a radio tower for a duke was off having adventures in Italy or somewhere. But P.E. class was miles and years away, lost forever.

The rain and sleet never quite came. By evening the wind had mostly driven the clouds away to leave it cold and clear, just about perfect weather for radio transmission. She had gone up to the operations room to check on things—and found Louis de Vendôme lounging there, with a few of his attendants standing by, looking bored.

"Mademoiselle Tillman," he said, standing and sweeping his impressive hat from his head as he bowed. "I have been waiting for you." *For some time* went unsaid.

"I've just come from dinner. If you needed me, Henri or Sylvie could have sent word." The brother and sister, a clerk and seamstress in the duke's staff at the Castello who had shown some aptitude, were on duty this evening. She'd come up to check on them—the weather was too good, so *someone* should be up here practicing.

"I bid them return to their duties. I beg your indulgence if I have overstepped."

"Their duty is here, my lord. So, yes. Overstepped. Now, if you'll excuse me—" She wanted to move past him into the room, but he didn't seem inclined toward getting out of the way.

This could become ugly. Terrye Jo knew she could take care of herself, though with four or five of the Frenchmen it wasn't a sure thing, even if they underestimated her—which they were likely to do. But still.

"As I say," the nobleman said smoothly, "I beg your indulgence. I am expecting the imminent arrival of His Royal Highness."

"Monsieur Gaston wants to inspect the premises?"

"That . . . and he wishes to make use of them. And you."

"I'm not sure I like the sound of that."

"Your *professional* services," Louis said, his perfect courtier's smile twitching downward for a moment, then returning to its place. "He has arranged to communicate at this day and hour."

Terrye Jo thought about it for at least long enough for the smile to start to disappear again, then she said, "All right. Fine. I assume he has a prepared call sign and frequency?"

"He has...whatever he needs. He will clarify all when he arrives."

It was clear that Louis de Vendôme had no idea what she meant. It was a fair guess that he didn't truly understand how radio communication worked at all, but that was just as well.

"I'd better fire up the set," she said, and this time he stepped aside to admit her to the room.

It was cold as usual, but everything was in order and put away except for two freshly sharpened Number 2 pencils, a block of paper and the small penknife that substituted for a pencil sharpener. On the pad, in what looked like Henri's hand, were the words *pardonnez-moi*, as if they'd be blamed for abandoning their posts. They were not accustomed to saying *no* to princes.

The set was an impressive-looking thing, with more decoration than any radio deserved to have, but that was the seventeenth century for you; inside it was really very simple. They'd installed a very sensitive dial with gradations that adjusted a tuning capacitor for the receiver. It was the responsibility of the on-duty operator to carefully note any transmissions and the dial position showing their frequency. The transmitter had a similar adjustment mechanism: the dial and a sliding bar controlled a spark-gap rig based on an old instruction book from the 1920s published by the National Bureau of Standards. They'd found it in Terrye Jo's dad's attic, where it had survived water damage and the Ring of Fire. The whole thing was powered by a bank of six Leyden-jar capacitors under the table, set in a wooden frame with a trough below, big enough to hold the contents of a jar if it should ever break. There were two knife switches on the front of the rig to engage or disengage them, and a sturdily built telegraph key mounted on a heavy wooden block, connected to the box by an insulated wire.

It would have been more impressive to have everything open. The transmitter, when powered, created a blue corona around the spark gap that was too bright to look at when the gain was all the way up—but maybe it was better to keep everything in a carved box to maintain the illusion, Wizard of Oz-like. It was for job security if nothing else. It was best that most folks, especially princes, didn't realize just how simple it all was...in the right hands.

She put on a pair of earphones and plugged them into a jack on the front of the box. There was a little volume control on the earphone cord. She turned it up and slowly moved the dial to a known position to see if she could pick up the transmitter from Bern, just as a baseline.

Thus when Gaston d'Orleans arrived she didn't notice. She knew that Louis was standing a few paces behind her at the door, as if he didn't want to get any closer to the wizardry. Gaston, on the other hand, seemed to have no fear—and a childlike curiosity.

She reached for one of the pencils without looking, and instead of the familiar wooden shaft, she touched a smooth, warm hand. She jerked her hand back and stood up, pulling the earphones off her head.

"What remarkable instruments," Gaston said, holding a Number 2 in his hand. "Tisond . . . Tisonger . . ."

"*Ticonderoga*," Terrye Jo said, giving the "I" the proper long sound. "It's an Indian name. Native North American." She looked from Gaston to the small shelf that held two boxes of authentic up-timer pencils. When transcribing a telegraph message, a good old Number 2 was much more useful than a quill and ink.

"Ty-son-de . . ."

"Ti*con*deroga. There's no cedilla under the c, Highness. I think there's a small company in Magdeburg that has started to make pencils, but they're not as good as the genuine article." She thought about it for a moment and added, "if you'd like one I'd be happy to make you a present of it."

"I graciously accept." He gave his most charming smile, glancing at his loyal follower Louis. "But let me not disturb you. I assume circumstances are fortuitous for us to send a message this evening?"

"I'll need some information."

"Ah." He reached into a sleeve and drew out a small rectangle of paper and handed it to her. "This is the . . . frequency? Yes. And the call sign."

Terrye Jo nodded approvingly. Louis was leaning very slightly forward to see what was written, showing more curiosity than she would have credited him with. She set the card on the table in front of her and put the headphones back on. She slowly moved the dial to the frequency Gaston had indicated. There was some small amount of background noise, but it was in a relatively clear part of the radio spectrum—a good choice by whoever had picked it.

GJBF, she sent. *GJBF, GJBF.* She wasn't sure what

the JBF was for—something something France, she supposed—but the G was probably for Gaston. *GJBF. CQ CQ.* CQ was the signal for anyone listening to respond.

She looked up at Gaston, who was watching intently. There was no immediate response; the frequency was quiet. She looked down at the card, and checked the position of the master dial. It was set correctly. He'd told her nothing about who might be waiting for the message. She imagined some guy, dressed like the prince, waiting by a set somewhere far away.

GJBF GJBF GJBF, she sent again. *CQ CQ CQ.*

She waited another several seconds and was just about to tell Monsieur Gaston that there was no response—and then she heard something. It was faint and halting, as if being transmitted by someone with little skill on a telegraph key. It certainly wasn't a "fist" she recognized. To a trained operator, the "fist" was the style and pattern of a sender—not quite as unique as a fingerprint, but like the sound of a human voice, they could be told apart.

GJBF, she heard. *SPAR SPAR KN.*

It repeated once more, and she wrote it down on the pad and showed it to Gaston. SPAR was a call sign, one she didn't recognize. But Gaston did.

"That is my servant in Paris," he said, laying a finger on the pad. "SPAR. Well done, mademoiselle. Are they ready to send?"

"They're waiting for you, Highness," she answered. "That's what the KN means."

"Ah. *Bon.* Ask them about the queen."

"All right . . . anything specific?" He didn't answer, so she shrugged. She sent *GJBF SPAR COMMENT VA LA REINE? KN.*

There was another long pause, and then slowly, almost painfully, there was a response, beginning with *SPAR GJBF*. She copied it down, letter by letter, onto the pad.

LA REINE A UNE POLICHINELLE DANS LE TIROIR, she wrote. *The queen has . . .* something in the something, but she wasn't sure. She sent *GJBF SPAR QSM—please send the last message again.*

"Is there any—" Gaston said, and she held up her hand. She was fairly sure that princes weren't used to having that happen, but she needed to hear what was being transmitted. The message was as before. When it had been fully transmitted again she lifted the pad and showed it to him.

Apparently whatever something was in the something, it meant something to Monsieur Gaston. His expression went pale, and then hardened into a tight-lipped anger.

"You're sure that this message was sent, Mademoiselle Tillman. This *exact* message."

"I had them repeat it. Your servant isn't a very good telegrapher, but this is what he sent. I have no idea what it means."

"A *polichinelle* is . . . a sort of puppet. A marionette. My servant says that the queen has a puppet in the drawer—it is a common expression. It means . . . that the queen is pregnant."

Terrye Jo smiled. "A bun in the oven," she said in English. "*Un p'tit pain dans le four*," she translated. "I guess it doesn't make any sense in French."

"It is not an expression we use, mademoiselle. But yes, the sense would be the same." He held the pad tightly, and for just a moment she thought he might slam it down or throw it at something. But instead he placed it on the desk and slowly, carefully adjusted the lace of his cuffs.

She heard *QSL* in her headphones. *Can you acknowledge receipt?*

Without looking away from Gaston, she reached her hand to the telegraph key and sent, *GJBF SN. ENTENDU. Understood.*

"What was that, then?"

"I told them you'd gotten the message. What do you want me to send now?"

"Ask them...where is the queen now?"

Terrye Jo nodded, and turned again to face the radio set. *GJBF SPAR OU EST LA REINE? KN*, she sent. *SPAR GJBF RECLUSION HORS DE PARIS.*

"She is away from Paris," she said. "In...seclusion?"

"But where?"

GJBF SPAR OU? She sent, asking where.

SPAR GJBF UN GRAND SECRET SOUS LA ROBE ROUGE.

"I'm not sure what that means, Highness," she said, showing him the pad again. "The secret is under..."

"*Beneath the red robe*," Gaston said. "Richelieu. He has sent her somewhere in secret. He knows where she is, but my loyal servant does not. Very well. Send him...tell him that as he loves me, it is paramount that he locate her and report to me. *At once.*"

GJBF SPAR TROUVER LA REINE ET SIGNALER IMMEDIATEMENT, she sent, and then added *IMMEDIATEMENT TOUT DE SUITE PAR ORDRE G*. She figured that would be enough for them to get the *at once* part of his orders.

SPAR GJBF ENTENDU SN.

"They got the message."

"Good. Excellent." He turned on his heel and walked to the door, then turned, as if he'd forgotten something.

"Was there anything else?" she asked.

"No. Not tonight . . . ah." He looked at Louis. "Attend me," he said. "But by all means pay her."

Without turning, she reached for the key and sent *CL—closing down*. In her earphones she heard *SN*.

Louis reached into an inside pocket of his cloak and took out a small pouch which rattled. He dropped it onto a chair without a word and swept out after his master. Terrye Jo had a moment's urge to pick it up and throw it at his head. The abrupt end to the conversation and the way he'd left money for her—not by handing it over but by leaving it behind—felt vaguely insulting.

Gaston had worked hard at charming her, but she was very much like a Number 2 pencil: a tool. This was an unequal relationship, and he'd just shown her who was the prince and who was the servant.

SN, she thought. *I understand.*

Chapter 7

Marseilles, Provence

"Now *that* is a view."

Philippe de la Mothe-Houdancourt, governor of Bellegarde, leaned on the rampart of Florentine limestone that comprised the sea-facing wall of Notre-Dame de la Garde, basilica and fortress of Marseilles, and took a deep draught of sea air. From up here, a few hundred feet above the sprawl and stink of the city, the air was clear and the sky was deep blue. The sun sparkled on the Mediterranean Sea . . . and somewhere beyond to the west, over the horizon, was Spain.

"It is beautiful. When I think of my city, Philippe, I think of it this way." Cosme de Valbelle, Seigneur de Brunelles, came up to stand by his young friend. "I'm surprised you've never been up here."

"There are a great many places I have never been. This is quite a remarkable place: a fortress that is also a church."

"The monks of Saint Victor didn't want to give it up,

65

but it's a perfect place to build a fort. Our lord François thought so a century ago, and it's been defending the city against all comers ever since—outsiders and insiders."

"Do tell."

"There have been plenty of intrigues in Marseilles over the years."

"But none since it has become the firm possession of *la Famille Valbelle*, or so I understand."

Valbelle smiled. "That's more my great-uncle and father's doing. Nowadays I merely offer good government and fair trade." He made an adjustment to the lace on one cuff. "Everyone wins, even the Church."

"I'm sure His Eminence is pleased."

"You know very well that Cardinal Richelieu is a great friend to my family, and I am loyal to him and to King Louis. I have made certain that he knows that, and that our family is properly represented at court. But... you're not here to question that, are you, Philippe?"

"No. Of course not. I am here on behalf of my lord Tour d'Auvergne, Marshal Turenne. Some of your vaunted commerce—" he waved a hand toward the port below—"provisions and equips our forces."

"So you think there'll be war?"

"My dear Cosme," de la Mothe answered. "There is *always* war. In the best instance it is possible for men to bring it about on terms of their own choosing."

"If it were up to me, the terms I would choose would be accommodation. War is bad for business, and we here in Marseilles gain nothing by fighting with Spain or Savoy or Naples or, honestly, anyone else." He sighed. "But if the cardinal wills it, then we must needs obey."

De la Mothe looked back out across the city. Valbelle was a politician: a former *conseil* of the city, now merely a private citizen. But no one achieved any office in Marseilles without his help or consent. So it had been for decades. Cosme de Valbelle, the second of the name, had been elected for the first time in 1618 when he was in his early forties, and for a second, shorter term a few years ago. Now the first consulship was in the hands of the Sieur d'Aiglun, a bland nonentity. But no one—not de la Mothe, not Turenne, and certainly not the cardinal himself—had any illusions about who really ran the city.

Valbelle loved to perform the stately pavane, the game of *bons mots*, rather than get to the point. De la Mothe, for his part, had spent too much time in military service—fifteen years, man and boy—to be anything less than direct; but he knew that to achieve anything with Valbelle meant to play the game.

"Your note said that you had someone you wanted me to meet."

"Yes. It's part of the reason I invited you to la Garde. She's up here receiving some sort of medical treatment from the priory's hospitaller; she didn't trust the quacks and frauds down in the city."

"'She'?"

"Yes, *she*. The lady is an *up-timer*, Philippe. And a very fierce example of that unusual race. I'm sure you'll find her interesting."

Interesting was hardly enough to describe how Philippe de la Mothe-Houdancourt found Sherrilyn Maddox when he first met her that soft early-autumn day in the fortress-priory above Marseilles. She truly was fierce.

When Valbelle led him into the priory, passing beneath the escutcheon of François I and the lamb of the Apostle John bearing the Christian banner, the first thing he heard was the sound of feet on stone. He was on his guard at once, and nearly drew his blade when someone came running along the vaulted gallery. The person was in loose-fitting clothing with a queue of hair neatly tied behind, and came to a halt a few paces away, bent over slightly with hands on thighs, panting as if the exercise had been difficult.

He removed his hand from the hilt of his sword and looked at Valbelle, perplexed.

"Give it a moment," the older man said quietly.

De la Mothe said nothing and waited. At last the other person stood up straight. Though dressed in a long-sleeved blouse and some sort of pantaloons, he could see at once that it was a woman. Not unattractive, but she had clearly made no particular effort to enhance her appearance. Without saying a word—or asking leave of either Valbelle or himself—she walked somewhat gingerly to a stone bench that ran along the gallery and dropped to a seat.

"Sorry," she managed. "Still trying to get back in shape."

De la Mothe understood the words, but wasn't sure of the meaning. "Allow me to present myself," he said at last. "I am Philippe, Comte de la Mothe-Houdancourt, Governor of Bellegarde, General of France." He made a leg.

"Sherrilyn Maddox," she said. "Thuringian Rifles. Glad to meet you." She extended her hand, and when he took it with the intent of offering his lips she grabbed his palm and shook it.

When this unusual introduction was over, she let her hand fall to her sides and looked him up and down.

De la Mothe was dressed in proper attire that befit a count. He had left off his breastplate and other armor, retaining only his blade—and not the one he used when fighting with the cavalry. He had donned his best wig, and bore a decoration of the *chevau-légers* that he had earned at Saint-Martin-de-Ré a decade before.

"I hope I've not offended you, Comte. Monsieur. I'm not sure what title I should use."

"Do not trouble yourself, Madame—Mademoiselle—"

"Just call me Sherrilyn. My students at Grantville High had to call me 'Ms. Maddox,' but most people just stick to my first name."

"Then you may call me Philippe."

"Suits me fine," she answered. "Would you sit down, Philippe? Monsieur Valbelle said you had something you wanted to talk to me about. I was just running a few laps—this knee" she slapped one of her legs— "has been giving me problems, and I'm not a damn bit of good to anyone if I don't get back to form. No less than Harry Lefferts took me off the first team."

"Ah," de la Mothe said. "*That* is a name I know." He looked at Valbelle, and then stepped over to the bench and sat near the up-timer. *Lefferts* was a well-known troublemaker, who had made the acquaintance of the cardinal and had been tied to all kinds of mischief since the Ring of Fire. From what he heard, there were even young bravos in the Italian cities who styled themselves after him—*lefferti*, they called themselves.

"Everyone knows Harry and his Wrecking Crew," Sherrilyn said. "Well, that's pretty much over. The band has broken up, and there's no plan to get it back together. To be honest, Comte—Philippe—I'm a bit at loose ends right now."

De la Mothe was struggling with the idiom and looked up at Valbelle—but the older man had walked away along the gallery, leaving him in the company of the up-timer. "I'm...not sure what you mean. But if you are presently without a position, I expect that I could find something for someone of your talents to do."

"What did you have in mind?"

"You mentioned the Thuringian Rifles. And the, eh, 'Wrecking Crew.' I am certain that your weapons expertise would be invaluable to us."

"And by 'us,' you mean..."

"Myself and my commander. Henri Tour d'Auvergne. General Turenne."

"*Turenne*?" She frowned. "The guy who carried out the raid against our oil fields at Wietze? The guy whose troops killed Quentin Underwood?"

De la Mothe took a deep breath. "...Yes. He did command the raid on Wietze two years ago."

"I'm not sure I'm fond of the idea of *working* for him. Of course, you're not the enemy anymore, are you? Now we're friends with the French. And Quentin Underwood was a dick who got caught up in our German vacation. Still, I'd have to consider the merits of the idea."

"My lord of Turenne has no designs on your USE, Sherrilyn, nor on the armies of your allies. We *know* who the enemy is."

"And who might that be?"

"Spain."

"Huh. And where is Turenne now?"

"His army is encamped outside of Lyon. The—king—has ordered him south to keep watch on the

Spanish. We believe that the Count-Duke de Olivares, the Spanish King's minister, is preparing an invasion of France in cooperation with . . . certain elements."

"But not the USE."

"No. Certainly *not*. Olivares' chief ally is—may be— the king's brother. Monsieur Gaston. We do not know his whereabouts. He was most recently in Lorraine and the Franche-Comté, but he has relocated—possibly to Madrid, or even Rome. He has a peculiar skill at making trouble."

"Sounds like Harry Lefferts."

"I can see the comparison," de la Mothe said. "But as versatile as your friend Lefferts might be, Monsieur Gaston is infinitely more devious. And he plays at intrigues with the crown of a kingdom at stake. Our task is to help stop that."

"How do you expect me to help?"

"Over the past two and a half years, my lord of Turenne has been slowly retraining a body of troops to use the newer weapons that up-time technology has made possible. It has not been an easy task: skills and habits borne of a lifetime cannot be easily discarded."

"You did well enough at Wietze," she snapped. "Your General Turenne seemed to know exactly what the hell he was doing there, and he got what he wanted."

"Yes, that is true, mademoiselle. Sherrilyn. But a raid is not a military campaign, and a small, fast-moving force is not the same as an army. The Spanish are still exceptionally well-armed and numerous, and muskets can kill a soldier just as dead as a Cardinal rifle. We learned a great deal from the Wietze raid, but many of those under arms were not a part of that action.

"We could use someone with your skill and expertise to help train them, to cure their bad habits and teach them good ones. And also to pick out...the best of them for particular duties."

Sherrilyn laughed. "You want me to train down-timer soldiers. That's rich. You expect a bunch of professional soldiers to listen to *me* tell them what to do?"

"Monsieur de Valbelle told me that before the Ring of Fire you had been a teacher. Surely there are some aspects of that experience that would be helpful."

"I taught girls' P.E. at Grantville High," Sherrilyn said. "I blew a whistle and got a bunch of girls in line so they could do exercises and play basketball. I hardly think it's the same."

"Why?"

"Because...because they were teenage *girls*, Philippe, and they were afraid of me. These men aren't likely to see me in the same way."

"You might be surprised."

Sherrilyn leaned her elbows on her thighs and shook her head so that her hair, tied back in its queue, swung back and forth. "Philippe, I was born in 1965. For the last four years I've been in the seventeenth century, and unless the same crazy thing that put me here comes along and puts me back, I'm going to spend the rest of my life here. I get surprised pretty much every day, usually in a bad way, but sometimes..."

She gave him an appraising look, from wig to boots. He wasn't a bad looking man; he was a little younger than she was, and had obviously made an effort to look good for the day—maybe even for this meeting. He smelled less like the average seventeenth-century nobleman than she expected, and other than the

Durante nose and a few pox pockmarks—universal, other than for those who had gotten vaccinated in the last few years—he was easy to look at.

"Sometimes," she said, "the surprise is a good one."

"So you will accept."

"I didn't say that. But I'll think about it. How much time do I have to decide?"

"I leave Marseilles the day after tomorrow. We can have a spare horse . . . or two, if you require a lady's maid to travel with you."

"A lady's maid? Are you serious?"

He looked serious. In fact, he looked embarrassed at her reaction. "It is a few days' ride back to Lyon, Mademoiselle Sherrilyn, and you would be in the company of . . . the entourage would be all men, other than you."

"So?"

"It is only that there is some . . . possible appearance of impropriety."

"After the Wrecking Crew I don't think there's anything more improper that can happen to my appearance. I don't have a 'lady's maid,' Philippe, and don't know what I'd do with one. And if you're worried about someone of your troop making, what, an inappropriate advance . . . if they survive the experience, they'll survive with two broken arms. Or legs. Whichever is more painful, especially on horseback. Maybe one of each."

De la Mothe couldn't help but smile. "I think you mean it."

"Damn straight."

"Very well." He stood and sketched a bow. Valbelle, the perfect courtier, seemed to already realize that the interview was over, and was walking slowly back to meet him. "I shall await your reply."

Chapter 8

Marseilles

Sherrilyn had come to Marseilles with an introduction arranged by Estuban Miro to a Jewish doctor, Bonnel de Lattès. She'd gotten some nasty looks from some of the men in the Jewish Quarter—*imagine, a single woman without escort!*—but Bonnel had received her very kindly, and sent her and a bundle of medicines to Pont de Garde. There the priory had welcomed her, quizzed her on up-time—everyone seemed to still do that, even four years after the Ring of Fire—and gave her personal space. Apparently the Jewish doctor was well-regarded among the religious, having practiced some real medicine there over time.

Bonnel had visited her twice there while she rehabbed in the only way she knew how: fresh air and exercise and patience. It had dulled the memories of the Wrecking Crew's last campaign, and she might have stayed a while longer had Bonnel not introduced her to Cosme de Valbelle, who told her he might have a job for her.

De la Mothe's offer was interesting. She was a little concerned about whether she was the right person for the job: not that she didn't know her stuff—she did, that was for sure. And the offer paid well—his messenger later that afternoon had told her exactly how much Turenne was willing to spend to hire an up-timer gym teacher to work for him.

Truly, it came down to the idea of working for Turenne—and, by extension, Cardinal Richelieu. Since Grantville had been dropped into Thuringia more than four years ago, the enemy had consistently been France and the villain had always been Richelieu.

She'd been raised on adventure movies about the Three Musketeers. Richelieu was the fork-bearded red-cloaked devil who controlled the puppet king and manipulated everything and everybody to the advantage of church and country. The reality was different from that, of course. Not only was the cardinal a more complicated figure—Harry had told her that—but there really was a D'Artagnan, and he was supposed to be way different from the books and movies.

Richelieu had done a damn good job of trying to tear apart the USE from the get-go, so his villain status wasn't exactly fiction either. Wietze...that was just part of it. There had been battles on sea and land and in the air, leading to the big fight at Ahrensbök a year and a half ago.

It really was above her pay grade. Treaties and the Union of Kalmar and all of the business of the little princess's marriage...Sherrilyn knew that the world had changed from what it had been even in '31 and '32. But Harry would say what she was thinking: that she was a grunt, a regular soldier, not anyone significant.

Decisions were made by bigger people on a bigger stage. People like Ed Piazza and Mike Stearns made decisions . . . a high school principal and a coal miner before the Ring of Fire gave them field promotions.

A little destiny, or luck, or freakin' magic pixie dust, and it could be her instead of Ed or Mike.

All of this introspection led her back to the question: could she really think about working for Turenne and Richelieu?

If they really considered Spain as an enemy—which Sherrilyn certainly did, especially after the Crew's rescue of Frank and Giovanna on Mallorca—then the answer actually could be *yes.* And since she really was likely to have to deal with this bum knee for life, and since Philippe de la Mothe wanted to give her a chance to teach—something she understood—and since the pay was damn good—then the answer was probably *hell yes*.

But she was *really* going to need a whistle.

She took the job. It wasn't a difficult choice: the pay was good and the opportunity to do something— anything—was compelling. She knew that she could have stayed as long as she liked, but time was marching on.

On the day she prepared to go it was cold and brisk. Her cell, only a few extra blankets more luxurious than the ones the sisters occupied, was filled with sunlight. She packed her gear, which didn't amount to much. Before leaving the room she turned to look at it one last time. There was really no evidence that she'd been there at all.

"Sherrilyn?"

She turned to find a sister standing in the doorway: Sister Amelia, a tiny, middle-aged woman who had been exceptionally kind to her—she had arranged the extra blankets. Sherrilyn put down her pack and embraced the nun.

"I'm so glad you came by," Sherrilyn said. "I didn't see you in the refectory, and I would have been sad to leave without saying goodbye."

Amelia smiled—her *secret smile*, Sherrilyn thought. "Oh, never fear, daughter. You'd not pass through the gate without my blessing."

"I appreciate it."

"And how is your knee?"

"It aches rhythmically, but Dr. Bonnel's plaster seems to help. I'll manage."

"Good, good." She folded her hands. "I've actually come to let you know that you have a visitor."

"A visitor? Who—did the doctor come up?"

"No. It is a...member of his community, I think. He does not wear the hat, but I think...well. He is in the courtyard."

"Did he say what he wanted?"

"Only to speak with you. If you would prefer not to meet him, I can give your regrets—I can tell him that you have already departed. If you hurry, you can save me prayers at confession by making it true."

"It doesn't sound threatening. I'd be happy to meet him."

"I will accompany you, of course."

"Of course. But I can take care of myself."

"I am certain. But I will accompany you. I am curious—so I will face extra prayers at confession after all."

Now it was Sherrilyn's turn to smile. She picked up her pack.

"Lead on."

The priory had a large open courtyard, flanked by four passageways, with solid walls on one side and plain, solid pillars on the other, ending in doors leading to other parts of the complex. Inside was a square area forty or so feet across where the sisters had planted flowers and herbs. There was a single stone bench in the middle; as they approached, she saw a modestly dressed man patiently sitting and waiting. He was middle-aged, with a carefully trimmed beard and moustache. There was a gray skullcap on his head (as opposed to the pointed, peaked *Judenhut* that she'd sometimes seen in Marseilles). But from his looks he might have been Estuban Miro's cousin.

Sister Amelia settled onto a bench and drew out her rosary. Sherrilyn set her pack beside her friend and walked out into the courtyard.

"Mademoiselle Maddox," he said, standing up. "I am so pleased to meet you at last."

"What can I do for you, Monsieur—Monsieur—"

"My name is Seth ben Adret," he said. "I am a humble soap-maker by trade, but I come as a friend of Dr. Bonnel—and of another mutual friend."

"I have a lot of friends."

"The . . . principal," ben Adret said. "Your former principal."

Principal, she thought. Did he mean Harry Lefferts? . . . Then she realized what he was trying to say, and practically slapped her forehead. He meant Ed Piazza—the former principal of Grantville High School, who was now president of the State of Thuringia-Franconia.

The Principal. It was like the name of a Batman villain. "I haven't talked to him for some time."

"I understand. But please be informed that he is aware of your presence here in Marseilles, and the employment opportunity you have just accepted."

"Huh. Is he trying to tell me not to take it? Because it's none of his damn business whether I take a job or not. If this is some sort of loyalty test—"

"No, no, Mademoiselle Maddox," he said, putting his hand up. "He is not telling you that at all. Indeed, he wishes you the best of luck in the position—there is no enmity between your new employer and . . . your previous one."

"All right then. But *he* sent you to talk to me?"

"Yes. He wanted to let you know that he had not had a letter from you for some time and would welcome one. Or more."

Sherrilyn thought about it for a moment, frowning. Before she could frame an answer, Seth ben Adret stepped forward and took her right hand in both of his. She was surprised enough not to react or pull away immediately.

Sister Amelia, who had seemed to drift off into a nap, was sitting forward, moving to get up. Out of her sight, though, ben Adret had slipped something into her palm: a small square object, perhaps two by three inches. He withdrew his hands, letting them fall to his sides, and fixed Sherrilyn with a steady gaze.

She didn't know what to make of it, but tucked the gift—a small, leatherbound book—into her sleeve, and nodded.

"He is sure that you will do well in your new role," the Jewish soap-maker said. "He knows that it is trite to say so, but wherever an up-timer goes, the United States of Europe goes with him. Or her."

"Thank you," she said. "And please thank the principal when you communicate with him. I'm glad to hear that he hasn't forgotten me."

"On that," ben Adret answered, "you can be sure."

De la Mothe's troopers went out of their way to respect her person and her privacy as they traveled. She wasn't sure if they were genuinely intimidated by her, by the cachet of an up-timer, or if the comte had warned them of her statement to him regarding broken limbs . . . or if he'd simply told them to be polite. But she was allowed privacy whenever they stopped to rest.

Late in the afternoon, the first day out from Marseilles, they stopped near a creek to water the horses. She separated herself and went a few dozen yards away to attend to her personal needs, after which she reached into a pocket within her pack and drew out the book that ben Adret had given her.

It was sixteen pages in length and carefully and beautifully printed in tiny type. The first fourteen pages consisted of a long list of common words that she might use in a letter about her assignment, but which were . . . descriptive, possibly sensitive. *Rifle. Troop. Attack. March. Reinforce. Siege.* There were hundreds of other, nonmilitary terms, but those caught her eye. Next to each one was another reasonably common word: *Shovel. Chorus. Invite. Vacation. Draw. Broil.* It was a cipher—not an especially clever one, but something she could use to send sensitive information.

God damn it, she thought. *Ed—the "Principal"— wants me to be a* spy. *De la Mothe says that Turenne has no designs on the USE, but Ed Piazza wants to make sure.*

The last two pages contained a set of substitution codes, a dozen of them, each keyed to—of all things—TV shows, all seemingly from the 1990s. To indicate which code she used, she'd have to include a reference to a character on the show: Buffy, Mulder, Cooper (that one took her a minute, then she remembered *Twin Peaks*); Lois; Sipowicz; Munch; and so on. It was a long way from unbreakable, but without any real computing power it would be hard.

It could also get her killed. Even having this little book could get her killed. What the *hell* did Ed Piazza think he was doing?

But she knew the answer to that question, even as she stowed the little book back in the inner pocket of her pack. He was watching out for the interests of the USE. It was true in a way, what ben Adret had said: wherever an up-timer went, the USE went with it. There were about three thousand up-timers in the world, a tiny little drop in a fairly big ocean, and there weren't going to be any more of them. In five years, in ten years, that number would be even smaller . . . and not all up-timers felt loyalty to the last vestige of the world where they'd grown up. Some, and she counted Harry Lefferts among them, had really gone native—this was their time not just by circumstance but by inclination.

God damn it.

One of de la Mothe's troopers called out to her, walking slowly along the river bank, not seeming to want to get too close. Sherrilyn smiled to herself; the guy must be attached to his limbs.

"I'll be right there," she answered, stepping back into view with her pack slung over her shoulder. *The USE goes with me*, she thought.

Part Two

The Virtue Of Fortitude

A noble and steady purpose of mind

Chapter 9

March, 1636
Lyon, France

It had taken all winter to sort them out.

When Sherrilyn Maddox first arrived at Marshal Turenne's headquarters, she expected to find an army camp—men in tents or barracks, with the marshal himself living rough with his troops. She had heard of his common touch... all the way from Marseilles, in fact: the men in her escort had made a great display of it.

But Turenne himself, and his staff, had engaged a very handsome villa outside of town where they were accommodated in quite comfortable style. It was fully staffed, and Sherrilyn was given her own room. It was a simple solution to a problem she had been concerned about: how to doss down with a few thousand men.

"You are comfortable?" he asked the day she arrived. She was walking around her room, pacing it out, looking at the furnishings and wondering what might break if she sat or leaned on it. Turenne had just come in from a ride: he had mud on his boots and hadn't taken the spurs off. He took his leather riding gloves off and tucked them in to his belt.

"More than comfortable, my lord," she said.

"Marshal is fine. Sherrilyn Maddox, isn't it?" He gave the name a surprisingly American pronunciation. "Colonel Maddox from now, I think."

"That's quite a promotion."

"It is what I had in mind." He looked down at his boots, as if noticing them for the first time. "I am very pleased to have you here at last. I know that de la Mothe explained my interest in having you come here."

"I admit to skepticism."

He stepped into the room, avoiding the delicate carpet and settling himself onto an armchair. Sherrilyn came and sat nearby.

"That is quite understandable," Turenne said. "I know de la Mothe told you that I needed someone to help train my troops—to teach them to fight like a modern army. But I realize, and I am sure you realize, that if each has a Cardinal rifle in his hands and knows how to shoot it, that is more than sufficient."

"I've done the math. Three shots a minute—three thousand men or so, that's nine thousand rounds a minute at a range of two to three hundred yards. Even if your men were lousy shots—"

"They're not."

"Even if they were, your average tercio would never reach the front ranks of your force. And a cavalry charge wouldn't get there either. If they really *can* shoot, then you have everything you need. The Spanish have no idea what you can do, do they?"

"The Spanish do not think too deeply about anything,"

Turenne answered. "I suspect that they would not expect much from a few thousand French troops against the mighty *Tercio Español*. With the proper cavalry support they would expect themselves to be unbeatable. If they come up against us—"

"Is that what's going to happen, Marshal? The Spanish are going to invade France?"

"I don't know. The cardinal clearly has some inkling that it might happen—otherwise why would we be deployed here? It's a long way from Paris—or the Dutch frontier—or anywhere else but Spain or Savoy." He made a gesture with his hand. "Really...it's a long way from just about everywhere."

"Keeps the boys out of trouble."

"Oh, believe me, mademoiselle, they make their own trouble. But it is a much smaller amount of trouble than they might make in sight of Notre-Dame de Paris.

"But to the point. The men can shoot; the rifles are accurate and deadly. My subcommanders have trained them well. I don't need you to help with that."

"Then..."

"When the Spaniard crosses the Pyrenees, as he surely will, it may not be with trumpets sounding and banners flying. We will need to know what he intends to do and where he intends to go. It will be this for which we will need your expertise. I believe the up-timer term is 'small unit tactics'—infiltration and precision attack at a distance. One rifle—one shot."

"Snipers."

"I have heard that term used, yes. I originally thought it meant a sort of hunting exercise, but I have come to understand it as something far more deadly and effective. My men can shoot, yes, but not all of them can perform this mission." He pointed at Sherrilyn. "I want you to find the ones who can."

And so she had. She had divided them into groups of twenty to see which ones met the minimum standard: decent eyesight, skill in the manual of arms, and careful use of their weapon. Once she could see which ones could *see* the broad side of a barn, she picked out the ones who looked like they had a chance of actually hitting that barn with reasonable skill. Those whose marksmanship—and poise—impressed her made it into a second, smaller group.

Turenne's quartermaster went to the marshal to complain on the first day regarding the extravagant waste of powder. Turenne thanked him and ignored him. He appeared each of the next two days, still hopping mad at Sherrilyn for squandering resources—and each time the marshal heard him out and turned him away. The fourth time he appeared at the villa there was a short closed-door meeting from which he emerged chastened: that was the last time anything was said about it.

She taught her little group of thirty-five every trick that the Wrecking Crew had managed to use during its active career. The hardest lesson was convincing them to think for themselves (as opposed to simply thinking *about* themselves—which mostly involved thinking with what was in their breeches.) There were thirty-one left after that lesson.

By the spring there were only twenty-four, for various reasons—but it was worth all the powder and shot, all the sidelong looks, the snide remarks, and the two brawls.

To fill out her company—*Maddox's Rangers* was what they decided to call themselves—there were sixteen regulars who could handle themselves well in a close-in fight. A winter's worth of conversations with Turenne's sergeants and NCOs helped pick those guys out.

It wasn't exactly the varsity at Grantville High—but it was what Turenne wanted.

It was just a matter of putting it to use.

> March 28, 1636
> Lyon, France
>
> *Dear Ed:*
> *Thanks for sending me the nice going-away gift when I decided to give up Marseilles for this place. It sure seemed like a good idea at the time, but I'd rather have some soft Mediterranean breezes than the wind off the Massif Central. One winter in this place would probably be enough. It's colder than old Mr. Mulder's classroom at the high school, when he'd leave all the windows open.*

Mulder had never been a teacher at Grantville High. That was a keyword from the cipher book, telling them what page to use. *Windows open* meant that the army was in camp, and hadn't been given orders to deploy anywhere.

> *Things have been pretty smooth here. The best part has to be the food. The boss treats us very well, nothing but the best. He's even*

> *arranged for the best forks and knives to*
> *be put in all of the troopers' hands, and*
> *they've all learned to eat with them. Some*
> *of them are still a little sloppy, but mostly*
> *they put the food in their mouths.*

The connection between Mulder and the windows had been clever. This reference was a little less subtle—*forks and knives* meant weapons, and the best weapons had to refer to the Cardinal rifles. And they'd been given to all the men, and they all knew how to shoot.

> *The head cook comes up with amazing reci-*
> *pes. They told me that originally the food*
> *wasn't fit to eat—it made people sick—but*
> *you know how it is with cafeterias. After*
> *a while, if you start with good ingredients,*
> *you can make a pretty good meal. I'm a*
> *believer, and so is he.*

Recipes was a cipher-replacement for *ammunition*. The comment about making people sick was a reference she hoped he'd understand, going along with the word *believer*. Their engineering expert was Johann Glauber, a chemistry wizard who had found a way to replace the mercury fulminate in the percussion caps with something more effective and far safer.

Glauben, of course, was the German word for "believe."

> *It's a little harder than working for you,*
> *but I guess teaching is teaching. You get*
> *the students lined up, you blow the whistle*

*and you watch them run. You can't make
an omelet without breaking eggs, but at
least I have a few cartons. Well, two cartons at least.*

She was guessing that the average down-timer
wouldn't know that an egg carton held a dozen eggs,
so that the key number here was twenty-four—the
number of special troopers she was training.

There wasn't any easy way to explain to Ed exactly
what she was doing by using the cipher since most of
the substitution terms weren't useful in this context.
It was probably going to take a few letters back and
forth in order to get the hang of it—if someone didn't
figure out that she was sending in code.

I am not cut out for this, she thought, and nearly
tossed the whole thing into the fire. What was the
benefit? She could convey a few general things, and
would be risking that Turenne, or someone else in
the camp, would figure out that she was spying on
them. That sort of thing could get you killed . . . after
some very nasty things happened to you.

But I think you'd like these guys, she finally
wrote. *The boss has kept them busy digging,
enough for twelve main drags, but that's
like running laps on the track.*

The *main drag*, the principal road through Grantville, was Route 250; 12 x 250 was 3,000. Maybe he'd
get that reference, maybe not. As for *liking these guys*,
she was trying to tell Ed that they were probably not
enemies of the USE.

If they were going to catch her spying, this letter would surely do it. She decided to close it out before she wrote something even more transparent.

I'll look forward to your letter.
>   *Best regards,*
>   *Sherrilyn Maddox*
>   *Gym Teacher to the Stars*

Chapter 10

March, 1636
Turin

Just after Twelfth Night, Monsieur Gaston and his entourage had departed the Castello del Valentino. The duke and duchess were relieved—at least in private—and life returned to normal.

In the workshop, Baldaccio paid more attention to Terrye Jo than ever, trying to bring her his own peculiar brand of seventeenth-century science. On the long winter nights he turned his attention to the stars: a new telescope, with hand-ground lenses from a new glass factory in Magdeburg, had arrived during the second week in January, and the *Dottore* had arranged to have it mounted on the top of one of the corner towers. He would go up late at night wrapped in a ridiculous fur coat and peer through it, taking crabbed notes that he would transcribe onto astrological charts. There was a tussle when he pulled down a portion of the latticework supporting the antenna;

whatever his professorial chops, his researches didn't trump Terrye Jo's radio. By the next evening it was up again. He had a personal interview with His Grace to clarify the matter and it was never repeated.

Undeterred, Baldaccio had shown her the horoscope he'd cast for her, explaining that the "imbalance in her humours" (or some other damn thing) resulted from having Venus in Scorpio or Jupiter in retrograde, and that she'd have to stop pining for Monsieur Gaston and find a proper man to bed with if she wanted to get everything back in balance.

She held back from strangling Baldaccio or dropping a heavy weight on his head. Meanwhile, Artemisio offered to slit his nose and ears.

"No one will know who did it, *Donna*," he said. "And I shall console you in your misery."

"*Everyone* will know you did it," she answered. "And I won't need consoling."

He gave her a sad expression that he must have practiced. She was unmoved.

As the winter wore on Terrye Jo spent some time getting to know *GJBF*. He—she supposed it was a he: the sender communicated exclusively in French, so it probably wasn't an up-timer—was slow at first and, while he was accurate, he didn't use most of the standard contractions and shortcuts all telegraphers knew. She worked with him and his speed and familiarity gradually improved.

The handle *GJBF*, it happened, stood for *Gaston Jean-Baptiste de France*—Monsieur Gaston himself had picked it out. *GJBF* called himself a *créature*, which Terrye Jo thought sounded very demeaning, as if he was the lowest kind of servant. But *GJBF* explained that it pointed at a particular kind of relationship, one in which responsibility went both ways: *GJBF* was completely loyal to his patron, and Monsieur Gaston owed his *créature* a certain kind of protective care when he "came into his inheritance."

Terrye Jo came to realize more and more what that meant. Gaston's "inheritance" was the throne of France. He had been exiled from his own country for conspiring against it, but instead of hanging him or beheading him or shooting him like a rabid dog, King Louis and Cardinal Richelieu had finally sent him into exile—four years ago, not long after the Ring of Fire. It didn't make any sense to Terrye Jo. She asked *GJBF* why Monsieur Gaston was still alive and he seemed shocked that she'd even ask.

Gaston wasn't her patron and his brother wasn't her king. Duke Amadeus and Duchess Christina weren't her duke and duchess either: the duke was her boss, no more and no less. But it still made her feel uneasy. This was political intrigue, maybe leading to treason, and it passed through her radio, *SPAR* to *GJBF* and back again. The queen of France was pregnant; she was hidden somewhere; and *GJBF* was trying frantically to find out where. If he found out he would tell her, and eventually that news would find its way back to Monsieur Gaston . . . and then something would happen.

She felt bad for the queen and told the duchess about it. Christina had given birth to a daughter in November. Amadeus had hoped for a son, of course, but was very happy that the duchess had made it through childbirth. Terrye Jo knew that a daughter meant that Christina would likely be pregnant again soon.

"Hm," the duchess said to her when she expressed

her concern about Queen Anne. "I don't know why you'd feel that way. She's been in danger from my brother Gaston for years."

Terrye Jo had found her in the nursery. Most of the time the little princess—Margherita Violante—was in the care of nursemaids, but Christina was unusually affectionate for a seventeenth-century noblewoman. Terrye Jo wondered to herself if this was a result of the Ring of Fire, or whether she'd been this way with the other children. Whatever the case, the duchess was in the nursery quite often, not simply having the baby brought to her.

She had sent the nanny on an errand at once, as soon as Terrye Jo had mentioned the French queen's name. Now she stood looking over the crib, where her infant daughter lay quietly sleeping.

"But now that she's pregnant—"

"She's been pregnant before. The poor thing has never carried to term. Why should this time be any different?"

Christina didn't seem terribly worried or sympathetic. In a way she sounded like a mean girl from Grantville High.

"This is the first time since the Ring of Fire," Terrye Jo said. "Maybe there's an up-timer doctor."

The duchess thought about this for a moment. "That's possible, I suppose. Someone from your people might be able to help her—but again, some women simply can't bring a child to term. It's a defect in their bodies. There's been so many problems, I wonder why Louis hasn't just put her aside, sent her back to Spain."

"I thought he couldn't do that."

"With God all things are possible," she answered,

crossing herself. "Without issue, the marriage could be considered unconsummated, and His Holiness could set it aside on petition. Lord knows he could have found a more suitable partner."

"Suitable?"

"More...fertile. More able to draw him out. Though at the time we all thought..." she let the sentence hang.

"It seems pretty underhanded."

"My dear." Christina said. "You are so delightfully naïve. This sort of thing happens all the time. Anne has been unhappy in France; some is her own doing, some is Louis'—he never understood how to treat his queen. Some of her unhappiness is due to our mother: she couldn't stand the idea that anyone would come between her and her son. And then there's the cardinal." She frowned. "I'm sure he'd rather that my brother have an heir, and it's a positive wonder that he hasn't arranged it somehow. But Louis was always..."

"Always what?"

She didn't answer for several moments, as if she was trying to find the right word. The little princess whimpered very quietly, and Christina reached out a hand to touch her daughter's forehead.

Terrye Jo had an idea what Christina wanted to say, but didn't know what they called it in the seventeenth century.

"Sensitive," the duchess finally decided.

Sensitive, Terrye Jo thought. *That's a good word.*

"Sure. But maybe this time it's different."

"I doubt it. In fact, if there *is* issue, I would have to be convinced that Louis is the father. Some women are defective; some men are defective as well."

"So... Monsieur Gaston—"

Christina held up her hand. "My dear Teresa. I shall give you a piece of advice, and I trust you will take it. It would be far better if you simply did the work that our duke or my royal brother has set you to do without question or concern, and let it go at that. Gaston will return this spring, I am sure of it, and things will take their course. It would be best for you not to oppose my brother... or my husband."

"I never intended to oppose anyone."

The duchess gave her a long, hard, appraising look, but it wasn't any more fierce than a middling-scary drill sergeant.

"I shall take your word, Teresa. We will speak no more of this."

Up-time, when she was little, Terrye Jo would journey far from Grantville in her mind with the help of the radio. Her dad had told her the usual stories about listening to Pirates games late at night with his little transistor—but this was the 1980s, and she had better equipment: a boom box that her uncle had bought her for Christmas. It could pick up Pittsburgh, and Wheeling, and even Detroit if the weather was right. Hearing the words *The Great Voice of the Great Lakes* coming out of the tubby little box late at night made her realize how *big* the world was and how small Grantville was.

It was still small, and in a way *this* world was even bigger—no airplanes, no superhighways, only a few coal-powered trains. Things were farther apart, and the radio spectrum was far more sparse. But it wasn't empty: especially in the last year there had been more and more broadcasts of one sort or another—the messages were almost all in the clear, and mostly in German or Amideutsch, with some French and Italian mixed in. During her shifts in the radio room she found herself returning to her former diversion. She would start at the bottom of the dial and slowly move up, listening for some operator's signal out in the dark, most often sending dots and dashes in short, fitful bursts with lots of errors and *QSM*s requesting a re-send.

It was boring stuff. Weather reports, gossip, sometimes the death of a nobleman or the birth of his child...no baseball games, no world news reports, no entertainment, just the steady and unsteady signals of Morse code sent out into the night. *Here I am*, the signals said. *Here we are.*

One cold spring night in late March she had gotten about a third of the way up the dial when she heard a clear, firm signal—a fist she hadn't heard before, an operator who knew what he was doing. The other guy wasn't too bad, but the first one was a real pro. She assumed it was an up-timer at first, someone who had learned to send before the Ring of Fire. But she realized that there was no reason to think that—anyone who spent a few months working at it could become proficient. Henri could already send and transcribe almost as fast as Terrye Jo, and most of the other operators weren't far behind.

The messages were in French. They used expressions and phrases that she didn't completely understand, but after listening for a half an hour she was able to start making sense of it. One of the senders was speaking for someone he called *Le Maréchal*; the other referred to *Le Cardinal*.

It was high-level stuff, and it was coming in the clear.

The idea that she was listening in on something that should have required a security clearance was a bit scary. She certainly knew who *Le Cardinal* must be—that had to be Richelieu, so that end of the conversation was in Paris. *Le Maréchal* was in Lyon, over the mountains; there was some sort of army there, a couple of hundred miles from Turin.

Were they getting ready to invade Savoy? She knew very well what Monsieur Gaston thought of Richelieu, and Gaston was on very friendly terms with the duke...

But Victor Amadeus would know if there was an army on his border, ready to invade, she thought. *Of course, Lyon isn't* exactly *on the border with Savoy.*

Why were they there? France's main war theater was Lorraine, and if anything they'd want troops in the field facing the Low Countries or the USE. What was the point of having an army hundreds of miles to the south?

In any case *Le Maréchal*, whoever he was, had a damn good telegraph operator working for him.

She noted the transmission frequency on her pad, intending to check in on it again the next night, and was about to sign off when she heard a snippet that made her sit up. The operator for *Le Maréchal* commented that the *entraînement spécial*—'special training,' whatever that was—had been going very well ... and that *Colonel Maddox* had been an excellent investment.

Maddox, Terrye Jo thought to herself. There was no way to be sure, but ... it couldn't be Ms. Maddox—Sherrilyn Maddox, her old nemesis and P. E. teacher? It might almost make sense, though. Maddox had joined Harry Lefferts' Wrecking Crew, so she was

out there somewhere; why not with a French army? Did that mean that Harry and his posse were all there too, teaching *Le Maréchal* their own particular methods for raising hell?

She didn't know what it meant, and wasn't sure if it was relevant, and even if it was if she should tell Amadeus, or Monsieur Gaston, or someone in Magdeburg.

After moving the dial away from that frequency, she broke one of her own firm rules for the radio room. She took the top sheet from the note pad, and the two sheets underneath that might have an impression from her pencil, and tucked them away in an inner pocket. If she'd learned anything from history at Grantville High—or in the few years since the Ring of Fire—it was that wars sometimes got started by accident. One piece of information, overheard by someone or interpreted the wrong way, could lead to the worst kind of consequences.

When Sylvie came in at midnight to take her shift, Terrye Jo said nothing about it. The other did not seem to notice the missing pages...but as she made her way up to her quarters they felt like a leaden weight.

Chapter 11

April, 1636
Sacra di San Michele, Savoy

At the ruined abbey of San Michele on the south side of Mount Pirchiriano, two soldiers stamped their feet and blew on their hands to try to keep warm. By the calendar, spring was three weeks old—but the snow on the ground and the icy wind put the lie to it.

"What did we ever do to Monsieur to get posted here, Jacques?" asked the younger soldier. He was tall and trim, and affected the same style of moustache and beard as his master.

The other man, shorter and older, turned aside and spat by way of answer. He had seen a considerably greater number of seasons, and didn't bother much with fashion. He also didn't ask questions anywhere near as much.

"Are you sure that he will be here?" Jacques continued.

"He told us he will come, Pierre, then he will

come. I know better than to disobey him." He gave his young companion a hard look as if to say, *and if you have any sense, you'd best do the same.*

"Why in this God-forsaken place?"

"Hah." Jacques scratched his beard. The ruins fit that description pretty well: the big stone structure with a tall tower and stone outbuildings sprawling all over the side of the hill was completely abandoned. "*God-forsaken.* You have the makings of a court fool, my young friend. There hasn't been very much of a presence up here since some pope or other threw the monks out of here ten or fifteen years ago... though I don't know how blessed it was when there *were* monks up here. But the answer to your question should be obvious even to a clown—it's miles from everywhere, but commands a good view of the road that leads over the mountains from the west all the way to Turin. A perfect place for a secret meeting."

"And we're here..."

"To make sure it stays secret," Pierre said. "The young bastard will be coming from *that* way—" he pointed west, toward the road that bent toward the little village of Bussoleno—"and Monsieur is traveling from Tuscany and should come up *that* way." He pointed in the other direction. "Then, I would guess, we will journey together to Turin."

"Seems like a lot of trouble to go to. But maybe he likes the view, Pierre."

"Shut up."

Before Jacques could respond, there was a high-pitched whistle. Jacques and Pierre drew their swords and stepped next to the tower, each looking in a different direction. After a few moments, two horsemen approached, climbing the hill in plain sight. Even from the distance, Jacques could pick out the livery of the house of Vendôme.

The two men put up their swords and approached.

Louis de Vendôme, Duke of Mercoeur, cut a fine figure. Tall and handsome, he was an excellent horseman and—Pierre and Jacques knew—a talented swordsman. During the last few years as he had accompanied Monsieur Gaston, there had been numerous occasions for him to demonstrate that skill in affairs of honor. The soldiers knew their place and stood respectfully as Louis dismounted. He was traveling light and fast, with two gentlemen in waiting and a valet, who dismounted and followed in turn. The servant caught the reins of the horses and led them carefully up the slope behind the others.

"Is he here?" Louis said.

"Not yet, Your Grace," Pierre said. "We have been watching for him."

The nobleman turned away, looking down the road and then up toward the towering, broken façade of the abbey.

"God-forsaken place," he said.

Jacques smirked at Pierre, out of sight of the duke; Pierre scowled at him, then turned to the nobleman. "Yes, my lord. But it is as His Highness commanded."

"Yes, yes." He kicked the base of the tower, loosening mud and snow from his boots. "We're going to go inside. Keep careful watch and alert me when he approaches."

"Of course, my lord."

He said nothing further, but beckoned to his two gentlemen companions. They began to walk up a narrow stone stair toward an arched portal that led to the interior.

The valet, holding the reins of the horses, looked at Pierre and Jacques, as if they might tell him where to stable them. When they didn't respond, he led them slowly around the base of the abbey to a place out of the wind and out of sight of the road below.

When Monsieur Gaston arrived a short time later, Louis and his companions had had a chance to walk around the ruins, and had located a place that had probably served as a refectory for the monks. It had a number of broad tables and benches, weather-beaten but largely intact; when the monastery was closed down, the lower windows had been boarded up, keeping most of the weather out. There was evidence that some animals had made their lairs there, and someone not too long ago—probably during this winter—had built a fire in the hearth, but the place was otherwise deserted.

"Charming," Gaston said as he came down the little stair into the refectory. Louis had been giving his attention to some of the carvings in the stonework while his gentlemen lounged on the benches, their feet up on the tables. They scrambled to their feet and offered a leg to the prince, earning a scowl from Louis; they were supposed to be attending him.

Louis was even more annoyed that the two ruffians set to keep watch hadn't warned him of Gaston's arrival. But he was determined to show none of this to the prince.

"Good day, Uncle. I trust you had a pleasant journey."

Gaston drew off his riding gloves and slapped them on his thigh, then tucked them into his belt. "Oh, yes. *Bracing.* But this venue will afford us some privacy."

Louis nodded. "That it will." He gestured to his retinue. "Go make yourself useless elsewhere."

They bowed and made their way out of the refectory, closing the heavy wooden doors behind them.

"It's so hard to find good help," Gaston said.

"Nearly impossible. But it's all my father could spare. At least they both speak passable Spanish, so they were helpful eyes and ears in Madrid."

Gaston gestured to a table, and the two men took seats opposite. "And how was Madrid?"

"Boring. His Majesty scarcely lets anyone see him directly; Olivares makes sure of that. It's all...what is that up-timer expression? 'Hurry up and wait.' Even the count-duke took over a week to give me an audience."

"Cheek. But what you would expect from a Spaniard?"

"Just so."

"What did he say?"

"It is as informative," Louis answered, "to relate what he did *not* say. Señor Olivares commended you on your wisdom with regard to support for Cardinal Borja. He allowed that his master the king continued to be troubled by the apparent disrespect shown to his royal sister by your royal brother, and was fretful about the recent actions of some up-timers on Mallorca."

"Interesting. Did he elaborate on that last?"

"Not in any detail. Apparently some prisoners taken during the—unrest in Rome, as he termed it—had escaped custody, and one of the king's most trusted *hidalgos* had accompanied them."

"Apparently he cannot find enough good help either," Gaston said, chuckling at his own wit.

"As you say, my lord. In any case, he is curious as to the effect a male heir might have on the political situation in France, and on your own situation with respect to our king."

"He knows *exactly* what a male heir would do," Gaston said. All trace of humor had left his face. "The count-duke de Olivares would be extremely unlikely to receive my envoy should my royal sister-in-law bring a healthy son into the world."

"He noted that your brother—and the cardinal— are being extremely careful on that account. Indeed, he asked me if we knew anything of Queen Anne's whereabouts. His master sought to correspond with her, and had been told by his envoy in Paris that such letters could be sent to the cardinal and they would be duly forwarded."

"I assume King Philip was dissatisfied with that answer."

"*I* assume," Louis said, "that King Philip had not actually posed the question. In any case, Olivares assumes that we know no more about Anne's location than he did. I demurred, and I hope that I conveyed the sentiment that if we did know, it was nothing we were prepared to share with him at this time."

"Clever."

"Thank you, Uncle. I don't know if I convinced him, but I might have planted a seed of doubt. In any case, I made it clear that regardless of the outcome of this ... diversion ... you were not prepared to fade into obscurity, and further, you considered the count-duke a friend and ally."

"What was his response?"

"That he was gratified, but that friends and allies sought mutual objectives as a result of mutual assistance."

"A *quid pro quo*. What does he want?"

"Oh, a great deal. A very great deal. Were you to ascend the throne, he would want you to publicly disavow Pope Urban; to make peace in Lorraine and remove the threat to Hapsburg troops in the Germanies; to permit free passage of Spanish troops through French territory—"

"Indeed!"

"Yes, Sire. And, of course, eradication of heresy in His Most Christian Majesty's domains—both here and abroad in the plantations. The other . . . requests . . . were merely conversational; but this last one seemed to be of particular moment. There I think he speaks not as the minister, but as the servant of his king."

"Let me speculate," Gaston said. "He wants France to be rid of the Huguenots."

"Essentially."

"You didn't commit to anything."

"Of course not. But neither did he. Olivares is canny, Uncle—very much like the cardinal. The Spanish face the past, by and large, but I think he stands apart from the rest of the court. He may even have a radio machine."

"The Spanish have no radios. They consider them tools of the Devil, and the Ring of Fire a work of Hell. They may even be right in that estimation."

The duc de Mercoeur paused for a moment to evaluate his uncle, trying to discern what was meant by the statement.

"That is their official policy," he continued. "But the count-duke seemed altogether too well informed. I would not underestimate him. I did not see any up-timers at the court, or in Olivares' household, but as we have seen, the skill required to operate the machine is modest. In Turin, the up-timer woman was training *servants* to do so."

"All right." Gaston ran a finger across his moustaches. "The count-duke de Olivares could be a very powerful ally, as I suspected. But we shall have to hold him close, or he could turn on us. My mother said as much."

"And how does the queen mother?"

"She frets about everything, and chafes at being in Florence. She would rather be back in Paris, but knows that it is unlikely to happen, even in the case that a new royal heir is born. I can't see her returning as long as the cardinal is alive. But even if she could, she would want to take back her old place.

"My brother the king would never permit it, and if I were king . . . I am not Louis, my Marguerite is much different from Anne, and enough years have passed by. We do agree on one thing: that the cardinal must go. I made no commitments to her other than that."

"You know that our family supports you completely in that matter, Gaston."

"The House of Vendôme has been made to suffer at his hands, Louis. I am sure your father will relish seeing him fall."

"He would be glad to help in any way. So would my brother and I."

"I know, my good nephew, and I prize your loyalty. If Richelieu were brought low, one way or another, I could even accept my exile and my brother Louis could reign in peace. I would be content, for France would be delivered from its tyranny. We will also be able to curtail the influence of up-timers—they are no good for France, and they will have to be swept away as well."

"Up-timers."

"Yes," Gaston said. "They have stolen France's glorious future and replaced it with one that does not belong to this world and this century. We can take that back. And we will."

Louis de Vendôme did not reply, and kept his face impassive, but while Gaston seemed utterly sincere in his assertion that he would be satisfied, Louis could not help but believe otherwise. Disposing of Cardinal Richelieu was his white-hot ambition, but supplanting his brother as king of France was scarcely less so. As for the business of the up-timers—if that was the means of his desire, then so be it. Louis did not care one way or the other.

But the kingship . . . that was something else.

You will never surrender that ambition, my good uncle, Louis thought. *My father will never be king, and will never try to seize the kingship. Though more capable than any of his brothers, his mother was Gabrielle d'Estreés . . . and thus he cannot be more than a* légitimé. *Now he is content. But you?*

No, Louis concluded. *Never. You will never surrender the notion that you are more capable than my namesake—that the throne and crown rightly belong to you. This is about Richelieu—but it is more about* you.

It has always been about you.

"That is most generous of you," Louis said at last. "I am sure the Fates will treat you kindly."

❖   ❖   ❖

Monsieur Gaston could barely contain his anger. He crumpled the sheet of paper in his hand and hurled it to the floor. The messenger flinched; but to his credit he stood his ground. He had ridden all the way from Paris by arrangement. Gaston had demanded that the Count of Soissons, his *créature* in Paris, send word of what he had learned by courier—in case anyone happened to be listening.

But the information Soissons had sent was no information at all.

"Questions," he said. "*Questions.* They outnumber answers. Your master has been deficient. He would not permit this message to be . . . what is the word? *Broadcast.* Sent by radio. Yet it is without information."

"I am sure he has told you whatever he knows—"

"He falls short," Gaston interrupted. "What does he say? What does his message tell me? I am merely informed that Madame is still with child, and is still in seclusion. What *is* of consequence is that your master has still not deigned to tell me *where she is*. Where? Some palace, some convent, a roadside tavern, a fisherman's shack on the coast of Gascony? I know she is not in the Louvre, and has not been since she became pregnant. But that is all I know. He caused you to ride all the way here to tell me that he has nothing to tell me."

"I am sure," the messenger said, "if Monsieur le Comte de Soissons knew this information he would certainly have conveyed it. And I am here," he added, more forthrightly than many who would stand in Monsieur's presence, "because Your Highness commanded my master to send me."

"Hah." Gaston lifted his chin and looked down the end of his Bourbon nose. "I assume your master *commanded* you to say that. My cousin of Soissons would like nothing better than to retain information that I want . . . but while he is devious, and while I am sure that he places his own goals above mine, I do not think he would keep this from me. Ultimately, he wants what I want. He does not know. But he must find out."

"I am sure that he is straining his efforts, Your Highness."

"Tell him . . . tell him that he must not rest until he learns where the queen has gone. My dear brother Louis' dalliance has proved fruitful—and if this child defies the odds and lives to term, and if, God help us, the child is a son . . ."

The messenger bowed his head.

Gaston made a fist. He gestured at the man. "Tell my lord of Soissons that his prince expects nothing short of success. And when we find out where she is . . ."

He bit the sentence off and turned away from the messenger, gripping the ornate carved back of a chair tightly enough for his knuckles to turn white.

"Your Highness?"

"That is all," Gaston said, not turning. "You may go."

Gaston noted with indifference when the door quietly closed, and he knew that he was alone. He walked slowly to his escritoire and sat down. He picked up his penknife and sharpened his quill, then drew a sheet of foolscap toward him, dipped the quill in ink and began to write.

> *M. le duc de Vendôme*
> *My dear brother César:*
>   *I trust that you are well, and eager to pursue the work we have set before our-selves. The time we have awaited is nigh, for reasons of which we are both aware.*
>   *I have made certain provisions, the details of which you already possess. When I have the requisite information, it will be promptly conveyed to you. When at last we meet we shall glory in the rebirth of the kingdom we both love . . .*

Chapter 12

May, 1636
Louvre Palace
Paris, France

It had been almost an afterthought: when the radio message came early in the morning, and was transcribed and placed into the cardinal's hands, he put aside everything and prepared to depart. In his haste he had almost left the watch sitting on his desk in its prescribed place, a finely crafted instrument ticking away the seconds beneath the exquisite sapphire glass.

Richelieu had often picked up the timepiece, a gift from a courtier who had obtained it in some way from some up-timer. It bore the name *Cartier*, the family surname of the prestigious watchmaker of a Paris that never would be—but it put Étienne Servien in mind of the great explorer who had uncovered the mysteries of the North American coast a century ago.

When he took it up, turning it this way and that to best catch the light, Richelieu seemed lost in its depths. It seemed to Servien that the minute work-ings cast a spell upon him, reminding him that time was fleeting (as the philosophers were eager to say).

The day of the message, however, permitted no time for reflection, no time to be ensorcelled by *Grantvilleur* wonders. Servien knew its contents at once, though it was passed to him sealed—the sender, a coded name, told the entire story. He entered his master's study, finding him bent over his work table upon which was spread a great map of the Germanies.

"What is it?" he said, without looking up.

"A message, Eminence." Servien proffered the sheet of paper, folded once and sealed. Richelieu glanced at his intendant, took the message, and upon noting the name on the outside quickly slit it apart and looked at it, his eyes darting down the sheet and then back at Servien.

"Who else knows of this?"

"Other than the radio operator and myself, no one."

"You are sure."

"I came directly to you, Eminence," Servien said. "The call came in not ten minutes ago."

"There is no time to lose. Present yourself to Monsieur de Saint-Simon, if you please, and inform him that I will wait on His Majesty presently."

"As you wish."

"And, Servien . . . I need not say that you are to speak of this to no other. We did not expect this for some time, but neither did our enemies."

"If they know of it at all."

"I do not doubt that they do, despite our best attempts to keep it secret." Richelieu permitted him-self a smile. "But if all is well, they will be unable to interfere. All that I have worked for, these past few years, will reach its fruition—and there will be nothing that *Monsieur* can do about it."

Richelieu was admitted to the king's presence without announcement or ceremony. At this early hour King Louis was untroubled by the court, and often spent his time with one or another project that ill-befit a monarch. The cardinal was not about to gainsay his master and the use of his time—but it meant that he might be in the dairy, or the stable, or a carpenter's or smith's shop rather than the royal apartments.

"Ah," the king said, without turning around from the bench at which he sat, working on some project. "Monsieur Saint-Simon, I trust you found—"

Richelieu cleared his throat. Louis turned suddenly, his face set in a mask of displeasure, as if annoyed that he might be disturbed by any but his first gentleman of the bedchamber, the young Saint-Simon—the latest favorite upon whom he had heaped honors and titles. Few would stand before the king when he was thus annoyed; Richelieu merely waited patiently.

"Ah. It's you."

"At your service, Sire," the cardinal answered, bowing, then folding his hands in front of him. "We have received a message."

"A message?"

"*The* message," he said. "The one we have been awaiting."

"Really!" The king stood, losing all interest in the project that had been occupying him. "Really. We are—we are somewhat early, aren't we?"

"Shorter than the customary term, my king. But

I am informed that all is well in hand. I intend to depart at once and ask your leave to go."

"At once? I—"

Monsieur de Rouvroy, Seigneur de Saint-Simon, swept into the room at just that moment from the other hallway. He held a basket filled with tools and bits of metal and leather and began talking at once. "I think I found everything you wanted, but it was a bit of work, so I beg your pardon for being late, but—"

He stopped suddenly, noticing the presence of Cardinal Richelieu.

"Oh."

Richelieu looked at him, stony-faced, his anger visible in his eyes. The young man reddened.

"You have our leave to go," Louis said without turning. "Go—go find yourself something to break your fast."

"As Your Majesty wishes," he said. He set the basket on the king's work-table and backed slowly out of the room, never taking his eyes from Richelieu.

When he was gone, Louis rolled his eyes. "You have frightened the man, Eminence. He's quite harmless, really."

"He is Captain of St. Germain and Versailles. He should not frighten so easily. I should have expected a trifle more decorum."

"Saint-Simon and I had set about a—a project. I do not think he expected anyone else to be here."

"I shall not trouble Your Majesty for very long."

"No indeed. And I am sure he will find something to—to amuse himself while I am gone."

"Gone?"

"Yes. Of course. I will accompany you, Richelieu. I wish to see what has—come of our efforts."

Richelieu paused. He had not expected this response. "My king, it had been my intention to leave at once. I do not think the proper guard could be assembled quickly to escort you. I intended to travel in haste—"

"I don't think we need any of that, do we?" The king looked away from his minister, as if he was distracted by something on the escritoire. Richelieu could not see it clearly but knew what it was: a small cameo locket bearing the likeness of his queen. Now that matters regarding the heir had been arranged, the king seemed much more at ease with a display of affection toward Anne, even in something so trivial as a keepsake.

"I don't think I take Your Majesty's meaning."

"I believe that we can dispense, dispense with an honor guard. I can be prepared to ride within the hour."

"But . . . the safety of the royal person—"

"I shall take care to be armed and attired. I have ridden to war before, as you know. My lady the queen is more than—more than a month early in her labor, *mon cardinal*, and even if my enemies suspected that she is with child, they do not expect her to give birth *now*. It is all a surprise. I shall ride as one of your gentlemen-at-arms."

"I hardly think that is appropriate, Sire."

"Oh, nonsense." He furnished Richelieu with a royal wave and favored him with a smile. It was truly a wonder. Richelieu had seen Louis in every disposition, but in most cases he was distracted, suspicious or unhappy—his oncoming fatherhood had returned him to the lightheartedness of his youth. "I—I am sure that your guard-captain can find me an appropriate set of clothes. I will be just another member of your escort—at least until we reach the chateau."

"I am sorry to disagree with Your Majesty, but I believe that this exposes you to unnecessary risk. There is a radio at Baronville. A message can reach you in due course and you can make your progress in state when the child is born. There is no need—"

"Need? You speak—speak of need?" Louis faced him directly. Richelieu immediately sensed a subtle change in his royal master's mood. He was all too well versed in the way in which Louis could instantly shift from one affectation to another.

At this delicate stage, he thought to himself, *I must tread very softly* . . .

When Richelieu did not respond, the king continued, pointing a finger at him. "For a quarter of a century I have been king of France, and through all of it I have had to respond to *needs*. To my—to my mother and her interminable demands; to my sisters, and their requirements for proper marriages; to my feckless brother, who can no longer live in this realm, but to whom concession after concession was extended while he let his henchmen go to the gallows or the block . . . to the Huguenots, to the pope, to every foreign nation that placed demands on my realm.

"And now at last I have what we most desire: an heir to the throne, an end to the intrigues of my lord of Orléans and all of his—his sycophants and coconspirators— and the queen tied by the strongest apron-string of all to this realm instead of the realm of her birth, the realm—the realm of Spain. You would deny me the pleasure of being present when that happens?"

"Your Majesty, I—"

"Answer me, Monseigneur, if you please. You would *deny me this*?"

"No," Richelieu said. "No, of course not. My hesitation derives not from selfishness but from care for your person and your safety. Of course you can take care of yourself as a gentleman and soldier." He offered a deep bow. "If I have offended, I humbly beg forgiveness."

While his head was still inclined, he could not see Louis' face, but his posture altered and relaxed.

"No," the king said at last. "No, my old friend." A hand came out and took his, and Richelieu stood straight. The king was smiling again. "You have not offended," Louis said. "Your concern is most—most understandable. But all is in order. I shall be perfectly safe in your company."

Chapter 13

Paris

The balcony doors were open to the crisp spring air, contrary to the admonitions of all down-time physicians. The view was magnificent: he could see the imposing façade of the church of St. Eustache, now nearly finished after a century of on-and-off labor.

Claude de Bourdeille, Comte de Montrésor, was fond of St. Eustache. His grandfather had been also. Most people only remembered the Seigneur de Brantôme for his memoirs and writings—entertaining, yes, but a trifle too lurid and explicit for the common person's tastes. Yet he had had an artistic eye as well as a critical pen, and he would have been very pleased to see the great church in this almost-complete state.

As for the rest of Paris, and the rest of France... Montrésor was not sure what he would have thought of that. The Ring of Fire had changed everything: politics, culture, science, and—for those who did not understand what divine or infernal purpose might have brought up-timers into this century—religion as well.

What Montrésor was not fond of was waiting. Or, to be honest, being summoned: the letter from Louis de Soissons had been insistent, almost to the point of rudeness. Louis was a prince of the blood and acted the part. He was a Bourbon to the hilt, as arrogant as his royal cousins. No lesser person would have commanded Montrésor's attention.

Montrésor had almost reached the limit of his patience when the count himself swept into the room. He walked to where Montrésor stood near the doors.

"Claude. So good of you to come."

"I could hardly refuse. But you should realize that I have been observed." He waved out the window. Down below, on the Rue Saint-Antoine, near the steps of St. Eustache, there was a man loitering. He was plainly dressed and was looking up at the balcony.

Louis, Count of Soissons, stepped closer and looked down.

"Quality. One of the cardinal's finest. Servien—and not the one who stays so close: his older cousin Abel, the one that styles himself *Marquis de Sablé.*"

Montrésor sniffed. "They are all the same."

"They are *not,*" Soissons said. "But it is of no matter." He reached into his doublet and drew out a sheet of paper. "They can watch all they want. I have news, and shortly your master will have it as well."

"What news?"

"Our friend in the red robe is on his way to see the queen give birth. He has just received a message by radio, and has left the city."

"Where is he going?"

"Somewhere to the west, not terribly far from Paris, Claude. I'm not sure just where. The queen—and soon the next king of France, assuming the blessed event is successful."

"Monsieur will be glad of the knowledge, but he will not be pleased that the birth is imminent."

Monsieur, the title given to the heir to the throne, currently belonged to Gaston d'Orleans, the king's younger brother. Montrésor had the honor at the moment to be Monsieur's favorite, which was enough to keep him away from his beloved Paris. He had spent altogether too little time here, in part due to the constant suspicion of Cardinal Richelieu. Ever since Montrésor had decided to attach himself to Monsieur Gaston, his comings and goings had been carefully watched by the spies and intendants and other little creatures employed by the red-robed menace who ruled this kingdom and its weak-willed king. As a result he had thought it best to remain by Monsieur's side or at his estate in the country, depriving himself of the pleasures of the great city—and incidentally depriving the cardinal of information on his friends and activities.

Soon, Montrésor thought to himself, *that will all change.*

"How did you get this information, did you say?"

"A radio transmission. There is a radio at the chateau."

"And you have a spy at the Louvre who relayed the message. Very clever, *Monsieur le Comte*—I am surprised that you could break Richelieu's security—"

"I didn't, Claude. I merely intercepted the transmission." Soissons smiled. "I have intercepted all the transmissions."

Montrésor frowned, baffled. "I don't understand. If you... intercepted the message... then how was it received by the cardinal?"

"You don't really understand radio, do you?"

Montrésor put on his best expression of noble disdain, as if the entire matter was beneath him. "Some up-timer matter. I'm sure it is a wonder."

Soissons sighed. Gaston—Monsieur Gaston, who should have been, and might someday be, king of France—was arrogant, petulant, self-absorbed and at times ruthless: but at least he wasn't an idiot. The count wondered how long Montrésor—elegant, cultured Montrésor, who was near cousin to an idiot—would last as Gaston's favorite.

"A radio message," Soissons said patiently, "is not like a letter. It is like a town crier—one that speaks a different language that only its recipients can hear."

"I don't quite understand."

"The town crier goes from place to place and gives out the news," Soissons said. "Except *this* one speaks—I don't know, Catalan. And no one in the town square speaks Catalan except one person, and he understands what the crier says."

"So you bribed the Catalan speaker."

"*No*," Soissons answered. "No. I found someone who speaks Catalan and hired him. So when the crier gives the news, I hear it too, and understand it."

"So... the people where the queen is in seclusion are sending you messages as well?"

"Yes. No, not exactly." Soissons ran a hand through his hair. "The radio there is broadcasting—shouting—a message. Richelieu is receiving the message, and *so am I*."

"Is that possible? I thought a radio talked to another radio."

"A radio talks to all the radios that might be listening at the time. They use a code, but it's primitive enough that it was easily broken. Everything His Eminence hears, my radio hears as well. He has no idea that I am listening in, of course—but now I know where he is going."

"I assume that you are having him followed."

"No."

"No?"

"Better than that, Claude. If all goes well, our good cardinal will never reach his destination."

Forêt de Rambouillet

César, duc de Vendôme, *légitimé de France*, sat on his charger, appreciating the quiet moment that occurred just before battle. To call what was to come a *battle*, of course, was an exaggeration at best; but the quiet was reassuring nonetheless. The weather enhanced the quiet. The rain had mostly gone, replaced by a faint drizzle and a fog that shrouded the late afternoon light.

This feeling joined with the elation he felt to be back in France. He had been away from his beloved country, having left in haste four years earlier, just after the arrival of the infernal Ring of Fire, exiled from France for perceived offenses against the crown. But it was not his younger half-brother, the king, who had exiled him. It was his advisor, his minister, the very incarnation of the Devil Himself: Richelieu.

He hated that name and hated the man who owned

it. He had made sure to teach his sons to hate him as well—just as Hamilcar had instilled hate into his sons in ancient Carthage. Louis, who was now with César's other half-brother, Monsieur Gaston, and François, who sat on his own horse beside him, had learned the lesson well.

"Father."

César sighed, the quiet broken. "What is it, François?"

"Do you ever think about fate, Father? About what might have been?"

The duc de Vendôme smiled and looked at his son. François at twenty reminded him very much of himself at the same age: tall, handsome, smart—and ruthless. *A fine trait*, he thought to himself.

"I should like to say 'never,'" he said. "But the truth is that I think about it all the time. The God-cursed up-timers have made us all consider what might have been and what might never been. There have been so many changes since they arrived...but imagine if they had come thirty or forty years earlier. Things might have been different. *Very* different."

"Do you think you might have been king?"

"I don't know." César reached up and smoothed down his long moustaches. He kept them in a style a few years out of date in France; François was far more trim and in fashion. "I am the eldest son of King Henri. My mother, your grandmother, was the king's first and greatest love—perhaps his only true love: Gabrielle d'Estrées. When she died, still as his mistress, he held a state funeral."

"La Belle Gabrielle."

"Just so. My father always thought she had been

poisoned, along with my youngest brother who died with her. He mourned her death most piteously—I was not quite five years old, but I remember that he was inconsolable. The procession included every person of note, and made its way to St. Denis for the funeral mass—and then out to Saint-Ouen-l'Aumône where she was interred at Notre-Dame-la-Royale de Maubuisson in solemn ceremony. It was a wonder."

"The queen must not have been happy."

"Hah." César leaned aside, hawked and spat. "She did not arrive for a year thereafter. King Henri did not marry for love, just as he did not embrace the One Faith from piety. He became a Catholic to become the king of France and he chose a wife to give him offspring. The old brood mare gave him just what he wanted: sons and daughters, my brothers and sisters. The queen—the lady Marie—brought us all together, princes and princesses of the blood and royal bastards. No one ever forgot their status. I was constantly reminded of it, and so was my brother Alexandre."

His fist clenched where it held the reins of his horse. The mount, sensing the motion, stirred and neighed quietly. César ran his free hand gently through its mane and it quieted.

"Monseigneur Richelieu has much to answer for."

François knew that his father and his uncle Alexandre had run afoul of the cardinal and they had both been sent to the Bastille for a plot against him. Alexandre had not survived the experience.

"And he *will* answer," César said. "Most assuredly. With the intelligence given us, we are here to make sure of it. You and our other fine gentlemen—" he waved behind at the troop of horsemen waiting quietly in the fog—"can do whatever you wish with the guardsmen who travel with him: but Richelieu is *mine*."

As the last statement hung in the air, there was a high-pitched whistle in the distance.

César de Vendôme turned to look back at his troop. He raised a gloved hand and gestured toward the road, lost in the fog ahead. The men pulled forward the hoods of their cloaks and, at a signal, galloped together toward their quarry.

Chapter 14

Chateau de Baronville, Beville-le-Comte

Katie Matewski took the queen's hand by the wrist and looked at her watch, counting the pulses as the second-hand swept around. The watch had belonged to her mother and had probably cost $10 back in the day—but now it was a priceless up-timer artifact, a jewel of the clock-maker's art crafted in miniature and wrapped around an up-timer's wrist.

Despite her now regular contractions, Queen Anne took notice of the watch, as if it were part of the French crown jewels.

"My ladies are still suspicious of you," she said. "They would rather that a proper midwife handle this duty."

"Imagine if I were a man," Katie said after a moment. She took a pencil from the pocket of her coat and made a notation on the chart by the bed.

Anne looked shocked. "A *man*? For a *birth*?"

"Well," Katie answered, "*I* was delivered by a man. So were my brothers and sisters and cousins and . . .

well, most doctors are men, Your Majesty. At least where—when—I come from."

"*Doctors*, yes..." A contraction made her tense; she bit her lip. "But this is no matter for *doctors*."

"It is, up-time. But I suppose it's really the province of women in this time. No matter—I'm here now, by arrangement, and it all seems fine. There are a dozen things I wish I could do but the technology isn't here...but how do you feel?"

"I don't think I've ever been asked that question during childbirth."

"First time for everything, Majesty."

Anne reached down below the sheet and tentatively touched the outside of her womb, winced, and lowered her hand to the bed, clenching the sheets.

"The little one is strong."

"That's good."

"He will be a forceful little prince."

"If he's a boy."

Anne frowned. "I have had masses said for months and have sent donations to many shrines in France with requests for their prayers. He *will* be a boy."

I hope you're right, Katie thought to herself. "Yes, Majesty."

There was a small commotion at the door. Madame de Chevreuse, who had been sitting quietly with her rosary across the room, had moved with astounding speed to stand in the way of a pair of men who appeared intent on entering.

"Let me pass," said the one in the lead, who was wearing a bishop's vestments. "I am here with my brother Achille on behalf of His Most Christian Majesty to witness the birth."

Madame de Chevreuse stepped aside. The two men entered the room. The bishop was an impressive gentleman of middle age dressed in episcopal finery, though he wore no hat. He walked to the bedside and offered a bow to Queen Anne; she extended her hand, letting go of the sheet. He took hold of it and when she made to bring his episcopal ring to her lips, he placed his other hand on hers and smiled.

"Majesty, I am so glad to be received by you today."

"Thank you for being here, Your Grace. The Bishop of Chartres is most welcome in our chambers."

"It is my honor to visit so distinguished a guest within my diocese."

"You honor—" Another contraction struck; they were coming close together now. Katie wanted to step forward but decided it could wait for pleasantries to be concluded. "You honor us with your presence, My Lord d'Étampes de Valençay."

"I have said regular masses for you and your child. In the interest of your comfort, we shall repair to the side and stay out of the doctor's way." He looked from Anne to Katie.

"Please remain close, Your Grace."

"I shall be no farther than a few feet away, Your Majesty."

Anne let go of his hand and turned her head aside. Sweat beaded on her forehead. As Bishop Léonore and his brother withdrew, Katie stepped forward.

"With your permission, Majesty," she said, "I would like to check your dilation."

Anne pulled the sheet aside. "When the next king comes into the world," she said, gritting her teeth, "his arrival must be visible. Madame Katie, attend, *s'il vous plait.*"

Near Saint-Arnoult-en-Yvelines, France

Fifty miles is a stiff ride, even for experienced horsemen. The king was accustomed to riding to the hunt. But that had become a stylized affair, with pauses and servants and luncheons. No one with the pedigree of the Most Christian King of France had to work very hard or ride very fast. As for the cardinal, though trained as a soldier and a skilled horseman, he was no longer in practice.

But the need was great, and the motivation was strong: aches and pains be dispensed with and weather be damned. By mid-morning the sun had been shrouded by clouds; by the time they entered the Forest of Rambouillet the ground was cloaked in fog.

At last, late in the afternoon, Cardinal Richelieu called a halt in a clearing beside the road. The dozen Cardinal's Guards took up their customary positions. One of them dismounted and walked over to where the cardinal stood next to his horse. Servien was nearby, attending to the mounts' harnesses.

"This is exhilarating," the king said. "Exhilarating." He pulled off his gloves and shrugged his shoulders, adjusting the cloak of the Guard.

"I am gratified to hear it, Your Majesty," Richelieu said. "I trust you are holding up well."

"It's like a hunt," Louis answered. "Except, except that there is no quarry."

Richelieu didn't answer, but raised one eyebrow. *There is a quarry, my king,* he thought. *It is all of your enemies.*

"Do you think she has given birth yet?"

"It is difficult to say, Majesty. If she began her labor early in the morning, it would be close now. I directed Léonore d'Étampes de Valençay, my lord bishop of Chartres, to attend the queen. He will be at the chateau by now."

"I am sure that Anne will be pleased to have a, a man of his stature on hand."

"He is very good in such situations. His brother is not quite as subtle, but Achille is as brave a man as serves Your Majesty. If there is any trouble at Baronville, he will be a good one to have on hand."

"Trouble? What sort of trouble?"

"I expect none . . . but I am inclined to be careful, Sire."

"That is most wise, my friend. I—"

Somewhere nearby in the foggy gloom there was the sound of a high-pitched whistle.

"What was that?"

"I am not sure," Richelieu said. He turned away from the king and signaled to the captain of his guard.

And then, as if it were a passage from a costumed drama, a score of mounted men, hooded and weapons drawn, burst from the wood on either side. The scene erupted into chaos. Those Guards who had not dismounted urged their horses into the fight, moving to form a protective ring around Richelieu and the king.

"Who dares to attack thus?" Richelieu shouted. He stretched out his hand and drew a flintlock pistol from his saddlebags.

"Don't worry," Louis said. "There is not a bandit alive whom I cannot best in combat." He ran a half-dozen steps and swung himself up onto his horse, drawing a sabre and placing himself in the path of a handful of oncoming attackers.

Richelieu was too stunned to respond. All around him, Cardinal's Guards were engaging in close combat with the attackers. His own men were getting the better of them, but two of them had already fallen. Of the four that were charging toward King Louis, two were drawn aside by Guardsmen. All wore cloaks with hoods that hid their faces, but the two that came closer were familiar in some way. There was something about the way they sat their horses, Richelieu thought—or something more simple: the shape and length of their arms and legs...

The first of the two remaining attackers rushed headlong at Louis, who was partially turned away. With skill and grace that surprised even Richelieu, the king turned with precision and swung his blade, knocking the man from his saddle and onto the ground. Blood gushed from the man's side; the wound was probably not fatal but severe enough to take the king's assailant out of the action.

The second attacker, just behind, seemed enraged by the act. He charged forward, hurling his strength and momentum into the thrust of his sword. King Louis, off balance due to the powerful blow he'd just struck, was unable to deflect his opponent's blade in time. The sword point entered his chest, easily penetrating the tabard and shirt below it and driving into his heart.

The wound was instantly fatal. From ten feet away, Cardinal Richelieu watched as the swordsman's hood flew back, revealing his face—and it was then that he recognized him: César, duc de Vendôme, *légitimé* de France.

"Treason!" he cried.

In the dim light Cardinal Richelieu could see that Vendôme recognized who he had stabbed. A look of surprise and horror crossed his features. Clearly, he had not realized the identity of his opponent, garbed as the king was in the uniform of a Cardinal's Guard.

It was still treason. Richelieu cocked his pistol with both hands.

In the moment before he struck the blow Vendôme recognized the man who stood between him and his target. But it was too late to stop—much too late. Even if it had been possible to consider restraining the killing stroke, years of experience in combat put it beyond question. Louis XIII was no fop. He was a strong man with skill and experience in sword work. To stop would have simply been suicide.

The king was not the man he'd wished to kill, and for a moment the duc de Vendôme regretted the all-consuming hatred of Richelieu that had distorted his vision. Even wearing the uniform of a guard, César should have recognized his sovereign. He knew Louis very well and had sparred with him personally. The way he sat his horse, the way he handled his blade . . . He should have heard the voice, the one he had known since they were children together. Maybe that would have stayed his hand.

But the moment of regret was brief. They were still in the middle of a fight and the duke had other opponents to deal with. One, in particular. As the king fell from his seat to the forest floor, Vendôme drew the sword from his victim, and turned his attention to Richelieu.

Who, he saw, had a pistol aimed directly at him.

The cardinal fired. Though he was a man of the cloth and not very familiar with personal combat, Richelieu had steady nerves. The shot did not go wild but struck Vendôme in the head. Unfortunately, the ball glanced off rather than penetrating the skull, sending the duke's hat flying. His face covered with blood, Vendôme half-slid off his saddle. Richelieu did not think he was dead—not yet—but he was certainly stunned. He began to reload the pistol.

But before he could finish reloading a ball struck him. The shot seemed to come from nowhere. It was quite possible the man who fired it had no idea where it had struck.

"Kill them all!" Richelieu heard someone shout. He was sure it was not one of his own men. "Leave none alive!" And then, as if the mercy of the Lord descended upon him as the dew of Hermon, Armand-Jean du Plessis, Cardinal-Duke de Richelieu, fell into blackness.

Chapter 15

Clairefontaine-en-Yvelines

Servien had followed the lead of Jean d'Aubisson, the youngest member of the Cardinal's Guard, who knew the area far better. The two of them had half-dragged, half-carried Richelieu away from the scene of carnage in the deepening twilight, and somehow had managed to get him onto a horse. The cardinal was in shock: but old habits took over, and he managed to grip the reins as they escaped.

Servien had watched his king fall, and had caught a glimpse of the man who had committed the deed. It was a scene that would be etched into his memory forever—in particular, the shocked expression on his face. Perhaps the cardinal could have made something of that, but Servien was not sure.

A path made scarcely visible by the rising moon led through the woods. Any obstacle—a fallen tree, a deep hole, a crumbling slope—could have stopped their passage, but somehow the young guardsman was able to lead them along without incident.

When they were well away, Servien asked, "where are we going?"

"A safe place, I pray. There are several along our route—particular friends and clients. This is the closest— in Clairefontaine."

"Is it close?"

"Four miles, perhaps five."

Servien looked aside at Richelieu, scarcely visible in the gloom. "I don't know if His Eminence can ride that far."

"Do not speak of me as if I am not here," the cardinal whispered. He did not turn his head, and his hands did not move from where they clutched the reins.

"I'm sorry—" Servien began.

"No argument," Richelieu said even more softly. "Ride."

It was closer to five miles. The woods gave way to a clearing with a small village; d'Aubisson rode toward the church, where the porter admitted them into the courtyard. Servien was accustomed to his master being pale, but when they assisted him in dismounting, Cardinal Richelieu's face was almost ghostly. Though the day had been warm, with night a chill had come into the air; his cloak was pulled tight around him, and his soutane was stiff with blood, stained black in the faint moonlight.

They half-carried him along a gallery into the chapter-house, where hooded monks awaited them. They moved to assist, but Richelieu waved them away. Servien and d'Aubisson carefully helped Richelieu onto a sturdy dining table: only then did the cardinal permit the religious men to approach.

One of the monks threw back his head to reveal a middle-aged man, bearded but well groomed and tonsured; his face was without emotion, but Servien thought he could see the beginnings of tears in his eyes. He ran his hand along the soutane, which was badly rent near the cardinal's waist. He took Richelieu's hand, grasping it in a slightly unusual way, as if there was some significance in the grasp.

"Is it mortal?" Richelieu whispered.

"I cannot tell yet," the monk answered. "It is . . . it is very bad. But I will do what I can."

Richelieu's eyes closed, then fluttered open, darting from place to place. It was dark in the refectory: a nearby cresset held a torch, and one of the other monks held a lantern, bringing it close so that the wound could be examined.

"Brother," Servien said. "Perhaps this might be better done in some better place?"

"I do not dare move him," the monk answered.

"Servien?" Richelieu's voice was almost a whisper.

"I am here, Eminence," Servien said, coming close. He touched Richelieu's left hand, and the cardinal's glance focused on it; slowly, with what seemed to be great effort, his eyes lifted to look at him.

"Servien. This . . . there are matters that must be addressed."

Servien looked at the monk. "The good brother will attend to your wounds, Eminence. Then we will find and punish the villains that committed this heinous act."

"Not just that." Richelieu began to move his other hand, reaching inside his cloak: the motion obviously pained him, and the monk grasped the hand and tried to lay it beside the cardinal's body. With a surprising

strength, Richelieu pushed it away, while simultane-
ously seizing Servien's hand.

"Please, Eminence—"

"My watch," Richelieu whispered. "I must find my
watch."

The monk looked from his patient to Servien.
"Your...watch, *mon cardinal*?"

"Yes. Servien. My watch. Please take it." With his
free hand he gestured toward an inside pocket.

Servien reached in and withdrew the watch, the
beautiful up-timer gift. It was shattered, probably
destroyed beyond repair. The musket-ball had evidently struck the face and had dented the case. The
sweep did not move, and the hands were set to a
time about ninety minutes earlier when the duc de
Vendôme had attacked.

"It is badly broken, Eminence."

"Yes. Of course," Richelieu managed. He closed his
eyes and took a great heaving breath and let it out:
for a moment Servien thought it might be his last, but
presently he opened his eyes once more and focused
on his *intendant*. "Of course it is broken. But...it still
serves a purpose. It records the time of the attack."

"I don't understand," Servien began, and then,
a moment later, he did. He knew exactly why the
cardinal had drawn his attention to the timepiece.
"When we were attacked," he said, "and the watch
was shattered—that is the time when the king died."

"Yes," Richelieu said.

Servien considered the matter for a moment. Under
French law, the timing of the child's birth didn't really
matter. Even if the baby was born after the death
of King Louis, if it was a boy he still inherited the

throne. But the law was one thing, political reality
another. Gaston was very likely to claim that the child
was not really the offspring of Louis XIII, anyway,
but a bastard born out of some illicit affair of the
queen's. If he could add to that claim the further
argument—specious as it might legally be—that since
no child existed at the time of the king's death he,
Gaston, inherited the throne by virtue of being Louis'
younger brother...

At least with some sections of the French nobility,
if not the fussier bureaucrats, that added claim might
have some weight. In any event, there was certainly
no harm in being able to establish the timing of the
child's birth with respect to the king's death.

He slipped the watch into a pocket. The cardinal
extended his right hand toward Servien, who bent to
kiss it, but Richelieu frowned and spread his fingers
apart. "No, no," he said. "My episcopal ring, Servien.
Take it."

"Eminence, I—"

"*Take it,*" the cardinal commanded. "You may use it
as a token of my authority. You must go..." He took
another great breath and continued, "you must go to
our intended destination. Tell the queen of the terrible
events and the perpetrator of this infamy...and the
hand that must be behind it. And upon your life," he
added, squeezing Servien's hand tightly, "protect the
watch. It is evidence of..." Richelieu shuddered, as if
being struck with some great blow. "Evidence of..."

"I understand, Eminence," Servien said. "But I am
loath to leave your side."

"I am in good hands," Richelieu said quietly. "I
am in God's hands."

"It pains me to leave you."

"You and your family have always been loyal to my person and to the realm of France," Richelieu said, his voice scarcely louder than a whisper. He seemed almost spent with the effort. "Now you must perform one more duty for me."

Servien took the watch and ring and secured them within his vest. They lay there, near his heart, a heavy weight. He looked at d'Aubisson and then back at his master. Now there were tears in *his* eyes.

"I will obey your command, Eminence," Servien said. "And I will pray for your recovery and look forward to our next meeting."

This side of Heaven, he added to himself. Looking down at Cardinal Richelieu, struck down by a vicious attack, his life in peril, he wondered if there would ever be such a meeting.

"You know what you must do. Go," Richelieu said, with a wave of his hand. It was a familiar gesture, but it was a shadow of the one to which Servien was accustomed.

He bowed deeply, and he and d'Aubisson took their leave. Servien wondered whether he would ever see his master again.

Chapter 16

Paris

It began as nothing but a rumor.

The absence of both king and cardinal was scarcely something unusual; but their absence for more than a few days—without information about a royal progress, or some other such event, was certainly out of the ordinary.

When it became known in the fall that the queen was with child, bells were rung in every church in Paris and across France. Masses and prayers had been said continuously through the winter and early spring in hopes that a new prince would be born. It was common knowledge that the queen had retired to some quiet place to have her child, after the many difficulties and disappointments that had accompanied earlier pregnancies. It was widely rumored that His Majesty had gone recently to join her.

But when no word had come either of prince or king, stories began to circulate. The king had taken ill (as he had done six years earlier while on campaign in Savoy); the queen had chosen to flee to Spain to have her baby, and the king and his minister were in pursuit...and so on.

At last the rumors had coalesced, like bits of iron gathering around the poles of a magnet, to a story that had reached Paris from the countryside to the south. There had been a battle, or an ambush, and some villain had struck down the king and all his party—including Cardinal Richelieu and several of his guardsmen. Rumors on Paris streets were usually unreliable...but sometimes they came true.

On a cool May afternoon, a large procession of mounted soldiers with Urbain de Maillé-Brézé, Marshal of France, leading, approached and then entered the Porte Saint-Germain. The marshal was a serious, imposing figure, rarely given to levity or joy in public; this day he was particularly somber.

Twenty feet behind him was a carriage bearing the royal arms, and word soon spread that it bore the king—or, more precisely, the body of the king. Covered carts followed the royal conveyance, carrying the remains of other victims of some terrible battle—or ambush—in which His Majesty had been involved.

The procession made its way slowly into the city, stopping for no one, crossing the Pont Neuf and turning into the gardens of the Tuileries, where it was met by guardsmen from the palace of the Louvre. Not long afterward, a proclamation was given to the criers to announce all over Paris. Louis, Defender of the Faith and Most Christian King of France, was dead—like his father, the victim of a violent murder.

But where was his minister, Cardinal Richelieu?

Where was his queen? And to whom did the crown now belong—to an infant prince or to an exiled brother?

Turin

SPAR SPAR SPAR CQ CQ CQ.

Terrye Jo heard it and recognized the fist at once: it was GJBF, signaling with an intensity that she could almost feel. Henri was standing nearby; it was nearly the end of her afternoon shift—the dinner bell hadn't rung yet but would do so soon. The duchess had recently begun to insist that she appear at meals in "appropriate" attire, which meant something other than flannels and jeans and work boots, so this time of the day had been assigned to one of the junior operators.

GJBF SPAR KN.

SPAR GJBF NOUVELLES IMPORTANTES POUR MONSIEUR.

GJBF SPAR, she sent back. *BON ATTENDEZ POUR LUI.*

She took off the headphones before GJBF replied. "Henri, go and find Vachon." Vachon was Monsieur Gaston's valet, who had been making life hell on the serving staff since the prince returned to Turin. "Tell him that—" her first impulse was to say, *tell him that his master should get his ass up here at once*, but realized that she shouldn't, and Henri *couldn't*, say anything like that. "Tell him that I am receiving an urgent message for His Highness, and ask that he convey my respects to his master and that he should come at once."

Henri's eyebrows went up. Monsieur Gaston had

visited the radio room a few times in the last several days, mostly in the evenings and not by arrangement—he came and went as he pleased.

"That sounds a little too much like a demand," she said after a moment.

"It does, Mademoiselle Teresa."

"Very well. I . . . damn. Tell Vachon that there is a message for the prince, and that I will receive it and bring it to His Highness personally unless he'd like to come up here and get it directly."

"He won't like that either."

"Will he like it less than the first version?"

"No, this is better."

"Good. Go." She waved toward the door and put the headphones back on.

GJBF SPAR, she sent. *KN.*

SPAR GJBF NOUVELLES IMPORTANTES POUR LE PRINCE, she heard, then a long pause. *LE ROI EST MORT.*

A chill came over her. She hesitated over the telegraph key, and then sent: *QSM. Send it again.*

SPAR GJBF LE ROI EST MORT.

That was not the message she had been expecting. Ever since their first exchange, she had been waiting for word that the queen of France—the woman she'd worried about, and that the duchess had seemed to dismiss so casually—had given birth to a child. Terrye Jo understood the situation much more clearly than she had done in the fall. A prince would replace Gaston as the king's heir; a daughter would be cause for celebration, but wouldn't change the political situation.

The death of the king, though, promoted Monsieur Gaston to king of France.

Apparently Henri knew how to speak to a valet, and apparently Vachon—for all his arrogance—wasn't about to get Monsieur Gaston angry. It took no more than twenty minutes for him to appear in the radio room. Terrye Jo expected Louis to be with him—but Gaston came completely alone.

"Good afternoon, Mademoiselle Tillman," the prince said. He came over to stand next to the bench, and waved Terrye Jo back to her seat as she began to stand. "I am informed that there is an important message."

She handed him the transcription pad, on which she had written the words *LE ROI EST MORT*. "This came in from the telegrapher GJBF."

Gaston looked from the pad to Terrye Jo and back to the pad. His Guy Fawkes face made an attempt at shock and sorrow, but she wasn't convinced. It was a put-on: it was as if he already knew that something had happened.

"My brother is dead," Gaston said, placing the pad on the bench. "What else does my *créature* have to say?"

"I'll ask for details," she answered. She turned away and settled the headphones on her head.

SPAR GJBF COMMENT EST-CE ARRIVE? How did it happen?

GJBF SPAR UNE EMBUSCADE DANS LES BOIS.
She wrote down the message. Gaston watched the pencil as she noted each letter. "They were attacked in the woods," she said. "An ambush."

"The king would go nowhere without an escort," Gaston said. "If he was attacked, it wouldn't be a lone assassin like our father. It would be an armed troop."

"Shall I ask if there is more information, Highness?"

"If you please."

She sent an inquiry. After a moment GJBF began to send a description. There was a lot of it; she could keep up, but her correspondent had to stop at intervals. Gaston watched her write each part of the message, then stop and go back, going over it as GJBF repeated it.

At last she sent an *SN* acknowledgement and turned away from the radio set.

"He has told me what he knows," she said. "Apparently the king was riding out from Paris in the company of Cardinal Richelieu, and there was an attack by a large group of armed bandits. There...were no survivors, and a group sent out afterward found the bodies. They have returned to Paris with the king's body."

"And the cardinal's as well?"

"It wasn't mentioned, Highness." She looked at the pad, running her finger slowly down the long message. "The king and a number of guards. That's what he said."

"Ask him," Gaston said. "Ask if the cardinal's body was recovered."

Terrye Jo looked at Monsieur Gaston curiously, but after a few seconds she turned her attention to the radio and sent the question.

The answer came back quickly: *NON.*

"No," she said. "It wasn't recovered."

Gaston made no secret of his anger this time: whether or not he was upset by the news of the king, he was clearly upset that the incident had not killed Cardinal Richelieu. It was almost as if...

"He is certain?"

"I made sure to have him repeat the message, Sire. The soldiers were his guards—Cardinal Guards—"

"The Cardinal's Guard. Yes. They have a distinctive uniform."

"Your servant said so. He said that the king was dressed as a Cardinal's Guard."

This time it was even more confusing: Gaston was upset, but in a different way—she wasn't sure why—but she was even more convinced that this report wasn't a surprise for him.

He knew this was coming.

"The king is dead," Gaston said at last. "I am now king. I shall have to proceed to Paris at once." He turned away, adjusting the lace on his cuffs. "There is much to do. I . . . may require your assistance."

"The duke made it clear that I am to help you in any way you require, Highness," she said. "If there is a message—"

He turned back to her. "I will need a skilled telegrapher in Paris. It is my wish that you accompany me."

"I'd have to discuss that with Duke Amadeus—"

"I shall speak with him, mademoiselle." He walked to the door. "You should prepare to leave as soon as possible," he said, and left the radio room before Terrye Jo could answer.

Lyon

Turenne's commanders tramped up the hill through the rain to the villa, stomping into the entry room with their muddy boots. The marshal had arranged for three grooms to be on hand to clean them, so as not to ruin the carpeting in the ground-floor morning room where the council was to take place.

He was not much inclined toward that sort of meeting. Turenne's army was as much a modern, professional force as Sherrilyn had seen down-time: particularly over the winter and into the spring, it had become more and more like the sort of army that the USE was developing—organized, well supplied, with specific tasks and responsibilities. It still had some good old-fashioned seventeenth-century brawling (and the occasional duel: that was illegal in France, but Turenne turned a blind eye to it—he would rather have such deep-seated feuds resolved in camp than on the battlefield); but by and large, it was a well-delineated chain of command, with a small number of senior officers that dealt directly with their marshal and handled their respective departments.

Thus, when he called the commanders—including her—together for a *conseil de guerre*, it was an occasion. It took a little time for them all to assemble, and a little longer for them all to settle into seats. She found a place in the back near Johann Glauber, Turenne's munitions expert and the man who had developed the new percussion caps. Most of the commanders steered clear of him. He was a little wild-eyed and had a sort of persistent chemical smell around him that tended to spook down-timers.

When the marshal came into the room they all got to their feet. He was accompanied by another man who bore a distinct family resemblance, though he was older and a little more weathered. Most of the people in the room knew who he was, and some of them doffed their hats to him. He caught Sherrilyn's eye and seemed to fix his attention directly on her, as if there was no one else in the room.

"Most of you are acquainted with my older brother Frédéric," Turenne began. "As prince of Sédan and duc de Bouillon, he outranks me—everywhere but *here*." He smiled. "I thought his insights would be valuable.

"We have received confirmation of something that some of you may have already heard. Our sovereign lord, King Louis, is dead." Turenne took his hat off and bowed; everyone else did likewise. "There was an attack of some sort at some distance from Paris, on a party that included His Eminence Cardinal Richelieu and His Majesty. The king's body has been conveyed in state to Paris, but there is no word on the cardinal—whether he is dead or alive, there is no news." The officers began to murmur, and Turenne held up his hand, quieting them.

"There is no way to know," he continued, "who might have performed this criminal act. The person who benefits the most from the king's death is his brother, but I have intelligence that indicates that he spent the winter in Tuscany with the queen mother and is now visiting his sister, the duchess of Savoy, in Turin."

"He was behind it," de la Mothe said. "You can count on it."

"There is no way to know that. It is possible that a group of Spanish horsemen ambushed the king's party; there are certainly *agents provocateurs* for Spain within our borders, reporting to—or working with— the marquis de Mirabel, King Philip's ambassador in Paris. It is known that in the past he corresponded with Her Majesty."

"There is no reason to believe that the queen is complicit," the duc de Bouillon said quietly. His voice was very similar to Turenne's, quiet but forceful. "At least at this time."

"She wouldn't benefit from his death," de la Mothe said. "With the king dead, Gaston would have no more use for her—he'd send her back to Spain."

"These are reasonable inferences," Turenne said. "But there is a further complication: the queen is with child, and is due within the month. Monsieur Gaston has no son: if the queen gives birth to a boy, he would be Gaston's heir. That makes her either valuable—or *vulnerable*."

"I have a question," Sherrilyn said, raising her hand. The other commanders turned to her; she lowered her hand to her side, feeling a bit silly at the gesture.

"Frédéric," Turenne said. "It is my honor to present my commander of sharpshooters, Colonel Sherrilyn Maddox, a *Grantvilléuse*."

Bouillon made his way across the sitting-room to where she sat. As he approached she stood, wondering if she should bow or curtsey. Instead she stuck out her hand and he took it, offering a firm grasp. Before he let it go he turned it this way and that, as if examining it.

"A pleasure," he said at last, letting it go. "Henri has told me a great deal about you, and I have made the up-timers a matter of personal interest. I have collected reprints of a number of interesting books from your wondrous future world."

"We seem to fascinate lots of people."

"You do," he agreed. "You certainly do. Now. Mademoiselle Colonel. What is your question?"

"I'm just a hired gun here, but most of your—most of the marshal's—troops are Frenchmen. Their loyalty is to their king, I'd guess; and now their king is going to be Gaston. What does that mean for us?"

Bouillon smiled and turned to face Turenne. "An interesting question, Henri. What do you intend?"

"It is my decision," Turenne said. "But that is partly why I have assembled you here—to advise me. I do not trust our new king: but he is, or soon will be, our king nonetheless. Cardinal Richelieu assigned me here, and gave me specific directions. Until I know the circumstances of this criminal attack upon our late monarch, I must assume that those directions are still in force.

"Indeed, he provided me with a letter to be opened in case he was killed or presumed dead. I have opened the letter, and it informs me of the hidden location where the queen is secluded, awaiting the birth of her child. I am instructed to use my judgment in this matter, but if I believe the persons of the queen and the child to be endangered. I may, if I deem it prudent, choose to interpose my forces between them and the danger presented.

"Spain remains the greatest danger to our country, to our queen, and to the prince—or princess. If the cardinal is still alive, the Spanish are a danger to him as well."

"What does that mean?" Sherrilyn asked. "We're going to deploy against an invader? Or are we going to go looking for this marauding band of outlaws that killed the king?"

"I will need to decide," Turenne said. "I don't know if finding the king's killers is practical."

"I agree. And I agree with the comte de la Mothe,"

Sherrilyn said. "From everything I've heard about Monsieur Gaston, I have to believe he was involved in this attack."

"And not the Spanish?"

Sure, she thought. *This could have been Pedro Dolor. He could have pulled this off. But it doesn't feel right... it's something he* could *do, but not really his style. It's too obvious, too direct.*

"I'm not sure," she said. "But I *do* think we need to be where Monsieur Gaston—King Gaston—can't take control of our forces. If that means marching toward the Spanish border, then we'd better do it. Unless..."

The duc de Bouillon, who was still standing next to her, stroked his chin. "Indeed, Mademoiselle Colonel. Unless what?"

"Unless we think that Gaston isn't legitimately the king. Unless we think we don't owe him allegiance."

The room was completely quiet.

"What are you suggesting, Colonel?" Turenne said. "You can speak freely here."

"If you don't want Gaston to be king, Marshal, you can make that happen. I don't know if it's the right thing to do, but it's in your power. In our power."

"You're talking about civil war," Turenne said quietly. "It ripped our country apart half a century ago. People take sides. Innocent people die. It exposes us to the predations of France's enemies—and believe me, Colonel, France has enemies. Is your USE prepared to take sides in such a conflict?"

"I—I don't know."

"Does the principal know?"

The question caught Sherrilyn by surprise. She wasn't sure what Turenne was asking—what he implied.

"I have no idea. I don't work for him anymore, Marshal. I work for *you*. Do you want me to ask him?"

"Have you not done so already?"

"No. You've clearly read my mail," she said, putting her hands on her hips. She was a little bit scared, but refused to show any of it. "I haven't asked him a damn thing. I'm guessing that the United States of Europe doesn't have any interest in nation building, but they'd also prefer that there wasn't *another* war going on—there are enough of them happening already."

"So they will stand by and watch," Bouillon said. "They will treat Gaston's actions, direct and indirect, as no more than a sort of *coup de theatre*."

I stayed in the back, Sherrilyn thought, *to stay out of the way; and now I'm center stage.*

"I can't say. I don't speak for the government. And other than personal contacts, I don't speak *to* the government." *I'm really not a spy, damn it*, she thought. *Really not. Just someone trying to get along.*

And next time I see you, Ed, I'm going to punch you in the mouth.

"Are you looking for advice?" she asked.

"Why, naturally," Bouillon said. His voice had a bit of an edge to it, but his smile—the Tour d'Auvergne smile, the one Turenne employed to great effect—was broad and cordial. "Say on."

"Turin is over the mountains, right? A couple of hundred miles. If Gaston is coming from there to France, he'd come this way." Turenne nodded. "If you're worried about being conflicted in your loyalty to Monsieur Gaston, then the best thing is not to be along his route. Wherever we go, whatever we decide to do, let's not meet up with him."

"We have a radio, Colonel," Turenne said.

"Does *he*?"

"There is some indication that he does, and that he has a confederate in Paris with whom he has been in contact. Could he not simply... send us an order?"

"He'd have to know how to find us—our call sign, I guess, and our frequency. I was never in the Signal Corps, so I don't know the details. But there are a hundred reasons why radio contact fails; the best reason is if we just go off the air. Then he'd need to find us—and we could work hard at not being found."

Turenne beckoned to his brother. Bouillon gave Sherrilyn a slight bow and walked to join him; they conferred very quietly for a few moments. Then Turenne turned to his assembled commanders and said, "You have twenty-four hours to break camp and be prepared to move. The quartermaster and his assistants will organize transportation for equipment not otherwise assigned, including your laboratory, Professor Glauber." He nodded to his "alchemist," who looked stunned by the possibility. "We will travel as light as possible, particularly the infantry; tell the men to take only what they must."

"Where are we headed?" de la Mothe asked.

It was Turenne's turn to offer the Tour d'Auvergne smile, which he bestowed in Sherrilyn's direction. "It remains to be seen," he said. "We will go where we're needed."

By the first gray light of the new day, Maddox's Rangers were ready to ride. Turenne was there to see them off—most of the rest of the officers were still asleep, though a few were working on plans to get their units ready to pull up stakes.

"You will give my respects to those whose lands you traverse," he said. "If they take issue with you—"

"They shouldn't."

"They *could*. I know that you will keep the men in line and I won't receive a report of lands laid waste. But the southerners tend to be prickly about armed forces crossing their territory. Still, I don't think anyone will be so foolish as to—"

"Start something."

Turenne smiled. "As to *start something*. Up-timers always seem to possess *le mot juste*. Before I send you on your way, do you have any last minute advice?"

"Actually, yes. I'm concerned about the up-timer team up north, the folks working on the steam engines. They need to know about the king's death."

"Surely they know."

"But there are others who *don't*. Before you go silent, I'd like to ask you a favor—send them a message about King Louis' death and the succession of Monsieur Gaston. But don't encode it: send it in the clear."

"Because..."

"Because it'll be overheard."

"By 'the principal.'"

"...Yes. And others. They need to know, Marshal. I don't think they're our enemy—your enemy. France's enemy."

"Plenty of people will overhear, Colonel."

"I don't think that's a problem. Do you?"

Turenne thought for a moment, and then smiled again. "No. I do not."

Chapter 17

Chateau de Baronville, Beville-le-Comte

The ringing of bells awoke Anne from a restful sleep. She could feel the deep pain from labor still, but her exhaustion had been deeper. Even before opening her eyes she reached down to feel her chest: after seven and a half months it felt strange to be without the life that had inhabited her womb.

Strange, she thought. *And wonderful.*

She knew that the infant would be with a wet-nurse nearby; yet she wished to hold her son, to look upon him. He had only been in her arms for a few short minutes just after his birth before he had been taken away and she had descended into sleep.

She opened her eyes to see the young woman who had been her midwife and doctor: she was sitting in a padded chair, dozing, a coat wrapped around her. It had clearly been a long night for her as well.

"*Mademoiselle* Katie," she said, and when the young up-timer woman did not answer, she repeated herself, pitching her voice somewhat louder.

Katie Matewski stirred and then awoke fully, startled. She looked across at Anne and rose quickly, shrugging off the coat and coming to the bedside. "I...I beg your pardon, Majesty," she said in passable French. "I must have drifted off."

"Do not trouble yourself. Tell me—why are the bells ringing?"

"I'm not sure, my lady. I can go and see. Are you in discomfort? Are you—"

"I am very tired, but I seem to be well. Please go and inquire, and give my compliments to my lord of Uzès." Uzès was the first gentleman of the bedchamber: he was the first on hand at the queen's arising and the last on her retirement.

"By your leave," Katie said. The curtsey was not exactly to court standards, complicated perhaps by the fact that the young lady was dressed in a man's trousers. If this had been a down-timer, a subject of the kingdom, there might be some slight affront—but she was an up-timer, from whom all sorts of informalities were expected.

Katie opened the bedchamber door and stepped into the outer room. Mazarin was there with Uzès and another man whom she had never seen. He was dressed for travel and looked as if he had come far and ridden hard.

She closed the door behind her. The three men stopped their conversation as Katie appeared.

"How does the queen?" Uzès asked.

"She has just awoken," Katie said. "I haven't examined her yet but she seems well. I had a little nap myself, but left word that I should be notified if there was any problem with mother or child."

"The baby is doing well," Mazarin said. "But grim news has arrived."

"Is that why the bells are ringing?"

"Yes," Mazarin answered. "There has been an ambush. The king is dead."

"Dead? What happened? An—an ambush?"

The stranger gave a bow. "*Mademoiselle*, my name is Étienne Servien. I have the honor to serve His Eminence Cardinal Richelieu. We were on our way to this place when we were viciously and violently attacked. My master was severely wounded, and His Majesty the king was slain." He was distraught as he spoke the words.

"The queen must be told," Katie said.

"More than that," Mazarin said. "She must be made ready to travel, and right away. We must leave Beville-le-Comte as soon as possible: there may be a further attack on her person."

"And the baby—"

"He is in terrible danger," said Servien. "He is the king of France now, and he has many enemies, none greater than his uncle. It is certain that Gaston was behind the attack. The assassins were led by César de Vendôme, the king's—and Gaston's—eldest brother, a *légitimé*. Gaston will now seek to have himself crowned king."

"He can't do that," Katie said. "Can he?"

"He *can*," Mazarin answered, "though he should not. But this is a circumstance often governed by power, not propriety."

"So who *exactly* is Vendôme? I thought we were talking about Gaston."

"César de Vendôme is the king's eldest half-brother,

mademoiselle," Mazarin explained. "Before Louis and Gaston were born, King Henry the Fourth of fond memory fathered three children by his first mistress, Gabrielle d'Estrées. César is the oldest of the three. His younger brother Alexandre died in prison several years ago, and his younger sister is now the duchess of Elbeuf. They were all declared *légitimés*—recognized for their royal blood, but ineligible for further preferment. In a different world, César de Vendôme might have been king of France; while in this one, he has become a regicide."

"Did he become king in my 'different world,' Monseigneur?"

"No," Mazarin said. "He is just as much a bastard in your up-time history. He engaged in further intrigues, including participation in a cabal against *me*." He smiled briefly, the strange twists of time and history bemusing him and pushing aside the gravity and tragedy of the situation. "He has many grudges against Cardinal Richelieu, and evidently had enough resentment against his lord king that he did not hesitate to put him to the sword as well."

"Will he attack us here?"

"No," Mazarin said. "Because we will not be *here*. We will be elsewhere."

Near dawn, the royal party was assembled in the chapel of Baronville to baptize the child. The first wan light was straining to pass through the thick glass windows. The room was lit with several small candles. Anne, less than twenty-four hours after childbirth, looked radiant and regal, wearing a traveling dress that hung loosely on her frame, a beautiful necklace that reflected all the light in the room, and a small circlet on her head. She held the baby—the *rightful king of France*—in her arms, and to Katie she looked like the most beautiful woman in the world.

Achille, the brother of the bishop, stood beside her, in the full regalia of a knight of Malta, his hat tucked under one arm, his hand on his heart.

The rest of the group, including Monsieur Servien, stood nearby, except for Mazarin, who was to assist Bishop Léonore in the baptism.

Katie had found a dress to wear. She realized, just a little before the gathering in the chapel, that she didn't feel proper dressing casually in church, even if it was just for a short ceremony; old habits died hard.

The castle servants had been gathered into a choir, and as Bishop Léonore entered the chapel, they began to sing. Mazarin, who waited near the altar, his hands joined in prayer, accompanied them.

Si introiero in tabernaculum domus meae si ascendero in lectum strati mei si dedero somnum oculis meis et palpebris meis dormitationem et requiem temporibus . . .

Lord, my heart is not haughty, nor my eyes lofty; neither do I exercise myself in great matters, or in things too high for me . . .

Katie didn't recognize the psalm, but the hastily-gathered singers gave a good account of it; the bishop made his way forward with little ceremony, until he reached the front of the chapel and turned to face the others. He carried his bishop's crook and wore his alb and surplice; he had intended to perform the service after the baby's birth, but probably wasn't planning to do it under such strained circumstances.

"I welcome you to this solemn occasion," he said. "Beloved in the Lord, when the Savior sent out his Apostles, he said unto them, 'Go ye, and teach all nations, baptizing them in the Name of the Father, and of the Son, and of the Holy Ghost: teaching them to observe all things whatsoever I have commanded you.' He that believeth and is baptized shall be saved. Through baptism men are cleansed from their sins, made partakers in the meritorious redemption of Jesus Christ, taken into the society of the faithful and into the Church of Christ, fitted to obtain a share in all the treasuries of grace, with the management and administration of which Christ has entrusted his church.

"Your Majesty," he said, bowing to Anne, "it is an honor to receive you here in the sight of God, and to receive your son, a gift from God, the source of all life, who seeks to bestow His life upon him. What name do you give to this child?"

"Louis," she said. "Louis Dieudonné—a gift from God."

"What do you ask of God's Church for Louis?"

"Baptism—the grace of Christ."

"Louis," the bishop said to the baby, and then looked directly at Anne. "Dost thou desire to obtain eternal life in the church of God through faith in Jesus Christ?"

"He does," she said.

"Who shall stand as godparents for this child?"

Katie stepped forward from her position to stand beside Achille.

"We will," Achille said.

"Are you ready to help the parents of this child in their duty as Christian parents, in the sight of God and within the body of the Holy Catholic Church?"

Achille was ready to answer the second question, but Katie said, "We are ready." It drew a sharp look from the knight of Malta, but he softened it to a mild wry smile.

The bishop dipped his right hand in the baptismal font and then stepped directly in front of Anne.

"The Lord himself has appointed baptism with water, accompanied by the invocation of the Trinity, to be the outward sign of the grace which is communicated through this blessed sacrament. It is thereby intimated that as the body is purified by water, so the soul is purified by this sacrament from whatever in it is displeasing to God.

"Now, the community of Christ welcomes this child with great joy," he said. "The Lord Himself hath said: 'This is life eternal, that they may know thee the only true God, and Jesus Christ, whom thou hast sent. If thou wilt enter into life, keep the commandments, and that thou shalt love the Lord thy God with all thy heart, and with all thy soul, and with all thy mind, and thy neighbor as thyself.'"

He drew a cross on little Louis' forehead, and then as Anne unwrapped a bit of the swaddling, upon his breast. "Receive the sign of the holy cross, to remind thee that thou openly profess thy faith in Christ crucified, and glory not, save only in the cross of Jesus Christ our Lord; and to remind thee that thou love from thy heart Him who hath died on the cross for thee, and that as He bids thee thou shouldest take up thy cross and follow Him."

Bishop Léonore leaned forward and breathed very softly on Louis' face; the baby looked up at him smiling. "May the powers of darkness, which the divine

Redeemer hath vanquished by his cross, retire before thee that thou mayest see to what hope, and to what an exceeding glorious inheritance among the saints, thou art called."

Mazarin handed the bishop a small towel, with which he wiped his hands. Léonore then placed a small bit of salt on the tip of his right index finger and touched the baby's tongue. Louis made a small frown.

"Louis," the bishop said, "receive this salt as an emblem of wisdom; the Lord grant it thee unto everlasting life." He then laid his hand on the baby's forehead.

"O God, thou author of all wisdom, look graciously down on this thy servant Louis and preserve him ever in thy fear, which is the beginning of wisdom, through Christ our Lord. *Amen.*" He then touched Louis' ears and mouth and said, "*Ephphatha*, that is*, be opened. As the Savior gave the power of hearing and of speech to a man that was both deaf and dumb by the use of these words, and by touching his ears and tongue, so may he strengthen thee through his grace, that thou mayest be ready and willing to hear his words, and mayest joyfully proclaim his praise.

"Does Louis now and for all time renounce the lusts of the flesh, the lust of the eyes, and the pride of life?"

"He does," Anne said.

Mazarin handed the bishop a small dish that had oil in it; he dipped his fingers in it and touched Louis' breast and forehead.

"For the war against evil, and for the practice of good, thou needest strengthening through the grace of him who hath redeemed us from our sins. Therefore

I anoint thee with the oil of salvation in Christ Jesus our Lord. *Amen.*"

He then touched the edge of his stole to Louis' cheek and said, "Louis, receive the white raiment of innocence. Preserve it pure and unspotted until the day of Jesus Christ, that thereby thou mayest enter into eternal life.

"In the name of the Father, and the Son, and the Holy Spirit, I baptize thee Louis Dieudonné, the Gift of God."

Anne wrapped the baby once more, then took the bishop's ring and kissed it. He placed his hands over hers and smiled.

"Majesty," he said. "I am in great fear of what might come next. I wish you would reconsider your course, and remain here, or accompany me to Chartres as my guest."

"I wish I could accept your offer," Anne answered. "But a prince who would stoop to killing his own brother would not scruple to kill a woman and child." She looked up at Mazarin. "I am in safe hands."

"My brother has offered to accompany you, I know. He has pledged his faith to Holy Mother Church, but I dispensed him from any duty he owes to my see so that he can go."

"I am most appreciative, Your Grace."

"I wish I could do more."

"You have done a great deal already," Anne answered. "I would only ask that you pray for us as well. All of us." She glanced back at Katie. "We are in God's hands now. All of France is in God's hands."

"Indeed, my Queen," the bishop said. "But you always were."

The last that Katie and the rest of the royal party saw of Château Baronville was of Bishop Léonore and the servants of the castle standing outside watching, as their carriage pulled away into the morning light. The duke of Uzès and the bishop stood a little apart from the others, and as they watched, Léonore made the sign of the Cross.

Chapter 18

Dear Dad,

Today we arrived at the Castle of Miolans in Saint-Pierre d'Albigny. It's in the mountains, about halfway between Turin and Lyon. Monsieur Gaston doesn't exactly travel light: he has a half-dozen gentlemen at arms, along with servants and guards—as well as his wife and her ladies in waiting and servants and whatever. And me.

He is headed for Paris, where he's going to become the king of France. You might have heard by now that the king, his brother, is dead; there was some sort of ambush. I can't tell you more than that but I'll know more when we get there. He decided that he needed a telegraph operator and I was drafted.

I have to tell you about this place. It's a fortress in the mountains that belongs to the duke of Savoy. A while back they *turned it into a prison, and the prince had to take a tour, and asked me to come with him . . .*

"Monsieur," the warden said, fawning painfully. "I cannot adequately convey how *honored* we are to have you visit."

"I will soon no longer answer to that title, *Monsieur* LeBarre." Gaston said. "As you know."

"Of course," LeBarre said. He was a short, sweaty man with stubby fingers and deep-set eyes in a pudgy face. "Of course. My deepest, sincerest apologies."

Gaston's facial expression did not change from the very slight smile, and he did not answer.

"Majesty," LeBarre added, looking at Gaston and then down at the floor.

"Quite." Gaston's smile inched slightly upward. "Show us your wonderful fortress."

LeBarre bowed slightly and then scurried away. Gaston followed leisurely, along with his entourage.

"Our *château* was built more than six hundred years ago, Majesty," LeBarre said, glancing over his shoulder to see if the prince was following. He was in luck. "It belonged to the family Miolans, who have since emigrated to the New World, and now it is the property of His Grace the duke. His grandfather . . . or was it great-grandfather? Or possibly great-great-grandfather?"

"His *ancestor*," Gaston said.

"Yes. Of course. My apologies. His Grace's *ancestor* converted it for use as a prison. *My* grandfather was a warden, then my father, then my uncle—"

"Not you?"

"I was too young," LeBarre said. They had reached the end of a corridor, where a guard in a metal cuirass and helmet stood guard in front of a banded oak door. He held a stout halberd, and had a brace of pistols. "But I came into the position when my uncle . . . when there was an unfortunate accident."

He fumbled at his belt and drew out a ring of keys; from where Terrye Jo stood, it looked like a stage prop from a play. The guard stood aside, and LeBarre inserted a large ornate key into the door lock. He turned it and, with the help of the guard, swung the door wide to reveal a broad set of stone stairs leading down.

And from below, they began to hear noises: moans and cries, as if from people in pain or despair, mixed with the sound of rattling chains.

Terrye Jo was at once reminded of a story that made the rounds of the sensational "newspapers" that were always on racks at supermarket checkout counters up-time. Some miners—or some guys in a submarine—found a crack in the earth or at the bottom of the ocean and through it they could hear the moans and cries of souls suffering in Hell. The sounds from below made her think of it.

"If Your Majesty wishes, we can tour the dungeons," LeBarre said, looking pointedly at Terrye Jo and adding, "though it might not be suitable for . . ."

"She is an up-timer," Gaston answered, looking back at her. "I am told that the entertainments of her time depicted many things far more barbaric and violent and shocking than anything we might witness here."

LeBarre looked unconvinced. Terrye Jo was so surprised by the exchange, particularly Gaston's response, that she didn't answer for a moment. Finally she said, "How many prisoners do you keep here, Monsieur LeBarre?"

"Let me see." He scratched his chin. "Winter was somewhat cruel to us this year," he said. At that moment there was a particularly painful scream from somewhere beyond the door. "I believe we have one hundred and sixty-five at present. Thirty of them are in Hell—"

"Excuse me, monsieur?"

Gaston smiled, as if he already knew something she didn't.

"That is one of our *dungeons*, mademoiselle," LeBarre said, smiling unctuously. "Hell, Purgatory, Paradise, Treasure, Little Hope and Great Hope. Hell is for the . . . most particularly recalcitrant."

"I am sure that its punishments are suitably severe to warrant the name," Gaston said.

"We would not want to disappoint the duke," LeBarre responded. "Of course."

"Of course," Gaston repeated.

"But I am sure they would be . . . *tame* compared to your up-timer entertainments," he added, with the slightest bow to Terrye Jo.

She gave an annoyed glance at Gaston and then looked away.

No, she thought. They hadn't had dungeons in the twentieth century, unlike the civilized seventeenth. But they did have genocides and Holocausts. They'd had wars that killed millions of people. They'd had weapons that could destroy the whole world, and her country had been the only one that ever used them. TV was full of these things, and full of cop shows and Westerns and war movies and horror flicks. And sometimes they'd laughed all of that off like it was nothing.

"I'll take your word for it," she said.

> *I have to admit I was surprised what Gaston said about "up-timer entertainments." Nothing like having a down-timer look at a movie review book and decide that we're all into homicide and zombies and whatever. We're so used to thinking about all the civilized stuff we lost and how much more violent and primitive down-time is, that it's hard to see up-time the way they see it.*
>
> *So we toured the dungeons, and they were pretty much what you'd expect, but worse. There's one thing that ties us together though, up-timers and down-timers: after a while we're indifferent. LeBarre, and the prince, and all the down-timers just took the dungeons in stride. It was surreal, like a horror movie, except without the popcorn.*
>
> *It took us six more days to reach Lyon. Each place we stopped was another chance for Gaston to play the part of the heir advancing toward his kingdom.*
>
> *Then the fireworks started . . .*

Gaston was pacing back and forth, cursing under his breath. The only other person in the room sat patiently, almost indolently, waiting for Monsieur to return attention to him.

"I cannot believe that you are showing such recalcitrance," Gaston said at last. "De la Mothe. *Pierre.*"

He let his angry face relax into a smile. "In view of the changes to the realm, I need to know that I can count on every loyal subject."

Philippe de la Mothe-Houdancourt nodded, smiling in return. "I would not want you to believe anything else."

"Then you need to answer my question."

"I wish I could, Monsieur—"

Gaston stopped smiling.

"I wish I could, Your Royal Highness," de la Mothe said. "I wish I could tell you where Marshal Turenne's army has deployed. He did not choose to confide in me."

"You are on his staff."

"I *have served* on his staff," de la Mothe said. "I do not presently have the honor to be in his service, or indeed in his company."

"That much is obvious."

"It was his contention that there was an imminent threat from the Spanish. I would assume that the army has moved to intercept it."

"To the south?"

"I would assume so, Sire."

"I have installed my telegraph operator and her equipment," Gaston said. "She has been provided with the—code, is it?—for Turenne's telegraph. He—it—does not seem to be responding."

"There are a hundred reasons for a telegraph system to fail. These devices are based on up-time technology, Your Highness, but they lack the reliability of actual up-time equipment."

"*My* telegraph operator says that the equipment is *remarkably* reliable, Philippe. There are only a few ways in which they can fail. And one of them is simply turning the device off. Is that the problem? They *turned it off*?"

"It would have to be disassembled during maneuvers, Highness. If the army is on the march, there would be no way to use it."

"So the army is on the march."

"As I said—"

"He did not confide in you." Gaston began to pace once more. "They have headed south. Not toward Paris, but south."

"That is my impression, Highness."

"I had hoped to have it accompany me on my progress to the capital." He stopped walking. "Very well: he shall have to come to Reims for the coronation, to give fealty to me once I have come to the throne."

De la Mothe did not answer. For several moments Gaston frowned at him, as if expecting some acknowledgment, but none was forthcoming.

"You shall travel with me, my lord de la Mothe. As we travel, you will bring me up to date on Turenne's army."

He wasn't real happy with Lyon. I heard about his interview with de la Mothe, who got left behind or something; he's like a nobleman out of The Three Musketeers: *a dandy with lace and a fine wig, with a big nose, the kind that gets you into fights when someone makes fun of it.*

We're still on the road to Paris now, but I'm posting this from Dijon, where the bishop has what they say is a reliable service. I hope it gets to you soon, and I'll write again when I get to Paris. Like just about every place else down-time, I'm amazed at the places I'm going. There are supposed to be up-timers there—maybe I'll see someone I know.

I know you're worried about me and want me home. I want you to know I miss Grantville and I miss you, but I have to make my own way. I feel like I'm at the center of big things, but I think everything will eventually work out.

Say hi to everyone for me.

Love
Terrye Jo

Part Three

The Virtue of Prudence

Government by the dictates of reason

Chapter 19

May, 1636
Magdeburg, USE

"There's just no relief, is there, Rebecca?"

Ed Piazza leaned his head on his hands and rubbed his temples. It had been a long year: the Crown Loyalist revolt, the uprising in Saxony, the war in Poland, the business in Italy, Lefferts' antics in the Balearic Islands, whatever was going on among the Turks—and now this.

"Relief." She laughed. "Try being one of God's Chosen People for a few years and you'll understand what 'no relief' means. This—pfah!—this is just diplomacy."

"I'm trying to figure out what the ruckus in France means for us," mused Piazza. He rose and went to the window of his office. Like the office itself, the window was on the small side and provided no view of the Elbe, as was considered prestigious. Instead, the window looked out over an alley.

On the positive side, the alley was kept much

cleaner than most such in the USE's capital. If Ed opened the window and leaned out, he'd be able to determine the reason for that unwonted tidiness. Just half a block to the south he'd see part of the royal palace and, beyond it, Hans Richter Square.

He didn't mind, though. Given the pollution in the Elbe coming from the factories south of the city, the river was not all that nice a sight anyway. And the political situation called for as much discretion as possible. The unpretentious office tucked away in an unpretentious (if very large) government building was just part of that. Since the collapse of the counter-revolution launched by the Swedish chancellor Axel Oxenstierna a few months ago, the precise nature of political authority in the United States of Europe had become...

Murky, he thought. *Let's leave it at that.*

Wilhelm Wettin was still the prime minister, even though he'd been up to his neck in the Swedish chancellor's plots and schemes. Luckily for him, though, he'd balked at outright treason and been pitched into a cell by Oxenstierna. That had been enough—just barely—to save him from the imperial wrath that came down on the plotters after Gustav Adolf recovered from his brain injury and Oxenstierna was shot dead by Colonel Hand. Where many others had been stripped of their titles, positions—even their lands, in some cases—Wettin had come out of it officially unscathed.

Still, in the real world the prime minister's authority was now threadbare. The political coalition he'd led, the so-called Crown Loyalists, was in outright tatters. Most people expected that when the next election was held—which would be soon, even if no specific date had been set yet—the Fourth of July Party would come back into power. And although no public announcement had yet been made, it was an open secret that Mike Stearns had already told the emperor that he did not intend to run for office again.

Which left, as the most obvious person who'd assume the post of prime minister if the Fourth of July Party won a majority in Parliament, the man who was currently the president of the State of Thuringia-Franconia—Ed Piazza. Who'd moved to Magdeburg weeks earlier, leaving the running of the SoTF in the capable hands of the province's vice president, Helene Gundelfinger.

In fact if not in name, Piazza was running a shadow government whose claim to being a "shadow" was thin at best. Still, he tried to keep up appearances. Hence the humble office—and hence also, the fact that he was using that humble office to deal with foreign affairs. Rebecca was here because she was serving him for the time being as his informal (and very unofficial) secretary of state.

All things considered, alleys do not make for interesting scenery. After half a minute or so contemplating its nonexistent wonders, Ed turned away from the window and moved back to his desk.

"I know that King Louis XIII was never what you'd call our friend," he said, easing into his seat, "but Gaston is a real wild card. He came down on the side of Borja, and from what I've been able to tell, he's had his hand in every major plot against his brother for a dozen years. He's *got* to be involved in this."

Rebecca gestured toward the stack of paper on Ed's desk. "The intelligence reports say that it was a band of outlaws that attacked the cardinal's party. Gaston was not there. He may have been visiting his mother at the time."

Ed flipped through the sheets until he pulled out the one he wanted. "Let's see. Marie de Medici. Does that name mean what I think it means?"

Rebecca shrugged. "Intrigue and conspiracy. Medici ... Strozzi ... Colonna ... they're pretty much all the same."

"Great. She strikes me as a real beaut. Louis exiled her too, from what I read."

"Just before the Ring of Fire. She forced him to choose between his mother and his minister. She'd been dominating his life ever since Henry IV was killed, and I think Louis was tired of it. He wanted Richelieu to take care of things for him so he could hunt and paint and act like a king *looks*."

"He always was a bit of a wimp, I guess."

Rebecca hesitated for just a moment, as if she was trying to locate the definition of the word *wimp*. "You underestimate him, Ed. Do not take the portrait of him in that *Three Musketeers* movie for good coin."

"Which *Three Musketeers* movie? There have been a jillion of them."

"Don't be silly. The one with Charlton Heston playing Richelieu. The rest—*pfah*." She made a dismissive gesture. "The real Louis XIII is—was—quite an athlete, for one thing. He rode to war in Mantua, and against rebellious Huguenots. My impression was that he simply didn't like the day-to-day parts of the role and wanted to leave those to Cardinal Richelieu."

"Who is—who was—very good at it."

"Is, I think."

"The report says the ambush party killed everyone," Ed said. "Richelieu's dead also, isn't he?"

"The body of the king was carried back in state," she answered. "It was buried in a great ceremony. Nothing was said about His Eminence the cardinal. Certainly someone so important would have been publicly laid to rest as well."

"Big funeral."

"With bishops and archbishops. Several of each, I would expect. There are a few there now, from what we hear—but not the number that *would* be there to perform the memorial for the man who's run the whole country for a dozen years. So if he is dead, the body hasn't been recovered."

"Or he isn't dead at all. He's . . . I don't know. He's Elvis? Is that what you're telling me?"

"I'm not sure I understand."

Ed leaned back in his chair. "Elvis. Elvis Presley. He was a singer, a big star performer. They called him 'The King.' When he first started he was young and strong and everything, every girl's dream." He smiled; Rebecca frowned. "Anyway. As he became more and more famous he got fat and—strange. Eventually he died, big funeral . . . they turned his house into a museum—Graceland, the king's home. Except that over time people kept reporting that they'd seen him here and there—"

"Performing?"

"No, but there were people *pretending* to be Elvis, dressing up like him. But that's not what I meant. There were 'Elvis sightings.' He was washing dishes, or waiting for a bus, or shopping, or something else. So the rumor started that the king wasn't dead at all.

It was some sort of giant hoax. He was working for the government undercover; he was getting ready for a big comeback; organized crime needed to believe he was dead."

"Ed," Rebecca said. "Are you trying to tell me that in your so clever up-time world there were people who believed that someone who was *dead* was secretly alive? A popular figure, an—an entertainer—had somehow made up his own death?"

"You'd be amazed what things people believed up-time."

"I guess I would. So . . . you think that Cardinal Richelieu is dead and people think he is still alive."

"Or he is alive, and is content to have people think that he is dead."

"People like Monsieur Gaston," Rebecca said. "I have met Richelieu. He's a brilliant man, Ed—one of the most perceptive men I've ever met—and quite charming, too. Even cut off from his base of power, he would be a formidable enemy. If he is still alive, he is Gaston's enemy. As is the queen, wherever she is."

"Our ambassador in Paris said that there's a rumor at court that she's gone back to Spain with the baby," Ed said. "I don't believe it, but it's the sort of thing that would be put about to discredit her."

"By Gaston's people."

"No doubt. So if she's not in Spain—and not in Paris—then where is she? And where is Richelieu?"

"You mean, 'Elvis.'"

"Yeah. Elvis in a red robe." He smiled. "Well, considering some of the stuff he was wearing at the end of his career, it wouldn't be too far off. It would have to be covered with sequins, though."

Auxerre, France

"Look at the happy family reunion," Artemisio said, looking out the window at the group at the edge of the trees that bordered the courtyard, sheltering from the rain.

"His brothers?" Terrye Jo pointed down at the three men.

"Donna Teresa!" He pulled on her arm. "*Attento.*" He gestured, and she squatted down, below the level of the window.

They were in the loft of the almoner's house of Saint-Germain d'Auxerre, looking over the inner courtyard. Monsieur Gaston had been installed at the bishop's palace, and most of them remained there, while Gaston and his gentlemen-in-waiting had come here. *To view the frescoes*, he had said to his wife before departing.

Terrye Jo would have been just as happy to stay and read, but Artemisio Logiani—who had somehow attached himself to Monsieur Gaston's party as a household servant—was determined to follow along, and begged her to come with him.

If the frescoes are beautiful enough to be viewed by a prince, Donna, he had said to her, *then I must compare them to your loveliness.*

Which somehow, impossibly, had led to their present location. While they were walking around the edge of the courtyard, trying to keep dry, a party of horsemen had arrived at the porter's gate. Artemisio had pulled her aside into the almoner's house, and they had made their way to the upper floor.

"A bird's-eye view," he had said.

"Of what?"

"We shall see."

But not be seen, she thought now, wondering if she'd been pulled into a Mark Twain adventure. *Hell,* she added: *the whole freakin' seventeenth century is a Mark Twain adventure.*

"His brother and his *father,*" Artemisio said. "Interesting."

"Why?"

"Monsieur Louis de Vendôme's brother François, and his father the duke, César, are exiled from the realm. His Majesty the king—" and here Artemisio stopped and crossed himself, looking toward heaven like a side character in a Renaissance painting—"sent the duke away for conspiring. Well, actually, Cardinal Richelieu did it, but that's the same thing. And now *here he is,* with his two sons. Who knows what they're here for."

"But *this* is what you came to see, isn't it, Artemisio?"

"Well," he answered, "not necessarily *this,* Donna. I didn't know what it was about, but I heard...you know how servants talk..."

"I certainly do."

"Well, I heard that something big and important was going to happen when we got to Auxerre. And here we are, and here it is." He peeked very carefully over the sill, and Terrye Jo did likewise.

The three men—clearly Louis, she could clearly make out his features, and two others, one young and one older—seemed very happy to be together. The older one, the duke, was speaking to his two sons. He paused for just a moment and looked around, as if he was trying to determine if he was being spied upon.

Terrye Jo and Artemisio ducked back down.

"What do you think this big and important thing might be?"

"Well, you know," Artemisio said. "It's all above me. But if I were to guess, I'd say that the duke is here to pledge allegiance to Monsieur Gaston—and get a pardon."

"Father," François said quietly as they walked slowly down the stairs to the crypt. "This is a perfect place for Gaston to betray us."

"Yes," César de Vendôme said. "It is." He did not look away, but continued to stare straight ahead, walking slowly down the stairs. "But he would not go to all this trouble—at least at *this* point—to do so. He still needs us."

By now, several weeks after he received the ball fired from Richelieu's pistol, the duke's injury had completely healed. As was often true with head wounds, it had initially looked much worse than it really was. His son François, on the other hand, was still recovering from the great gash in his side left by the king's sword. He was lucky to have survived at all.

"For what does he need us?"

The duke shook his head. "I am not sure. But there is still something."

"I am not sure either—"

César stopped walking and turned to his son. He leaned close, so that their escorts could not easily hear.

"Do you trust me, my son?"

"Of course. With my life, Father. You know that."

"Then you must rely on my judgment. Now and in the near future. Gaston d'Orleans has *already* betrayed me after a fashion. It is now our task to make sure that when he pulls the noose tight, his own neck is caught in it as well."

François was accustomed to his father's stern gaze: it was how he always pictured him—proud, noble, with a hint of scarcely concealed anger. This expression was different in a way: totally serious, focused, intense.

"I will do whatever you ask."

"Then I ask now that you do nothing. And say nothing. I want you to remember that our time will come, François."

"I understand."

César stood straight, and they began to descend once more.

In the Abbey of Saint-Germain d'Auxerre, beneath the frescoes in the crypt, the monks had placed the sub-prior's chair on a small platform. It was something short of a throne, but was sufficiently elevated above the floor that it gave the appropriate separation that the prince desired.

The Vendôme men walked through the open area and between a pair of tall support pillars, looking straight ahead at Gaston d'Orleans, presumptive king of France. César did not spend a moment of attention on anything other than the figure of his half-brother.

He acts as if it is a throne, he thought to himself. *Though Louis would not have received me thus if I had returned to court.*

He put the thought from his mind: he leashed his anger and curbed his desire to draw his sword. The gentlemen in waiting radiated hostility: it was if they found his presence an affront.

He is not the king, César thought to himself. *He wishes to be. He may be. But not yet.*

He stopped a few paces from the dais and made a leg. François, a step behind, did the same. Not a deep obeisance, but a mark of respect rather than homage.

"My Lord of Vendôme," Gaston said. He seemed eerily calm and composed. "Welcome. Let me be the first to welcome you back to our realm, Brother," Gaston said. "I trust that you found our safe-passage sufficient to your needs."

"It was most satisfactory, Your Majesty. I cannot adequately express my gratitude for permitting me to return to France."

"Ah, César." Gaston gestured, and César rose to his feet and approached the throne. "It has been too long." Gaston placed his hands on the man's shoulders.

"We both know why that is the case."

"Yes. We do." César met Gaston, glance for glance, enough so that the king-to-be looked away, dropping his hands to his sides.

There was an extended moment of silence. Finally, without looking up, he said, "My companions, please leave us."

"Sire—" the nearest one began, but Gaston looked aside to him with a glance that silenced him.

The four gentlemen-in-waiting bowed and backed away, never taking their eyes off César de Vendôme and his son.

"François," César said without turning, "you have leave to go as well. His Majesty and I have matters to discuss."

It was clear that François did not want to leave his father alone; but he also bowed and backed out of the room. When his footsteps began to echo on the stairs, Gaston settled back in his chair.

"This is rather quaint, isn't it?" he said, spreading his hands out. "The abbot's chair. Nicely padded—the old man has hemorrhoids, apparently, and it hurts for him to sit overlong. Two monks carried it all the way down here for their king."

"You don't have that title yet."

"*Yet.*" Gaston smiled, cat-like. "A trifling distinction, one that should only trouble us for a short time."

"I cannot believe your insolence and arrogance, Gaston. I have half a mind to run you through."

"Anger ill-becomes you, César. And I know—we both know—that you are not that foolish or self-destructive. I arranged for your safe passage back into France, you and that headstrong son of yours. *He* certainly wants to run me through.

"And after all the effort to bring you back into France, you would be forced to flee . . . and even if you were able to escape the kingdom you would be condemned as a regicide. Twice over." Gaston smiled again.

"You knew he would be with the cardinal, didn't you?"

"Eh?"

"You *knew* that Louis would be in Richelieu's entourage. And neither you nor that snake Soissons saw fit to tell me."

"Would it have made any difference?" As César began to reply, Gaston held up his hand and sat up straight. "No, please, let me answer. Of *course* it would have made a difference. It would have prevented you from carrying out your mission—from doing your duty."

"I wouldn't be too sure of that."

"*I* would." Gaston snickered. "You intrigued against Louis, César. We all did. It made for good sport, even if it was surpassingly easy. But we all loved him in one fashion or another. It was Richelieu we hate. The devil in the *robe rouge*—he was your target. He was your duty. He might be spared if the king commanded it: and make no mistake, Louis *would* have commanded it.

"Where *is* he? He didn't make the grand funereal entrance into Paris with my lord of Maillé-Brézé. You didn't leave him out on the road at Saint-Arnoult-en-Yvelines, I assume, to be torn apart by the wolves and feed the maggots? Because they *didn't find a body*, César. They didn't even find the damn *robe rouge*."

"You're remarkably well informed. You tell *me*."

Gaston stood up and walked away, turning his back on César. If he had the least concern that he might actually be run through, he showed none of it. He walked slowly along the wall as if he was admiring the frescoes.

"No," he said without turning. "You tell *me*, César. Tell me where the red-robed bastard spawn of Satan is. He was not found at the ambush site: not him, not his body, not a fold of his cloak or a lace from his boot. *Where the hell is Cardinal Richelieu?*"

"I don't know."

"You don't know." Gaston turned around. He laughed, a cruel, cackling sound. "*Magnifique.* You don't know where he is. Were you, or were you not, specifically and categorically directed to *kill* him?"

"I was. I was *not* directed to kill our brother the king. You have used me to commit a foul act—and it would not surprise me, Gaston, not a bit, if you arranged for Richelieu to escape."

"What? Are you—are you accusing me of saving his life?"

"Your schemes are so deep and complex, I should not exclude the possibility. I am a simple soldier, Gaston—"

"Spare me. You are nothing of the kind."

"You are no fit judge. What you are, is—"

"What I *am*," Gaston said, "is the next king of France." His voice was icy calm, where he had been agitated before. "I will soon be your lord and sovereign, César, my lord of Vendôme, and I urge you to make no mistake: if you see fit to oppose *me*, you will not find yourself dismissed and sent into noble exile—you will meet the same fate as your brother Alexandre. Or worse. *Much* worse. And much, much sooner."

"Are you threatening me?"

"Of course I am, you idiot. I am giving you my royal promise that I will prosecute you as the true and vile murderer of my older brother Louis, the most puissant sovereign of the kingdom of France. It will be proclaimed at court; it will be announced on every street corner and printed in every newspaper, and it will be broadcast on the up-timers' radios for everyone in Europe and beyond to hear. Be assured that I will do so, beyond doubt—unless you do, and *continue to do*, exactly as I direct."

"You're in it as deep as I am."

"There you are mistaken. I am involved, yes: no doubt, for you would accuse me, and it would be inconvenient for you to be prevented from speaking. But no, I am not in as deep. Blood is on *your* hands, César. Mine—" he extended his hands, examining the fingers in turn—"only bear the king's signet."

César did not answer. There was nothing for him to say; and even if there was, this was not the place to say it. Gaston had brought both of them to the place they now occupied—Gaston, the prospective king; he, the prodigal, returned to his native land.

He had allies and he had resources. This was a trap but it was not yet a prison. Bringing up the name of Alexandre was a deliberate provocation, like poking a caged bear, intended to make him angry and to deprive him of cold reason.

As the moment stretched out he realized that he would be safe from Gaston's betrayal exactly as long as he remained useful. His half-brother would not dispense with him until that was no longer the case—but would not tolerate him a moment longer.

The clock was ticking but midnight had not yet arrived. It was not clear how much time he had, but he reassured himself that if he passed up this opportunity to end Gaston's life, that another one would appear.

There were, after all, innumerable ways to kill a man.

"Yes, Sire," he said. "I understand."

Chapter 20

Southern France

Étienne Servien made all possible speed away from Beville-le-Comte. Richelieu had been clinging to life when they had parted; God only knew whether he was still alive. His young Guard companion had not accompanied him to the queen's place of retirement, but at Servien's direction had been sent on his way back to Paris to seek out Tremblay and inform him of the events at Yvelines.

D'Aubisson had the advantage of youth and skill—he was a professional soldier—but at least in principle Servien had the signet of the most powerful man in France. It would not protect him as well as a good sword or helmet or hauberk, but it would have to do. No one needed to know that Richelieu hovered close to death—or that he had already passed on. Not even Servien himself knew.

It was on a need to know basis; Servien did not apparently need to know. He had specific orders, issued long ago and reinforced in his last conversation with Richelieu.

You know what you must do. Go.

He was to make for Pau, the fortified capital of the province of Béarn, and present himself to the comte de Brassac et de Béarn. Neither Tremblay nor Richelieu had ever told him why: Servien, for his part, was not inclined to pursue the matter further—it was not in the repertoire of an *intendant* to ask questions, particularly on serious matters.

Pau was near the Spanish border; Béarn was nominally a part of the kingdom of Navarre, but it had come into the realm of France along with its most famous scion, King Henry IV of revered memory, who had been born in the Fortress of Pau.

It explained nothing about his own mission: why Béarn, what the comte might do for him, what—if anything—could be done about the duc de Vendôme or his likely employer, the duc d'Orleans. Word of the death of the king would reach Paris soon if it had not already done so. Rumors about the death of Richelieu would certainly follow. It was critically important that doubt in the matter persist as long as possible.

As for his own fate, Servien was pragmatic. There was nothing he could do—nothing, truly, that he *should* do, other than ride toward Pau, following Richelieu's orders to the last.

To the last, he thought. *Apt.*

You know what you must do.

Go.

Paris

Long before Maillé-Brézé returned in state with the body of the murdered king, long before rumors of the ambush on the road began to circulate—long before it became apparent to most of those intimate to the circles of power in the capital that something had *happened* and something was *wrong*, Père Joseph, the cardinal de Tremblay, took action.

Cardinal Richelieu had arranged with Tremblay that he would send a message by radio upon their arrival at the Château Baronville. The slightly premature birth of the heir, if God had chosen to grant the kingdom a son, would work to their advantage: the prince, if prince he was, had not been expected for almost a month, and there were matters to attend to before the king's (and therefore the cardinal's) enemies were able to counter them. The radio was a marvelous up-time blessing, Tremblay knew; some in the clergy were dubious about whether it was somehow a tool of the Devil, but many of those learned men had the same feeling about all of the up-timers.

Theological debate was one thing. Pragmatic state politics was another.

When the message did not come in the evening, Tremblay was willing to ascribe it to the lateness of their probable arrival, or a malfunction of the radio, or uncertainty about the result—perhaps the queen was still in her labors, or there was as yet nothing to report. When the message did not come on the following morning he was more troubled.

A day later, when a few whispers began to traverse the Louvre and make their first ventures into

Les Halles and elsewhere, Tremblay began to make provision for what the world might be like if Cardinal Richelieu was not in it.

Jean d'Aubisson had turned nineteen years old two days after Lady Day; he had been the youngest and least experienced of the cadre of Cardinal's Guards in Richelieu's escort on the journey to Beville-le-Comte. The others had joked with him, telling him that he certainly couldn't expect to be a personal man-at-arms to the *robe rouge* until he could at least grow a proper beard. It had led to a few shoves and more than a little ill-feeling: however much the other Guardsmen professed their desire for simple, innocent fun at his expense, it came across more angry and resentful. He was the youngest, but he was also the most agile, the fastest blade, the best dancer ... truly the best looking, with no comparison among the weary and scarred veterans that wore the red-on-white tabard and maroon cape of the Guard.

What he never expected was to be the only survivor.

It took a night and part of a day for him to reach the outskirts of Paris. He had left his maroon cape and most of the other accoutrements of his uniform at Claire-fontaine. The passing of a few coins had obtained him nondescript traveling clothes; a little creative tailoring dispensed with insignia of rank and any identification of his family's personal heraldry. He could have chosen an entirely different identity—but it would have meant giving up his fine mount and his weapons to sustain it: and he wasn't about to surrender either.

He would be a simple, anonymous gentleman at arms, a provincial, perhaps in service to one of the lords who were even now streaming into the city at the rumor of the king's death. He was scarcely noticed as he entered at the Porte Saint-Antoine, riding close enough to be mistaken for a member of some troop attending one of the *noblesse de robe* who even now returned to their townhouses in Paris, riding far enough away that no bailiff or sergeant might decide to put him to work.

To go directly to the Palais-Cardinal would certainly have drawn attention, and possibly unwanted recognition. Instead, d'Aubisson went to the parish church of Saint-Étienne-des-Grès just off the Rue Saint-Victor, and hired a messenger to send a particular message to Cardinal Tremblay—a coded signal of distress, long rehearsed and memorized among the Guard.

It took only a few hours for Tremblay himself to appear: not in pectoral and full regalia as a cardinal of the Church, but in his more accustomed attire as a Capuchin monk—gray hooded robe and sandals, coming into Saint-Étienne-des-Grès as a simple penitent. D'Aubisson was waiting for him in the alcove that held a black-painted limestone statue of the virgin, *Notre Dame de Bonne Délivrance*, the black Madonna of Paris.

"An interesting choice."

D'Aubisson prided himself on his observational skill, but he jumped when Tremblay spoke from just a few feet away.

If he were bent on taking my life, d'Aubisson thought, *I would be dead on the floor.*

"Why do you say that?" he asked, recovering his composure.

Tremblay—in the more familiar habit and persona

of a simple monk, came up to stand beside him, looking up at the statue. It was almost life-size, and set up on a plinth; the Blessed Mother smiled beatifically down at them, at once familiar and otherworldly, her expression impossible to read.

"This is where De Sales made his confession almost fifteen years ago. The Black Madonna...an object of veneration. Rather public, don't you think?"

"It is easiest to be hidden in plain sight."

"Pithy. An up-timer expression."

"And quite accurate in your case, wouldn't you say...Brother?"

"I assume that you have no intention to offend or antagonize. But do not try me, boy. Walk with me."

They left the alcove and began to walk slowly along the ambulatory, gazing up at the woodwork and stained glass as if they were awestruck penitents. At Tremblay's direction, he provided a short, succinct description of the events in a low voice.

"We might be under observation," Tremblay said to him. "But they shouldn't be close enough to hear. Still, there is a chance that someone may have followed me here, or be spying on us now. But there is nothing to be done."

"Where is my good friend and our patron's servant Étienne, then? Is he still with him now?"

"He was to ride out after I did."

"And not accompany the...dignitaries."

"No. He said that he was going to Pau, of all places. You do trust him," d'Aubisson added.

"Of course," Tremblay answered. "Well, at least as much as I trust anyone. Yourself included."

"I feel as if I should be insulted."

"Don't trouble yourself," Tremblay answered. "We must assume the worst—and we must also assume that the longer his enemies lack certainty about his situation and whereabouts, the better our lives will be."

"What do you intend?"

"I have a mission for you to undertake, my fine young friend," Tremblay said. D'Aubisson could scarcely make out the priest's face within the hood; the day was overcast, with lowering clouds that made the gloom in the church nave shadowy and ponderous.

But he did hear a very soft and cynical laugh.

"I am eager to serve."

"Good. You will take a message to a person I designate in a place I will reveal. The destination of that message will be the place to which the party will first travel."

"How do you know that?"

"Her Majesty will be invited to consider this possibility," Tremblay answered. "Indeed, she will choose it."

"How can you be sure?"

"It is very simple," Tremblay said. "One of her closest companions works directly for me."

D'Aubisson didn't seem surprised.

Tremblay reached into his sleeve and withdrew a small cloth scapular on a woven string. It bore a painted image of the Blessed Virgin with a crimson heart surrounded by a golden halo. He touched it to his lips and held it out to d'Aubisson.

"Wear this under your clothing, young man. Go— as soon as you can—to the Auberge Écossaise in Evreux. Present yourself to my…colleague, Brother Gérard. Tell him that he should shortly expect a very important visitor, who will need to be protected. He will know what to do."

The young guardsman nodded. He took the scapular, kissed it, and put it around his neck, tucking it below his blouse.

"And then?"

"Return here. We have much to do."

Chapter 21

Pau

If Servien had been given to lyrical prose, he might have been moved to write about the sweeping vista visible from the plateau upon which the capital of Béarn was built. Beyond the town he could see the Pyrenees, verdant and sculptured against the backdrop of a late spring sky, like the frame of a grand tapestry that held the fortified castle and settlement that surrounded it. The beauty of the place—serene and quiet, far from the bustle and grime of Paris—might have been enough, had he the temperament for it, to forget the seriousness of his mission.

As Servien paused on horseback with the scene before him, he allowed himself a grim smile. Of all the things he was, a lyrical craftsman of prose was not one of them and the mission was not far from his mind. The Pyrenees, beautiful as they were in the sunny afternoon, merely marked the boundary between his native land and its greatest potential enemy, the kingdom of Spain.

He wondered for just a moment how much Spain might be involved in this: whether Monsieur Gaston had enlisted France's rival in order to gain the throne—and what price the Spanish would exact for their assistance.

Then he shrugged off the thought and concentrated again on the mission, following the road that led steeply down toward the river and the town for which he was bound.

When he reached the drawbridge to the Castle of Pau, which was lowered to give access to the town, he was approached by a soldier in Brassac livery. Servien had already dismounted from his horse; the soldier looked bored and disdainful, as if dealing with petty civilians from Paris was not part of his brief.

"I have business with Monsieur le Comte," Servien said. "I would be obliged if you would direct me to him."

The soldier smiled, showing what few teeth he had. "Business with the comte, is it? Well, then, monsieur. You must realize that His Lordship is an extremely busy man."

"He will receive me."

"Perhaps yes, perhaps no. Perhaps today, perhaps next week—"

"Yes," Servien interrupted. "And today. You may tell him that I come at the behest of Cardinal de Tremblay."

"I do not know that name."

"That His Lordship does not confide in you is not my concern. You may take my message to him and be rewarded; or you may be difficult and recalcitrant, and afterward be punished."

He looked dubious, possibly weighing the possibilities of *reward* in view of the lack of dignity at being an errand-boy.

"Despite your stubbornness, I shall reward you as well. Now, if you please, I should like to enter."

At last the soldier determined that it was above his pay grade to interfere, and looked over his shoulder, making a gesture to some unknown person on the nearby battlement. Then he turned and began to walk across the drawbridge, beckoning Servien to follow.

Tremblay's name carried a particular cachet. Within a few minutes a groom had emerged to attend to Servien's horse, and Servien himself was escorted by a gentleman—who gave the soldier a disdainful glance, but only after Servien had made sure to provide him with coin—into the castle.

It was a beautiful place, more palace than the fortification it had been centuries earlier. He was led along a wide, airy corridor covered by a paneled vault and crowned by an exquisite chandelier; on the wall he passed a large tapestry showing a royal hunting-party that his gentleman guide identified as being Francis I, king a century past. At last they came to a grand staircase and into a wide salon, which held a great table made of a slab of highly polished stone, and a set of plush armchairs drawn up before an elaborately sculpted fireplace decorated with the quartered arms of Béarn and Brassac. Despite the sun outside it was still chilly, and a banked fire was burning, helping to cast off the chill. The gentleman bowed and left him there.

He was alone only for a few moments before a middle-aged nobleman entered from another doorway.

Servien offered a gracious leg and waited to be addressed.

"I am Louis de Galard de Béarn, Sieur de Semoussac, the comte de Brassac et de Béarn," the man said. "You have invoked a powerful name in order to be admitted to my presence, monsieur. I am sure that you are ready to explain yourself. To whom do I speak?"

Servien looked up at the comte. He was in his midfifties, fit and strong but gone a trifle to overweight. He wore his clothes well, and was clearly attentive to his toilet. His glance was not hostile, but it was unwavering. Servien had not been told what Tremblay's relationship was to this nobleman, but it was sufficiently cordial to allow Servien to be admitted to his presence.

"My name is Étienne Servien. I come at the instruction of Cardinal de Tremblay, my lord," Servien said. "But I serve as *intendant* for my master, the cardinal de Richelieu." He reached into his wallet and withdrew Richelieu's signet, and walked across the *salon* to present it to Brassac.

The comte took the ring and examined it, paying particular attention to the inscription within and the stone without.

"This would not leave Cardinal Richelieu's finger except in dire emergency," he said at last, handing back the signet to Servien, who put it away at once.

"My master instructed me to take it as a surety to others that I speak on his behalf," Servien said. "He lies in peril, having barely survived an ambush while riding. His Majesty the king was traveling with him."

"The king?"

"The . . . late king," Servien said, looking down at the polished floor and crossing himself. "His Majesty was killed."

"Who could have committed such a heinous deed?"

"His murderer was his half-brother, César de Vendôme. I witnessed it with my own eyes, my lord. But Cardinal Richelieu believes he acted on behalf of another. I am inclined to believe it as well."

The comte de Brassac walked slowly to the great table and ran his index finger along it, following the whorls and patterns almost absently.

"The cardinal de Tremblay was wise to send you to me, monsieur. The duc d'Orleans has some unsavory alliances and could make some injudicious choices now that the kingship is his."

"It is his by possession, my lord, not by right."

"What do you mean?"

"The rightful king of France is his nephew, the son of King Louis and Queen Anne. He was born a few hours before his father was murdered."

"How can you be sure?"

"I am sure, my lord. It is indisputably true."

"Does Gaston know this?"

"I do not think that he does, my lord, and even if he did I cannot expect that his course would change."

"And where is Monsieur now?"

"It is my understanding that he wintered with his lady mother in Tuscany, and has most recently visited his sister in Turin. If word of the king's death has reached him—or if he has already been informed of the deed—he is most likely *en route* to Paris."

"And the queen and . . . the young king?"

"They have departed the place where Her Majesty

was in seclusion. I do not know their present where-abouts."

Brassac thought for several moments, then looked directly at Servien. "Some provision will have been made. I shall have to return to the capital in due time. What are your orders, Monsieur Servien? Or your plans?"

It was Servien's turn to think. The answer did not immediately present itself; he had followed Trem-blay's—and Richelieu's—instructions to come to Pau and inform the comte de Brassac of the terrible events in the forest of Yvelines; he had not even had time to think past that.

His king had been murdered; his patron was dead, or near death. When he returned to Paris—if that did not prove unwise—he could contact his cousin Abel, the Marquis de Sablé...but for the moment he had no place to go: his duties had been discharged.

"I have neither orders nor plans, my lord."

"I believe I can make use of your talents," the comte said. "In the meanwhile, you are a welcome guest. You have ridden far, and you must have time to think."

Servien had never been given much to reflection on his future. The present had kept him busy in his role as *intendant*. He knew, and his cousin Abel had frequently reminded him, that there would certainly come a time when his patron would no longer be there to employ him, but this fact was pushed out of his mind in his day-to-day interactions with the cardinal. While Richelieu was alive and in power, he refused to give it a second thought.

Now that he was gone, Servien found himself in the uncomfortable position of considering what uptimers called "Plan B."

Over the next few days he was comfortably accommodated as the guest of the comte de Brassac within the Château de Pau. He was given the freedom of the place, to walk where he would, without restriction.

The comte neither demanded nor required anything of him. He suspected that Brassac was sensitive to his own restlessness, his desire to take some action—but there was nothing for Servien to do, from Pau, right now.

It didn't make waiting any easier. But it was unclear to him just what the comte was waiting for.

Three nights after his arrival at Pau, Servien found himself in an upper hall of the Château at vespers, admiring a particularly impressive tapestry depicting the famous Field of the Cloth of Gold, a great knightly contest and tournament from the previous century. It took him far away from the conflicts of the present day; it was a restful pause in the quiet of the early evening.

As he stood there trying to identify some of the more famous participants in that long-ago ceremony, he became aware of a murmuring sound not far away. It was almost too soft to hear; but he made it out—a man's voice, speaking a Latin prayer in a steady, regular cadence. He considered leaving, but curiosity overcame him; he walked slowly and quietly along the hall until he came to a slightly open door. Light spilled into the hallway from the room beyond.

He was hesitant to interrupt; he moved the door very slightly to see what was within and saw before him a small chapel. Below the crucified Savior was an ornately carved *prie-dieu* and a small table; something—he could not see just what—was laid upon the table, and the comte de Brassac was kneeling on the hassock, his back to the door, softly praying. At the soft creak of the door he stopped and turned, and noted Servien.

After a moment's pause he continued the prayer—an *Ave*—to its conclusion, then picked up the object from the table and tucked it within his vest. Standing and genuflecting, he turned to face his guest.

"You find me at my devotions, monsieur."

"I apologize for interrupting."

"It is nothing. I... merely had need of counsel."

"I hope you found what you needed." Servien glanced from Brassac to the now-empty table, and then back to the comte.

Brassac looked ready to move on, then seemed to reconsider. "Please close the door, if you would. I thought I had done so, that I might not disturb others. But perhaps it is fortuitous that you came upon me."

Servien did as he was instructed. He walked into the room, crossing himself as he faced the *prie-dieu*.

"I have not explained to you why Père Joseph... the cardinal de Tremblay... directed you to come here in case of emergency. I have been trying to decide what I might share with you, but I have concluded that in fairness, it is appropriate that I explain."

Servien did not answer, waiting for Brassac to continue.

"Cardinal de Tremblay and I, and others whose names you would know, share a common interest in the defense of the realm and the crown. We belong to a... society for the maintenance and protection of our beloved country. Its name is the *Compagnie du Saint-Sacrement*—the Company of the Blessed Sacrament."

"I cannot say that I have ever heard of that society, my lord."

"It is a *secret* society," Brassac said. "And your master was aware of it, but we do not count him among our members."

"Ah."

"The Company is devoted to the Crown of France," the comte continued. "We have known for some time that the queen was with child, and that there were... forces looking to intercept the succession."

"And kill His Majesty the king?"

"Every monarch has enemies, Servien. King Louis was no exception. But if your question is whether we expected this attack—the answer is definitively *no*. Gaston was always a threat, but has been exiled for many years. As for Vendôme... there is no question that he is capable of regicide, but his greatest enemy was your master, not his brother the king."

"I think you underestimate his desire for revenge, Monsieur le Comte. You and your—Company—seem to have overlooked an obvious alliance."

"We are not the only group seeking to protect crown and kingdom. And we cannot be everywhere."

Servien bit off an angry reply: he was without his patron, in the presence of a member of the *noblesse d'épee*. He wanted to give vent to his frustration and bitterness, his resentment that the world had been turned upside down.

Brassac was telling him of a society that pledged to protect the crown and defend the kingdom... *but they were not in the Forest of Rambouillet, at Yvelines, when Vendôme and his men rode out of the dark and struck down King and Cardinal.*

"*Kill them all...leave none alive,*" he heard in his mind.

"You seem dubious, Monsieur Servien."

"I do not intend to convey that sentiment, my lord."

"Then..."

"I entreat you to continue, Monsieur le Comte."

"Our worst fears have not been brought about," Brassac said. "If what you say is true, the infant king and the queen mother still live, but are in peril. We will do everything we can to protect them."

"May I ask a question?"

"By all means."

"What position do you hold within this Company?"

"I am its superior."

"And Cardinal de Tremblay?"

"He is a member of our society. An important one."

"I am gratified to hear that he is so highly regarded," Servien said. "And now that you have revealed the existence of this secret company to me...what happens next?"

"You mean," Brassac said, "do I swear you to secrecy with a blood oath? No. Nothing of the kind. It would be my preference that you keep its existence secret; I know that you are familiar with the business of keeping secrets, and thus I have no doubt of your ability in that regard. But I will not foolishly compel you. Do whatever you like with the information."

"Just that. 'Do whatever you like.'"

"Just that." Brassac reached within his vest and drew out the object he had concealed there: a cloth scapular on a woven string. It bore a painted image of the Blessed Virgin with a crimson heart surrounded by a golden halo. He touched it to his lips and then handed it to Servien. "This is our emblem: the Sacred Heart. It is one of our methods of recognition.

"When you entered, I was praying to our Holy Mother that others in our Company were executing their instructions, making efforts for the defense of France in the face of these events. I shall return to Paris after word of the king's death officially reaches us; until then, I must leave matters in the hands of others."

"Including the cardinal de Tremblay, I assume."

"Yes. Most especially including the cardinal de Tremblay. And in the meanwhile we watch, and wait."

Chapter 22

Maintenon, France

Mazarin had become accustomed to the idea of intrigue, of deception in plain sight, as a part of his career within and without the Vatican. His relatively recent association with Cardinal Richelieu, the man who—in some other future, never to be reached—would pass the mantle of ministerial authority to him, only enhanced that acclimation.

Most of those who saw the small party of seven—himself, Achille d'Étampes de Valençay, Queen Anne and her infant son, her lady-in-waiting the duchesse de Chevreuse, the up-timer doctor, and the Savoyard servant—saw nothing but a noblewoman and her entourage traveling from place to place. Mazarin wanted to continue that way—they could not move quickly by carriage, with a mother just out of childbed and an infant only a few days old—but it was also clear that they could not avoid all contact for fear of arousing suspicion.

A full day's travel brought them as far as Maintenon, a small town on the banks of the Eure. It lacked any sort of reasonable hostelry, of the sort suitable for a traveling noblewoman, much less the queen of France.

As the servant attended to watering the horses by the side of the road, Mazarin and Achille held a conversation.

"It seems simple enough," the knight of Malta said. "Maintenon is the home of the Marquis de Rambouillet; we will go to his manor house and request lodging for our honored lady."

"Whom he will immediately recognize."

"Not necessarily," Achille answered. "She is recently widowed; she will wear a suitable veil. I would be more concerned about you, Monseigneur."

"Me? Why me?"

"You are . . . better known than any among our company, with the exception of Her Majesty."

"It doesn't matter." Mazarin took off his hat, examined it and flicked a tiny bit of road-dust from the brim, and placed it back on his head. "If we choose to stay with the marquis, word will reach Paris that we have been there. His wife is the renowned *salonnière*."

"And he is likely to speak of it."

"The marquis and the marquise have their own . . . diversions," Mazarin said. "But I suspect that such news would be passed on in short order. We cannot go to Maintenon."

"We cannot reach Dreux before nightfall," Achille said. "We must go to Maintenon."

"Why Dreux? Why have we chosen this direction in preference to all others?" The morning of their departure from Baronville, Mazarin's principal concern had been for Anne and the infant; he had let the other man determine their direction.

"Which way would you rather go, Monseigneur? We cannot go toward Paris—Her Majesty has many enemies there. There is nothing to the south or west."

"And to the north?"

"Ultimately, the Low Countries," Achille answered. "Her aunt in Brussels."

"You wish to travel to the court of *Lady Isabella*? Are you mad? The Hapsburgs are the enemies of France."

"The Spanish Hapsburgs certainly are, I'll admit that," he said. "But perhaps not the Austrians. And the king in the Low Countries—that's another matter entirely."

"It is a terrible risk."

Achille laughed and looked away from Mazarin toward the carriage. The up-timer nurse, who had disembarked to stretch her legs, looked curiously at the two men.

"Tell me what part of this venture is not risky, Monseigneur. We travel in the company of the queen, who may be in danger from anyone she meets and has only *us* to defend her. Her husband and his chief minister have been slain by assassins, led by an exiled bastard prince who—I do not hesitate to remind you—is still somewhere nearby, and has two dozen men for each one of us.

"Has anyone explained all of this *risk* to Her Majesty? Do you believe she truly understands?"

"I am extremely well acquainted with the queen, monsieur," Mazarin said. "There might have been a time when she was innocent with respect to such things, but it is far in the past. She understands completely what is happening, and what our situation has become. Do not underestimate her.

"I wonder sometimes if we understand it nearly as well."

Achille was right: there was no other choice than the Château de Maintenon. And he was also right to note that Mazarin was better known than he was; therefore, it was logical for Achille, rather than Mazarin, to approach the château and request lodging for his mistress and her company, while they waited without.

Mazarin's introduction to Achille's lack of diplomatic skill came with the arrival of a troop of a dozen horsemen, their hauberks and helmets dappled with the wan light of the last quarter moon. The carriage had remained on the lane near the château; Mazarin stayed on the top bench with Artemisio while the others stayed within.

The leader of the horsemen approached the carriage, holding his hand up to keep the others at a distance.

"Good evening," Mazarin said.

"Monsieur," the man said. "Good evening. You are . . . companions of the knight of Malta, I presume."

"He has made your acquaintance."

"I found him arrogant, demanding and—"

"I can just imagine. Achille is impetuous—"

"To say the least."

"And undiplomatic. But . . . I thought it best to have him approach with our humble request."

"A troublesome choice."

"May I have the courtesy of your name, monsieur?"

"My name is Charles de Sainte-Maure; I am the Marquis de Montausier. Monsieur de Rambouillet, who is not in residence at this time, is my . . . he is the father of my intended."

"Congratulations."

"*Merci,*" the man answered with exaggerated courtesy. "Who is the distinguished lady on whose behalf the knight of Malta is so eager to offend?"

"I would invite you to step inside our carriage and find out."

"Very mysterious," he said, "but I shall humor you." He dismounted and walked toward the carriage. "Who are you, and who could be so important?"

Mazarin did not answer, but looked down toward the carriage door, which had been opened slightly from within. Montausier stepped up and opened it, then stepped in. A moment later he stepped out, his face transformed by surprise.

"Please follow me," he said without looking back at the carriage.

"They did not treat me with proper respect," Achille said, placing the bread crust on the plate before him. "I'm sorry, Monseigneur. I cannot accept an affront to my dignity, or the honor of my order."

Mazarin looked from Achille to Montausier.

"No particular offense was given to him," Montausier said. He picked up his wine goblet and took a sip. They were sitting in the nearly deserted dining hall of the Château de Maintenon; the queen had been comfortably lodged in quarters upstairs. The candles had burned low in the candelabras.

"With respect," Achille said, "I beg to differ."

"Is this how it is going to be?" Mazarin said. "We are trying not to attract any attention. Is that not meaningful to you?"

Achille shrugged. "I do not quite see your point, Monseigneur."

"Diplomacy is not one of your primary skills," Mazarin said. "We should consider ourselves fortunate that the marquis is not in residence."

"He has gone to Paris," Montausier said. "The king is dead."

"You don't say."

Montausier seemed to be considering whether Mazarin was serious or not; but after a moment he smiled. "Yes. Of course you know that. Is Her Majesty aware of . . ."

"Of course," Mazarin said. "And she is in great danger. It is why we are here."

"If you had merely explained yourself . . ."

"I was very clear—" Achille began, but Mazarin held his hand up.

"My Lord de Montausier," Mazarin said. "I have no other choice but to trust in your discretion. Tomorrow we must be gone from here, and no one must know that we tarried with you. Monsieur Gaston is likely not in the country, but his spies likely *are.*"

"Now that he is to be king, he can command anyone he wishes."

Mazarin stood suddenly. "He is *not* the king of France, my lord. He may believe that the crown belongs to him, but it does not. It belongs to that infant upstairs. As long as the baby lives, *he* is the king of France.

"With respect, My lord Marquis, I ask you to remember that."

Montausier was taken aback, enough that his hand moved down toward his scabbard. With a glance at the standing Mazarin and the still-seated Achille, he stopped that motion.

"I give you my word," Montausier said at last.

Chapter 23

Pau

In the last few days, Servien had been thinking a great deal about the comte de Brassac, and his revelations concerning the Company of the Blessed Sacrament. Brassac, he was sure, had violated a principal rule of the Company by revealing it to him, and of his membership in it; but these were difficult, extraordinary times.

He wondered if there were others, elsewhere in the country or beyond, who were just learning of the society.

The servant found him in the library, examining a family history of the Château de Pau's most famous resident—Henry of Navarre, who had been born here and had embraced the True Faith so that he could become king of France.

"Monsieur le Comte asks that you attend him at once," the servant said. "By your leave, monsieur."

"Of course."

As they walked down the great staircase, Servien said, "Do you know what this is about?"

"I do as I am commanded, monsieur."

"A wise course."

The comte de Brassac was waiting at the bottom of the stair with a younger man who shared his features; indeed, Servien—a careful observer of such things—would have thought that the comte, at half his age, would have looked thus.

"Allow me to present my oldest son Alexandre. He brought me a report that might interest you as well. My son, this is Monsieur Servien, *intendant* to His Grace the cardinal-duc de Richelieu."

The man offered a polite bow, which Servien returned. The three began to walk toward the inner courtyard.

"We have visitors," Brassac said. "They are very well armed and trained—and led by an up-timer."

"An army?"

"Not in the normal sense," Alexandre answered. "But given their arms and equipment...well, if any two dozen horsemen could be considered an army, then this label might fit."

"How can I be of service?"

"Very simple, Monsieur Servien. I need you to tell me: are these friends or enemies?"

They emerged into the bright May sunlight to find four riders still mounted, with more than two dozen in Brassac livery keeping close watch upon them. Three were subordinates, but clearly well-equipped as Alexandre had said; they remained still, a few feet apart from each other.

The fourth, a somewhat older woman, dismounted as they approached. She seemed to favor one leg very slightly; at first Servien attributed it to the cavalry sword at her waist, but he concluded that it was in fact a weakness of some sort—perhaps an injury. Still, she walked very steadily to where the comte, his son, and Servien stood.

She nodded to Alexandre, who acknowledged it.

"You must be the comte de Brassac," she said. She glanced at Servien, but didn't have anything to say to him.

"Louis de Galard de Brassac et de Béarn," Brassac answered. "The rest of your command is outside the château?"

"This is my honor guard," she answered. *Maddox's Rangers*. In service to Marshal Turenne. I'm Sherrilyn Maddox. Colonel Maddox to them; you can call me Sherrilyn." She stuck her hand out, and neither Brassac nor Alexandre seemed to know what to do; Servien extended his hand to her and took it, and found a firm, steady grip.

"I am Étienne Servien, *intendant* to the cardinal-Duke de Richelieu," he said when the handshake was over. "You must be the up-timer of which so much has been heard."

"You know her, then," Alexandre said.

"Not personally," Servien answered. "But I do know that the marshal engaged the services of a *Grantvilleuse*"—he made sure to use the female version of the noun—"to train some of his troops."

"Is Marshal Turenne planning to invade my lands?"

"I wouldn't call it an invasion," the up-timer answered. "We're here at his direction. The rest of the army is on its way; we're just the advance guard."

"And what are his intentions?"

"Your boss," she said, looking at Servien, "assumed that there would be trouble coming from the south. When we heard about the death of the king, we packed up and began to move down here. If there's any sort of invasion, my lord, it won't be by the marshal—it'll be by the Spanish."

"And how do I know that you are, indeed, from Marshal Turenne's army?"

She placed her hand on the hilt of her sword. Everyone in the courtyard tensed; but Brassac held up one hand. Maddox seemed to realize that she had sent the wrong signal.

"If I may be permitted to draw the sword to show it to you, my lord."

Brassac nodded. The up-timer looked around her, then slowly drew the blade from its scabbard; she brought it to her shoulder, then extended it, flat across her right forearm, with the hilt so that Brassac could grasp it.

He picked up the sword and examined the guard, which bore the d'Auvergne crest; he noted an inscription along the flat of the blade nearest the hilt.

"A generous gift from the marshal," Brassac said, and offered it back, hilt first. Maddox took it, saluted, and replaced it in her scabbard.

"I believe I have given good service in return, my lord," she said.

"No doubt." Brassac turned to Alexandre. "My son, please make these soldiers—and the rest of Colonel Maddox's command—comfortable. Colonel, I welcome you as our guests for the time being. As for the rest of the army . . ."

"I'm sure they'll find a place to camp."

Brassac turned with Servien and they stepped inside the building once more.

"So Marshal Turenne *is* invading," Brassac said as they made their way back toward the library. "After a manner of speaking. Perhaps he has news of which I have not heard."

"I'm sure the marshal would have the same question for you."

"An interesting response."

"May I ask a question, my lord?"

"Ask away."

"Who is the king of France?"

Brassac stopped walking. They were at the foot of the grand staircase; he glanced from Maddox to Servien, and then back to the up-timer.

"He is the sovereign lord to whom your commander has pledged his fealty," Brassac said. "Your understanding may be more clear than mine. Perhaps you should answer the question."

"I asked you first."

"And I am a peer of the realm and you are a hired soldier. I know that you up-timers are known for their forthrightness, Colonel Maddox, but you and your command are in my home, in my lands. Courtesy extends so far, and then stops. Who do *you* believe to be the king of France?"

"I'm not sure," she said at last. "Marshal Turenne wasn't sure either. It's why he moved his army so that Monsieur Gaston could not take command of it."

"Where is Gaston now?"

"Again, my lord, I'm not sure. We heard that he was traveling to France from Turin, where he was a guest of his brother-in-law the duke of Savoy. I imagine he's in Paris by now, or close to it." She took a deep breath. "And now, Comte, maybe you'll answer *my* question."

Brassac did not respond, but looked at Servien; the *intendant* inclined his head and spoke.

"The king of France," Servien said, "is an infant child, ten days old, the son of His Highness Louis XIII and Her Majesty Queen Anne. He was born just before his father was ruthlessly murdered before my eyes."

There was a very long silence, then Maddox spoke. "When we passed through Toulouse, there was a royal herald or something proclaiming Gaston d'Orleans as the king. He's to be crowned in two weeks or so at Reims. Does he know about this baby?"

"We believe he does," Brassac said, looking at Servien. "We believe that they are in terrible danger."

"From Gaston?"

"Or his agents. It is unclear whom he has chosen as allies, or what he has promised them. When do you expect your commander to arrive?"

"At least ten days from now. They move at good speed, but it's still an army. And that's if they don't meet up with any opposition."

"That is not what I fear," Brassac said. "The question is whether the Spanish themselves will invade before they arrive."

She smiled slightly. "The marshal assumes that before the Spanish march over the mountains with their tercios, they'll send a scouting party to check things out. He thought we might be able to stop them."

"Stop," Servien said, "meaning—"

"I think you are being disingenuous, Monsieur

Servien," Brassac said. "Colonel Maddox's 'Rangers' consist of the best marksmen in Marshal Turenne's army. 'Stopping' infiltrators on French soil means exactly what you would assume it means."

Sherrilyn Maddox smiled even more broadly. "It means target practice."

Paris

When word began to circulate of Monsieur Gaston's imminent arrival in the capital, members of the elite Cardinal's Guard began to absent themselves from the precincts of the Louvre, and from their barracks nearby. For fifteen years, the distinctive uniform of Richelieu's personal troops had been ubiquitous in Paris—Guardsmen were admired, feared, resented, the subject of rumor, and considered a law unto themselves.

Now they were almost impossible to find. This, more than anything else, was demonstration that the cardinal himself had fallen. It was said in the markets of Les Halles and the public places in the city that the new king, Gaston d'Orleans, would surely not retain him in his long-held post; it was Richelieu who had caused Gaston to be exiled from the realm.

And surely, it was said, *Gaston will be a better king than his brother. At the least he will provide an heir to the throne...something Louis had never done.* Had not even the most recent pregnancy, attended with so much fanfare, resulted in another failure? Surely if there was an heir, it would have been announced.

Gaston approached, and the guardsmen had seemed to vanish. Their disappearance was not mourned.

Chapter 24

Paris

As the carriage approached, Gaston could see the beautiful girl into which his daughter had grown. She sat astride a handsomely turned-out pony, her attire a perfect small copy of an adult's riding habit, topped with a feather-decorated hat that was completely *haute couture*.

Anne Marie Louise, Duchesse du Montpensier—*Mademoiselle de France*—mesmerized him; yet withal Gaston could feel Marguerite's smoldering anger. She had provided her husband with no children as yet; and this young child, all that remained of Marie de Montpensier, her husband's first wife, captivated him even though—or perhaps despite—the fact that he had not laid eyes on her in nearly four years.

When the carriage came to a halt, the young princess dismounted with assistance from her governess, the formidable Madame de St. Georges, daughter of his and Louis' own governess Madame de Montglat. With slow, measured steps she walked the short distance to where her father and stepmother sat waiting. She executed a perfect court bow, inclining her head and awaiting recognition.

"Rise, child," Gaston said. He stood—and again felt the disdain (or possibly more anger) from his wife; he ignored it. A servant scurried around to the side of the carriage and placed a stepstool; Gaston descended to the ground and stood before his daughter, helping her to her feet.

He held her hand for several moments, looking down at her and favoring her with his best smile.

"I have missed you so much, Papa," she said, doing her best to maintain her dignity; but she was ten years old, and appeared to be bursting with joy. "Your Majesty," she added, her eye catching the cold gaze of her stepmother.

"We do not need to be so formal in private," Gaston said. He glanced over his shoulder at Marguerite, whose expression said, *speak for yourself.* He ignored that as well. "I am so blessed to have you ride into our capital together."

"Thank you, Sire," she answered. She raised her chin proudly in a gesture that painfully reminded him of Marie, his first love, her mother. Holding her hand, he helped her up the steps into the carriage, where she settled herself in the seat opposite her stepmother. Gaston followed her and resumed his place next to Marguerite.

"Good day to you, Your Majesty," the girl said politely to the duchess of Orléans. "Am I to call you *Maman*?"

✧   ✧   ✧

The arrival of Gaston in Paris on that fine early May day was a cause for celebration. As far as any in the open carriage could tell, the citizens of the capital were delirious to see their new king, his consort, and his young daughter; if there were reservations among those in the crowd, it was to see César de Vendôme, Monsieur Gaston's older brother, riding behind the carriage with his two sons Louis and François: it was a sign of royal favor, an indication that their exile was at an end.

On Gaston's part it was a sly *coup de theatre*—César would have been happy to ride in the carriage with the king he had helped create, but Gaston had rejected the idea out of hand a few hours earlier before they had met up with his daughter.

"You will be better received if you are part of my escort, Brother," he had said. "You can thus adequately display the arms of your noble house, and show off your excellent horsemanship."

"I am to be reduced to the status of a mere guardsman?"

"I would hardly characterize it thus."

"It seems that way to me."

"Really." Gaston seemed already bored with the conversation. "I cannot be responsible for your perceptions, César. You are *légitimé de France*, a well-respected soldier and a member of my family and my household. Having you ride in the royal entourage sends exactly the right signal: that whatever your past infractions might have been, a new reign means an amnesty."

When Vendôme began to renew his protest, Gaston said, "If you would prefer not to enter Paris in my company, you are welcome to make your own way.

I was merely trying to portray you in the best possible light."

"My...infractions are based on the judgments of the late Cardinal Richelieu, as you know."

"Ah, yes. Cardinal Richelieu." Gaston had removed his glove and examined the nails on his right hand. "A shame that he was felled by assassins...he is dead, is he not, Brother?"

Vendôme had reddened slightly but said nothing.

"I think you had best leave perceptions to me, Brother," Gaston said. "You have an unfortunate tendency to see things less clearly than you should."

Terrye Jo rode into Paris some distance behind Monsieur Gaston and the other prominent figures. The others in the entourage accorded her some respect— she was an up-timer, after all, and had some scientific knowledge and wizardry at her fingertips—but she was still a servant, or an employee, or in some category that kept her at a distance from the front of the line. Still, she had been provided with some very nice clothing by the duchess of Savoy—not a woman's riding dress but a man's outfit tailored to her size and shape, complete with an ornate hat that she'd had to pin in place since her natural hair was too short and she refused to wear a wig.

Long before she could see most of Paris she smelled it. Bigger than Turin or Grantville or Magdeburg, Paris was one of the greatest cities in Europe—and that meant it was full of people and everything those people produced. The river reeked the worst; they approached from the west, passing along the bank as they rode through some sort of royal forest. It was almost a relief when the road veered away from the river to a wide gate. Beyond, she could see a large tower and at least a dozen churches—including Notre Dame, which she remembered from a picture in a book.

The rest of Paris was unfamiliar. No Arc de Triomphe, no Eiffel Tower. She wondered if there would be guys in little moustaches and berets playing the accordion, or if that belonged to the twentieth century too—or to bad movies.

"If only old Baldaccio could see us now, eh, Donna?" Artemisio guided his horse close enough to rub up against her; she had to keep herself from fending him off with a well-placed kick from her riding boot.

"He'd just be lecturing us on everything he knows."

"Or thinks he knows."

"Or that. Monsieur is getting quite the reception, isn't he?"

They were just passing through the Porte Saint-Martin and onto a fairly wide boulevard; people on either side were waving and shouting. She could see the Guy Fawkes mask that was Gaston's smiling face turning this way and that, acknowledging the crowd.

"They like seeing a real man," Artemisio said.

"As opposed to..."

"His brother," he said. "You know what they said about him."

"That can't have been true. He was married for twenty years, wasn't he? He—it—that sort of thing isn't something you could keep secret for that long."

"You might be surprised, Donna. I have heard a story that there is a *cavaliere*—a *gentilhomme*—here in Paris, a brave soldier and swordsman, respected by all, who is actually..." His voice lowered conspiratorially. "a *woman*. She has kept the secret for many years waiting for a chance to revenge the death of her brother, who taught her how to handle a sword."

"No reason that couldn't be true."

"Except that it's probably some story. Imagine, a woman swordsman!" He laughed, then stopped laughing when he saw Terrye Jo's frown. "What?"

"Why is that funny?"

"She would be a *down-timer*, Donna. I can believe it possible from someone such as *you*. But a down-timer woman disguising herself as a King's Musketeer or some such? Preposterous."

He gave the last word in his best impression of Umberto Baldaccio. Terrye Jo tried to keep her anger hot—but after a moment she couldn't help but laugh as well.

Even the reception of the procession at the Louvre was ceremonial. The guild masters of Paris and at least a dozen of the *noblesse d'épee* were on hand to greet Monsieur Gaston as he arrived. The noblemen saluted with their ceremonial swords, while the merchants presented their king-to-be with the honors of the city. Six noblewomen dressed in samite were present to welcome Princess Marguerite and Mademoiselle, the little Anna Maria Louisa. They executed perfect obeisances, and presented each of them with perfect white roses. It made for excellent theatre.

When all had disembarked and dismounted, the prince and his train walked slowly through the polite and approving crowds into the palace, going directly to the *salle de réception*. Gaston took up the king's seat, with Marguerite at his side, and his daughter on an ornate chair one step below. César de Vendôme stood at the same level, a sword in his hands pointed down at the floor. His sons took up positions one step below that. François, still feeling the effects of his wound, was a bit slower than Louis in doing so. Other nobles, both the *noblesse d'épee* of medieval origin and the more modern creations of the *noblesse de robe*, assumed positions according to their ranks and stations. When all were properly arranged (by their own act, or by the fussy direction of the royal masters of court protocol), the *salle* became quiet, and Gaston stood, looking out across the crowd.

"My dear countrymen, my lords and ladies. It is with great joy that I stand before you this day, to claim what is mine by right: the throne, crown and scepter of our beloved kingdom of France, and to be proclaimed Most Christian Majesty.

"But it is also with a heavy heart that I return to my native land, in the wake of the base and cowardly attack upon my dear royal brother Louis, whom men called 'the Just.' To say of him that he was pure of heart, and that our Father in Heaven smiled upon him and his reign as our sovereign, is to grant him a scarce fraction of that which was his due. We can be sure that his good works, his piety and his devotion to country and to the Lord God Almighty have given him a worthy place at the right hand of the Father."

Gaston paused for a moment, his hand upon his heart, his head bowed as if in humble prayer.

"As with our own blood kin, our devoted father Henri, he was taken from the mortal world before his work on this earth was done. As was true when that king was struck down by an assassin's hand, his heir—my dear brother Louis—had no higher duty than to carry on, and try to carry forth the labors that kingship imposes, a heavy burden upon the man who bears the crown and sits upon the throne.

"We do not know the identity of the craven assassins who performed this vile deed. I promise you, my countrymen and subjects, that no effort will be spared to find these criminals and cause them to suffer for their crimes—in a measure sufficient that when death comes at last, it will be a welcome surcease...and yet their pain in this world will be a mere foretaste of that punishment that awaits all regicides in the infernal region prepared for their eternal torment.

"No effort will be spared in finding all that were involved, even those who dare not show their faces again in our city.

"I take only a few more moments of your time this day, my friends, to announce a mark of my royal favor. Some years ago, the pernicious act of a hateful minister in service to our king caused loyal and brave members of a noble—nay, a *royal*—family to be cast into exile. This day we rescind that banishment, and welcome my dear brother César, and his sons, back to their native land. Dear brother, we grant you a pardon for whatever crimes are supposed to have been committed to cause such a false judgment. It shall be as if they have never been."

Vendôme turned at this and knelt before Gaston, who placed a hand on his head for a moment and then offered him his hand to bring him back to his feet. The two royal brothers embraced; Gaston spoke some words into Vendôme's ear, but no one else in the hall was able to discern what was said.

When Vendôme returned to his place, a mask of

calm upon his face, Gaston extended his hands wide in a theatric gesture.

"To you, my fellow Frenchmen, we pledge the loyalty of a devoted monarch, and offer you the assurance that we will be ever ready to offer an attentive ear to just entreaties, a pious heart in my supplication in your behalf, and a steady and strong sword in the prosecution of justice in our realm and beyond whenever—and wherever—it is needed. we ask only that you pray with us—and for us."

Though it would have been his preference to immediately take up residence in the king's apartments, Gaston recognized the need for propriety. Therefore, on his instructions, Vachon had established himself—and his royal master's effects—in a suitable guest suite. Marguerite had adjoining quarters, and his daughter not far away: not close enough to *anger* his wife, but close enough to *annoy* her. He loved Marguerite dearly... but he loved *La Petite Mademoiselle de France* dearly as well. The two women would need to learn to get along with each other.

His presence in Paris introduced a vast number of petitioners to his schedule, even on his first day at the royal palace; but Gaston was not interested, or prepared, to receive any of them. Still, there was one whom he could not refuse. Accordingly, late in the afternoon of his arrival, a distinguished gentleman presented himself at the outer door of Monsieur Gaston's apartments. He was admitted at once; the sitting-room was spare and nearly empty, but for Gaston himself and César de Vendôme, whom he had invited to be present.

There was only one chair, and Gaston occupied it, with his half-brother standing behind. The gentleman visitor offered a courtly bow.

"Be welcome, Don Antonio," Gaston said. "Be at your ease. What can we do for you?"

"I thank your Royal Majesty for taking the time to speak with me," said Don Antonio de Zuñiga y Davila, the Marquis de Mirabel.

He was a figure well known at the French court. For nearly fifteen years he had been King Philip of Spain's personal representative. Graying at the temples and with a carefully trimmed beard, Don Antonio was exquisitely turned out. He wore the ruff and extensive lace cuffs still in fashion at the Spanish court, with a silken doublet over which he bore the heavy collar and cross of the Order of Calatrava.

"It is our pleasure."

"Your words this afternoon were worthy of the highest praise, Your Majesty," he said. "On behalf of my master, permit me to extend the most sincere condolences on your loss. King Louis was a friend and brother to my own monarch, and it pains him greatly to hear of his death—and the manner in which it came to him."

"It pains us as well," Gaston said. "It is a regret that we have no Ravillac on hand to immediately punish." He glanced back at Vendôme, who said nothing and did not change expression—except perhaps to slightly clench his fists. If Mirabel noticed it, he gave no sign.

"The monk who murdered your royal father was mad, Your Majesty—but his act was performed in public, before many witnesses. This heinous deed took place elsewhere, as I am told."

"Indeed, yes. But we sense that you did not come merely to convey this, Don Antonio."

The Spanish ambassador looked slowly from Gaston to Vendôme and back. "I wish to discuss matters that are delicate in nature, Your Majesty."

"Our brother enjoys our most complete trust," Gaston answered, smiling. "Whatever you have to say to us, Don Antonio, you may say in front of him."

"As you wish, Majesty." He folded his hands in front of him, and then let them fall to his sides. "There are a few questions to which I am commanded to obtain answers. Most pressing is the location and condition of my master's royal sister, Queen Anne. Can you apprise me of her current whereabouts?"

"Ah. Regrettably we cannot."

"I see. I would have expected her to be here . . . it was understood that she was heavy with child and had gone into seclusion, as a . . . precaution due to her delicate condition. King Philip is eager to know that she is well, and whether she has given birth."

"We can readily understand your royal master's curiosity in this matter, Don Antonio. Regrettably, Queen Anne's seclusion was a closely-held secret, its location known to but a few."

"But not yourself."

"Unfortunately, we have been long absent from the land of our birth, señor," Gaston said. "So no."

"A few, including—"

"Our late brother," Gaston said. "And his minister."

"The distinguished Cardinal Richelieu. I have noted his absence as well," Mirabel said. "I am surprised that he was not on hand to welcome you to Paris."

"We, too, are troubled by his absence." Once again

Gaston looked back at Vendôme, long enough that it would be impossible for Mirabel not to take note of it. "That the queen and our brother's minister, as well as . . . others . . . are not in Paris is a matter of the gravest concern. It is no mere coincidence; and in view of the cardinal's long legacy of intrigue, we fear that there are darker connotations."

Mirabel's right eyebrow elevated, but otherwise his face remained a mask of diplomatic composure.

"I do not completely take Your Majesty's meaning."

"It would be improper to impugn the motives or actions of our royal sister-in-law in any way," Gaston said. "But Cardinal Richelieu's intrigues and plots are of such depth and are of such long standing that the most stalwart and clever can be caught up in them. It is impossible to say what role he may have had in the tragedy."

"You are suggesting . . . that he may have had something to do with the assassination of the king? It was understood that he was in the king's company when the party was attacked."

"And his body was not found among the dead," Gaston answered smoothly. "Nor was the body of his trusted *créature*, Servien. We find that somewhat curious, Don Antonio. Don't you?"

"I had not considered the matter, Your Majesty."

"It is no more than speculation," Gaston said, with a wave of his hand. "There is no evidence to support it . . . yet the queen is absent, the king is dead, and the cardinal is missing. We have no suitable explanation."

Mirabel did not reply for several moments; Gaston let his last words hang in the air, remaining silent while the Spaniard considered it.

"That brings me to my second matter, Your Majesty. I am empowered to offer any assistance that you might find useful in locating Her Royal Majesty the queen, and in uncovering the truth regarding the death of His Majesty."

"Assistance?"

"My master has servants whose methods are exceedingly effective in extracting the truth, Your Majesty."

Gaston's expression never wavered. "Please convey our sincerest gratitude to our royal brother for his offer," he said, "but we will manage with our own servants. And our own methods."

"As Your Majesty wishes," Mirabel said.

"Was there anything else?"

"There are some matters that require consultation, Your Majesty," Mirabel said. "But they can wait until after Your Majesty's coronation."

"Very well," Gaston said. "Then you have our leave to go."

Mirabel executed another courtly bow and withdrew from the room, not turning his back until he was outside the door. Vachon waited in the doorway, and after a few moments gave a curt nod, indicating that Mirabel had departed.

"Well," Gaston said. "*That* was interesting."

"I am glad you found it so," Vendôme said. "The Spanish wish to offer us—what? Inquisitors?"

"Or some such thing. I suspect that is only the beginning of their demands."

"Have you made some foolish bargain with them, Gaston?"

"I'm not sure I like your tone, Brother."

"You already have your noose around my neck,

Gaston. You can hardly threaten me further. I will take whatever tone I please—in private."

"I suppose I should thank you for that mercy," Gaston said. The smiling mask had gone. "In answer to your question, César, I have made no foolish bargains with the Spanish; but we must needs become more intimate with them than heretofore. They are our co-religionists, after all, and it is not clear to me that they are the enemy."

"Of *course* they are the enemy, Gaston. The Spanish would as soon slit our throats as take us by the hand."

"I don't think it is at all clear. Our chief enemy is not Spain: poor, backward Spain, last century's great power. We have far more to fear if we look east. The up-timers and their self-styled Emperor Gustav Adolf are a far more potent threat to our native land, César, not to mention his up-timer conspirators. A few years of exile may have blunted your perceptions even further than I previously thought."

"You think you're the soul of wit," Vendôme snarled. "I do not find you the least bit entertaining."

"I do not seek to entertain." Gaston rose from his seat. "I will want to know what Mirabel knows, and what he is telling his king. But what I most want to know is where Richelieu is, and where Anne is. Now that you have been granted a royal pardon, your movements should be much less constrained. Make whatever inquiries you can, and take whatever steps you need, but *find them*. Both of them.

"This isn't the last time we'll be taking questions from Don Antonio de Zuñiga y Davila, and the next time I should like to be better prepared."

"I have your leave to withdraw, then?"

"Yes, yes. Of course." Gaston turned away, waving his hand in dismissal. If he saw the anger in Vendôme's eyes he did not take note of it.

When his half-brother had gone, Gaston stood for a long time, looking about his largely unfurnished sitting room. He was angry: if there had been something breakable close to hand, he would have hurled it to the floor or against the wall—but there was nothing but a heavy chair.

You already have your noose around my neck, Vendôme had said.

"Yes," Gaston said to no one in particular. "And sooner than you think, Brother, I will take great pleasure in pulling it tight."

Chapter 25

Paris

Terrye Jo's initial accommodations were in a townhouse on the Rue Saint-Antoine, several hundred yards from the Louvre, near a big church that was under construction. When the traveling party from Turin was first settled, she was worried that construction noise was going to be a problem—there was a lot of hammering and sawing going on; but the workers seemed to knock off for lunch and dinner early, and didn't get to the job site until late in the morning and were gone well before vespers. They'd evidently been working on this church for a long time and didn't seem terribly interested in finishing the job.

The day after Gaston's grand entrance into the city, she received a visitor. She hadn't realized that anyone knew she was there—as far as she was concerned she was lost in the crowd that had followed the royal carriage into the capital. She asked the manservant who had been assigned to them if, in fact, the visitor was meant for *her.* "Yes," she was told, "he asked for you personally, mademoiselle."

The apartment had a sleeping chamber and a receiving room—evidently it was meant for someone more important; but it was there and she was there. She didn't have the time (or the inclination) to dress up in any way for the interview; the duchess would have been scandalized. *What the hell,* she thought, and settled for jeans and flannel.

The servant admitted the man. He was not an impressive fellow—he was dressed like a minor functionary, like a clerk or a scribe—but he seemed very nervous. He bowed and swept off his hat.

"Mademoiselle Tillman?"

"That's me," she said. "And you are—"

"You do not know me by name, mademoiselle. But I am ... GJBF."

The penny dropped at last. This was the man she'd communicated with by telegraph over the last several months while she was in Turin. This was Gaston's telegrapher in residence.

"Forgive me for not recognizing you."

He smiled. "I cannot see how you could have," he said. "I confess that I look nothing like my 'fist.'"

Somehow the comment—which, for all Terrye Jo knew, could have been meant completely in earnest—broke the ice, and they both burst into laughter.

"I'm Terrye Jo Tillman," she said, extending her hand. He returned the handshake. She gestured to the window bench, where there was room for them to sit.

"My name is Cordonnier," he said. "Georges Cordonnier. My father—and grandfather—are shoemakers," he added, smiling. "Only when I came to Paris was the surname truly necessary."

"Where are you from?"

"Soissons," he answered.

"What brought you to Paris?"

"I suspect, Mademoiselle—"

"Terrye Jo," she said. "Or Teresa: that's what the Italian speakers call me."

"Teresa," Georges said. He smiled as he said her name. "I suspect that I am in Paris for the same reason you were in Turin. To be a telegrapher. I was... dexterous, and a test was conducted. I was one of several who were chosen to be trained."

"I was wondering. There aren't very many up-timers in Paris, and overall there aren't too many of us who have telegraphy skill. I assumed you weren't from Grantville."

"No, Mad—... Teresa," he said. "I am not. But I hope to visit the city of wonders someday."

"It's not all that wonderful."

"To *you*," he answered. "It is hard for you to imagine, Teresa, what those of us 'down-timers' think of your home. What might have been commonplace for you in your future is often wondrous to us."

"No, I get that. But it's been, what, four and a half years. I assumed that nothing surprised anyone anymore. You're a telegrapher, Georges, and a good one." *Well*, she thought, *a fairly good one*.

"I fear that you must speak in the past tense now, Teresa."

"Why?"

"With your arrival, my services will no longer be needed. I have come merely because I wanted to meet SPAR, before I am sent back to Soissons and my father's workshop."

"Wait. You're going to resign?"

"I do not think I am resigning. Merely being reassigned."

"No." Terrye Jo stood up and walked away from the window; Georges stood up as well. "No. You're not being 'reassigned,' and you're not resigning. I didn't sign up to take your job."

"Then why are you here, mademoiselle? Teresa?"

"I—" She thought for a moment. "The prince—the king—wanted me to be in his service, as an expert." She turned to face Georges. "I can't fault his logic— no offense, Georges, but I'm a little bit more skilled, and I bet you don't know how to fix the equipment if it goes wrong."

"Fix it? You mean—open up the apparatus? On pain of my life I would not dare."

She smiled. "Yeah, I thought so. But you should understand this, and the king should get the message too. I'll tell him what I told Duke Amadeus; this isn't a job for one person on duty all the time. He needs a *team*—people to staff the radio at different times, or around the clock if he needs it. I'm happy to be the resident expert, as I said. But he'd be a fool to get rid of the best person he has on site."

He seemed even more nervous when she said the word "fool," and she realized that this was enough of a protocol violation to scare him.

"I would not go against the count's wishes, Teresa. Or the king's."

"Did he actually *say* that you were fired?"

"No, he didn't. He didn't actually *say* anything.

But your arrival...I assumed..." His face brightened. Clearly he had resigned himself to something that he really didn't want to do—to go back to Soissons and make shoes.

"I'd assume otherwise," Terrye Jo said. "Georges," she added, extending her hand. "Welcome to the team."

Well before Monsieur Gaston was to receive the members of the Court, the *Conseil du Roi* began to gather in the great Receiving Room. César de Vendôme arrived early; no one else had chosen to rise at Lauds for the meeting, and he was just as happy to review the battleground alone. The comparison was not a bad one, actually—the advisors to the soon-to-be-king were a mixed lot: councilors who had served his brother; returnees like himself; and others chosen from among the many capable men whom Richelieu had dismissed, marginalized or ignored. The *Conseil* would not be peaceful, he thought—better to understand the terrain before the battle was joined.

The room was broad and long, but dim: great damask curtains had been pulled to cover the large windows that overlooked the inner gardens. The place was clean and free of dust: Vendôme knew that Louis had been meticulous about such things. It was also musty and airless, for it had been used far less often than in former years. Richelieu was meticulous about *that*.

The cardinal-duke de Richelieu had much to answer for—*wherever the hell he was*, Vendôme added to himself.

He had been in the room for only a few minutes when another man came through the wide doors—someone Vendôme had not seen in a long time, longer than the time of his exile from France. The other looked pale and somewhat thin, as if he had been out of the sun for quite a while.

"My lord de Bassompierre," he said, offering a gracious nod of his head, enough courtesy for the newcomer.

"Your Grace." François de Bassompierre, fifteen years older than Vendôme, looked very well, actually, considering where he had been for a half-dozen years: the Bastille, for his minor role in the so-called "Day of the Dupes," when King Louis had chosen his minister in preference to his mother. Bassompierre was no common criminal, of course: but prison was prison, just as exile was exile—hard to forget, and harder to forgive.

"You look well, Bassompierre."

"I look terrible, my lord of Vendôme," he said. "But no matter. I received my parole and my invitation to wait upon the prince yesterday, and it cost no small sum of *livres tournois* to my tailor, my wigmaker and a half-dozen other parasites to become presentable for the king's *lever*. But I would not miss it for any weight in coin."

"I don't think any of us would."

Bassompierre shrugged. He walked to a side table, where crystal flagons of wine and exquisite glasses were placed. He poured himself a glass and took a long drink.

"You don't want to wait for the prince."

"I shall drink His Highness's health when he arrives," Bassompierre said, setting the glass down. "Whenever that is."

"So you are to be a member of the *Conseil*."

"You find that surprising."

"I do. But our new king has surprised us in many ways."

"As in his decision to invite you to return to France, Your Grace. A...pleasant surprise, to be sure, but a surprise nonetheless. There is much talk of it."

"I had not heard."

Bassompierre shrugged, as if he could care less whether Vendôme had heard of it or not.

As a *légitimé* and prince of the blood, César de Vendôme—exiled or not—outranked Bassompierre, a mere *gentilhomme*, a courtier and second-rate diplomat who had whiled away the last five years of his life in prison. But Vendôme's illegitimate birth allowed liberties that would never have been permitted otherwise. His indifference was a sign of that, and it irked Vendôme—but he refused to show his irritation.

"Perhaps this is merely a consultation, Bassompierre, and the new king will place you in the field once more."

"I rather think he could use my military advice, Your Grace. It would be good to have someone at hand with *actual* experience leading troops."

Vendôme's polite expression never left his face, but inside he seethed: all things being equal he wanted to walk over and strangle the older man—but of course all things were not equal. Before he could either respond (politely or otherwise), others began to arrive.

Claude de Bullion, the aged, portly minister of finance, came in alone. He looked around the room as if he were determining the cost of the drapes, the furniture, and the inhabitants. Vendôme despised him—but then *everyone* despised him: He had been a courtier since Vendôme was a child as a *Maître des Requêtes*—one of the royal officials who determined which petitions received the king's attention, and had been minister of finance for the last few years, keeping the exchequer afloat while Louis fought wars in Mantua, Lorraine and elsewhere. Both offices had made him absurdly wealthy and even more disliked.

Noyers and Épernon arrived together. François Sublet de Noyers, one of Richelieu's former *créatures*, was in charge of royal constructions—the *Bâtements du Roi*—and the duke of Épernon, a now aged soldier, had been decorated extensively by both Vendôme's father Henry IV and his predecessor. Épernon had been dismissed and exiled for some affair of honor a few years ago; Vendôme was a little surprised to see him back. Bassompierre saw the two men enter and immediately busied himself in conversation with the prince of Condé, who had come into the chamber unnoticed.

The comte de Soissons and Archbishop Gondi were talking in hushed tones as they arrived, with the comte de Montrésor trailing like a little pet hound. Soissons was beaming as he spoke, oblivious to everything else: Vendôme knew that he had been waiting for moments like this.

A few others entered—all in advance of the king-to-be. The last to arrive was Épernon's brother-in-law, Vendôme's half-brother Gaston-Henri, *légitimé* by Vendôme's mother's successor, Catherine Henriette de Balzac. Though he carried the name *Gaston* he went by Henri, their father's name; he had been Bishop of Metz since he was eleven—a few years after King Henry IV was murdered by the mad monk Ravillac.

As the councilors gathered in groups and settled into seats, the two half-brothers remained separate, acknowledging each other's presence with polite nods. None of the others thought it worthwhile to approach them.

"I think we're scaring them off," the bishop said at last. "None of them want to talk to us, César."

"I sometimes have that effect on people. You?"

"I move in many circles." Henri began to extend his right hand, on which he wore a beautiful episcopal ring; but he thought better of it and let the hand fall to his side.

"Including this one. Our brother—"

"*Half*-brother."

"Thank you for reminding me of the obvious. Gaston has chosen to add you to his council, then?"

"He's adding *you*, isn't he? He brought you back out of exile to serve him. He didn't have to send so far to bring me."

"And you came running."

"There may be a cardinal's hat in it, César. And you? What did he promise you? Or did he just have something for you to do?"

The comment sounded innocent and unassuming, but it caught Vendôme by surprise. His first thought was that it was that Gaston had put him up to this—to see what he'd say.

"Eh, César, *ne vous mettez pas dans tous vos états*," the bishop said, smiling, folding his hands in front of his soutane.

"I'll get as exercised as I *please*, Henri," Vendôme said, trying to keep a snarl from his voice. "My relations with our new king are none of your business."

"Everyone is everyone's business in Gaston's Paris, César."

"When I wish to share my private affairs with you," Vendôme answered, "I shall assign one of my servants to give you whatever trivialities that are of no consequence. Until then—"

He turned away, but Gaston-Henri grabbed his arm. Vendôme shook it loose with a jerk abrupt enough to make his half-brother stumble backward. He grabbed Gaston-Henri's shoulder and steadied him.

"You really must be more careful, Your Grace," he said. Then he hissed in his younger half-brother's ear, "What do you want?"

"I told you. A cardinal's hat."

"From me," Vendôme said. "What do you want from *me*?"

Gaston-Henri, the bishop of Metz, straightened his clothes, disengaging himself from Vendôme's grasp.

"Nothing," he said quietly. "Like most of the people in this room, César, I want *nothing* from you."

Whether Gaston's arrival was intentionally late, or if he simply felt that he had a more important place to be, Vendôme wasn't sure—but it was clear that his half-brother, soon to be the king of France, liked to make an entrance.

The members of the *Conseil* turned their attention at once to Monsieur Gaston, offering polite bows or making a leg. Gaston caught his eye; Vendôme inclined his head but made no further indication or gesture.

Gaston's smile never wavered as he acknowledged the obeisances of his councilors, but Vendôme could see that he was a bit annoyed at his own lack of deference.

"My lords," Gaston said at last. "We offer our apologies for being tardy. Matters of state," he added, allowing his smile to extend even further than usual.

Matters of state, my ass, Vendôme thought to himself. *One more toss with Marguerite, I'll wager.*

Pierre Séguier, the duc de Villemor, stepped forward and offered an additional bow. His chain of office, which marked him as the king's chancellor and keeper of the seals, jingled as he lowered his head and then raised it.

"Your Majesty's Council awaits your pleasure, Sire."

"Excellent, excellent," Gaston said, and walked to the great oblong table. He took his seat at its head, and the others gathered, taking various places. Vendôme took a seat at the other end, directly opposite Gaston, with Gaston-Henri to his left, much to the other's annoyance.

"There is much for us to discuss, monsieurs," Gaston began. "We will progress to St. Denis tomorrow to visit the grave of our dear brother." He stopped for a moment and looked down, placing his hand on his forehead in a gesture of grief. "But there are matters we must address immediately.

"Monsieur de Bullion," he began, addressing the minister of finance. "We have read your report on our exchequer with interest. It is certain that there are many areas that you address that have fallen short in their obligations to the Crown. Effective at once, you are to direct that these omissions be corrected, by force if necessary."

"Yes, Your Majesty," Bullion said. "It shall be done."

"In particular," Gaston added, "those of our subjects who derive profit from the *paulette* and the *lettre de maîtresse* should be informed that if they wish to continue under our patronage, they should...*encourage* their clients to live up to these modest requirements. Is that clear?"

"Abundantly," the minister said, smiling. "It will be as you command, Sire."

Both the *paulette*—a "voluntary" tax upon office holders—and the *lettre de maîtresse*, by which the crown derived revenue from craft guilds by recognition of mastership, were intrusive and much disliked (and often avoided). Such impositions were hardly uncommon: King Charles of England had been funding his royal government with such things since he dismissed his last Parliament eight years earlier. Richelieu had regulated them desultorily, depending on whether the affected party was a client or not.

"We are most grateful," Gaston said. "Now to the next item. Monsieur *le Márechal*," he said, addressing Bassompierre. To Vendôme's eyes, the man perked up like a bantam rooster with free rein in the henhouse.

"Sire," Bassompierre said. "If I may take a moment to extend my gratitude to your royal favor in freeing me from unjust imprisonment—"

"Yes, yes, a small matter," Gaston said, waving it away as if freeing him from prison after five years were simply a *small matter*. "Monsieur, we have a particular charge for you. A military force presently under the command of the comte d'Auvergne—*Marshal* Turenne—" he added the last almost as if with distaste—"has chosen to redeploy to the south without strict royal order. As it took place after my brother's death and before my return to the kingdom, it might be argued that this was a matter of military necessity. But now that the coronation is at hand, this force will need to be in the charge of someone with demonstrated loyalty to the Crown. What is more, he employs up-timers—and *their* loyalty is completely unpredictable.

"You will gather whatever staff you need and depart at once to take command."

"Does Your Majesty have any notion of its present location?"

"What information is thus far available indicates that it is in or on its way to Gascony or Béarn—somewhere near the Spanish border. We consider this very provocative, and ultimately contrary to France's interests."

"The Spanish border, Sire?"

"Yes. In the south, near a range of mountains called the Pyrenees. Perhaps you are acquainted with them, monsieur."

There was the slightest titter of amusement among the councilors; Bassompierre reddened very slightly.

"I believe I can locate them on a map, Sire," he managed to retort. "But surely the Spanish cannot be considered friends—so the presence of an army close to our border, provocative or not, is of no moment to them."

"Why do you say that the Spanish cannot be considered friends, Bassompierre? Have they insulted you personally in some way?"

"I . . . do not understand. The Spanish—"

"The Spanish," Gaston interrupted, "are an upright Catholic nation. Our sister is married to its king, while *his* sister was married to our late brother. Surely there are many other nations that might hold greater enmity to France than Spain."

"That . . . was not the opinion of your late brother, Sire."

There was silence from everyone else at the table. Bassompierre looked around at the other councilors; no one said a word, or betrayed any emotion—except Gaston himself, whose smile had vanished. He placed his hands on the table in front of him, palms down, the rings on his fingers catching the light from the candles in their sconces.

"Our brother is dead," Gaston said, and with a glance up the table at Vendôme, added, "as is his chief minister. What policies and positions they held are a matter of history. The crown rests—or soon will rest—upon *our* brow. It is *we* who will occupy the royal throne. It is *our* policies and positions which will govern.

"You may believe as you wish, Bassompierre; but if you wish to sit in this *Conseil*, and if you wish to continue to enjoy our royal favor, you will endorse them. You will carry out your direction without question, and without objection. Is that clear?"

There was a short, tense silence and then Bassompierre said, "Very clear, Sire. Very clear indeed."

Gaston looked down at his hands for several moments; when he looked up again, his smile had returned. "There is one other matter that we would choose to lay before you at this time, my lords. Since the ambush that occasioned our brother's death, nothing has been heard of the queen. It is difficult to believe that this is coincidence.

"Monsieur de Villemor," he said to the chancellor, "it is our wish that a proclamation be drawn up regarding our sister-in-law, commanding her to appear at Reims two weeks hence when we take upon ourselves the crown of this realm. There she shall be received with all honors due a grieving widow and queen. It is our royal wish—no: it is our royal *command* that she be present.

"What is more," he added, lifting his hands from the table and extending them in front of him, "if she chooses to absent herself from this august ceremony, it will be taken as an affront and a sign not only of our disfavor—but a clear indication of her *complicity in the death of King Louis.*"

Once again, the table was silent. Gaston folded his hands before him and looked directly at Villemor.

"When can the proclamation of our royal will be ready?"

"A day or two, Sire," Villemor said. "It will take some time to be distributed beyond Paris, but that can begin as soon as it receives the seal."

"You may begin at once," Gaston said. Again he looked up the table at Vendôme; clearly most of the councilors noticed this. Some seemed merely curious, but a few had expressions of scarcely concealed malice, as if they perceived a sign of royal favor.

If you only knew, Vendôme thought.

Chapter 26

Evreux

The Marquis de Montausier seemed almost obsessed with his own gallantry. After a night at Maintenon, he went out of his way to assist in guiding the queen and her entourage toward Evreux, arranging discreet lodging and assuring that the widow and child be left alone. Mazarin was reasonably sure that Montausier was keeping her identity secret; Achille was not quite as sure, making some effort to keep close to the marquis, scarcely letting him leave his sight.

"We cannot avoid trusting some that we meet," Mazarin told him.

"We shall endeavor to keep the number to a minimum," was Achille's reply; and then he launched into an extended tale of his service aboard Mediterranean corsairs against the Turks.

It took three days to reach Evreux, just prior to which they parted company from Montausier, who swore a personal vow of silence to Queen Anne. She received it with dignified courtesy, but insisted that she accepted it on behalf of her infant son—the king of France.

They reached the ancient town, located in a bend of the River Eure, in the late afternoon. As they came upon it, Mazarin halted their procession and drew Achille aside.

"You have some specific destination, I presume."

"Yes, Monseigneur. Arrangements will have been made."

"Arrangements? By whom?"

"A friend."

"Ah," Mazarin said. "We are enlarging the circle of those we trust. Who is this friend?"

"I . . . am not at liberty to say."

"I find that less than reassuring. Does our queen have some loyal servant in Evreux? Perhaps I should inquire, as she has made no representation to me."

"You do not trust me."

"I didn't say that. I . . . Monsieur Achille." Mazarin sighed, taking his time to reply. "I assure you that I am just as careful, just as suspicious, and just as tentative as you are about any step we take on behalf of the queen and the child."

"Our king."

"Yes. Our king, the child of two weeks that we are trying to protect. I want the same outcome you do. Yet when I ask for your trust, you are suspicious—but when you ask *my* trust, you expect me to accept it on its face and ask no questions. That may be well and good in the Order of Malta; but those rules do not apply here."

Mazarin frowned. "Are you prepared to include me in your deliberations? We all want the same outcome, Achille. All of us."

"Are you accusing me of—"

"I am accusing you of *nothing*."

Mazarin looked aside, holding the reins of his horse tightly; if he were not wearing riding gloves, certainly Achille would have noticed his white knuckles. He silently recited a *Pater Noster*, calming himself.

"It is necessary that you take me into your confidence, monsieur. At once, if you please."

"It is better that you do not know."

"No, it is *not*. Achille, I accept that I may be placing you in an uncomfortable position; but even so, for the sake of all we hope to accomplish, we must work together and keep as few secrets as possible. Either apprise me of our situation, monsieur, or prepare to part company from the king and queen mother. I shall not jeopardize their lives by the want of this information."

There was a short, tense silence, during which Mazarin tried to determine just what the knight of Malta might be thinking. The man was prideful and impulsive to a fault. Might he draw a weapon? Might he ride away—back to his brother, off to Gaston, or somewhere else? Or might he actually back down and tell Mazarin what was happening?

"How well do you know Cardinal de Tremblay, Monseigneur?"

"Cardinal . . . you mean, Père Joseph? The Capuchin, Richelieu's *eminence grise*?"

"The same. How well do you know him?"

"He is a rather private man," Mazarin answered. "He kept his master's secrets, and I assume he has kept some of his own. I also assume that becoming a cardinal *in pectore* has changed none of that."

"It was Cardinal de Tremblay's direction that I

accompany my brother Léonore to Beville-le-Comte when he came to witness the birth of our new king. He further indicated that I should take it as my personal responsibility to protect Her Majesty and the child."

"From . . ."

"Anything and anyone. My *personal* responsibility, Monseigneur. He made it most clear to me."

"This was before the murder of the king."

"It was three months ago, Monseigneur Mazarin."

Mazarin considered himself a fairly good judge of character. In addition to his religious vocation, the last year or two had taught him a great deal about human nature. But here was Achille, looking at him squarely and telling him this.

"Does this mean that Cardinal de Tremblay anticipated that event? Did he *expect* His Majesty and Cardinal Richelieu to be killed?"

"He planned for whatever contingency might present itself. He planned for the worst—and how to avoid it. That we are here, and not dead, means that the worst has not happened."

"Hosanna in the highest," Mazarin said.

"You mock me once again, Monseigneur. Do you doubt the truth of my account? Are you suggesting—"

"I suggest nothing. Pray continue."

Achille settled himself in his seat; his horse pawed the ground and shook its head.

"Cardinal de Tremblay was devoted—*devoted*—to the king and to the crown. You are well aware of the scope and depth of the precautions taken to protect Queen Anne and the child. Since that child is the heir, those precautions seem exceptionally well-founded. I am continuing to act in accordance with my last instructions."

"By guiding us here?"

"And other safe places, depending on our ultimate destination. The queen has more friends than she realizes."

"And the...how shall I put it? *Quid pro quo* for these favors?"

Achille's eyes flashed angrily, and once again Mazarin wondered whether he would attack or depart in a huff.

"The help is freely offered. It is true that some who would assist Her Majesty do so more out of enmity to Gaston than love for the queen."

"Or the king."

"Or the king," Achille agreed. "In the case of Evreux, it is a close associate of Cardinal de Tremblay. He will have been thoroughly briefed on recent events, and is ready to help protect and assist our party."

"Who briefed him?"

"I don't know. You may ask him yourself. That is, if you are sufficiently *informed* that you are willing to accompany me."

Mazarin intentionally hesitated long enough to make Achille frown in consternation. He had already made his decision, but wanted to keep the other man waiting. It was a sin of pride, for which he would say appropriate prayers...later.

"Please lead on," he said at last.

Magdeburg

Joe Tillman hadn't spent much time in government buildings up-time, and didn't make a habit of it down-time. If it hadn't been by invitation, he wouldn't be doing it now. The capital city's Government House was a busy place: lots of people going back and forth on errands lots more important than anything Clarence had for him to do.

He'd told his boss that he had to go up to Magdeburg for a few days to meet with Rebecca Stearns. Clarence had been working on a weld, and had lifted up his hood and given him a look that he might have used if Joe had told him he'd won the lottery and was quitting this crappy job: a nice mix of annoyance and disbelief—annoyance that he would want to take time off work, and disbelief that *Rebecca Stearns* would want to see *Joe Tillman*. Then he growled something, nodded, and dropped the welding hood back down and went back to work.

Magdeburg was a pretty amazing place, at least by down-time standards. It wasn't even Wheeling: not that Wheeling had been a great world-class city, but it was the big time compared to Grantville. When the Ring of Fire had brought his town back to this century, though, Wheeling—and everything else outside of Grantville—was gone.

Just like Dorrie was gone, and Gloria too.

Joe Tillman stood in the middle of the great open hall of the edifice, alone in a crowd. He wondered to himself what the hell he was doing there.

"Waiting for the train, Joey?"

He spun around to see his brother Frank standing a few feet away, his hat in his hand.

"What are you doing here?"

"Same as you, I expect."

"Train."

Frank walked over and took his brother's hand.

"Quite a building they put up here, Joe. Not quite the U.S. Capitol, but it's still pretty grand."

Joe didn't have any answer to that, but said again, "what are you doing here?"

"Like I said, Joey. Same as you."

"You mean?"

"When Rebecca Stearns sends you a letter and tells you she wants to meet with you in her office, you come runnin'. I certainly wasn't going to argue."

"Huh. She asked for me too."

"I know."

"You do?"

"Clarence told me. I was off in Saalfeld doing that offsite job, and when I got back he told me you'd left for Magdeburg. When I got home Lana had a letter for me. Clarence near hit the roof when I told him I was coming up here too. 'Has the woman gone plumb crazy?'" It was a pretty fair impression of Clarence Dobbs, and they both laughed.

"Maybe she has."

"Has what?"

"Gone plumb crazy." Joe looked around. "*Both* of us have an audience with the wife of the so-called prince of Germany. Damn. Do you think she's going to want to see us together, or..."

"I don't know, Joey. Maybe we should go *ask* her."

"Lead the way," Joe said, gesturing toward the long hall of offices ahead.

The wife of the prince of Germany, as Joe Tillman had called her—but not to her face—was more gracious and pleasant than he could have expected. He and his brother had stood in the outer office while her secretary checked whether she was busy, and then beckoned them to come in.

Rebecca Abrabanel had married Mike Stearns not long after the Ring of Fire, and now was almost as recognizable a public figure as her husband. She had been in the middle of all of the recent political intrigue—stuff that happened way above Joe and Frank's pay grades—but she still seemed genuinely excited to see them. She led them into her inner office, which was crowded and small, but very organized—*everything in its place*, Joe thought, *and lots of places*. They sat in two straight chairs facing the desk, and she armed each of them with a sturdy coffee-mug bearing the USE flag before sitting in her comfortable chair behind it.

"Thank you for responding so promptly," she said. "I suppose you're wondering what this is all about."

Joe didn't answer; Frank smiled and said, "Yes, ma'am, we were a little curious."

"And you should be. Do you read the newspapers regularly?"

"Is this some sort of test?" Joe finally blurted out. Frank looked at him, wondering how to follow that up.

"He didn't mean anything by that," Frank managed. "No offense."

"None taken. No, Mr. Tillman, this is not a test, but rather an invitation. I'd like the two of you to be a part of a . . . delegation."

"A what, now?"

"A delegation. I have been asked to travel on behalf of the government of the USE, to represent it at a rather significant event. The crowning of a new king."

"The king of France," Joe Tillman said. "Gaston."

"You *do* read the papers."

"I keep up," he said. "The old king was killed, right? Some sort of ambush. And his brother is going to take his place."

"That's right. He is to be crowned in Reims on the twenty-first of May. I will be accompanied by Colonel Hand, who will represent his cousin the Emperor, and who will present diplomatic credentials to King Gaston as our permanent representative. I am taking some of my staff with me, and I'd like to have the two of you along as well."

"You would," Joe said. "For what? Do you need some plumbing done at the consulate? There must be Frenchmen you could hire for that."

"Joey—"

Joe held his hand up. "No, this is important, Frank. Mrs. Stearns has decided that two pipefitters from Grantville are going to be a part of some *diplomatic delegation* so we can watch a king be crowned. All I can think is: why? And I bet I know the answer."

Rebecca sat patiently as the two brothers stared each other down. Frank looked uncomfortable—he didn't seem to like the idea that his brother was speaking so bluntly. Joe was more defiant.

"I think we should let the lady tell us," Frank said.

"No," Rebecca Stearns said. "Please, Mr. Tillman." They both looked at her. "I'm sorry. Mr. Joe Tillman. Tell me why you think I've invited two pipefitters to travel with me."

"It's about Terrye Jo."

"Joe—"

"Yes," Rebecca said, leaning forward. "That's right. It's about your daughter. For the past several months she has been working for the duke of Savoy and for the king-designate of France. There are things she knows that may be of vital importance."

"Things she might tell her dad that she won't tell a government minister."

"Just so," Rebecca said.

"Well," Joe said, "I hate to be the person to break it to you, ma'am, but my daughter and I aren't exactly on speaking terms right now. I had to bury her aunt and her mother while she was working hard for this duke. I don't think she'll be curling up on my lap and telling me secrets."

"I understand."

"You do. So..." Joe looked at Frank and then back at Rebecca, who didn't seem too surprised at Joe's answer. "So I still don't see what's the point."

"You act as if you haven't communicated with her at all since she left Grantville, Mr. Tillman. She came home after her tour of duty, before she went with the team that installed Duke Victor Amadeus' radio tower, and hasn't been home since—but you've received letters from her."

Joe's face reddened. "How the *hell* do you know that? Did you open 'em too and read what she said?"

"No. Of course not. But we do know that letters to you arrived in the Grantville post office. Savoy is a... place of interest for the USE at the moment, due to the duke's relationship with Monsieur Gaston. So *any* correspondence with *anyone* in Savoy is of interest to the government."

"So I got a few letters from Terrye Jo. All right. I confess. That doesn't mean we're talking."

Rebecca leaned back again and looked away. "Mr.

Tillman," she said, without looking directly at him. "Do you know how Michael and I met?"

"What does that—"

"Better answer the lady's question, Joey," Frank Tillman said. Joe looked at his brother, who was smiling very slightly, as if he saw where this was going.

"He brought you into town the day of the Ring of Fire," Joe said. "You and your father."

"That's correct," Rebecca said. "He rescued us from a band of mercenaries. My father was afraid for my life—and for my honor, but Michael and his friends treated us courteously and respectfully. Both of us. My father's heart was failing, but Dr. Nichols saved his life. Your people saved both of our lives.

"Fathers and daughters never truly stop talking to each other, Mr. Tillman," she said, turning back to face him. "Sometimes words fail, but the conversation persists. If you believe otherwise, then you are deceiving yourself. I offer you the opportunity to reunite with your daughter; I have my own motives, yes, but I do hope that your own self-interest will motivate you to agree."

Joe nodded, his anger draining out of him, replaced with an expression of sadness.

"What about me?" Frank said. "Why am I here?"

Rebecca smiled. "In case my arguments aren't strong enough, sir, I am counting on you to convince your brother that this is a good idea."

Chapter 27

Pau

After Maddox's Rangers had gotten themselves settled, they began to perform regular patrols south of the Gave de Pau, the river that ran south of the town. Servien assumed that this was with the consent—or, at least, the cognizance—of the comte.

The group of forty would ride out in the morning and return in the late afternoon; they would look as if they'd had some exercise, with evidence of maneuvers in the dense wooded hills in the Pyrenees foothills present in their clothing. Brassac did not make any particular observation regarding their activities until the end of their first week at Pau, when, shortly after their arrival—a bit later than usual—his manservant presented the comte's respects and asked Servien to attend him in his private quarters.

Servien attended briefly to his toilet, making sure that his attire was presentable and his hair and beard were combed, and then accompanied the man to the part of the chateau near where he had happened upon the comte's private chapel.

Colonel Maddox was in the comte's sitting room when Servien entered. The manservant bowed briefly and closed the doors, leaving Brassac, Servien and the up-timer alone.

"Monsieur Servien," Maddox said. She was standing next to a long, plain table that bore a heavy canvas sack.

Servien looked from Maddox to Brassac and raised an eyebrow.

"Colonel?" he said.

"I thought it best that you see this as well, monsieur," she said, and took the sack and dumped it on the table. What emerged was a disorderly pile of what looked to be boot soles, some of which had some fragment of the boot upper attached. Several were missing heels or parts of the toe.

"I am told that Monsieur le Comte employs an excellent *cordonnier*," Servien said. "Though some of these may be beyond repair."

Brassac sighed. "The royal court is known for its wit, Colonel Maddox," he said, and continued, "perhaps you should clarify for Monsieur Servien what he is looking at."

Maddox picked up one of the boot soles. "These are from the boots of a small group of Spanish scouts we—encountered—in the hills west of Oloron, perhaps twenty or twenty-five miles from here."

"And you knew that they were Spaniards..."

She reached into a pocket and tossed a wallet onto the table. Servien opened it and pulled out a number of rank insignia, all recognizable as Spanish.

"We've been looking for groups like this one. They

probably came down through Somport or St. Jean Pied-de-Port."

"How many?"

Maddox picked up a few of the items on the table. "I think it was nineteen or twenty."

"All dead."

"You're not suffering a bout of sympathy, are you, Monsieur Servien? I thought you'd been Richelieu's man."

"I assume you are being witty," Servien said. "I assure you that this is no time to try out for a position at the royal court. Even veteran jesters are having trouble finding a job."

Maddox shrugged and smiled. "Monsieur de Brassac, you're right on target with your comment about court wit." She turned back to Servien. "Yes, monsieur. They're all dead. We set a trap and led them into an ambush. Pretty simple, really: we let them see an obvious retreat from our sharpshooters' crossfire, and when they withdrew there our regular guys took care of them."

"And the boot soles?"

"To send a message," she said. "The count tells me that his man of business knows a tavern keeper in St. Jean who is used to dealing with Spanish traders and merchants; this sack will be delivered there. The message will be taken over the mountains quickly enough."

"Did you kill every man?"

"We can't be sure. It's possible that one or more of the scouting party got away."

"Did you lose any of your own company?"

"One of our men nearly broke his neck when he fell down into a gully, but that's just bruises. Their boys had flintlock muskets; we set up the crossfire to start shooting when they were more than a hundred fifty yards away. We dropped ten of them on the spot and the rest when they retreated. Our boys were out of range for the whole exchange of fire."

"Thus ending the invasion," Servien said. He picked up a sole from the table and looked at it.

"No, I don't think so," Maddox answered. "The invasion is still coming—probably soon. We just took away the element of surprise."

Paris

Gaston d'Orleans stood in the front-most pew of the Basilica of St. Denis, his hands clasped in front of him. He did not turn as the Archbishop of Paris, Jean-François de Gondi, entered the nave. The sweet, cloying smell of the incense being aspersed filled his nostrils as the archbishop entered his view. The cantor intoned the psalm: *"asparges me hysopo et mundabor, lavabis me et super nivem dealbabor"*—"Thou shalt sprinkle me with hyssop, and I shall be cleansed: thou shalt wash me, and I shall be made whiter than snow."

The prelate slowly made his way up to the high altar, followed by the other celebrants, offering a prayer to bless it. Without turning, he raised his hands toward the ceiling and pronounced a blessing on the congregation. A deacon stepped behind and carefully removed his cope and set it aside. To either side of the archbishop, the deacons knelt and sang: *"et introibo ad altare tuum ad Deum, laetitiae et exultationis meae, et confitebor tibi in cithara Deus Deus meus"*—*"I will go in to the altar of God: to God who giveth joy to my youth."* Then they ascended the steps and separated to the left and right while the archbishop genuflected and stepped forward to the credence table.

The introit, the *Kyrie* and the *Gloria* followed, along with the collects. Then Gondi raised the epistolary and began to read.

Custodite sabbata mea et pavete ad sanctuarium meum ego Dominus...

Dabo pacem in finibus vestris dormietis et non erit qui exterreat auferam malas bestias et gladius non transibit terminos vestros...

Ponam tabernaculum meum in medio vestri et non abiciet vos anima mea...

Ponam faciem meam contra vos et corruetis coram hostibus vestris et subiciemini his qui oderunt vos fugietis nemine persequente...

Conteram superbiam duritiae vestrae daboque caelum vobis desuper sicut ferrum et terram aeneam...

As the words from Leviticus were intoned, those near Gaston could see him growing more and more angry, particularly when Gondi intoned the nineteenth verse: *I will break the pride of your stubbornness: and I will make to you the heaven above as iron, and the earth as brass.*

King Louis' tomb was no more than an unfinished marble slab with the dates of birth and death and the Bourbon arms. A monument, a more grand and suitable memorial to the late king, had already been commissioned but its completion was months away at least.

When the mass was completed, Gaston and his party descended into the crypt to view the tomb.

When they approached, Gaston held up his hand and walked slowly to the slab, where he knelt and placed his hand on the marble. Tears welled in his eyes.

The archbishop stepped forward.

"Sire," he began, "I—"

Gaston rose and turned to Gondi. "A word with you, Your Grace," he said, grasping the elder prelate's elbow firmly. Gaston escorted the archbishop a few dozen feet away, out of the hearing of his companions. He released Gondi's elbow and stepped away. The archbishop looked alarmed; Gaston brushed a tear away and looked fiercely at Gondi.

"Is there . . . some problem, Your Majesty?"

"Leviticus," Gaston said. "Leviticus 26. *I will break the pride of your stubbornness: and I will make to you the heaven above as iron, and the earth as brass. This* is the message you choose to give to the congregants in the memory of my royal brother?"

"My choice from the epistolary is a matter of conscience, Sire. A prerogative of my office."

"You should tread carefully, Your Grace. If it is your wish to exercise your *conscience* on a regular basis, your tenure in that office will be shorter than you think."

"Are you threatening me, Your Majesty?"

Gaston scowled. "Why do people keep *saying* that? His Holiness confers the office of archbishop, Your Grace, but the king of France has something to do with the process. And with the current difficulty attending Pope Urban, I can assure you that I will have a *great deal* to do with it. A great deal."

Gondi looked at Gaston, aghast. "You are not king of France yet, Sire, and I will have a great deal to do with the placement of the crown on your head."

"And now you threaten *me*, Your Grace. You have no idea what is happening here." He lowered his voice. "You will know very soon. And if you have any notion regarding the coronation, I suggest that you lay it aside. Permanently. Do you understand?"

"Sire—"

"*Do you understand*, Your Grace? Do you completely understand me?"

"Every word, Sire."

"I will keep you to that, my lord Archbishop. Now, if you will excuse me, I must mourn my brother and *our* king."

Evreux

The Auberge Écossaise was a few hundred yards from the cathedral, at the end of a *cul-de-sac* in sight of the *plâce*. The carriage gate was ajar and opened as they approached; Mazarin and Achille looked at each other, but it was obvious that they had been observed.

Achille stepped down from the driver's bench, his hand near his sword. A short paunchy man in a Capuchin habit emerged from a door opposite; he glanced at Achille and held his hands up.

Mazarin climbed down and walked to the carriage gate and closed it.

"We have been expecting you," the Capuchin said. "Monseigneur Mazarin?"

"Your servant," Mazarin said, walking back toward the monk. "I am Jules Mazarin."

"Her Majesty is—"

Mazarin nodded toward the carriage.

"Convey my compliments, if you please," the monk said. "But with respect, we should get inside."

Brother Gérard bustled around the little pantry, placing mugs and plates. A loaf of bread and a quarter-wheel of cheese appeared from somewhere. Queen Anne sat in an armchair with the baby in her lap, watching, bemused. The others sat around the trestle table, staying out of the way.

"I had expected you to arrive two days ago," Gérard said, placing a crock of butter on the table along with a half-dozen spoons.

"We were unaccountably delayed, brother," the queen said. "But you come highly recommended."

Gérard began to cut slices of bread. "I accept the compliment with humility."

"It is occupational, I assume," Mazarin said. "Actually, it was our friend Achille who recommended you."

"Of course," Gérard said. He began to sit down, hesitated with a glance at the queen and then shrugged and sat. "He is a *confraternatarius*."

Mazarin looked directly at Achille. "Truly."

Queen Anne looked up. "Of what fraternity, brother?"

"I . . ." the monk looked flustered. "I thought you were aware."

"Perhaps you can enlighten us," Mazarin said. He had not taken his eyes off Achille.

Brother Gérard picked up a slice of bread and looked at it, then put it down. "I fear I may have already said too much. Clearly the cardinal de Tremblay would have told you if he meant you to know."

"Cardinal de Tremblay?" the queen asked. "What does—what does Père Joseph have to do with this?"

"A great deal. He sent word that you would be coming, and that Monsieur Achille, here, would be escorting you."

"It seems to have been arranged quite some time ago," Mazarin said. "Months ago. A plan has been in place—a plan of which I was completely unaware," he said with a nod to Anne—"to protect Your Majesty. It is apparently led by the shy and retiring cardinal *in pectore*."

"Not *led*," Gérard said. "But he is a principal part of the Company of the Blessed Sacrament. For the last several years, the Company has had as its particular charge the protection of the royal family of France."

"The king and queen," Mazarin said. "One failure, one success."

Gérard looked away. "Yes. I know."

"Brother Gérard," Anne said after a moment. "I do not hold you responsible for the death of my husband the king. There is one particular person to blame: César de Vendôme. My brother-in-law killed—" she looked away from the Capuchin and down at her son, who was whimpering and reaching for her. "He . . . Vendôme. The duc de Vendôme is the culprit."

"And we could not prevent it," Gérard said. "We are in a state of mourning, Majesty. It is difficult for us to bear that we have lost the king whom we had sworn to protect." He looked at the queen, almost desperately. "We will not fail you."

"I am confident that you will not," Anne said. "I am grateful for your loyalty."

"It is our duty," Gérard said. "And there are many of us. When you leave here you will travel to another place where another of our Company will receive you. We will continue to do so as long as you are in danger."

"That would make our progress easier," Mazarin said. He still had not taken his eyes off Achille. "Still, with the stakes so high, I would have liked it better if I had been informed of this plan."

"Monseigneur," Gérard said. "With the stakes so high, it is far more important that you *not* be informed... until absolutely necessary."

Madrid

Gaspar de Guzmán, Count-Duke of Olivares, was singularly unhappy with the news that the informants had brought. They confirmed so many of his worst fears: that a substantial force had been moved to just north of the Pyrenees; that the level of skill and capability of French arms—with the help of the devil-spawn up-timers—was far more powerful than he had realized; and that, despite Mirabel's assurances, Gaston of France was nowhere near as pliable as he had been led to believe. Not to mention that the finest scouts he had been able to employ were either incompetent or very badly outclassed.

He looked at the object sitting on his desk—the sole of a military officer's boot. The heel was partially separated, as if it had been twisted off. He wondered, once again, who might have once worn this particular boot—which of the hand-picked men sent over the mountains to scout possible routes for Spanish troops. He had picked it at random from a sack that had been left with a tavern keeper at St. Jean Pied-de-Port, at an establishment where men with tidbits of intelligence could pass them to one of his operatives.

He had long assumed that the French knew of this drop—but had left it untouched for the same reason he continued to use it: that such a conduit's existence benefited them as well as Spain. They might even know the identity of his man on site.

It was unclear to him at that moment just how he was going to explain all of this to his royal master. Philip was not always given to cool and measured reason—which, Olivares thought, was his prerogative. Still, with the Borja mess and the disagreeable situation in the Lowlands and the business last year in Mallorca . . . only with the upturn of Spanish fortunes in France had he received any indication that the Lord God on high still smiled upon his country.

But one tidbit of information from one particular informant had offered Olivares a ray of hope.

Gaston, with his cleverness and his guile, had overturned the balance of power in the kingdom of France—and would soon sit upon its throne. Richelieu was dead, though there were rumors . . . but there were always rumors. But he had somehow lost track of his sister-in-law Anne, child of Spain and sister of Olivares' king: it was even said that he had insinuated that she was somehow responsible for her husband's death. He had no idea where she was.

But Olivares knew. Thanks to the Capuchin, he *knew*. It was a piece on the board that *Olivares* controlled.

And at the proper moment, he would move it against the new king of France.

Chapter 28

Reims

The cathedral city was overwhelmed by visitors from across France and beyond, from dignitaries and foreign princes to common folk from the countryside who hoped to catch a glimpse of the new king of France.

They had begun to arrive two weeks earlier, when the date of the coronation had been set and proclaimed throughout the country. Word had traveled even faster than usual, due to up-timer wizardry: the newspapers and broadsheets had up-to-date information giving all the particulars, from the composition of King Gaston's royal council to the style and pattern of Queen Marguerite's dress.

The excitement regarding the coming of a new monarch helped to set aside the anguish at losing an old one. People largely wished to put it behind them and to expect, with almost naïve enthusiasm, that the new reign meant better times ahead.

Troops from the king's guard and officials from the

royal household came with the first arrivals, arranging accommodations for members of the court and important visitors. Despite the excitement, there was plenty of evidence of discord: the guardsmen spent time tearing down broadsheets that had appeared in the city, asking: *Where is Cardinal Richelieu?* and *What has become of our good Queen?*

The king and his entourage had an established residence: the Palace of Tau, a villa close to the great cathedral. Monarchs had stayed there for centuries, and the night of the coronation the royal ball would be held there. A week before the coronation, Terrye Jo's radio equipment was moved to the palace. Though the king's chamberlain assured her that she need not trouble herself to travel with the gear—*the accommodations are far from suitable, mademoiselle*—she wasn't about to let it far out of her sight.

Thus, she had a chance to see Reims transform itself from cathedral town to Super Bowl venue in a matter of a fortnight. And the *far from suitable* accommodations were impressive even if there was constant work going on—they found her a little chamber on an upper floor, out of the way, which had marble floors, a mahogany dresser and desk, and a feather bed. She felt as if she was sleeping in a museum, which uptime it probably was.

The day after she arrived, she received an invitation to visit the delegation from the USE. It was delivered to her by a very nervous acolyte, a servant of the archbishop of Reims; he seemed more afraid of her than anything else, as if she was a powerful wizard or something. He offered her the letter, bowed, and vanished before she could even thank him.

Consulate (Acting) in Reims
United States of Europe
14 May 1636

Dear Miss Tillman:
   I would be honored and pleased to have
you call upon me at our temporary residence
in the Hôtel de Ville tomorrow afternoon
at two. We here at our consulate have a
great deal to assimilate, and your insights
and opinions would be extremely valuable.
   I know that your duties may make you
unavailable at that hour, but if you can
oblige me I would be most grateful.
                With sincere regards
                Rebecca Abrabanel Stearns,
                   Consul (Acting)

When she had finished reading, Terrye Jo went to the window and looked out across the roofs and spires of Reims. It was a beautiful spring afternoon, full of noise and smells and scenery—not as grimy as Paris, not as remote as the Valentino, and a long way from Grantville: and here was an invitation written by Rebecca Stearns herself, a member of the USE Parliament and—even more important—Mike Stearns' wife. And she was a quarter of a mile away in the Hôtel de Ville, expecting Terrye Jo to come visit as if she was some sort of dignitary.

Your duties may make you unavailable... Mrs. Stearns had no idea. When the king arrived she might have something to do, but until then she was just an observer, sleeping in the museum and trying to stay out of the way of the laborers, merchants, entertainers, thieves, and gawkers that were filling every hostel, every stable, and every back alley of Reims for the coronation. She had plenty of time.

Artemisio had been excited to hear the news.

"We'll have to arrange a carriage, Donna," he said. "I'll ride up front with the guards, unless you want me to be inside—"

"Wait. *Guards?* Carriage? No one is getting anywhere in a carriage right now. It would take two hours to go the five hundred yards."

"Well," he answered. "It's hardly suitable for you to *walk*. Imagine what your dress would look like—the streets are muddy and filthy—"

"Dress?"

"Yes. You can't wear what you'll wear for the coronation, of course, but you have the one that the duchess had made for you—"

"I have a perfectly fine riding suit that she had made for me. And I'm not going to walk, I'm going to ride. And no guards: it's just down the avenue. I am pretty sure I won't get lost."

"You're going to *ride*."

"Yes."

"But surely not alone."

"I assume so." She waved the invitation. "She's only invited me, not the whole court."

"What would people think? You must take a servant, at the very least." He grinned. "I humbly volunteer, Donna. But I really think you should have an escort."

"Why?"

"Because—because, well, what if we are *attacked*?"

"Then I'll shoot them."

He continued to protest against the idea that she would wear anything but a formal dress and ride in a carriage, but she was firm. *You can stay here and I'll go alone,* she told him. *That's the other choice.*

In the end she stuck with the riding suit. It consisted of a comfortable pair of light-colored breeches, a lacy blouse with an armless buff coat over it with skirts that flared out over the hips and down to the tops of her custom-fit leather boots. The whole costume was completed by a wide-brimmed leather hat pinned up on one side and adorned with a bright-colored feather. The short sword at her belt was mostly there for decoration, but the flintlock pistol wasn't. She didn't expect problems; Artemisio was far more nervous than she was as they rode out of the stable, across the Place Royale, and along the crowded avenue toward the Hôtel, a broad building with scaffolding attached to one side—it was apparently being worked on even now.

They were expected. Their horses were taken by a groom; she hung her gun belt over her saddle (and Artemisio, with a bit of hesitation, did the same) and they entered the building, climbing a short set of stairs; their boots echoed loudly. They were met by a secretary—an up-timer, Terrye Jo thought, but someone she didn't recognize; she reached into her vest to pull out the letter from Rebecca Stearns, but the man waved it off.

"You're expected," he said. Somewhere within she heard a clock strike once, twice—she was just on time.

He led them up further stairs and onto an interior corridor. Officials were bustling back and forth; it was clear that a number of chambers had been emptied to allow visitors to take up residence; business was being transacted in the hallways. She drew more than a few looks—whether it was that she was an up-timer, or an armed woman, or some other reason she wasn't sure; but there was nothing to do but walk confidently, following the secretary to wherever they'd parked the USE delegation.

Finally they reached a suite of rooms at the end of a corridor, and they were shown in to a large sitting room. It was bright and airy, with windows overlooking the crowded square below. Rebecca Stearns rose to greet her as she entered, but before she reached her she stopped dead and looked directly at the man standing next to the USE minister.

"Hi there, sweetheart," he said. "You look...you look well."

Artemisio, standing in the doorway with his hat off and in his hands, didn't know what to do. Terrye Jo looked from her father to Rebecca, torn between shock and anger.

"I owe you an apology," Rebecca Stearns said. "I felt that I should tell you that Mr. Tillman—well, both Mr. Tillmans—were here, but they asked me not to."

"They did," she said.

"I thought you might not come if you knew I was here," her father said. "Frank wanted to go over to that palace you're staying in, but he didn't think they'd let us in."

"They probably wouldn't."

Shock won over anger, and Terrye Jo embraced Joe Tillman, father and daughter holding each other tight for several seconds. Terrye Jo looked toward the far end of the room and saw her uncle Frank standing there awkwardly, as if he didn't know why he was there. Finally he approached and hugged her as well.

Joe Tillman took a handkerchief from a pocket and wiped his eyes, exchanging a glance with Rebecca, who beckoned them to seats. Terrye Jo hesitated, looking toward Artemisio, who looked more uncomfortable than ever.

"My—manservant, Artemisio Logiani," she said. "He insisted I needed an escort."

Rebecca caught the attention of the secretary. "Perhaps Signore Logiani would like something to eat or drink," she said. The secretary took Artemisio by the elbow and steered him out, shutting the door behind him.

Terrye Jo took her hat off and sat. Her father looked her up and down. "You really do look good, girl."

"I've been keeping in shape, Dad," she said. "And the duchess of Savoy made sure I dressed well. Wait until you see what I'm wearing for the coronation."

"I think you described it in a letter."

"The dress she had made for me makes that one look like a cheap bathrobe," Terrye Jo said. "I asked her if I had to give it back afterward."

"Do you?"

"Have to give it back? No, but I have no idea where I'd ever wear it again." She smiled at her father, then made the smile go away. "I'm going to give you the benefit of the doubt, Dad, Uncle Frank, and assume that Mrs. Stearns has some reason for you to be here. I feel as if I've been ambushed, and I have no idea why."

"It was my idea," Rebecca admitted. She folded her

hands in her lap and looked directly at Terrye Jo. "I asked your father to come to France with me, and asked your uncle to come along to help convince him.

"For the past six months, Miss Tillman, you have been in the company of Monsieur—soon to be King—Gaston, and his close relation and ally Duke Victor Amadeus. I will be completely honest with you: I know that you have knowledge that may be vital for your country to possess."

"You're asking me to betray—"

"Not *betray*," Rebecca said. "I want merely to . . . obtain your opinion of certain things. I might also be able to provide you with some information you might not possess."

"Such as?"

Rebecca didn't answer the question. "In the past few days I have heard two rumors that I find disturbing. The first is that Cardinal Richelieu is recovering somewhere from injuries caused by the attack that killed the king. The second is that the queen—by which I mean Anne of Austria—is in flight, along with an infant son. If either of these is true, and I fear that *both* are true, then France is headed for civil war."

"I guess you think I'll more likely confide in my father than in you?"

"I thought it likely, yes."

The admission caught Terrye Jo somewhat by surprise. Her dad looked troubled, embarrassed, almost helpless, as if he'd been dragged into this against his will; he was obviously very happy to see her—there was no blame, no anger, just the same profound sadness she'd seen when she was last in Grantville.

He doesn't really belong here, she thought. *Not just*

here in Reims. He doesn't belong in the seventeenth century.

She looked down at her clothes, which really did fit well—they'd been made for her. She was completely comfortable; she had a profession, she had a purpose, she had a direction in her life that would never have been there but for the Ring of Fire. She *did* belong in the seventeenth century.

"So that's, what, the fig leaf. You ask the questions and I tell my dad all the secrets. You may have missed the news, ma'am, but we haven't been talking recently."

"You write him letters."

"You're reading my mail?"

"I asked her the same question," Joe Tillman said. He glanced at Rebecca and then back at his daughter. "She said that they didn't. Exactly. But they know that you wrote me letters."

"You didn't write back," Terrye Jo said. "I didn't know if you even got them."

"I did," Joe said. He reached into an inner pocket of his denim jacket and pulled out a thick envelope. "I have every one of them. I've read them each a dozen times. I . . . never knew what to write back."

Terrye Jo didn't have an answer to her father's comment. He had never been one to talk or write a great deal—while others bragged about their war service, he'd never had more than a few words to say about his time in Vietnam. As her mother became increasingly more ill, his anger grew but simmered below the surface—it took other forms, making it hard for anyone to reach him.

Her mother's inevitable death hardened it even further.

"I want to tell you it's all right," Terrye Jo said.

"But you can't."

Terrye Jo didn't say anything in reply.

"What do you want to know?" she asked. "I suppose that since you've dragged my father and uncle all the way here, you should get something for your investment."

Rebecca Stearns settled herself in her chair, smoothing her skirts with her hands. There was no doubt that Terrye Jo's comment was provocative, but she didn't appear to want to rise to the challenge.

"I don't want you to betray any confidences, or any duties you owe to the duke of Savoy or His Highness," she said at last. "I merely want to revisit the time you spent in Turin as a telegrapher."

"So I can say 'stop' at any time?"

"Yes."

"Then ask away."

"Miss Tillman, I understand that you served as telegrapher for Duke Victor Amadeus and then for Monsieur Gaston, both while he was in residence at Turin and during his progress to Paris after the death of King Louis."

"I stayed on at Castel Valentino after we built the radio rig for the duke." Terrye Jo smiled. "That's how I got Artemisio: he's one of my apprentices. He's actually very handy."

"Should I load my shotgun?" Joe Tillman said.

"Dad, if he was any sort of threat, I'd have shot him *myself*. Anyway, I helped build and set up the equipment at Castel Valentino, and the duke hired me to manage and take care of it. There wasn't really much to do, other than to train some of the down-timers as telegraph operators so we could keep the rig staffed at all times. When Monsieur Gaston turned up, we started communicating with someone specific."

"Who was that?"

"Well, his name is Georges Cordonnier, but I only just met him. He was a telegrapher working for the Count of Soissons in Paris; the Count of Soissons is—"

"I know who he is, Miss Tillman. What sort of messages did Monsieur Gaston send and receive?"

"Well, he was interested in certain things—what was going on in Paris. Georges—GJBF was his handle, it's all I knew until we reached Paris—was reporting on things like the queen's pregnancy and seclusion. Monsieur Gaston wanted to know how things were progressing and where the queen was staying—no one knew. I don't think Monsieur Gaston knows even now."

"He has issued a proclamation inviting her to attend his coronation," Rebecca said. "I do not expect to see her. Do you know if she is still carrying the child, or if it has been born?"

"I don't know."

"Gaston would certainly want to know if Queen Anne had a son. Even if he succeeds in his throne grab and proclaims the baby to be illegitimate, the infant will garner enough supporters to be a problem just because he exists. Particularly since Gaston does not have a direct male heir of his own—only a daughter who, under French law, is excluded from the throne."

"Up-time there was never a woman President."

"In any case," Rebecca continued, "you transmitted the report of the king's death. Is that correct?"

"Yes. The message came in toward evening, just before dinner. I sent word and Monsieur Gaston came at once."

"And he prepared at once to come and claim his inheritance. The end of his exile at last, with the king and Cardinal Richelieu dead. Assuming he *is* dead."

"I guess nobody knows that," Terrye Jo said. "I keep hearing rumors, and you said you'd heard them as well."

Terrye Jo looked as if she was going to say more, but didn't. When she fell silent, Rebecca sat forward again.

"And?"

"And nothing. Just rumors, I guess."

"Miss Tillman, there is something you aren't telling me."

"How do you know?"

Rebecca smiled. "I am my father's daughter, Miss Tillman. He taught me—and taught me very well, I would venture—to listen carefully to what people say, and take especial note of that which they do *not* say."

"You're an expert on words."

"My father is a Jewish scholar," Rebecca said. "Everyone in the Jewish race is an expert on words. Morris Roth told me that even up-time, putting three rabbis in a conversation would yield five opinions. At least.

"So I am assured that you are leaving something out. I would very much like to know what it is."

"I'm still working for Monsieur Gaston, ma'am."

"I do not ask you to betray any of his secrets."

"Well," Terrye Jo said, "it's just . . . when the news of King Louis' death came in—just that, that the king was dead, by an ambush in a forest—Monsieur made a show of being upset. But I got the feeling that he almost expected it. But he *really* wanted to know what had happened to the cardinal. Cardinal Richelieu. If his body had been returned to Paris along with the king's. When there was no information, he was angry. *Very* angry."

"Indeed."

"I just told you some things you didn't know," Terrye Jo said. "If this gets back to Gaston I'll not be working for him anymore."

"It is in strictest confidence," Rebecca answered. "We've been very careful here to make sure we're not easily overheard. And with your relatives here, there is an easy cover for your visit to our consulate. I think...we may need to have you show your father and uncle around Reims. I will be in touch with people back at home.

"Your information is very valuable, Miss Tillman," she added, standing up. Terrye Jo stood also, picking up her hat; the interview was clearly over. "I don't know what it all means, but I do know that there is more to this than is immediately clear."

"Thank you for inviting me," she answered, taking Rebecca's hand. "It's...well, it's great to meet you after hearing and reading so much about you."

"It is also my pleasure to meet you," Rebecca said, with a glance at Joe, who had stood up as well. "I've heard a great deal about you as well." She placed Terrye Jo's hand in her father's.

She looked at Joe—really *looked* at him. He was smiling, but seemed almost on the edge of tears.

"Come on, Dad," she said at last. "Let's go see the sights."

Chapter 29

The South of France

An army, even one with excellent organization and marching in good order, moves slowly and makes a great deal of noise. The army that Henri de la Tour d'Auvergne, the comte de Turenne, commanded was organized and ordered—not tearing up the countryside, for example—and was making no attempt to disguise its presence; it was not that difficult to find.

Surely, François de Bassompierre thought, *His Royal Highness could have found it himself if he wanted to.*

Bassompierre and forty men of the King's Musketeers had departed Paris the day after the first meeting of the *Conseil*. None of them were happy with the detail: it would prevent their attendance upon their new king in Reims. Bassompierre was not happy with the orders either—but a coronation, however grand, was a matter of a single day; good service to a king could bring handsome rewards for years to come.

His orders to locate Turenne's army and take command of it—expanded upon by written instructions drawn up by the duc d'Épernon for the king, ordering him to march it toward Paris—were simple, and finding the army would be simple. What happened after that could be simple as well.

It had taken almost two weeks, even in good weather and on good roads, for Bassompierre's party to make its way south into Languedoc. It was a fair assumption that a force the size of Turenne's would travel by the most reliable roads, traveling by way of Clermont-Ferrand, and would avoid the rough terrain to the south. That was the place Bassompierre hoped to intercept them at first; but news of the noise of their relatively ordered passage reached him while they were pausing at Limoges. Turenne had chosen to use the southern route after all and had already passed through LePuy and was marching toward Rodez, at least five days' hard ride from their present location. The encounter would have to be even farther south.

Twenty-five years old and a marshal of France, Bassompierre thought as his command rode steadily south, crossing the Dordogne near Souillac on a sturdy footbridge that might have been there when Jeanne d'Arc was crusading against the English invaders. *Twenty-five years old . . . does he dare to choose the course of foreign affairs?*

Bassompierre could not imagine it. Confronting and defying an arrogant cardinal, who had made it his life's work to bend a king to his will, yes: that sort of thing won you honors or landed you in prison. But defying the king himself? Yet that was exactly what it seemed.

They would soon find out.

Albi

The bishop of Albi was none too happy to have an army at his doorstep. Gaspard de Daillon du Lude was a young man—in his early thirties, from what Turenne could tell—and had only recently been confirmed in his see.

He had received the marshal with courtesy, and was relieved to hear that the military force had no intention of marching through the streets of his town but was merely passing on its way southward... meaning that whatever trouble faced Bishop Gaspard would soon be someone else's trouble.

"It would be my pleasure to show my cathedral to you, Monsieur le Comte," the bishop said, leading him up the steps and under a baldaquin that covered the south door of the Cathedral of Sainte-Cécile.

"This looks like a fortification, Father," Turenne said.

At the door the bishop turned and looked up, then back at Turenne. "As indeed it was. One of my predecessors, a few hundred years ago, converted a round tower into this porch."

"Forgive me for looking at this entrance with a general's eye. It looks as if it would be suitable for defending against all comers."

"The tides of war have swept through Albi many times, monsieur," Gaspard said. "But as for defending... this entire structure is built from brick rather than stone—there's precious little of that in the Tarn Valley. I doubt that it would stand up against any determined attack."

The bishop fell silent. He looked anxious, as if wanting to say, *and you're not planning on making such an attack, I pray.*

"Have no fear, Father. The Lord Most High protects your church, and I would not dare oppose Him. But it does seem a very...martial structure. The windows are high and fairly inaccessible; this entrance is well protected; and the bell tower is more than two hundred feet high—I'd like to see the view from there."

"It has been compared to a fortress," the bishop said. "But it is a house of God. I should not want to see it turned to...martial purposes."

"You have my word, Father."

Gaspard looked at him for several moments, as if trying to read the truth. At last he seemed satisfied, and led Turenne into the church.

Turenne would not have guessed, based on the austere and imposing exterior, that the inside of the church would have been so beautiful. Instead of being plain, it was incredibly ornate. Almost every pillar bore a statue, and the walls, ceiling vault and side chapels—dozens of them—were richly painted. There were no separate side-aisles or vaults, however—it was one huge unified space, from the south door to the high altar, separated from the nave by an exquisite rood screen.

His thoughts turned to war: of the destruction that had come to the Germanies over the last two decades, decreasing in ferocity only with the arrival of the up-timers. His own native land had not been ravaged in this way, of course, but there were churches and other buildings this beautiful, this majestic, that had been wantonly sacked and burned and destroyed. Standing in this place gave him some sympathy with the young bishop, who wanted his church to be as remote as possible from such violence.

"Monsieur *le Maréchal.*"

He realized that he had been addressed at least twice. He genuflected again and turned to face Gaspard, whose face was a mask of concern.

"I'm sorry, Father. Lost in my thoughts."

"It does happen in this place. Come, let me show you our mural of the Last Judgment."

At the west end of the nave, the curved walls that flanked the altar were covered with a beautiful mural painted in such detail that it seemed almost to jump out at him. It was, indeed, the Last Judgment in horrifying detail: Heaven along the top, Hell at the bottom; the Blessed on the left and the Damned on the right. The demons were engaged in prolonging the suffering of the resurrected dead who wound up on the right side, while the saints and angels supervised the arrival of those who had been taken up with the Lord. Those being punished were organized according to the Deadly Sins; he walked slowly along the walls and noted Pride, Envy, Wrath, Greed, Gluttony, Lust...

"Isn't there one missing, Father?"

"Yes. Sloth. We have always assumed that the painter was too lazy to finish it." Gaspard smiled. "We have no idea who he was, of course—it was a century and a half ago. But the blue paint that you see there and elsewhere—" he gestured toward the ceiling. "That's from our own *pastellieurs*. It's what made Albi rich in the past."

"This is a useful object lesson for your flock, Monsieur *L'Évêque*," Turenne said. "Scaring them into obedience."

"That is not what scares them, Monsieur *le Maréchal*," Gaspard answered. "They worry about losing all they have."

"To the last judgment?"

"To the depredations of greedy, violent men."

"I sense a certain amount of reproach, Father. I will remind you that I have given you my word that I mean no harm."

"No, monsieur," the bishop answered. "Not you. But there are others."

In the *Palais de la Berbie*, the bishop's palace—also structured very much like a castle—Bishop Gaspard took Turenne for a walk in his gardens; afterward, they sat on a covered terrace and sampled wine from a local vineyard.

"We are somewhat sheltered here," the bishop said. "I am eager for reliable news...we have heard that our good King Louis met with a violent end."

"That is regrettably true."

"And your march into the Tarn valley—is that a prelude to war? The up-timers—"

"The attack on the king was not the work of up-timers, my lord Bishop. It was the work of a band of outlaws. I know very little of the circumstances, except that Monsieur Gaston has assumed the mantle of kingship and will shortly be crowned in Reims.

"It was always the intention of Cardinal Richelieu that my command be sent south to prevent a possible attack by the Spanish—so if there is war, it will be my task to win it."

"I see." Gaspard took up his wine-glass and sipped. "Have you seen the broadsheets and proclamations that have even reached our remote area?"

"Proclamations? No, Father, I have not."

Gaspard gestured to a servant, who came close. He

whispered in the man's ear; the servant nodded and departed, returning a minute or two later with three pages. One was on crisp parchment and was carefully inscribed; the other two were single-sheet newspapers of the sort that were springing up all over Europe.

"Please tell me what you make of these."

The parchment was a proclamation from the new king-to-be. It commanded Queen Anne, the widow of his late royal brother, to present herself at Reims at his coronation—where she would be received "with all honors due a grieving widow and queen." There was no indication, at least in this royal command, of the consequences of failure to comply.

Turenne set it aside and picked up one of the broadsheets. It had various sorts of news, some of which dealt with places not far from Albi, such as Rodez or Clermont; but his attention was immediately drawn to an article near the top that suggested that the queen and her lover—*paramour* was the chosen word—Giulio Mazarini were complicit in the death of the king and the cardinal, and that they were both secretly in the pay of the Count de Mirabel, Spain's ambassador in Paris.

He placed it on the table before him, noting that Bishop Gaspard was watching him carefully to gauge his reaction.

The third document was even more scurrilous—it did not even pretend to be any sort of newspaper, but was rather a sort of declaratory screed. Richelieu, it suggested, had escaped the terrible ambush in the forest of Yvelines, and had gathered men and arms— including hundreds of men in his Cardinal's Guard— and was preparing to march to Paris to dethrone King Gaston when he returned from coronation in Reims.

"The proclamation, I assume, was sent to you. But how did you come by the other two?"

"Traders and merchants. There are several variations of these 'news papers' in circulation here in Albi and elsewhere nearby. Do they tell the truth? Is the queen...complicit? And what of Cardinal Richelieu? Is he in rebellion against the new king?"

Am I? Turenne asked himself. "I have heard nothing to indicate that the cardinal survived the ambush, Father. That his body did not lie in state may be because it was not found. That is a horrifying thought, but the truth may be that simple.

"As for our good queen, it is my understanding that she is—or was—in seclusion, awaiting the birth of a child. If she bore a son, then it would be the cause of great rejoicing. Even if you could attribute such a base motive to such a noble lady, what would be the possible gain in assisting in her husband's death? A helpless widow with an infant, with enemies all around—that would place her in enormous danger. So I do not believe that tale either, Father. I think it is base and scurrilous. You should take these and use them as kindling in your hearth."

"I wish I could be that confident, Marshal."

"Confidence wins battles, my lord Bishop. I assume that applies to battles for souls as well."

Before vespers, Turenne was escorted to the bell tower of the cathedral by a deacon, an older man who moved with the lithe grace of a younger one. He felt that he was in excellent shape, but Turenne had rarely seen a man ten years his senior go so nimbly up a long stairway; he must have had years of regular practice.

The tower room gave an excellent vantage in all directions. The slate roofs of the town were spread out like a tapestry, dappled by the sun down near the horizon. The deacon stood back, leaning against one of the support pillars, enjoying a few minutes of leisure; Turenne reached to his belt for his spyglass—

And only then he began to hear the sharp crack of rifle shots and the slower, more measured fire of muskets.

He took out the spyglass and focused toward the river, across which his army had camped. Even before he placed it to his eye he could see puffs of smoke. Somewhere to the north someone was firing on his troops. He couldn't make out anything distinctly; he resisted the urge to utter a very soldierly curse and went to the staircase, where he began to take the steps two at a time.

Chapter 30

Albi

Alain de la Croix, captain in the King's Musketeers, cantered slowly toward Marshal Bassompierre, who was consulting a map with two other men. His superior did not look up right away, which was a bit off-putting, but not unexpected: the gaunt, older man seemed to have a positive disdain for his entire subordinate command—and, as Alain had seen during the ride south, just about everyone else.

A few years in prison does that for you, I suppose, Alain thought. With no other choice, he waited patiently, waving at a few flies that seemed to want to take up residence in his horse's left ear.

Apparently the motion caught Marshal Bassompierre's eye, and he looked up from the map, fixing Alain with a scowl.

"Do you have a report for me, de la Croix?"

"Yes, my lord Marshal. We have located the pickets of Marshal Turenne's command."

"Well? Where are they?"

"On the outskirts of Albi, my lord. On the high ground overlooking the Tarn."

"Did they see you?"

"On your orders, sir, we remained hidden and observed. They are not numerous, but they seem alert and attentive, merely watching this road."

"Not numerous?"

"We counted two groups of three soldiers, monsieur."

Bassompierre snorted. "This young Marshal Turenne is very confident in his troops—or does not expect a reconnaissance in force. Very well; inform the men that we will advance in order."

It was as Captain de la Croix had described it. The pickets were lightly manned and made no attempt to conceal themselves; as Marshal Bassompierre and his staff approached, the musketeers behind, an officer came out into the road, his weapon held loosely in his hands.

"Good day, my lord," the man said. "I am Colonel Jean de Gaisson. May I ask your business?"

"I am Marshal François de Bassompierre," he said. "I am directed by his Majesty King Gaston to take command of this force. Take me to Marshal Turenne, if you please."

The man squinted at him as if the words made no sense.

"Did you not hear what I said?"

"Monsieur," the man answered, "I have no orders from our commanding officer on this matter. I can send word—"

"You will do as I command," Bassompierre interrupted. "You do not need to *send word* or do any other thing than as I command. Do you understand?"

"I understand very well, monsieur," the man said. "But I am following orders."

"Your orders are *overruled* by my orders, Colonel," de Bassompierre snarled back. He beckoned behind him; Alain de la Croix turned and nodded to the musketeers, who began dismounting and forming up.

"You say your orders are from..."

"King Gaston, you insolent oaf. I will not repeat myself. Escort me to Marshal Turenne. If you do not choose to follow those orders, you will suffer the consequences."

De Bassompierre cantered his horse a few feet to the right. A half dozen musketeers had formed a line, and had their weapons out, their slow-matches lit, and powder-horns in hand.

"We were not informed that the king's brother had been crowned," Gaisson said carefully. "And with respect, my lord, I advise against this."

"Advise against what?"

"A firefight, my lord," he said. He looked from Marshal Bassompierre to the six musketeers proceeding through the process of preparing their muskets to fire, and the thirty-odd more who were a few steps behind them. Then he began to walk backward, slowly and deliberately, keeping his weapon pointed downward.

The marshal's face reddened. He drew his sabre from its scabbard and began to charge the man, who turned and ran for the trees. A moment later, four shots hit the ground directly in front of Bassompierre's horse, causing it to rear.

The musketeers, and Turenne's riflemen, responded almost at once.

❖   ❖   ❖

Before Turenne reached the camp, his cavalry commander François Lefebvre galloped up to meet him. The firing had stopped by the time he reached the bridge across the Tarn.

"Report, Commander. And there had better be a damn good reason for this."

"He—they issued outrageous demands, Monsieur le Comte."

"Who did?"

"The commander." He gestured out beyond their camp. "He claimed that he had orders to take command of our army. Colonel de Gaisson offered to send a runner to fetch you, but the commander... initiated hostilities."

"And you responded."

"... Would you have wanted us to do otherwise, Marshal?"

"No. Of course not. What happened next?"

"After the commander charged Colonel de Gaisson, they fired in front of the horse, which reared. The musketeers managed a volley and one of Olier's men was hit. He returned fire. The enemy didn't stay in range for long." Lefebvre smiled, but quickly stopped when he saw his commander's stern glance.

"The... 'enemy'? How do you know them to be enemies?"

"They *shot* at us, Marshal. By your leave, that seems good enough to me."

Turenne did not answer, but rode past Lefebvre, galloping toward the place he had indicated.

A few hundred yards up the road he could see the picket where Lieutenant Olier and his company were crouched; Olier didn't stand upright, but did wave his hat; a musket shot rang out from beyond, but was off target or, more likely, fell short.

"God curse it," Turenne said, digging his boots into the stirrups and charging forward. He took his own hat off and raised it in the air, keeping the other hand on the reins.

It was the sort of thing a man did at age twenty-five; if he was ten or even five years older, he might not have considered it. But whatever was going on, he wasn't about to let it go further.

He heard a shouted command—but it wasn't an order to fire. He saw motion ahead of him, and a mounted officer, an older man with sunken cheeks, rode slowly out from cover, holding a sword across his saddle.

"Hold your fire," the officer said, tilting his head imperiously toward the troopers, crouched in cover.

"Monsieur," Turenne said. "I would be obliged if you would identify yourself."

"You must be the *Maréchal* de Turenne. Monsieur le Comte, your soldiers are most insubordinate."

"Perhaps you should explain yourself. And once again I ask you who you are."

"I am the *Maréchal* François de Bassompierre, monsieur, and I am directed strictly by His Majesty King Gaston to take command of your forces. I have ridden a considerable distance in pursuit of you, and I demand your compliance."

"To which end you have *fired* on my men?"

"They fired first."

"I should like to see those orders in writing. It is fortunate that any of your men are still alive."

"Four of them lie dead, Monsieur le Comte. You will answer to King Gaston for their deaths. Once again, and for the last time, I *demand* that you surrender your command to me instantly or prepare to—"

"Or prepare to be fired upon again?"

"Yes."

"Do not try my patience. Marshal Bassompierre, I invite you to join me in my tent to discuss matters; or I encourage you to leave the way you came." Turenne turned his horse away, wanting to show perfect confidence that he would not be shot at by Bassompierre's men. He was close enough that even a bad marksman could blow him off his horse, or worse.

He slowly cantered his horse away from the position, waiting for the shot, but it never came. Instead, he heard a hushed exchange and then the sound of another horse following him.

"No," Turenne said.

He had set two camp chairs outside his tent. Marshal Bassompierre sat in the other chair, and did not look happy.

"I am not prepared to return to the king with that answer."

Turenne set the parchment document on his lap. "You can take any message you like to Gaston. But he is not yet king, and that means that my orders—"

"Richelieu's orders?"

"The *king's* orders, monsieur. King Louis."

"He is dead, Monsieur le Comte."

"I know he is. But Gaston is not king yet, Marshal Bassompierre. Until he is, this—" he tapped the parchment—"is no order I am prepared to follow."

"He is to be crowned king at Reims, Marshal. This is treason."

"I . . ." Turenne picked up the parchment as if to examine it, then let it fall back into his lap. "I have considered that, since you told me that you were directed by Monsieur Gaston to take my command from me. But until I am informed that he has had the crown placed on his head, I do not consider myself obliged to follow his orders. The safety of the realm is in my hands, monsieur, and I will protect it with the force given into my charge."

"There will be a reckoning for this." Bassompierre stood; several of Turenne's men who stood nearby stepped forward, as if the elderly marshal might do something violent. "I will return to my master and inform him of your insubordination."

Turenne stood as well. "No," he said. "You will not. You and your troop will accompany this army to its destination. The men will be properly treated as soldiers of France, and you will be accommodated as befits your rank and station. I will await official word, and then decide the next appropriate action."

"And if I—and my force—resists this coercion?"

"Please, Monsieur *Maréchal*. Do you truly think that is even a choice?"

Chapter 31

Reims

Three days before the *sacre*, in which Gaston d'Orleans was to be crowned as king of France, he made his formal entry into the cathedral city of Reims astride a white horse, passing slowly under triumphal arches made of woven flowers into the *plâce* before the gate, which was packed with spectators. A gold-painted chariot drawn by a matched pair of white horses was driven slowly toward him; it stopped a dozen feet away and a woman in a white gown dismounted and walked slowly to stand before him, carrying a velvet pillow which bore an ornate key on a purple ribbon. She lifted it so that he could take the key; when he took it up, the crowd roared its approval.

On the morning of the *sacre*, Gaston arose before the first light crept over the horizon. Vachon had drawn a ceremonial bath for him in the great marble tub in the king's chamber in the Palace of Tau; he took his time in his preparations, suffering himself to be barbered and prepared before his valet dressed him in the many layers of royal vestments. When he emerged, Vachon assisted him in dressing in a shirt of Dutch linen, an overshirt of crimson satin and a long-sleeved robe of cloth-of-silver.

A few minutes after nine o'clock, Gaston descended to the ground floor of the palace, preceded by Séguier, the keeper of the seals, dressed in a gown and hood of scarlet, a white baton in his hand and a cloth-of-gold mortar-board upon his head. A dozen bishops were waiting for them; the Bishop of Laon, Philibert de Brichanteau—another man forced into exile by Richelieu, a middle-aged ecclesiastic from an ancient diocese, and only lately returned to his see—had been chosen to represent them. He stepped forward between the others, who had arranged themselves in two lines.

When he reached Gaston and Séguier, he thrice rapped the foot of his crozier on the marble floor and asked, "Who are you?"

"Monsieur Gaston, of the House of Bourbon, son of Henry IV."

A second time the bishop asked the question, and once again Séguier gave the same answer. He asked once more, but the third time, the keeper of the seals answered:

"Gaston, heir to the throne of France, whom God has given us as king!"

Bishop Philibert offered a respectful bow and turned away, followed by Séguier and Gaston; the other clerics fell into line behind. A dozen gentlemen ushers in white satin holding their maces of office lined the vaulted corridor between the Palace of Tau and the cathedral, and the steps of the procession matched the rhythm of drums and *hautbois*. The duc de Vendôme, acting in the capacity of chamberlain and carrying a naked sword held out before him, waited at the entrance of the church; the same questions and answers were exchanged, and at the final answer Vendôme turned and proceeded into the church, leading the keeper of the seals, Gaston, and all of the others between a line of uniformed King's Musketeers. When Gaston crossed the threshold a choir of monks began to intone Psalm XX, *"à faux-bourdon"*—*The king shall rejoice in thy judgment, O Lord.* Where the nave and transept crossed, Marguerite and her principal ladies, including his daughter Anne-Marie-Louise, awaited his arrival.

Archbishop Gondi waited before the high altar dressed in full episcopals, with the *ampulla* of sacred oil from Saint-Rémy held in his hands; four monks, dressed in white, held a canopy over him. The cathedral was full of dignitaries, domestic and foreign—representatives of lands from England and Spain, the Germanies and Scandinavia and Italy; *noblesse de robe* and *noblesse d'épee*.

When Gaston reached his queen, he took her hand and turned to face the rear of the nave. A herald, bearing a tabard with the coat of arms of the House of Bourbon, walked slowly forward toward the high altar. When they reached Gaston and Marguerite, Séguier raised his baton and spoke.

"Vive le Roi Gaston I de Nom, par la grace de Dieu Roi de France et de Navarre, très-Christian, nostre très-souverain seigneur et bon maistre, auquel Dieu doint très-heureuse et très-longue vie!"

God grant him a very happy and long life! Gaston heard those words echoing in his mind through the joyous cheers that filled the cathedral, echoing from one end of the nave to the other and from the floor to the vault of the ceiling. He had composed himself with the intention of showing no emotion during the ceremony, but he could not help but give way to a smile—the goal of his entire life was close at hand: soon, very soon, he would indeed be consecrated and crowned *très-Christian, très-souverain seigneur* . . . the Most Christian King of France.

After bowing deeply to the archbishop, Gaston settled himself into a gilded chair provided for him.

When the attendees were quiet, the archbishop placed the *ampulla* in the hands of an assistant and raised his hands in benediction, then returned them to an attitude of prayer in front of his chest, turning to face Gaston.

"Most gracious Majesty," he said. "Do you promise upon your honor to protect, defend and support the one true and universal Catholic Church and to promote orthodoxy in worship?"

"Upon my honor, I do so promise."

"Most gracious Majesty, do you promise upon your honor to protect and defend your realm, the laws of your kingdom and the ancient rights and privileges enjoyed by its subjects?"

"Upon my honor, I do so promise," he repeated.

A baron of the realm descended from the high altar with a beautiful and elaborately decorated volume of the Gospels; he stood before Gaston and lowered the book before him; Gaston placed his hands upon the open book, and kissed it once, twice, thrice.

Archbishop Gondi stepped back, not turning his back on Gaston, and turned his head toward the congregation.

"And do you, people of France, accept Gaston Jean-Baptiste de Bourbon, son of Henry, the fourth of that name, and brother of Louis, the thirteenth of that name, our late beloved king, as your monarch, and puissant lord and sovereign, Most Christian King of France?"

Shouts and cheers were the response.

He turned back to Gaston. "In consequence of the affirmation of your people, Your Majesty, and your acceptance of the oaths incumbent on the king, I shall, with your permission, proceed to invest you with the apparel and regalia of coronation."

Two gentlemen-ushers approached and stood before Gaston, who rose from his seat. The three men, with the archbishop behind, approached the high altar where the relics of the kingdom had been placed.

Gaston genuflected and then stood upright before the altar.

"The *moyenne*," Gondi said. "The imperial crown of France." He lowered it slowly to Gaston's head.

"*Le main de justice*," he continued, placing a gold scepter in Gaston's left hand; it bore a unique finial— an ivory hand bent in a blessing gesture.

The duc de Vendôme then approached, sword upright before him; when he reached the altar he reversed it, bowed, and placed it hilt-first in the hands of the archbishop, who in turn presented it to Gaston.

Vendôme then bent down and attached silver spurs to the heels of Gaston's boots.

"*Joyeuse*," Gondi said. "The sword of Charlemagne, and the spurs of knighthood. With these symbols, Majesty, you are accorded honors as the first peer of the realm, and the dignities of knighthood oblige you to seek truth, defend the law, protect women and use your strength and skill to do right as you perceive the right."

The spurs were then removed. Gaston kissed the sword on its hilt and returned it to Gondi, who took it back and placed it again in Vendôme's hands; he backed slowly down and assumed his former position.

"I now display to you the sacerdotal garments indicating your divine authority as king," Gondi said, gesturing toward the remaining items laid out before Gaston. "The monastic sandals and dalmatic; the tunic made of cloth-of-gold; and the royal mantle." He took up the mantle and placed it on Gaston's shoulders. "Upon your shoulders rests the blessing and the burdens of the realm of France."

Gondi then opened the *ampulla*, removing a small bit of oil with a golden spoon, and mixing it with the chrism prepared in the paten for the anointing of the king. The mantle was unfastened, and his outer garments were loosened by two assisting bishops, one of whom took the scepter from his hand. He then prostrated himself before the altar, his hands extended outward, his head bowed almost to the floor.

"The holy oil bestowed by Heaven," Gondi said. "The king alone on earth shines with the glorious privilege of being anointed with this oil." He reached into the paten with his right thumb, and placed a drop on the crown of Gaston's head, the top of his chest, and the palms of his hands; he then placed Gaston's hands together and raised him to an upright position, after which he touched Gaston's chest above his heart, then his left and right shoulders, and at last upon a spot just above his upper lip. When he finished the anointing, Gaston's clothes were returned to their proper positions. A pair of loose-fitting gloves were offered to him, so that no earthly thing might touch the holy oil; the scepter was then returned to him. At the direction of the archbishop, he turned to face the congregation.

He descended to the chair and sat, as his daughter Anne-Marie-Louise approached with a satin cushion in her hands, upon which was an ornate ring. Though she had been carefully rehearsed in this role, she too could not keep from smiling as she knelt before her father, lifting the cushion to him.

Gondi, who had descended to the level, took the ring and offered a brief blessing, then placed it on Gaston's gloved right hand.

"With this ring, Majesty, you are sealed to the realm of France as its sole and sovereign king. May your reign be long and happy, peaceful and prosperous. Long live the king!"

A thunderous shout of "Long live the king!" rang out from the congregation, spoken by subject and friend alike.

As the echoes died away, there was a commotion of some sort at the back of the nave. King Gaston was to have remained seated for the rest of the ceremony, as further hymns and adulations were to be performed; but in order to see what was happening he stood, holding the scepter in his hand. He exchanged a brief glance with Vendôme, who looked equally mystified.

The crowd began to part, and a group of richly dressed persons became visible, slowly approaching the new king of France. After a moment, one individual walked forward, coming at last to stand before

King Gaston. She curtseyed deeply, but never took her eyes off him.

After a moment, Gaston extended his right hand to her, aiding her to rise upright.

"Madame," he said. "We were not aware that you had returned to our sovereign realm."

"I could not stay away from the supreme pleasure of seeing my son crowned as king of France," she said. "Those things that were impediments to my return have been removed. Now, by your leave, I return—to be the first to offer you allegiance and fealty."

In the moment that stretched out, with Gaston holding his mother's hand, the new king of France considered the possibility of refusing and dismissing her—she had, after all, waged war against his brother, assumed unsanctioned privileges during and after her regency, and sought to undermine Louis' reign. Last winter when he had visited her in Tuscany, when they had discussed returning to France, he had demurred: she might seem to be here at his invitation or by his leave, but it was not part of the plan that had been set forth for the day of his coronation.

You want me to choose, Gaston thought. *You forced Louis to choose—and he decided to send you away. You play a dangerous game, Mother.*

"We welcome you back to our kingdom, Highness," Gaston said at last, releasing her hand. "And we restore to you your former honors, privileges and dignities." He handed the scepter to the archbishop and stepped forward, embracing his mother, who returned the affection.

"We will discuss this in due course, Mother," he hissed.

"Yes," she said. "I am sure we will."

Chapter 32

Picardy

The secrecy, the constant travel, the fear of discovery all preyed upon Anne as her little party made its way northward and eastward, moving from manor to guest-house to Capuchin hostel. Her infant son—*the king of France*, she constantly reminded herself, as she and her up-time companion and her single lady-in-waiting attended to the many needs a tiny child requires—had somehow become accustomed to it: he woke and slept and took milk from her breasts; he soiled his diapers. Katie had an *Américain* expression for it, and for the chores that went with it: *lather, rinse, repeat*, she said—it defied direct translation into French—but the meaning was clear enough and quite descriptive of the care the three women gave to the child that they hoped would return to the Bourbon throne.

Achille and Mazarin had a brief conversation after one particularly arduous day; they had both noticed that they had acquired a "shadow"—someone, or some group, following them, but never approaching closely enough to be recognized or confronted. It would have been the purest good luck to have avoided notice, particularly since the would-be king of France was looking for them.

They concluded, after their discussion, that they would not discuss this with their queen. *No need to add to her burdens,* Achille had said.

It was in Rumigny near Amiens, while staying a single night at the Chateau Cour-des-Prés after a long day of travel, that Anne first saw the proclamation that designated her an outlaw, an enemy of the state. They had learned of Monsieur Gaston's "invitation" for Anne to attend his coronation as king in Reims, a week or so earlier: it had apparently been circulated throughout the country, followed closely by a rumor that she had been involved in the murder of King Louis.

Achille had found a copy of the proclamation, reprinted in an Amiens broadsheet; he had ventured into the city for supplies and rumors, and returned to the old fortress at night to report it. He found her sitting in a dimly lit sitting room with Mazarin conferring in low voices, almost drowned out by the steady drum of rain. Anne looked up when she heard his footsteps.

Katie, who was sitting near the fire inventorying their medical kit, stood and bowed as if to leave, but Anne gestured to her to sit.

"You look as if you've seen something unpleasant," Anne said. "Please share it with us."

He drew a rolled bundle of cheap paper from

within his cloak, and spread it out on a nearby table. The others gathered around as he spread it out; Kate set a candelabra on the table, bringing the scene out of the shadows.

"I was in a tavern near St. Martin's Church near the Porte Gayant, and came across this. It's a newspaper—"

"I've seen one before," Mazarin said.

Achille looked at Mazarin, as if he was trying to decide the most prudent way to react. "I mention it only to say that this account is unofficial, but is obviously out in public." He pointed to a section on the lower left side of the front page. "The man who calls himself king of France has named you a traitor and a murderer, Your Majesty."

Anne looked closely at the broadsheet for some time, reading the badly printed words, her lips moving as she did. Her expression became more and more angry. When she reached the end she stood up straight and looked from one companion to another, finally resting on Achille.

"I do not have any way of responding except by deeds," she said. "I don't know if Gaston expected me to present myself and permit him to take the crown: but two things are clear: first, he does not know where we are at present, and second, he doesn't know where we are going."

"Where *are* we going, Majesty?"

"Wherever your . . . friends are available to give us refuge, Monsieur Achille. I assume you had a destination in mind."

"You know that is not quite true, my Queen. I do not know your ultimate destination."

"Well." She looked down at the newspaper once

again. "It is clear that my *ultimate destination* cannot be in France. Monseigneur Mazarin and I were discussing that when you arrived."

"And?"

"And," she said, "We have considered a number of alternatives. I cannot go back to Spain without being rightly viewed as a traitor to the realm. The Italian states are in turmoil—and even if they were not, Savoy is an ally of Gaston, and that is the closest approach to the peninsula. England has its own difficulties. Scotland is a long and dangerous voyage. And America..." she looked at Katie, who had looked up sharply. "It is even longer and even more dangerous, and I will not risk my son thus.

"That reduces our choices to the Germanies and the Low Countries—Brussels, Amsterdam, or the uptimers' empire."

"Amsterdam," Mazarin said. "Full of schemers. Brussels, full of Hapsburgs, begging Your Majesty's pardon. And I'm not sure how we would be received in Grantville or Magdeburg—I don't know if the uptimers, or Emperor Gustavus, would have any desire to be drawn into the internal politics of France."

"Schemers, Hapsburgs or neutrals," Anne said. "Is that what we have come to?"

"What have we come to," Mazarin said carefully, "is a choice. For the past few weeks, madame, we have been in flight from danger—real or perceived—and we have accomplished nothing but to remain out of the hands of the king of France."

"My son is the king of France," Anne said levelly.

"Your son is the rightful king, true. But as far as every court in Europe is concerned, the king of

France is Gaston Jean-Baptiste d'Orleans, son of *Henri le Grand*, fourth of the name—and it was confirmed not long ago when the archbishop of Paris placed the royal crown on his head.

"You know what Gaston is, Your Majesty. You know what he has always wanted—and now he has it."

"He is a usurper. He sits on the throne that belongs to my son. He—" She let the sentence trail off. She balled her fists, controlling her anger, as if she was trying to shape it into a weapon.

Mazarin leaned down over the table, rereading the proclamation in the newspaper. At last he looked up.

"Fifteen years ago, my queen, your husband and *his* mother went to war. Each had supporters, soldiers. Each wanted to become the ruler of the realm. They had two campaigns and, in the end, reconciliation. Queen Marie lost in the end, of course, as you well know: your husband chose his red-robed cardinal over his manipulative mother. But during the decade before her exile, the queen mother and the cardinal worked together—or at least reached an accommodation.

"I think it is possible that you could do the same with Gaston."

"Are you suggesting that we—surrender—to him?"

"Not surrender. Make peace. I believe that the uptimers no longer consider France an antagonist, but France still has many enemies, beginning with your royal brother King Philip. For France to descend into civil war over..."

"Yes? Please tell me, Monseigneur," Anne said. "We do not want France to descend into civil war over what? Over *my son*. Over his right to be king. Over justice. You are ready to give in because you do not want France to suffer. What about my suffering? What about *my* justice? What about my...my vengeance?"

Mazarin gestured to Achille, to Katie, and placed a hand on his own breast. "This is your army, Your Majesty. These are your paladins, your champions. There may be others, if we can find them. If Gaston's men don't find us first."

"What are you saying?"

"I...don't know."

"Oh, you know. You know very well, Giulio. Jules. You are telling me that you have lost faith in our cause. You no longer wish to serve me—so be it. Go back to Gaston, then. Go serve the usurper."

"I have no intention of doing anything of the sort. In the event that we continue to pursue the cause of your royal son, I am your man—now, and until the end. But I beg you to consider the other choice—not for yourself, not for your loyal servants, but for your son."

"Is that your *wise counsel*?"

"No. It is not. It is my wise counsel that you consider the alternatives before you, my Queen, and that you make a choice. Make sure it is the correct one."

Paris

Marie de Medici, the former regent of France and the mother of Louis XIII and Gaston d'Orleans, stood in the unfinished great hall of the *Palais-Cardinal* and scowled.

Above her on the east wall of the large room was a mural depicting the entry of the king and cardinal into the defeated city of La Rochelle—eight years ago during the suppression of the rebellious Huguenots. It was unfinished; the renowned architect Jacques LeMercier had undertaken to construct a great theater for the hall but had scarcely gotten underway.

The cardinal de Tremblay stood patiently, his hands tucked into his sleeves, watching the scene. The dowager queen—he refused to think of her any longer as the "queen mother," for that title truly belonged to another—had her ladies around her. None were so resplendent as Queen Marie: they were adornments, minor satellites orbiting the great luminary. Marie was clearly unhappy. Tremblay assumed that she was considering to what better purpose this room, and that wall, could be put. After all, Gaston was in the mural: but he was in the background, one among many beyond the two principals in the scene.

Gaston was certainly not in the background now.

Have a care, Tremblay thought. *This is not your residence. At least not yet.* But Marie de Medici did not appear the least bit interested in having a care.

She looked up and noticed him standing there, waiting to be noticed. Her demeanor changed: it became darker and more hostile, as if the sun had gone in behind the clouds. The crowd around her dispersed even before she waved them away. For his part, Tremblay did not wait to be called to her presence; he began to walk toward her, crossing the room with measured strides.

He had considered the possibility of emerging into the room through the hidden door in the muraled wall. It would have taken Marie by surprise, to be sure: but on reflection, he decided that if Marie didn't know about it—which was likely—there was no reason to provide any additional information.

When he reached her, he considered extending his cardinal's ring to her; but instead he simply adjusted the position of his *biretta*, as if to emphasize his status.

"Father," she began, and then said, "Your Eminence."

"Highness."

"Are you curious why I have summoned you?"

"I . . . do not recall being 'summoned,' madame. I merely thought it courteous to call upon you." He looked around. "Did you find the Palais du Luxembourg unsuitable?"

"My son . . . my late son turned that residence to other purposes. This place was vacant."

"Regrettably."

"As you say. Walk with me," she said, and began to walk slowly around the great room. "It is clear that it can be turned to better purposes."

"As you say," Tremblay said.

"Yes." She frowned; Tremblay's wordplay did not amuse her. "Cardinal Richelieu—are you pained by his death?"

"His *absence*. We do not know whether he has passed from this earth."

"He is *dead*," Marie said. "He would otherwise have made his grand return by now."

"As you say," Tremblay repeated. "I would not venture to argue with you, madame."

Marie sniffed, as if she did not believe it.

"You have not answered my question."

"I think you know my answer, Highness. We were close friends and associates for many years; his work is unfinished. In the world the up-timers describe, he had years yet to come—and up-timer medicine and God's grace might well have granted him more."

"This is a different world, Eminence. All things are changed: a new Heaven and new Earth, one might say."

"Not everything has changed," Tremblay said. "Right and wrong have not changed. His Eminence Cardinal Richelieu was ambushed and assaulted, madame. Whatever you think of him or his work, he has been a faithful servant of God and his king. He was attacked because of what he did for France because someone did not think it worthy."

"The king and cardinal were killed by rogues and bandits."

Tremblay stopped walking. Marie was a few steps beyond; she stopped and turned.

"Madame," Tremblay said levelly. "You truly do not believe that any more than I do."

Tremblay folded his hands in front of him and met Marie de Medici's glare with his own.

"I accept this explanation," she said. "So does the king."

"The king is dead."

"I meant Gaston," she snapped back.

"I know you did."

"You are being insolent, Cardinal de Tremblay: I find it quite unseemly. You would be wise to consider your position and mine and decide whether angering me is in your best interest."

"Are you trying to frighten me? Please spare me, Highness. I served Cardinal Richelieu for many years. You do not present anywhere near his menace."

"Let me be clear," she said. Her voice was level and icy. "I will not dissemble with you. This *Palais* was Cardinal Richelieu's official residence, where he conducted much of his business. To my surprise, I have noted that a number of things are absent from his chambers and office."

"Such as?"

"State papers. Diaries and personal records. They seem to have disappeared."

"Imagine." Tremblay folded his hands in front of him. "Well, Highness. I *do* have the cat. The one that the lady Rebecca Abrabanel presented to him several years ago. He had grown quite attached to it, and I see why—it's a very useful animal. Perfect for catching vermin."

"I do not care about some animal a Jewess presented to your master," Marie snapped. "You know exactly what I am looking for. What is more, while I may not scare you, *Cardinal*," she added, sneering, "Eminence, if you have taken crown property and this fact is discovered, your red beret will not protect you. And yes, this time I am most definitely threatening you."

"I find *this* unseemly," Tremblay said. "And if you wish to commence your return to Paris by issuing threats, you will most certainly meet with resistance. If I may be so bold, Highness, let me suggest that I would make a far better friend than an enemy."

"A friend? You were a friend to Cardinal Richelieu. That hardly recommends you to my affections."

"I am a servant of God, Highness, and I am a Frenchman. These are the first two obligations I bear."

Marie did not answer for a moment, as if she was evaluating him. While she considered her response, Tremblay thought about the long and difficult relationship between the former queen mother and the cardinal.

It had begun long before he received his cardinal's

hat. He had spoken for the clergy before the Estates-General when she was still regent for King Louis XIII two decades ago. He had entered service of the crown as her own almoner. He had risen to authority because of his skill, his intelligence and his devotion to hard work—and, as well, because of his love of France. He worked hard to exclude her most obvious sycophants from the councils of the king—but it was only when Marie tried to force her royal son to choose between minister and mother that she was driven into exile within, and then beyond, the borders of the kingdom.

She hated Richelieu. She made no secret of her feelings, and suffered exile because of him: but he was gone—and now she occupied his apartments.

Marie de Medici was not known for her magnanimity, her forbearance, or—God help her—her ability to contain her passions or emotions. She could be quickly roused to anger and that made her dangerous.

"This is a critical time for France, Eminence," she said. "There are many enemies and many perils. My son—" and Tremblay knew she meant Gaston. "He has to learn to rule, and is in need of support from all quarters—from places he has not even considered. He has waited all his life for the chance to sit upon the throne, but I confess that he is unprepared."

"Your Highness is most astute. But I should like to offer you a small bit of advice, if you will permit."

"I welcome your insights, Eminence."

"Gaston d'Orleans is experienced in the ways of the court." Tremblay meant "intrigue," but did not want to use the word. "But in the role of king, these ways are different than they are for a younger brother and rival, even an heir."

"I'm sure he is aware of that, especially now that he is king."

"I would not be sure," Tremblay said, and Marie frowned, not sure whether he was speaking about Gaston's skill—or his legitimacy as king. "Habits are hard to change," he continued. "But that is not the primary thrust of my observation. In his youth, Highness, your *first* son was attentive to your counsels. You will find your *second* son far less biddable: especially now that he occupies the throne."

"By which you mean—"

"You assured me you would not dissemble with me, madame. I think you know *exactly* what I mean. I shall take note of your concerns regarding the cardinal's papers, and will make some inquiries."

He offered Marie de Medici a polite and courtly bow, and then turned and walked away, leaving her alone in the unfinished hall.

Chapter 33

Pau

From the parapets of the Chateau de Pau, Étienne Servien and Sherrilyn Maddox watched the army approach in the cloud of dust kicked up by the passage of thousands of men and horses.

"I'm relieved," Sherrilyn said. "I bet *they've* got some news."

"True," Servien answered. "We have news as well. I wonder what they'll make of it, and what's going to happen next."

"Oh? Has the plan changed, monsieur?"

"Colonel Maddox," Servien said. "You have not been in contact with Marshal Turenne's main force for several weeks. There is no way to tell if he is still in command, or if he has received—or accepted—new orders."

"You mean changing sides to serve Gaston? He'd never do that."

"Are you sure?"

"I—"

Sherrilyn stopped herself as she began to answer. How well did she know Turenne? She'd been working for him for six months. She knew that he was a client of Richelieu...a *former* client of Richelieu now, she guessed:...and that he didn't think much of Gaston. But he was a Frenchman first and foremost.

Gaston was king now: crowned in Reims a few days ago—word had come to the comte de Brassac by radio. Turenne might know that, or suspect it—and he did not have the intelligence that Servien had brought regarding Monsieur's perfidy. He could have changed sides. He could be marching here on Gaston's behalf.

"I really don't know," she said at last.

"No. There is no way you can know, is there?"

"I'm just a soldier, Monsieur Servien."

"And I'm just an *intendant*. But we each have former obligations, do we not?"

"Yes," she answered. "But the difference is that you're a Frenchman. I'm a hired soldier. I'm an American, a citizen of the USE."

"You think that will matter?" Servien said. "You think that *Gaston* will have any scruples with regard to your citizenship, or your contractual status? Do you really think that it ever will? As for me—I rely upon the patronage of a person of authority, but my patron is likely deceased or, at least, out of power. I might as well be a foreign national.

"Marshal Turenne is a young man, Colonel. He has a role as a peer of France. He has his family to consider. It is unclear what he may be willing or able to do."

"Which leaves us..."

"On the parapets of the Chateau de Pau," Servien said, smiling. "Fortunately, if things don't go well, the border of Spain is nearby, you are well armed, and my Castilian is passable."

"Ever the pragmatist."

He offered her a perfect courtly bow. "At your service, Colonel."

Henri de la Tour d'Auvergne, the comte de Turenne, turned the shattered watch over and over in his hands.

"This is hard to accept," he said.

Servien stood at the head of the table. At Brassac's direction he had presented the watch to Turenne and explained what it was, and how it had come to be so badly damaged.

Turenne placed the relic on the polished stone table and laid his hand next to it; then he pushed it slowly toward François de Bassompierre, who picked it up and let it catch the gray light from the late afternoon sun.

"As hard for me," Bassompierre answered. He let the watch dangle by its broken chain and then flipped it and caught it in his hand. "If it is true that Louis left a son, then Gaston is no king. But he holds the *main de justice*; he wears the Bourbon crown; he sits upon his father's throne."

"It makes him a usurper and a traitor," Turenne said. "It makes the son of King Louis and Queen Anne the rightful king, wherever they are. If he and his mother are even still alive."

"I think we can assume that they are, Marshal," Brassac said. "Gaston d'Orleans would not hesitate to tie up that loose end. That no word has reached us here that he has found them—alive or dead—is a reasonable assurance that they are still at large."

Bassompierre slid the watch to Brassac. "If they turn up safe, monsieur, then we face the possibility of civil war."

"They will turn up safe."

"How do you know that?"

"I am not at liberty to furnish that information to you at this time, Marshal Bassompierre. But let me assure you that it is true. So I now have a question for you: who is the king of France?"

"Meaning—"

"Just that." Brassac fixed the old soldier with a steely glance. "A simple question. *Who is the king of France?*"

"There is no simple answer."

"I disagree. The answer is as simple as the question."

"If I respond in a way you find unacceptable, what will you do with me? Lock me in a prison? Believe me, though I would not choose that fate, it no longer presents any dread."

"I would hope that it would not come to that."

"And if it does?" Bassompierre made a fist of his right hand on the table. "What if it does, Brassac? Are you prepared for civil war? My friend Turenne here is too young to remember, but you and I are of another generation. We recall *le Grand Alcandre, Henri le Grand*, born in this very house. We were children during the War of the Three Henries—when *Henri le Grand* took Queen Elizabeth's shilling and drove his enemies from the field at Arques and Ivry. The Catholic League wanted another man to wear the crown because he was not of the true faith, but in the end even that was not an issue."

"'Paris is well worth a mass,'" Turenne said.

"Yes, well." Bassompierre looked down at his fist and snorted. "He may not have even said that; it may be a fiction of the Jesuits, who called him *le Hercule Gaulois* and every other damn thing. But my point remains: do you want this strife to return to France— now, when the stakes are higher, the weapons are more deadly, the evidence"—he gestured to the watch, which lay on the table between them—"so dubious?

"Consider this," he continued. "Gaston d'Orleans is no saint, God knows. But neither was Louis. It was Richelieu who was the devil. Now that he's gone, I would give serious thought to the possibility that Gaston would make a decent king. He's shrewd in his own way and he might be able to give this realm the one thing his brother apparently could not: a son."

"Louis *did* give France a son."

"Who was conveniently born just before he was slain by his bastard brother—on orders, you say, from Gaston himself. All I can say is *prove it*. What I see is a broken watch—which anyone could have broken at any time—a king on a throne, and a chain of reasoning that is as brittle and fragile as a newborn babe. You are a man of honor, Monsieur le Comte," he added to Brassac. "I would not sit in your house, at your table, and accuse you of being anything other than that. I am a practical man who loves his country and would not see it tear itself apart to displace a strong king with a weak regency. The last three kings of France have been assassinated: think about that. Would you care to make it four?"

Paris

"Have you read this?"

"Yes." Vendôme tossed the letter on the table. "I read it. Rather insulting, actually. I assume you're going to tell him to go to hell."

"I wish it were that easy."

"It *is* that easy, Gaston. You're the king now."

The king's apartments were still in the state of disorganization that Louis had left them: a small easel held a half-finished portrait; several books sat a low table, two of them opened and marked; a hunting-horn on its strap and a few bits of harness, with a pen-knife and an awl beside sat on an occasional table. The restless king, no longer restless, had left his varied diversions and interests half-finished.

Gaston was leaning back on a couch, his boots propped upon a fine hassock. He looked relaxed but worried: the sardonic half-smile had not left his face, but Vendôme knew that it was more of a façade than usual.

"No. It's not."

"What did you offer them?"

"The Spanish made no *specific* demands. They said that they would be satisfied to see me on the throne."

"These are the demands, then."

"So it seems. And Mirabel will be here in a few minutes to get my answer."

"Which will be to tell him to go to hell," Vendôme said. "What can the Spanish possibly do?"

Gaston did not answer.

"Gaston," Vendôme said. "I have known you for your entire life. At no time have you ever been completely truthful, completely true to your promises, or completely without an alternate plan. Have you made a commitment to the Spanish that you feel obliged to fulfill?"

"Let us say that I did."

"Then I would say, dear Brother, that you are a fool or a very good liar. And since I know you are both, I can imagine that it is the case. What? What did you promise, and *why* are you going to go through with it?"

"You don't understand."

"I understand very well indeed," Vendôme spat at him. "As if weren't enough that you planned Louis' death from the start—and got me to do it for you—now you're going to let the Spanish take our *country*? Are you mad?"

"You dare talk to me like that? It's been a month. A *month*, César. Where is Anne? Where is Richelieu? I have it on reliable information that the cardinal is assembling an army to overthrow me. Instead of lying dead in the Forest of Yvelines, he's got all of his Cardinal's Guard assembled and ready to march on Paris. That's what I'm dealing with, Brother. You've been useless."

He took his feet off the hassock and jumped to his feet, pointing his finger at Vendôme, who stood his ground. "You've brought me nothing—except excuses. I'm blaming Anne for Louis' death; maybe I should simply announce to the world the identity of the *actual* culprit."

"I don't take kindly to threats," Vendôme said levelly.

"At least you have the sense to know one when you hear it. Do you have anything new to tell me on the simple tasks I have set before you?"

"I think the Richelieu rumor is no more than that.

I believe he's dead, Gaston, and there are *agents provocateurs* circulating these rumors to make you anxious and worried."

"I'm not anxious and worried."

"Like hell you aren't. The devil has gone back to his master. As for Anne—"

"Yes. What about Anne?"

"Her seclusion was probably somewhere west of Paris; the day she went into labor was the day Louis and Richelieu died. They were on their way to see her. If you draw a circle around the city a solid day's ride, you take in a number of small manors and chateaux. I think she was somewhere near Chartres. My informants tell me that Bishop Léonore left the city for two days just afterward—and his brother, a knight of Malta, hasn't been seen since. I suspect he's with the queen."

"Marguerite is the queen, César."

"With Anne, then. But where she *was* doesn't matter; it's where she's *going*. Almost certainly she's looking to leave France."

"She could be headed for Spain."

"I doubt it. She'd be walking right into the wolf's den. Italy would be the same. England—not a very friendly place, especially for Catholics. That leaves the Low Countries and the Germanies."

"And?"

"I would guess that she's headed for the USE. The up-timers are unpredictable, annoyingly sentimental, and fond of the underdog. Of course, to give safe haven to Anne and possibly an heir to the throne brings them into direct conflict...but they might do it anyway."

"I agree," Gaston said. "Up-timers—everywhere I turn: with Turenne, with Anne, and now possibly involved in this...this treason. I think that after I speak with Mirabel, I should summon the USE consul to have a little discussion. Does that mean I'll be talking with the Jewess, the one who so charmed Richelieu?"

"I don't know if she's still in France," Vendôme said. "The permanent ambassador is a military man, the cousin of the emperor. His name is Hand. But I don't imagine he'll come out and tell you they're granting asylum."

"No," Gaston answered. "But what he *doesn't* say will give him away. These military types have no subtlety or guile." When Vendôme tensed, Gaston added, "present company excepted, of course."

"You are too kind."

"I am too patient." Gaston jabbed his finger at Vendôme again. "This has gone on long enough, César. You have a fortnight: two weeks to find our wayward queen and our rogue cardinal, if he still lives. If at the end of that time you have accomplished neither task, I will have to take drastic action."

Vendôme considered an angry reply, but instead nodded, turned and walked toward the door.

"Not even going to ask my leave to go?"

He stopped and didn't turn around. "I have a fortnight and a task. If you wish to waste my time with idle courtesies, then it makes my job harder."

Gaston did not answer; Vendôme stalked out of the room, closing the door behind him.

The Marquis de Mirabel was accustomed to waiting. It was an integral part of the diplomat's trade: every monarch, every minister, every nobleman of standing assumed that keeping an ambassador waiting was not only customary, it was *expected*.

At least the gentleman who had admitted him had escorted him to the gardens; it was a beautiful late-spring afternoon, and the noise and stink of Paris was invisible and well-nigh out of hearing. There was just the fragrance of flowers and the chittering of songbirds—a thoroughly bucolic setting.

The king of France appeared after he had been waiting for several minutes. Mirabel offered him a courtly bow, which Gaston acknowledged with a curt nod. He spoke briefly to the duc de Villemor, who appeared ready to accompany him, but after a moment the nobleman bowed and was dismissed.

He wants to keep this private, Mirabel thought. *So much the better.*

Gaston made his way across the garden atrium to where Mirabel waited, rather than beckoning him. Mirabel bowed even more deeply and awaited the king's command.

"Señor de Mirabel," the king said. "Rise. I thank you for answering my summons."

"I am at your command, Majesty," he answered.

"You are, are you." Gaston looked—and sounded—angry. *Angry people do stupid things,* Mirabel thought to himself. He did not let his face betray any emotion. "I received your—letter—this morning, and I must say that it does not betray any willingness to be *at my command*."

"I assure Your Majesty that I am a friend to the French Crown, and that His Most Catholic Majesty is a friend as well. But...I must remind Your Majesty that there are certain agreements in place, and now that the coronation is behind us it is incumbent upon me to discuss them with you."

"Such agreements were made before I was unexpectedly raised to the throne."

"That is certainly true," Mirabel said. "But you accepted my master's offer of help, and his financial assistance, based on the proposition that you would become the king of France—by accident or design. I think it only reasonable that His Most Catholic Majesty be recompensed for his trouble."

"The situation has changed, Mirabel."

"Indeed it has, Majesty. You are now in position to honor your part of the agreement. Unless, of course," he added, "you do not choose to do so."

"What would your master say if I did not?"

"He would doubtless be disappointed," Mirabel answered. "And angry. His Most Catholic Majesty is extremely disagreeable when angry...and yet, Your Majesty, there is no reason for things to reach that pass."

"As long as I accept your terms," Gaston said. "Surely you do not expect me to hew to all of them. As I said, things have changed."

Mirabel thought for a moment and said, "Let me ask you this, Majesty. Assuming that political exigencies do not permit you to fulfill all of your earnest promises, perhaps you can tell me which ones you are prepared and willing to accept."

"Would His Most Catholic Majesty be disagreeable with half measures?"

"I am sure that he would, Sire, but with due respect, he would accept half a loaf instead of no supper at all. But there may be a further incentive for Your Majesty to reconsider honoring your promises."

"A . . . further incentive?"

"Yes."

"Would you care to be more specific?"

"Humbly, I ask what terms you would be willing to accept. There are a number of conditions, but only a few of them are of paramount importance to my master."

Gaston thought about Mirabel's remark for several moments. "I shall have to discuss these matters with my *Conseil*, of course . . ."

"Of course."

"The revocation of my father's Edict of Nantes, all at once, would be extremely difficult; but I am certain that it could be set aside in the near term—perhaps within a year or two. There are more alternatives for those who dissent from the True Faith than there were in 1598."

"I believe that would be more than acceptable."

"And I have already spoken publicly in support of Cardinal Borja, and expect that most of our cardinals could be convinced to support him in place of the current holy father."

"It will please my master to hear this as well."

"I suspect, however, that it will be most unpalatable to permit Spanish tercios to pass through the sovereign land of France. I do not know if my *Conseil* would consent to that."

"Your council is there to advise you, Your Majesty—but are they not installed for the purpose of carrying out your will? They are answerable to you: you are not answerable to *them*. It was assumed that the departure of Cardinal Richelieu would bring our great kingdoms closer together—surely you know that His Most Catholic Majesty's troops are in no way a threat to France: they are to be deployed in the Low Countries."

"I do not doubt your master's *intentions*, Mirabel. But this is a sensitive subject. There are royal troops to the south, and I cannot but believe that a conflict would take place. I have dispatched a member of my council to take command, but I still consider the idea of Spanish troops crossing French territory to be a volatile situation."

"Your commander—that would be the *Maréchal* Bassompierre, yes?"

"Yes." Gaston looked at him, frowning. "Your sources of information are very good."

"I thank you for the compliment, Your Majesty."

"It was not meant as a compliment."

"Sire," Mirabel said, continuing without acknowledging the king's last comment, "if you have your own commander in place, I must register the protest of my government. A preemptive attack has already been made against Spanish troops, a circumstance that severely grieves my master. I assume that you gave no such order."

"No," Gaston said. "Not at all. Of course not. My order to Bassompierre was to redeploy his forces away from the border with Spain—and he has undertaken an *attack*?"

"This was some time ago, before you were enthroned."

"How do you know this?"

Mirabel sighed. "I assume that Your Majesty is familiar with the up-time radio technology. I received a message by radio that it took place."

"I was not aware that there were any radio sets in Spain."

Mirabel shrugged.

"You spoke of an additional incentive, Mirabel. You might be able to convince me more readily if you told me of this."

"Very well," Mirabel said. "I am aware that you are eager to locate Queen Anne and her son."

"So the baby is a son?"

He did not know that? Mirabel thought. "Yes, he is. You have not found them as yet, as I understand."

Gaston did not answer, but waited for the Spaniard to continue.

"I can tell you where they are."

"How?"

"My sources of information are very good," Mirabel said. Gaston scowled at having his words thrown back at him. "I assume that this information would be valuable to Your Majesty."

"That is a . . . fair assumption."

"Very well, Your Majesty. Then perhaps . . . we can now negotiate?"

After Mirabel had taken his leave, satisfied with the agreement that Spanish troops would be permitted passage through France en route to the Netherlands, Gaston sent for Vendôme and provided him with the information the Spanish ambassador had provided.

"Go," Gaston told his older brother. "Do your duty."

When they parted, neither king nor bastard prince had any doubt about what would happen when the queen was returned to Paris. The noose would be pulled tight, with Gaston's hand at the other end.

Chapter 34

June, 1636
Luçon

Jean d'Aubisson had always been the youngest, the newest, the least experienced member of the Cardinal's Guard; but in the last few months, that status had actually been an asset. Without the uniform, he was just another soldier in Paris, a member of some company or regiment, not of the most well-known one in the capital—which was just as well: most of the Guardsmen had disappeared from Paris, or had wound up in the brand-new prison of l'Abbaye, near Saint-Germain-des-Prés. It was said that the king was looking out for prominent members of the Guard, because he was certain that Cardinal Richelieu was somewhere building up a power base. The word that passed from man to man, from tavern to tavern, was that King Gaston was frustrated and angry that they were largely nowhere to be seen.

D'Aubisson knew where the missing Guardsmen

had gone; and d'Aubisson, as the youngest and newest and—by extension—least well known member of the Guard, had been able to remain in Paris in service to the cardinal de Tremblay. He was just another face in the crowd—a *gentilhomme* bringing his master a cup of wine, attending to his cloak and holding a cover over his head in foul weather, running errands.

But with the coronation of King Gaston now past, and the feast of Pentecost done, it was time for him to follow the others.

"Welcome, little brother, welcome!"

Jean d'Aubisson had no sooner dismounted than he was wrapped in a bear hug and surrounded by a half-dozen men. They were not dressed in any particular uniform, but they carried themselves as fighting men. He knew a few of them—Louis-Marie, Therrien, Guillaume—but there were several who were strangers.

It was well past vespers, dark and quiet. The group of Cardinal's Guards escorted d'Aubisson through the quiet courtyard to the entrance to the chapter-house of *Notre-Dame-de-l'Assomption*, the cathedral church of Luçon.

"Is that a beard I see, Jean?" Therrien asked. "You look like you've aged a year since—"

The older Guardsman did not finish his sentence. The last time they'd seen each other was when d'Aubisson had ridden out of Paris with his king and Cardinal Richelieu.

"I feel as if I'm much older."

"Well, you're not a boy anymore, are you," Therrien said. "No more than we are."

"And no less."

"*Oui*, that's true," Therrien answered. "Now. You're here in time, lad. Best get dressed."

"Dressed?"

Therrien accompanied him into an alcove dimly lit by torches, where a dozen Cardinal's Guard uniforms hung in neat rows.

"You know," Jean said, running his hand along the sleeve of one of the uniform blouses, "when I was a young page—"

"Not so long ago," Therrien said, undoing his vest.

"Not so long ago," Jean continued. "When I was a page, and I saw men going about the city in the uniform of the Cardinal's Guard, I wanted more than anything to be one of them. They were feared—but they were respected."

He took a hat from a shelf and looked at it, turning it so that its gold edging caught the light.

"And now it means nothing," he said after a moment. "The Cardinal's Guard. Our time is gone."

"Right and wrong, young Jean," Therrien said. He pulled his blouse off and picked up the uniform one, and began to shrug it over his shoulders. "Our time *has* gone. But it does not mean nothing. You are here because of what it means."

Once dressed, the half-dozen Guardsmen who had accompanied Jean d'Aubisson formed a small procession to walk along the ambulatory between the chapter house and the nave of the cathedral. Each was dressed in the uniform of the Cardinal's Guard; each carried a red beeswax candle.

As they entered the church, Jean could see that there were dozens more waiting, each in uniform and

each holding a candle. The nave was dark but for
them, the few votive candles in the side-alcoves, and
the candles on the high altar. They joined the line,
three to one side and four to the other.

From the rear of the church a small procession
began to move toward the altar. It was led by an
acolyte bearing a censer, from which he aspersed
incense; two others carried staves topped by crosses,
and yet another bore a silken pillow that held the
ducal coronet.

Behind them was the abbot of Luçon, and behind
him Joseph François LeClerc, Cardinal de Tremblay,
dressed in the habit of a Capuchin friar. Abbot and
cardinal looked neither right nor left. In the flickering
light of the church, Jean could see tears on many of
the faces of the Guardsmen, looking straight ahead;
he assumed that the clergymen noticed it too.

From above, the choir softly intoned the introit:
*"Requiem æternam dona eis, Domine; et lux perpetua
luceat eis."* Eternal rest give to them, O Lord, and let
perpetual light shine upon them. When they reached
the front of the line of Guardsmen, they parted:
two acolytes and Tremblay to the left, two others
and the abbot to the right. There was no bier, of
course: Cardinal Richelieu had died weeks ago, and
only persistent rumor and the king's paranoia had
kept him alive. Instead, a stand bearing a portrait of
Richelieu in his full episcopal garb had been placed
at the crossing of the nave and transept.

"'Cast thy care upon the Lord,'" the abbot said,
when the introit had been sung. "'He shall sustain
thee.' In death is there life eternal; and those who
shall give themselves over to God will be sustained

by Him, and brought forth from the grave to sit at His Right Hand.

"Grant him eternal rest, O Lord," he continued. "Thou art praised in Sion: and unto Thee shall the vow be performed in Jerusalem. Thou that hearest prayer, unto Thee shall all flesh come."

The acolyte with the censer slowly moved forward, swinging it back and forth over the portrait.

"O God, whose property is always to have mercy and forgive, we humbly pray Thee on behalf of thy servant Armand Jean which Thou hast commanded to depart out of this world; deliver it not into the hands of the enemy, nor forget it at the last, but command it to be received by the holy angels, and to be carried into the land of the living; and forasmuch as he hoped and believed in Thee, let him be accounted worthy to rejoice in the communion of Thy saints."

"Glory be to God," the Guardsmen intoned, and it was echoed in the choir.

"I would not have you be ignorant, my brothers in Christ. Comfort one another with these words. 'For we believe that Jesus died and rose again: even so them who have slept through Jesus, will God bring with him. For this we say unto you in the word of the Lord, that we who are alive, who remain unto the coming of the Lord, shall not prevent them who have slept. For the Lord himself shall come down from heaven with commandment and with the voice of an archangel and with the trumpet of God: and the dead who are in Christ shall rise first. Then we who are alive, who are left, shall be taken up together with them in the clouds to meet Christ, into the air: and so shall we be always with the Lord.

"We gather here tonight in the presence of the Almighty to give thanks for the life of a true servant of the One True Faith, a prince of the Church and a child of God. Armand Jean du Plessis, Cardinal-Duke de Richelieu et de Fronsac, walked upon this earth for fifty years and seven months; at the age of twenty, he took vows as a Carthusian monk, and two years later was consecrated here as Bishop of Luçon.

"For nearly twenty years our good bishop was a loyal and trusted servant of the king of France, of the Holy Father, and of the good people he served. In the fullness of time he would have done even greater things in their service, but a cruel fate was visited upon him. Now he has gone to the land where there is no pain, no strife and no cruelty. As the apostle assures us, those who remain faithful in the Lord shall be taken up on the last day.

"As the psalmist says: 'Yea, though I walk through the valley of the shadow of death, I will fear no evil: for Thou art with me, O Lord.'"

"Thy rod and Thy staff comfort me," the Guardsmen and choir responded.

"Grant your servant, O Lord, eternal rest, and let light perpetual shine upon him. His soul shall dwell at ease. We ask in the name of your son Jesus Christ, King of Glory, that you deliver the souls of all the faithful departed from the hand of hell, and from the deep pit: from the lion's mouth and the blackness of darkness. Let Saint Michael the Standard-bearer bring them into the holy light which you promised of old to Abraham and his seed."

"For ever and ever, world without end, Amen," the Guardsmen replied.

"Accept, we beseech you, O Lord, merciful Father, the oblation which we offer unto Thee on behalf of thy servant Armand, whom Thou hast delivered from the corruption of the flesh; and grant that he may be restored and absolved from all the errors of this mortal state, and in eternal rest may await the day of resurrection."

"Let light perpetual shine upon him. Grant unto thee, O Lord, in memory of whom the Blood of Christ is received, eternal rest."

"Grant, we beseech Thee, Almighty God, that the soul of Thy servant Armand, may be received by the angels of light, and carried to the habitations prepared for the blessed."

After the mass was done and the Guardsmen had filed out singing, Jean and Therrien returned to the sanctuary. One of the alcoves held a shrine to the Blessed Virgin, and the two Guardsmen knelt on the hassock and prayed quietly for some time.

"What will we do now?" Jean asked at last.

Therrien crossed himself. "I'm not sure what *I'm* going to do. There is no more *we*, my friend . . . Perhaps I'll go home. Gascony. It's beautiful in the summertime."

"I'm from Paris," Jean said. "My mother and her sisters were from there. I'm not sure I have any place to go."

"You could stay with the old crow, I suppose."

"Cardinal de Tremblay?"

"That's the old crow I was talking about, yes. Haven't you been his manservant, or messenger, or some such? The last of us to leave the city to come here, to say goodbye to the cardinal. Why don't you go on doing that?"

"I don't think it's even safe for him anymore in Paris. So . . . you mean that we're just going to go our separate ways."

"There's no reason to stay." Therrien made to rise, but Jean grabbed him by the arm.

"There's *every* reason to stay. The man who killed our cardinal is still walking abroad, safe and in service to the new king. To the usurper."

"First," Therrien said, shrugging off Jean's grasp and getting to his feet, "the man you're talking about is a peer of the realm, a prince of the Blood. And second, those are dangerous words. Even coming here, tonight, is dangerous: if the 'new king' has spies among us, he will now know the truth. His bitterest enemy, his brother's minister, is in the ground and food for worms. If you don't want to join him straightaway, I suggest you find somewhere else to be."

Therrien genuflected and crossed himself again. "The Blessed Virgin may protect you and light your way, my friend. But you'll find more safety in becoming someone's *créature*—the old crow, or someone else."

"You know," a voice said from behind, coming slowly into the light from the Virgin's *prie-dieu*, "I think I could become weary of being called the 'old crow.'"

Cardinal de Tremblay came into view, his face etched in flickering light and shadow, partially hidden by the hood of his Capuchin robe. Jean scrambled to his feet, while Therrien took a step back.

"I beg your pardon, Eminence," he managed to say. "I didn't know you were there—I didn't mean—"

"I suspect, young man, that you meant exactly what you said: that associating oneself with a new patron is the best course, and that I am a possible choice. But you must keep this final secret: that you know nothing of the whereabouts of Cardinal Richelieu. As indeed you do not—this was not a funeral mass, but rather a requiem and offertory. We come not to bury Caesar, but to praise him." Tremblay smiled. "Shakespeare so often knew the right words to say, even if he showed poor taste by writing them in English."

"You have my word as a C—" Therrien began, then stopped. "As a gentleman."

"I promise as well," Jean said.

"That is good enough for me. Now. *Requiescat in Pace* to my old friend—and *pax vobiscum* to you, and to the rest of your brethren. As for you, my son," Tremblay said, placing his hand on Jean d'Aubusson's shoulder, "if you are willing to take the risk, you would be welcome to continue in my service."

"Eminence, I would be honored."

At matins, the quiet, empty church was dark, but for the lights on the altar and the flickering of the presence lamps in the side chapels. Tremblay knelt, his eyes well adjusted to the dimness; the Blessed Virgin gazed down at him beneficently, her hands spread in a blessing, her face etched by the intermittent light.

He had been told by the brother who had attended Richelieu in his final hours that the man had never given in to his injuries, though he knew they were mortal; at last, soothed by the monk's ministrations, he had drifted into a painful sleep, apparently troubled by dreams. His last words, whispered during some moment of lucidity, had been, "Armand—Armand for the king." But Tremblay had not seen the body, of course—that was weeks ago in any case.

The prayers he had offered were not to be answered, if what the monk had told him was true. He had come to accept that; the outcome he most wanted, the blessing he most ardently sought, was beyond the capacity of the Blessed Mother or her Divine Son to grant. Death for a simple mortal, even one so exalted as his former master, was a final judgment. It was a final grace as well, perhaps, for Cardinal Richelieu had endured illness and pain in his service to his king, now also beyond the mortal pale. The last chapter of their deeds on earth had been written.

It would not be beyond him to have arranged all of this... Tremblay thought, but dismissed it; all that he had heard suggested that even the great Cardinal Richelieu could not have escaped death, nor avoided detection.

And surely, he added, *he would have tried to contact me.*

Sighing, he got to his feet and genuflected. The canon of the church of Luçon had marked the grave with a blank stone: only he and a few others would know the final resting place of Armand Jean du Plessis until it was time for the world to know. Until then the world would be kept ignorant. He deserved a state funeral and interment in a place of honor in Notre-Dame de Paris: but for now it was better that the usurper Gaston be kept wondering if he had died at all.

When Servien parted from his master, it had been a final parting. Tremblay's parting had been unwitting: neither of them had known that it could be the last time they would see each other.

They would all meet again in Heaven . . . if the Blessed Virgin or her Divine Son permitted.

Chapter 35

Picardy

It was less than ten miles from Rumigny to Amiens, not half a day's journey even in Queen Anne's much-traveled carriage. But in the early morning it had begun to rain, causing the roads to clog with thick, sticky mud that made progress difficult.

The rain came with a thunderstorm, first a distant echo but growing in intensity as it came closer. The lightning was impressive: Achille sat on the box, watching it cascade across the sky—every time it cracked and the thunder rumbled he had to strain to control the horses. It made him wonder whether it might be prudent to turn back: but it was only ten miles—then eight, then five, and once Amiens was closer ahead than Rumigny behind, the prudent course was to press onward.

The road was largely deserted: most sensible travelers were not abroad in the storm. But on at least three occasions the bright flash of lightning showed one or more horsemen behind—never approaching but keeping their distance.

"There's going to be trouble at Amiens," he told Mazarin when they stopped to water the horses. They were out of the rain, but only just: an overhang from the roof of a half-collapsed barn provided shelter from the downpour.

"That's a welcome bit of news," Mazarin answered. From the carriage they could hear the cries of the baby, who had not been pleased with the crack and rumble of the storm.

"Well, I don't make the news, Monseigneur. I just report it."

"Our new-found friends?"

"I'm afraid so. I can't imagine anyone else would be fool enough to ride out in this storm."

"You mean other than us."

"You would rather have stayed in Rumigny?"

"It would have kept us dry—" Mazarin removed his hat and tipped a long rill of water from it, then settled it back on his head. "But I agree, it would not have changed the situation. You have a safe location in Amiens, I assume."

"I hope it is still safe." Achille looked back at the carriage. "But I think that any pretense of secrecy is gone. Someone knows where we are."

"And who."

"And who we are, yes," Achille agreed. He adjusted a strap on the harness near him. "And I know what you are thinking."

"Do you, now?"

"You continue to suspect me, Monseigneur." He held up his hand before Mazarin could respond. "Despite protests to the contrary. When we reach Amiens I will have words with my contact there; I will report faithfully what I learn."

"I don't suspect you."

"You don't? You should. Not because I am disloyal, but because you should suspect everyone. Should our noble lady return to her proper station, she will need someone to act as her Richelieu, eh? Were you not the next minister of France, in the up-time history? And . . . more?"

"That future is gone, Achille. It will never be, because the past that created it no longer exists. I am Queen Anne's protector, as are you, as long as we can manage it. As for a position at court . . . that is too far distant to even consider."

"Yes," Achille said, giving the horse a gentle pat and climbing up onto the box. "Isn't it."

They entered Amiens at Port Gayant, after passing through the *faubourg* of Vignes. The city skyline was dominated by the great cathedral's two towers, one higher than the other, thrusting above all the other buildings.

The rain had not stopped but the storm had driven south and east and largely left them behind. Achille guided the carriage along a narrow lane and into a partially covered courtyard; he climbed down from the box to the rough cobbles; a young groom was waiting to take charge of the horses.

Mazarin was holding the carriage door slightly ajar; Achille could hear the baby crying from inside.

"Are we stopped for the night?"

"Blessedly, yes," he answered. Mazarin opened the

door and came down the step, hunching against the dripping rain. "My lord king is out of sorts."

"I can imagine. Actually, Monseigneur, I don't *need* to imagine—I can hear him."

"Inside the carriage there is further evidence of his upset. I am relieved to be in the open air, rain or no."

"We should get His Majesty and the queen inside," Achille said.

"Yes, certainly." Mazarin stepped up and handed down Madame de Chevreuse, who carried a heavy rucksack. Katie was just behind. "By the way, where are we?"

"*La Maison des Fleurs*. A safe hostelry, I hope."

"I hope?" the duchess of Chevreuse said.

"On the list," Mazarin added, ignoring the duchess. Achille nodded. He turned and sloshed to the front of the carriage where he began to undo the harness.

"I smell bread," the duchess said. "Shall we get inside and confirm it?"

The common-room of the *La Maison des Fleurs*, two floors below the guest rooms, was nearly empty, other than a servant who brought them wine and bowls of stew of indeterminate origin. Within a few minutes the queen and the baby, accompanied by the duchess, prepared to move upstairs; Mazarin went with them to make sure all was secure, leaving Katie and Achille alone.

"Should I be worried that there's no one else here?" she asked.

"Perhaps. You know—"

"We are being followed."

"You know."

"You seem surprised. Both you and Monseigneur Mazarin have been speaking in low conspiratorial tones, and you spend a lot of time looking around. If we're not being followed, you guys are just bad actors."

"We didn't want to worry the queen."

"What, you think she isn't worried? Achille, she's *terrified*. You must see it too—every night we stop and she looks around like it's Custer's Last Stand." At his blank look she said, "Sorry. Like this is where she'll have to make her final defense of the baby and herself. So who's following us? Soldiers?"

"I don't think so," he said. "They'd be more rash, riding in and making a big show of it. No, it's a small group. There's probably a reward, and they want to collect it."

"That's just great. Can you stop them?"

"It is my intention," Achille said. "But they have to make an attempt."

"How did they find us?"

"As I told Monseigneur Mazarin, it is a wonder that they have only just found us. Unless they have been following us all along and have finally gotten close enough."

"Are they close enough now?"

Achille thought about it for just a moment, then said, "I believe so."

"What are we going to do?"

"Stop them," he said. "Or die trying."

Anne was rocking her son, who was whimpering very slightly. The thunderstorm had frightened the infant king for a time; he had refused to be held by anyone other than his mother, and she had only just gotten him settled.

The door opened and Achille entered. He had clearly been out in the rain. He shrugged off his wet cloak and tossed it on a settle, followed by his hat, which dripped slowly on to the floor. Katie picked them up and found a peg to hang them on.

He gave the semblance of a bow to Anne and dropped into a seat. "I hate this weather," he said.

"Rain makes the crops grow," Mazarin said.

"I'm not interested in the crops. But I *am* interested in this." He reached into a sleeve and pulled out a scrap of parchment.

Mazarin picked up the parchment and read through it. It was a portion of a letter, from its appearance— the second and final page. At the bottom of the sheet was a signature: *CVB*.

"Where'd you find that?"

"Someone dropped it. I picked it up."

"Oh?"

"He was spying through the window. He'll sleep awhile. Apparently there are a number of people in Amiens looking for us."

"That's what I think it is, is it, Achille?"

"What is it?" Anne said. "What's on the page, Monseigneur?"

"It's a signature. If I am not mistaken," he added, "it's the hand of César de Vendôme."

Anne stood in alarm, still holding Louis. The baby began to fret again. "He knows where we are?"

"I fear so. When I came through, the common-room was empty: not even a tap-boy or serving-girl."

"We must get out of this inn," Anne said. She handed the baby to Mazarin and began to gather things from the room, with help from the duchess of Chevreuse. The two women looked alarmed and afraid.

"You look quite calm, sir Knight," Mazarin said.

"I'm just catching my breath. Give me a moment. If I were to hazard a guess: someone has betrayed the Company of the Blessed Sacrament. Much to my surprise, I don't hesitate to add. But there it is."

Anne stopped gathering.

"Would you care to reveal the identity of the betrayer, monsieur? Or is he sitting in front of me?"

Achille's face, which had been bemused, became serious. "No, Majesty. He is not." He reached into a pocket within his vest and drew out another piece of parchment. "This is all the direction I was given: a list of safe places, and instructions to carry out if your life was in danger. I regret only...that I assumed that I could keep you safe."

He stood and drew his weapon. Mazarin began to step forward to interpose himself between Anne and Achille, but realized he was still holding the infant king.

But Achille made no move toward the queen; instead he walked to the door and placed his weapon at the ready, his back to his companions.

"And now," he said, glancing over his shoulder, "I shall prepare to be the first one slain in your defense."

The common-room was now only nearly empty; it was occupied only by a single Capuchin friar, sitting at his ease with a mug of ale and a mostly-empty plate in front of him. The door to the street was blocked by two burly soldiers, well-armed and wearing unpleasant grins.

"Brother Gérard," Achille said. It was the monk that had hosted them in Evreux; he looked as if he had been out in the rain. Achille's sword was in front of him as he descended the last few stairs. Mazarin was just behind; he had a pistol in his hand, but held it pointing downward. The other members of the queen's party remained behind, in sight but in position to run back upstairs.

"Monsieur Achille." Gérard took a drink from his mug, and wiped his mouth with the sleeve of his robe. "Well met."

"I would not characterize it thus. Perhaps you will explain yourself."

"What is there to explain? The queen—*pardonnez-moi*, the dowager queen—is a wanted woman. A traitor to the Crown, along with all of her companions. A fine reward is given for her return."

"You would take Gaston's thirty pieces of silver."

"*King* Gaston, if you please," the Capuchin said. "Your gift for metaphor is unparalleled, Monsieur Knight. Yes, it is true that King Gaston has offered a handsome reward for the safe delivery of his dear sister-in-law and his nephew.

"It is his intention," Gérard continued, picking up his mug, examining it and then setting it back down on the table, "to settle Her Majesty in some convent where she can live out her days, praying for his health and the peace and stability of the kingdom of France. Oh, and incidentally, to *hang* the rest of you—except your up-timer nurse, whom—for the sake of peace—he would have escorted to the boundaries of his realm and delivered into the USE."

"And the infant? The king?"

Gérard smiled, very slightly. "What infant?"

"The—" Achille began, and then he stopped and glanced up at Mazarin. "You would not dare."

"Please do not go on about what I would or would

not dare. But we were not speaking of that, were we? I merely detailed what King Gaston intended for Queen Anne, and for the rest of you, safely delivered into his hands."

"I don't understand."

"I do," Mazarin said. "Our Capuchin, here, is not interested in Gaston's reward, is he? Brother Gérard works for someone else."

"Really?" Achille frowned, pointing his sword at Brother Gérard. "Who?"

"I would assume that he is in the pay of the king of Spain. Am I correct, Brother?"

Achille frowned even further, as if the idea had not even occurred to him.

"It is small wonder that your future was so brilliant, as the up-timers account it, Monseigneur Mazarin," Gérard said. "You are so much less dense than this knight of Malta. His Most Catholic Majesty is eager to have his sister return to her native land, and would honor her and welcome her son. The rest of you would be more likely to receive the king's mercy were you to come quietly."

"You're going to take the queen back to Spain?"

"I believe that's what I said," Gérard said. "Really, weren't you listening?"

Achille walked slowly across the common-room toward Gérard, but stopped when one of the soldiers at the doorway raised his musket, aiming directly at him.

"At this range," the Capuchin said laconically, "even that woefully inferior musket would blow quite a hole in you."

"Not before I take your head off your shoulders," Achille answered, but he hesitated.

"Care to try?"

"Achille..." Mazarin began. He still held his pistol ready, but made sure it was in plain sight and pointed down at the stairs.

"No," Anne said after several tense seconds. "There is no need for bloodshed. I would not see anyone die on my son's account."

She came slowly down the stairs past Mazarin, her son swaddled and held gently in her arms.

"No," Achille said. "No!"

"Achille—" Mazarin said, but it was too late: the knight of Malta had already launched himself at the Capuchin, who was barely able to stand before Achille landed on him. The man aiming another musket discharged it, striking Achille in the leg just as he leapt across the table.

Mazarin pushed Anne behind him and fired at the other man at the door who was aiming his musket at her; the shot went wild, but the man ducked for cover behind a nearby table.

"Get back upstairs!" Mazarin shouted without turning, and cocked the pistol for another shot. Anne retreated a few steps, and the baby began to howl at the noise and the smoke from the weapons.

Mazarin was torn between keeping himself between Anne and the musketeers, and finding cover for himself. The man who had fired his weapon was going through the drill of reloading: opening the breech, adding a cartridge... Mazarin knew it would be thirty seconds at least before he could aim and fire again. The other man, however, was primed and ready. Meanwhile, the wounded knight of Malta was grappling with the Capuchin, sword still in hand, blood spouting from his leg.

For Giulio Mazarini—Jules Mazarin—it seemed as if time had slowed down. Various thoughts crossed his mind: what he might have done to prevent this from happening; how Anne might escape this; what else might be awaiting them, just beyond the door to the street.

I'm sorry, Your Majesty, he thought. He wanted to turn around, to embrace her, to keep her safe from harm—but in a moment the musketman at the door would discharge his weapon at him, at her, or at Achille d'Étampes de Valençay—

Then, still in slow motion, three shots rang out. The two musketeers crumpled, and a rifle bullet grazed the floor near Brother Gérard's head. They had come from the direction of the kitchen.

César, duc de Vendôme, stood with his two sons behind him. Each held a Cardinal rifle that had just been fired.

Chapter 36

Amiens

The Capuchin yielded, and Achille got weakly to his feet, pointing his sword at the monk's breastbone. He was unsteady, and bleeding from a wound in the leg. Mazarin wondered how he could be standing at all.

"My lord de Vendôme," Mazarin said. "You have found us."

Vendôme gestured, and his sons went to the musketmen; one was clearly dead, the result of a rifle shot. The other had been hit in the chest and was badly hurt, despite a fine cuirass.

"You have had quite a time, Monseigneur Mazarin," Vendôme said. "King Gaston is in a state. But when he learned of your whereabouts, he ordered me to come and find you."

"And so you have."

"Yes," he said. He set his rifle, butt-end down, against the wall, and took up a mug from a nearby counter. He drank deeply and set it back down, wiping his moustaches with the back of his hand. "I have."

He exchanged a long glance with Anne, who held the baby tightly. Her anger was not concealed in the least.

"You have us at a disadvantage."

Katie stepped past the queen and came down the stairs and made her way across the room to Achille. He had not moved from his position; neither had the Capuchin, except to put his hands over his face to protect himself.

"We do. But at least I'm not pointing any weapons at you."

"Those are just there for show, I suppose."

"No. They are there to *shoot people*," Vendôme said. "Just not you. Any of you. Unlike this fellow here," he added, gesturing toward the cowering Capuchin on the floor. "He would have taken great delight in it, for which he would have been severely punished."

"Why?"

Vendôme walked across the common room and nodded to Achille, who had lowered himself into a chair; Katie, ignoring the drama, had begun to pull aside the leg of his breeches.

He gave the monk a swift kick; there was a cracking sound, and the man cried out and whimpered. "Because that is not what his master would want."

"You seem well informed," Achille gasped out. "About what His Most Catholic—" Katie evidently touched some particularly painful spot on his leg, and he grimaced.

Vendôme turned away from consideration of the monk lying on the floor, curled in a ball. "Are you trying to imply something?"

Achille did not reply. Vendôme shrugged.

"Are *you* working for the Spaniard now?" Mazarin asked.

"No. Not in the least."

"Then you are simply the usurper's creature. If you wish to take Her Majesty into custody, you must be prepared to kill even more people. I am sure you will be amply rewarded—but it is on your head, monsieur."

"You are right, Monseigneur. It is on my head—but I do not take the coin of the Spanish king, neither do I wish to be answerable to my brother Gaston."

"You've already done enough on his behalf," Achille said through gritted teeth.

"Achille—" Mazarin began, wondering if the knight of Malta would be afforded similar treatment to what Vendôme had done to Gérard.

"No," the duke said. "Though I recognize a condescending tone when I hear one, Monseigneur Mazarin, I accept this knight's condemnation. It is a matter of great regret that my sword took my brother's life. I never intended anything of the sort."

"You admit to killing King Louis," Mazarin said, glancing up the stairs at Anne.

"It would do no good to deny it. Of course I do— and Gaston has used that fact to control me from that time forward. It is time for that to end.

"I would speak with Her Majesty, but I understand her reluctance. I freely admit to, and offer no apology for, the death of Cardinal Richelieu. He has been a plague upon this country for a dozen years, twisting my brother Louis to his own purposes. Killing him was a matter of honor and duty.

"But it is a matter of great regret that Louis, my brother, met his end at my hands. There was strife and discord between us; I might have wished that his reign be shorter, and at one time would have preferred that Gaston be king in his stead. Having seen him in the role, I regret any such desire.

"Louis' death was an accident, and I grieve that I caused it. But as a man of honor, as a peer of France, I cannot deny the act. *I killed the king of France.* It cannot be undone . . . but it can be atoned for. I come here today to offer Queen Anne a choice.

"She can have my head, Monsieur Mazarin, if she wishes it."

His two sons turned to look at him in alarm. François stood up next to the dead man he had been examining and said, "Father—"

"No. Be silent," he said, holding up his hand. "It is her right. My sons will not intervene if you, or your wounded friend there, wants to take my life. I killed the queen's sovereign lord and husband; a life for a life is just.

"But if she will forbear, I offer something different: I offer her, and her son, my allegiance. My sons will offer the same. We will aid her in her cause and escort her to whatever destination she wishes."

Mazarin was not sure how to reply at first; he stood there, speechless, trying to read Vendôme's expression. The man was a schemer, a jaded and disillusioned military man, who had been brought up as royalty in a royal court, the oldest son of the king of France—yet he wore his parentage, a badge of shame, every day of his life.

He had been constantly reminded of it, no doubt: *Henri le Quatre* had reached down and pronounced him *légitimé de France*, making him royal but never capable of sitting upon the throne.

And now...

"Forgive me," Mazarin said at last. "It is difficult for me to believe you. I know, I know," he continued as Vendôme began to reply, "you can pronounce your honor and give your word, and your willingness to sacrifice your life is a powerful argument for the truth. Yet if you were to be spared you would be close to our infant king—close enough to betray him later."

"You impugn my honor, priest."

"I'm afraid I do, my lord. But you know it's true: what you have said, though a revelation, might be just what you would be expected to say. It is the sort of thing that Gaston d'Orleans would say if he were in your place."

Vendôme was angry: it was burning and fierce, a few paces away, framed with the sort of hauteur only great nobles could muster. Mazarin was sure that Vendôme would be capable of killing him, or ordering him killed, for no better reason than his tone of voice.

Into your hands, O Lord, he thought. *This is the last hand of cards.*

Somehow, though, the order did not come. Priest and nobleman remained standing, silent, each waiting for the other to break the silence; both were surprised when it was interrupted by someone else.

"My lord of Vendôme."

Aña Maria Mauricia, Queen of France, Hapsburg princess, mother of the legitimate king of France, placed her still-crying infant son in the hands of Katie Matewski, who had ascended the stairs toward her. She then came to stand beside Mazarin.

"My lady, this is no place—" Mazarin began; and she turned her attention to him and silenced him again with a glance.

Vendôme gave a proper courtier's bow. Anne waited for the gesture to be complete, her hands folded in front of her, her face set in a serene expression. The weeks of travel had worn down her attire, but at that moment she was as regal and as beautiful as Mazarin had ever seen her.

"My lord of Vendôme," she said. "Father Mazarin does Us a great service by his concern, and shows his care for Our son by his caution. He speaks thus to you not out of anger or spite, but out of loyalty to His Majesty whose mother We are.

"You are right to offer to pay for your transgression with your life. Killing a crowned king is no slight matter, regardless of the cause or the circumstance. When Our father-in-law, your father, was slain by the mad monk Ravillac, the monk's body was torn apart by teams of horses as a lesson to those who might contemplate such a vile act.

"To simply take your head would be a mercy in comparison . . . and yet even the satisfaction of revenge would not return Our husband and sovereign Lord. *Mea est ultio, dicit Dominus: Revenge is mine, saith the Lord.*"

She crossed herself, slowly, deliberately.

"I do not want your head, my lord of Vendôme." The pride and demeanor of the queen seemed drained from her, along with the royal pronoun. "If the situation were not so dire, I would spurn your offer of allegiance and assistance and dismiss you to perdition as the Lord does on Judgment Day: *Et qui non inventus est in Libro vitæ scriptus, missus est in stagnum ignis—Whoever was not found written in the Book of Life was cast into the lake of fire.*

"But you know, and I know, that I, a poor woman with few allies, cannot afford to do so. Therefore I spare your life freely given and accept your offer of support and assistance."

She stepped directly before the duc de Vendôme. She reached out hesitantly to touch his face, which had shed a few tears as she spoke.

And then she drew back her hand and slapped him directly across his right cheek. A heavy ring she wore left a deep welt; she returned her hand to her side, and her body shook with fury.

"Your allegiance to the rightful king is accepted, and perhaps someday he will reward you according to your just deserts. But do not ever presume to believe that I will do so—or ever call you friend."

Vendôme reached up to touch his face; his hand came away with a small smear of blood. After a moment he went to one knee and looked up at her, placing his hands together before him.

Anne placed her small, delicate hands around his great heavy ones, and accepted his oath.

Chapter 37

Pau

"Are you sure, Colonel?"

Sherrilyn Maddox leaned over the table, which held a detailed map of Béarn. "Yes, Marshal. I'm sure. I believe I can recognize a military formation when I see one. A regiment of cavalry and three full tercios—or, what passes for a full tercio these days: fifteen or sixteen hundred men each."

"Why do you think they're here?"

She looked up at Turenne.

"You're asking my opinion."

"Yes. Does that trouble you?"

"As long as you're not troubled by my answer. High politics is not exactly my stock in trade, Marshal."

"If I wanted the opinion of someone whose stock in trade was politics, I would ask Monsieur Servien." Turenne leaned back in his chair, pyramiding his fingers. "So. I assure you that I shall not be troubled by your words, Colonel Maddox. Why would a regiment of cavalry and three tercios of infantry be crossing the Pyrenees?"

"I can only think of two reasons."

"Which are?"

"The most obvious one is that they're invading."

"And the other?"

"That they're marching into France by invitation. But that would have to come from the king, I suppose."

"The king—well, the man who sits on the throne— sent Marshal Bassompierre with orders to move the army north, away from the border. Evidently Monsieur has made some sort of _arrangement._"

"Spanish troops on French soil seems like a bad idea."

"It's a terrible idea. Even if they are _intended_ for war in the north—even if Gaston believes that they are merely intending to transit our lands—they might find it to their liking and remain. He is permitting the enemy to occupy his country. Neither our late beloved king nor Cardinal Richelieu would have ever permitted such vulnerability.

"Perhaps," Turenne said, glancing at the map, "the Spanish commander will see reason."

"I don't know why you want to give him the chance."

Turenne frowned. "This is not a scouting mission, Colonel: if we seek to prevent the Spanish forces from moving north, it will come to a battle, not an ambush. That means ordered troops; it means a parley. I _will_ give them _the chance_, Colonel Maddox, because that is the way war is conducted. _Perhaps the Spanish commander will see reason._"

"As opposed to attacking us—"

Turenne stood up, making Sherrilyn stand up straight.

"The only way regular troops can attack us is from ordered formations," he said. "A tercio is not a commando unit. It can be a devastating fighting force—but not against *our* ordered formation. From a hundred and fifty yards away, we can hit them effectively—but they cannot hit us."

"They must realize that."

"It will enter into their thinking, I trust. But they may attack nonetheless. And if they do, we will show them exactly what *we* can do."

Near St. Jean Pied-de-Port

Five miles south of St. Jean Pied-de-Port, the advance scouts located the Spanish cavalry. Turenne's army of twenty-eight hundred was still north of the town; the scouts had orders to avoid engagement and report back. A few of the Spanish cavalrymen loosed shots with their pistols, but it was no more than a waste of ammunition.

Column formations are vulnerable: an army is only effective when it is arranged in its proper ranks. For a tercio, that meant a series of *cuadros*, infantry squares with musketeers in groups—*mangas*—at each corner, to provide crossfire to anyone bold enough to charge against the *cuadro*. Sherrilyn would still have been willing to take out the infantry while it was still making its way down the narrow, winding roads from the Pyrenees passes. The Spaniards were enemies—weren't they?—and there would be no need to fight them in the field. But the marshal was willing to let them form up, *cuadros* and *mangas*, pikes and muskets, cavalry arranged on the flanks, the Cross of Burgundy standard fluttering from the standards.

In the morning light, they looked impressive. Marshal Turenne, Marshal Bassompierre, the comte de Béarn and Sherrilyn sat on horses on a hill overlooking the field; below, the French army had been drawn up in a narrower formation, four ranks deep. The Spanish cavalry—a few hundred horsemen armed with breech-loading pistols and sabers—was deployed at the right side of the line.

From what Sherrilyn could see, the French riflemen looked determined and serious, while the Spanish seemed confident. They could see they had numerical superiority. They knew that the tercio was the strongest infantry formation in existence, and had been for more than a century. They thought—they *knew*—that they would win.

The analysis had only one flaw: they were at least six hundred yards away. There would be at least two minutes of volleys that they couldn't answer.

Her own troops were on the slope above the battle line; their targets, if they presented themselves, would be the officers—the *alfareces*—in their plumed hats.

Alexandre de Brassac, the comte's son, was moving slowly out from the French lines, with a Béarn banner in his stirrup—crows and bulls quartered on a yellow field, with a crown on top: there were fancy heraldic terms, but Sherrilyn didn't remember them. He had a piece of white silk tied to the top of the staff. A Spanish officer, also on horseback, journeyed out to meet him. After a bit of bowing and doffing of hats, they spoke, and the Spaniard handed Alexandre a scroll. He glanced briefly at it, doffed his hat again, and rode quickly back and up the hill to deliver it to his father.

"Tell me what you've learned," Brassac said.

"There are three tercios deployed," Alexandre answered. "The one in the center is the *Tercio de Infantería en Navarra*; its commander is Don José García Salcedo, and it's at nearly full strength. Don José is in charge of this expedition. The other two are the *Tercio de Fuenclara* and the *Tercio Nuevo de Valladolid*. Fuenclara was in Germany and was badly beat up; it's under a thousand men—Don José has placed it on his left. Valladolid is a new tercio, raised within the last six months; it's a little over half strength, but it has two *cuadros* of veterans who fought in Italy."

"Don José is an old cavalryman," Brassac said to Sherrilyn. "He's one of the smartest field commanders the Spanish have in their employ. We must be especially careful of him."

"So he's a high priority target."

"If it comes to that," Turenne said.

"I don't know why you think it's *not* coming to that, Marshal," she answered. "Those boys look like they're ready to attack. And they think they're going to win."

"We are engaged in a parley," Turenne said. "Monsieur de Brassac, if you would continue." His glance at her sent a clear message: *shut up and listen.*

She shut up and listened.

"Don José's envoy presented the compliments of his commander, as well as this document." He gestured to the scroll. "It claims to be a safe-passage for his troops, by order of his king, with the kind consent of our king."

"Gaston," Brassac said.

"He is named in the document. It's not signed or sealed; it refers to a...radio conversation."

"A radio—" Brassac read through the document: it was a parchment written in Spanish, formal phrases and proper diplomatic terminology. It bore the signature of Gaspar de Guzmán, count-duke of Olivares. "This could be a complete fabrication."

"Or it could be what Señor Garcia Salcedo assures me it is."

"What was your response?"

"What you instructed me, Father. I told the envoy that I would bear this document to you, and deliver your response."

"And what did he make of that?"

"He was unsurprised. But he acted as if this was an inconvenience, nothing at all. Indeed, he told me that if we were not disposed to let their forces pass, it would be necessary for them to force the issue."

"He told you they'd attack?"

"As I said," Alexandre answered, "he implied that they did not consider us a threat. When I asked him for clarification of the term 'forcing the issue,' he said that they would be required to 'sweep us aside.'"

"Sweep us aside. *Vraiment. Bien*," he added, "they're in battle formation," Turenne said. "Colonel Maddox is correct. They are ready for a fight. If they were not prepared to enforce their will they would remain in marching order."

"What are your orders?" Alexandre asked.

"Tell the envoy that, with due respect, we do not accept this document: not from any question of its legitimacy, but because we do not take orders from the usurper. Gaston," Brassac said, taking a deep breath, "Gaston d'Orleans is not our rightful king. His promises have no value."

"He's not going to like that answer," Sherrilyn said.

"That is the answer I propose to give," Brassac said. "Unless you wish something else," he said to Turenne.

"No," Turenne said. "That is the answer I would have you give."

Turenne looked at Bassompierre, as if expecting defiance or protest. The old marshal looked grimly from the young marshal to the comte de Brassac, and after a moment he nodded his agreement.

Alexandre took one last glance at his father, then turned his horse and rode back down to the field, where the envoy from the Spanish side waited.

The Spanish officers conferred for several minutes while the troops waited. It was obvious that they were in no hurry to attack and had no fear that the French might make a move while they discussed their options.

To Sherrilyn, who hadn't been present for a battle—at least not with the French—it was almost surreal: each side's toy soldiers were set up on the field, their helmets and cuirasses reflecting the sun, the horses neighing and pawing the ground . . . and no one was moving. It was like a football game before the referee blew the whistle.

With one significant difference, she thought. *When the whistle blows, these guys will try to kill each other.*

Then the whistle blew: three blasts on a horn from the center tercio, followed by three blasts from each of the flankers, and the Spanish cavalry began to move across the field toward the French line.

She looked at Turenne and the comte de Béarn, whose expressions hadn't changed.

"Now we will see how good they are," Turenne said, and rode down toward the center of the line.

The Spanish cavalry was heavily armed and armored; it took them a few moments to get up to speed. Thirty seconds after they began to move they had covered a quarter of the distance to the French line; thirty seconds later they were more than halfway.

Thirty seconds after that, the French line, armed with Cardinal rifles, began to fire. Every fifteen seconds another volley erupted from the formations on either side, striking the cavalrymen and their mounts with devastating effect: each time the front rank retired in order, and the loaders behind the line reloaded their weapons as the other ranks stepped forward.

The Spanish cavalry on each side had been expecting to strike the Frenchmen, firing a pistol caracole and then attacking with swords and the momentum of their charge. There was no pike square opposing them. But by the time their pistols were in range, too many of them were wounded or unhorsed, utterly dispersing the charge. Those who remained turned aside, trying to ride out of range of the French rifles—which continued to fire, volley after volley.

Then the horns blew again, and the infantry began to advance.

Paris

When King Gaston came to the telegraphy chamber, Terrye Jo was ready and waiting. Several in his entourage seemed tentative and perhaps even a trifle afraid: but the king himself was accustomed to the up-timer technology. The hum of the radio set did not disturb him in the least.

She stood, not removing the headphones, but Gaston waved her back to her seat. He gestured to the others with him.

"Mademoiselle Tillman is very skilled with this device," he said. "My lord of Soissons, did you discharge the man you had working for you? I understand he was quite inferior."

"No . . . no, Sire. Mademoiselle Tillman asked that he be retained."

"Indeed." Gaston looked from Soissons to Terrye Jo, one eyebrow raised. "And why would that be?"

"Because, Your Majesty," Terrye Jo said, removing the headphones and laying them carefully on the table, "as at Turin, no one can attend the equipment at every hour of the day and night. Monsieur Cordonnier—"

"He has a name, does he?"

"Of course he does. Everyone has a name," she answered. And then added, "Your Majesty."

"Yes. You are correct, mademoiselle," the king said. "But most names are not worth remembering."

There was a titter of laughter. Terrye Jo did not laugh, and did not find herself moved to smile.

"Have I offended you?" Gaston asked.

"No, Sire," she said. "Not me. But I do not wish to waste Your Majesty's time. By your leave, we should proceed."

The duc d'Épernon frowned—*glared*, actually, Terrye Jo thought—at what he must have perceived as impertinence. She returned his stare.

"Then let us proceed," Gaston said, waving at her to sit.

Terrye Jo sat down and put the headphones back on, tuning the radio set to the frequency she'd been given.

GJBF CQ, she sent. *CQ CQ CQ.*

"Any response?" D'Épernon said. "Is there—" He stopped at a gesture from his king.

GJBF. GJBF.

GJBF HDAT, she heard at last. *HDAT. KN.*

HDAT was the call sign she had been expecting to hear: *Henri Tour d'Auvergne, Turenne.*

"Go ahead, Sire," she said.

"I would speak with Marshal Bassompierre. Tell the telegrapher to summon him."

HDAT GJBF LE ROI DESIRE PARLER A BAS-SOMPIERRE KN.

There was a pause, and then she received a response: *LE MARECHAL TURENNE DIRIGE L'ARMEE. LUI SEUL PARLERA POUR L'ARMEE.*

GJBF HDAT QSM. Please repeat, she sent. *QSM.*

HDAT GJBF BASSOMPIERRE NE DIRIGE PAS. LE COMMANDANT EST MARECHAL TURENNE. KN.

"Majesty," Terrye Jo said. "I am told that Marshal Bassompierre is not in command."

"Has he not reached Turenne's army?"

GJBF HDAT EST BASSOMPIERRE LA?

HDAT GJBF OUI came the response. *PORTANT LE COMMANDANT EST MARECHAL TURENNE ET C'EST LUI QUI PARLE POUR L'ARMEE.*

"He has. He...I am told that Marshal Turenne is in command, Sire, and only he will speak for the army."

"I ordered Bassompierre to take command! Is he violating my orders?"

"I'm not sure, Majesty. I only know what I—"

"Yes, yes. You only know what you receive. Well, send them *this*: Bassompierre is to take command of Turenne's army, and he is to march it northward at once. Those are the orders of the king."

Terrye Jo nodded, and began to send. It was a long message; at several points she had to stop and repeat parts of it—it was clear that HDAT, whoever he was, couldn't quite keep up.

There was a lengthy response. She wrote on her pad, crossed part of it out and wrote more.

"What is it?"

She didn't answer, looking at the pad and then at Gaston.

"Come, girl, out with it," Gaston said. "What's wrong?"

"The army, Sire. It is on the march, but not northward. And it says—he says, the telegrapher—that the army is under the command of Marshal Turenne, and that it does not answer to you but rather to the true king of France."

Gaston reddened, angry. "What in the name of God does that mean?"

"They call you usurper, Sire. They say—they say that the true king is the..." she ran her finger along the writing on the pad. "The true king is the son of King Louis and...and Queen Anne."

Chapter 38

Paris

The convent of the Capuchin Friars was located on the Rue du Faubourg St. Honoré, a relatively recent addition to the royal city. It consisted of a group of buildings surrounding a central courtyard and bordered by an iron fence on the street side. The entrance was through a gated arch; the collegiate church was opposite, with the chapter-house to the left and the brothers' cells to the right. In a city of churches, it hardly stood out as unusual—one more steeple among many.

Indeed, it was the perfect place for the Company of the Blessed Sacrament to meet.

Most Parisians and most Frenchmen had never heard of the Company. The duc de Ventadour had founded it in the spring of 1630. His Grace had just escorted his wife in her retirement to the Carmelite convent, and found diversion in the establishment of this secret, pious confraternity. It had multiple goals:

encouragement of piety among its members; charity among the needy and poor in the king's city; and the promotion of the True Faith. Encouraged—covertly— by King Louis, it had never quite been recognized by letters patent despite a number of quiet petitions requesting the same. Cardinal Richelieu had favored its works but given it no official sanction, though his most trusted advisor, Père Joseph—now Cardinal de Tremblay—was a Companion and presently served on its nine-member council.

The abbot of the Capuchins knew that the Company met on its premises, in a small chapel accessible through a false door in the sacristy of the great church, decorated by a beautiful depiction of the Savior's Sacred Heart. He had one of the four keys to that door; the lay superior and the ordained spiritual director each possessed a key as well. The fourth key, almost since the formation of the Order, had hung from the *cingulum* of Père Joseph himself.

On a cool late spring night, when the streets of Paris were cloaked with fog, the cardinal de Tremblay and Jean d'Aubisson were conveyed to the entrance of the Capuchin church in a closed carriage. The brother porter looked curiously at the young former guardsman, but Tremblay nodded and he admitted both of them without a word.

The two men made their way through the grounds into the main nave. The vespers office was over and the hall was largely vacant—a few oblates were attending to the altar candles and preparing the church for the night offices a few hours away. As they made their way down the main isle after kneeling and genuflecting, others stepped away; Tremblay turned left and walked up two steps and into the sacristy, d'Aubisson just behind.

Someone was waiting near the door: Philippe d'Angoumois, the Capuchin prior, another of the nine overseers.

"Brother Prior," Tremblay said. "I apologize for being tardy. A few matters required my attention."

D'Angoumois looked from Tremblay to d'Aubisson. "I will vouch for him."

"It is in no wise that simple, Eminence. You are here with someone outside the Company—it is bad enough that you brought him into the Convent—"

"I will vouch for him, Philippe, and that is an end to it. With the superior away from Paris the baton belongs to me, so the decision belongs to me."

"What does he know?"

"Enough."

D'Angoumois was dissatisfied with the answer, but looked away. "Your arrival was not noted, I trust."

"Not as far as I know. Gaston's spies are everywhere; the man has a positive talent for intrigue." He smiled. "I humbly offer that I have some skill in that area as well."

"I never doubted it, though since you are not alone—"

"Enough," Tremblay said. "I assume the others are waiting within."

"Yes. We would not begin without you."

"I daresay you would not."

D'Angoumois reached within his cassock and drew out an unusual key: instead of a straight bar, it was truncated by a small stylized flat plate like a seal, a splayed heart with lines radiating out from it. He placed it not where a normal door lock might be found, but directly on an almost-invisible indentation in the Sacred Heart in the portrait before him, pressing it inward; there was a mechanical click, and the door swung inward to a slight push. Beyond there was a narrow hallway, lit by a small flickering torch.

The prior led the way. Tremblay followed with d'Aubisson, who at a gesture closed the door quietly behind them.

The secret chamber where the Company met was small, mostly occupied by a long wooden table inlaid with ceramic tiles. Each tile depicted one or another saint, each a blessed hero of France: Saint Louis, the just and noble king; Saint Denis, the patron of Paris; and a number of others. At the head of the table was an empty chair; a small ivory baton sat on the table in front of it.

Before taking his seat on the far side between a man in episcopal dress and a lay person in noble's finery, d'Angoumois picked up the baton and carried it to the foot of the table, where Tremblay took his seat before the inlaid tile that showed Saint Bernard of Clairvaux, the great and charismatic twelfth-century divine.

At a gesture from Tremblay, d'Aubisson took up a position behind him. The others looked curiously at Tremblay but offered no challenges.

"I have just returned from Reims," he began. "I was allocated a rather inconsequential place in the procession. Our self-styled king is not much interested in cardinals *in pectore*."

"There was no affront to your person, I trust," d'Angoumois said.

"No, nor to my dignity, but there wasn't much chance of that. It is my impression that Gaston has not yet drawn up his list of royal enemies. The dowager queen mother, though..." he gave a gesture as he let the sentence trail off, while members of the council frowned and muttered.

"She has taken up residence in the *Palais-Cardinal*, in case you were unaware," he said. "Apparently she has not found the Palais du Luxembourg to her liking." Before her exile on the Day of Dupes, Luxembourg had been her home in Paris.

"I believe she appreciates the irony of it. But of course she was hoping to find some plowshares to beat into swords—to use against my lord of Richelieu. She was disappointed, I am happy to say."

"You would not have called us all here, in the absence of the superior, to merely pass on gossip of the royal court," d'Angoumois said. "Nor, Eminence, would you violate our secrecy with an outsider without good and just reason. I am sure we would all like to know what that is."

"You are correct, Monsieur l'Abbé. You are all apprised of the news regarding the healthy son born to our good Queen Anne.

"The fact remains that Gaston is on the throne," Condé said. "And the queen and her infant son have vanished. I know that we had made provision for this circumstance—were they protected?"

"That...is the true reason for calling this meeting. Our protection was extended as planned, up to a point. I regret that I bear some distressing news. It seems that we have a turncoat in our ranks."

There was silence in the room after he said it: the

members of the Company looked at each other, then back at Tremblay.

"The turncoat himself is not among us. It remains to be seen whether anyone here has any connection to him. But I have learned that he has been taking the coin of Olivares, by means of the Spanish ambassador in Paris, the marquis de Mirabel, who has told my lord Gaston what he knows."

After further silence, Condé said, "He'll have sent his hound after her, then."

"The duc de Vendôme—"

"The duc de Vendôme will clearly stop at nothing to achieve his aims," Condé said. "He is already a regicide. He will not hesitate to kill again. Queens... princes..."

"The duc de Vendôme," Tremblay repeated, patiently, "is no particular friend of Gaston. The man who styles himself king of France has done his best to make sure that he holds Vendôme's life in his hands. There is only so much a man like that will tolerate—and I believe his tolerance is at an end."

"What does that mean, exactly?"

"It means that the fate of the kingdom of France is in the hands of a legitimated royal bastard who has nothing to lose. Is that clear enough, my lord de Condé?" Tremblay leaned back in his chair. He closed his eyes, rubbing them with his fingers. "Is it clear to you that all of our planning, all of our prayers, all of our ambitions have come to this?

"We have no control. *No* control over events. It has come to this, and we have come here to consult over those events." Tremblay opened his eyes and picked up the ivory baton, turning it in his hands so that its faceted edges and gold-chased ends caught the candlelight. "We might as well douse the candles and put up the chairs and go home."

"Did you come here to tell us that, Eminence?" d'Angoumois said quietly. "To tell us that the Company of the Blessed Sacrament no longer has any purpose?"

"I wish I knew how to answer that, Abbé. Truly I do."

"I rather expected a more positive answer."

"I am so sorry to disappoint you."

"Damn it, Eminence, that's not good enough." Condé pushed back his chair and stood, walking to stand next to Tremblay's seat. "You tell us that the queen is—or soon will be—in the hands of the duc de Vendôme. You tell us that the king—that Gaston—is not the rightful monarch of our land, and that he is complicit in the death of his brother and Cardinal Richelieu. And what you have to offer in return is indifference—of helplessness?"

"What would you have us do?"

"Fight," Condé said. "*Fight.* If Gaston is not the king, then we should fulfill our vows to protect the one who is."

"By . . . riding out to join him? Wherever he is?"

"That may be necessary. If the Spaniard knows where to go—if Vendôme knows—if the king knows—then we can know as well. Are you ready to exert whatever influence you have to find the queen and her son?"

"How shall I answer you?"

"I offer you two choices, Eminence. Either say yes and we will all know what to do; or say no, and hand me the baton. The Company—" he gestured along the table, at the expectant faces there—"awaits your answer."

❖   ❖   ❖

Colonel Erik Haakonson Hand knew that the role of ambassador would be an uncomfortable one, but the unease of the present situation was worse than he would have imagined.

He had not yet presented his credentials to King Gaston. After Rebecca Stearns, who had led the USE delegation for the coronation in Reims and reception in Paris, left for home, he had made application to the chancellor's office to arrange a proper presentation— but had been put off several times.

It made his summons even more surprising.

There was nothing for it: his full dress uniform was in order, with the appropriate military decorations of the kingdom of Sweden, augmented by the red, white and blue sash of the United States of Europe; the gold-chased ceremonial sword that wouldn't cut a rindy cheese; white doeskin gloves on a sweltering hot day in the airless Palace of the Louvre. He'd endured much worse, and looked much more foolish.

He was admitted to a small reception room at the east end of the *Grande Galerie*, the long closed arcade that Henry IV had built between the Tuileries palace and the old Renaissance structure of the main Louvre Palace. He was left in the company of a bishop, Gaston Henri, a royal brother—one of Henri's many illegitimate sons. Hand knew of him but had never had occasion to meet him, and wasn't sure why he was present.

"Your Excellency would find it tiresome to remain alone," the man told him when he asked that question.

"I have had many solitary periods in my life, Your Grace," he answered.

"That is as may be, Monsieur Colonel," the bishop said. "But I am here by my royal brother's command."

A few minutes passed in silence.

Hand stood up and walked slowly around the room, examining the bookcases and art objects; occasionally he would reach up to touch something gently with his left hand. The right remained crookedly at his side.

"Are you injured, Excellency?"

"I'm sorry?"

"Your right arm. You favor your left."

"Ah." Hand turned to face the bishop. When they had been sitting together the effects of the old injury were far less pronounced; the other man was observant, perhaps deliberately so. "I led an attack during a battle and suffered an injury. Rather a permanent condition, I regret to say."

"Could not an up-time doctor fix it with—" he gestured, vaguely. "Whatever wizardry they possess for the purpose."

"Not as yet," Hand said. They had examined him, but had said—regrettably—that most of the capability to address the damage remained up-time and inaccessible. "But there is always hope."

"Yes, of course." Bishop Gaston Henri folded his hands and looked piously off into the middle distance, as if posing for a portrait.

"Your Grace, do you know if I will have an opportunity to present my credentials at this time?"

"Have you not done so already?"

"No. I have been making every effort, but . . ."

"The royal bureaucracy moves very slowly, Excellency. My brother the king has many demands upon his time, and is keeping all of his ministers quite busy. He—"

Whatever else the bishop intended to say regarding

the king was suddenly cut off when the doors opened and Gaston walked into the room. Two gentlemen-ushers stepped just inside; the bishop was on his feet and offering a low bow, which the king ignored.

"You have our leave to go," he said to Gaston Henri without turning. The bishop bowed again—and was ignored again—and scurried out of the room. The doors were closed, leaving Hand and the king alone.

Erik Hand was a blunt and forthright man, accustomed to plain speaking with his cousin Emperor Gustavus Adolphus; but he knew that the first words would have to come from the king.

"Colonel Hand, isn't it?"

"Erik Haakonson Hand, if it please Your Majesty," he said, giving a bow of his own.

"No salute?"

"I regret to say that an injury renders that difficult, if not impossible. I appear before you as a civilian, and appointed representative of my government."

"Your government," Gaston said. He curled his lip in amusement, or perhaps distaste. "Ah, yes. The United States of Europe. Our . . . new neighbors."

Hand wasn't sure how to respond to the comment.

"I am curious, Colonel," the king continued. "How long do you think you could keep the secret?"

"Secret, Majesty?"

"Yes." He stared at Hand, all impression of amusement gone. "The secret of your government's involvement with the traitorous queen and her companions to undermine my authority as king."

"I beg your pardon? Are you accusing my government of involvement in a matter internal to your kingdom?"

"Did I not just say so, Colonel, or is your hearing as impaired as your right arm? *Yes*, I am accusing your government of conspiracy. I believe that even now she is in your sovereign territory. She must be returned. *At once*."

"I cannot say that she is in the USE, Your Majesty," Hand responded. The suddenness of the attack, and the rude approach, caught him unprepared—but he kept his composure. "There is no official word that she has been granted asylum, or even that she has requested it."

"How utterly convenient."

"I am sure that you do not seek to make any improper accusation, Majesty," Hand said. "It would be in contradiction to your well-known sense of fairness and honesty."

"I make no improper accusations. Only proper ones."

"Once again, I cannot speak to the matter."

"Cannot, or will not?"

Hand felt himself slowly getting angry, but restrained it. "Cannot," he said. "I would ask how you have reached this conclusion—and the source of your information."

"My source is impeccable, monsieur. And I reach this conclusion by means of irrefutable logic." He pointed a finger at Colonel Hand. "The traitress is clearly fleeing the country. Where can she go? Not Spain or other Hapsburg lands: she would never be welcome there. Italy? It is in chaos. England? A servant of the One True Faith would be as endangered as the radical Protestants my brother-in-law so rightly imprisons. She would similarly avoid Holland, where Catholics are unwelcome.

"That leaves one choice: your nation of up-timers and heretics and—and whatever else lurks there. She is seeking refuge in your country. *I want her back.*"

"I am in no position to make that request, Majesty."

"And why not? Are you not the deputed representative of your government in Paris?"

"I am the *appointed* representative, Majesty. You have not yet accepted my credentials."

Gaston stared at him angrily for several moments. "Are they in your possession?"

Hand slowly reached inside his coat. From an inside pocket, on the right side so that he could reach them with his left hand, he drew out a thick envelope that bore the official seal of Emperor Gustavus Adolphus—the Swedish coat of arms, lions quartered with a trio of crowns, surrounded with other decorations of the House of Vasa. He offered it to Gaston with a slight bow.

The king of France accepted the envelope, pulled it open and discarded it as he drew out a thick sheet of parchment which also bore the royal seal.

"Your credentials are accepted," Gaston said, scarcely looking at the paper. "You are dismissed, Colonel Hand. Do not presume to call upon me until you can report the impending return of the former queen of France."

Near St. Jean Pied-de-Port

At least since the Battle of Pavia, the tercio—especially when at full strength, and arranged properly in groups of three: one forward, two to each flank—had dominated the battlefield. To serve in a tercio was the highest aim of every honorable Spanish soldier; many in the ranks were volunteers, and some had foregone higher positions in other, less prestigious formations to march beneath the Cross of Burgundy. Despite the occasional setback, the tercio had demonstrated superiority over many opposing deployments, and the best of them were proof against concerted cavalry assaults.

In the space of ninety minutes south of St. Jean Pied-de-Port, that reputation was utterly and completely torn to pieces.

With his cavalry in tatters, García Salcedo began to slowly advance his heavily armed infantrymen. The men in the *mangas* carried snaphaunce muskets, many of them custom-made and beautifully built; but they knew very well that beyond sixty or seventy yards, a shot fired from their weapons was a waste of ammunition. They were under orders to hold their fire until the enemy was close.

Many of them died with their muskets in their hands, still waiting the order to fire.

The well-trained pikemen in the main body of each tercio continued to advance, perhaps confident in the expectation that they would be able to push back the enemy.

But when they came within a hundred and fifty yards, they arrived in the accurate range of the Cardinal rifle. Every fifteen seconds thereafter—and their march rate required nearly two minutes to reach the French line—roughly two thousand rounds were poured into their front ranks. For almost a minute their advance remained steady, despite the casualties: it was at this point that Turenne gave some thought to ordering his men to retire, to make the *alaberderos* have to cover even more ground to reach their enemy. But the decision was made for him; first the understrength infantry on the wings, and then the proud *Infantería de Navarra*, began to break and run. Once begun, the greatest commander on Earth could not stop it.

His tiny cavalry force was eager to charge into the fray to cause the rout to continue, but Turenne refused to issue any such order. Instead, he directed them to find Garcia Salcedo and capture him, along with any other officers they might turn up.

By the time the sun was low on the horizon, de la Mothe had turned up at the marshal's field tent, escorting three Spanish officers. They looked dusty and tired, as if they had been in the thick of the fight; one had a bandage wrapped around his head.

Turenne stood when they entered. The officer with the bandaged head carefully removed his hat and bowed. He was a veteran, perhaps ten years older than Turenne. He looked a bit surprised at the age of his opponent.

"May I ask," he said in passable French, "to whom I have the honor of speaking?"

"I am Henri de la Tour d'Auvergne, Comte de Turenne," the marshal said. "Are you the commander of the Spanish forces?"

"What remains of them." He slowly drew his sword from its scabbard and handed it, hilt first, to Turenne. "I am Don José Garcia de Salcedo, in service to His Most Catholic Majesty Felipe Cuatro."

Turenne took the sword, examined it, and then offered it back to Garcia Salcedo. "Your men fought bravely today, señor. If you will permit, my medical staff will assist them. With respect, I must ask that you remain as our guest."

"You will not accept my parole."

"Regrettably, not at this time. But I am sure that the matter will be satisfactorily resolved in due course."

Garcia Salcedo seemed only mildly disappointed with this answer. His command was in tatters, and it was clear that he was not in any particular hurry to return to Spain and explain it to his master.

"You have committed an act of war against the government of Spain," he said at last. "I hope you are prepared to defend it."

"It is not we who have begun this conflict, Don José," Turenne answered. "We are on the sovereign territory of France; you launched an attack upon us. You, señor, have committed the act of war, and what you have to show for it is a shattered command and the regrettable deaths of many honorable men. And your sword. I hope you are ready to justify it."

"To—to whoever you claim is the rightful king of France?"

"No, Don José," Turenne said. "To His Most Catholic Majesty. I expect he will demand a *personal* reckoning."

Part Four

The Virtue of Justice

Unto every man, his just due

Chapter 39

June, 1636
Magdeburg

Gustav Adolf, King of Sweden, Emperor of the United States of Europe, rose to his full height more quickly and suddenly than anyone else in the paneled conference room would, or could, have expected.

"He said...*what?*"

Ed Piazza barely kept himself from smiling. Estuban Miro was more uncomfortable, and less amused.

"According to Colonel Hand," Miro said, "Monsieur Gaston—'King Gaston,' as he now styles himself—accused us of harboring Her Majesty Queen Anne and her infant child in our territory."

"And *are* we doing so?"

"No, Your Majesty," Miro said. "At least not so far as I know."

"You are now the spider at the center of the web, Don Estuban, since Francisco Nasi moved to Prague. I realize that you are newly come to this position"—Gustav

Adolf smiled thinly—"which is in any event not yet an official position so long as Wettin remains prime minister. Still, I must ask: how soon can I assume that you know what is happening everywhere in our sovereign lands?"

"At all times?"

"That would be my preference," Gustav Adolf said. "Do I underestimate you?"

"I cannot say," Miro answered. "I thank Your Majesty for your appreciation of my talents, but no one can have that level of expectation. Still, as far as I can tell, Queen Anne has not sought asylum in the USE, and we have not granted it."

"Then why does the self-styled king of France issue this accusation?"

Don Estuban looked at Piazza, who shrugged. "From what I've been able to determine," Ed said, "Gaston's motives are often muddled. But in this case I think he's throwing stones everywhere he can in the hopes of flushing his quarry."

The emperor resumed his seat. "I suspect you're right. The queen worries Gaston not for herself but because of her child—who under established French law is the rightful heir to the throne."

Miro nodded. "In essence, Gaston is demanding that we choose sides. As will Queen Anne, if she surfaces and asks us for asylum."

"And what is your advice?"

Miro looked uncomfortable. He glanced at the president of the SoTF but Piazza's face was blank of any expression.

"I think you should really ask the prime minister's advice, Your Majesty," Miro said.

"I already have," Gustav Adolf replied curtly. "Two

hours ago. Now I want your advice." He swiveled his head to bring Piazza into his blue-eyed gaze. Rather cold gaze, at the moment. "And yours, Edward."

"I think we should refuse to respond to Gaston's accusation one way or the other. Simply send him a note to the effect that this is not our affair. The dispute over the succession is an internal matter to the kingdom of France, with which we are not at war."

The emperor's head swiveled back to Miro. "And you?"

"I agree with President Piazza, Your Majesty."

Gustav Adolf grunted. "Regardless of what official stance we take, what do you think? Surely we think this child is the rightful king of France?"

"If we decide that's true," Piazza said, "and act on it, that would certainly count as us 'taking sides' in the matter."

"Yes," Gustav said. "It would. I likely do not need to ask what the fate would be for Queen Anne and the child if they were returned to the custody of Gaston."

Neither Miro nor Piazza made any reply.

The emperor rose to his feet again. The movement, this time, was relaxed. "As it happens—not really to my surprise—your advice matches that given to me by Wilhelm Wettin. So, having to the best of my ability"—the grin that came here was as cold as his gaze—"maintained constitutional decorum in this odd political situation we have at the moment, I will . . . What's the proper word? Instruct? Recommend? Urge?"

Piazza smiled. "You can't go wrong with 'urge,' Your Majesty."

"Urge it is, then. I will urge the prime minister to send a diplomatic reply to King Gaston along the lines we've discussed. Then we'll wait and see how he responds. In the meantime, Don Estuban, I want you to direct all your efforts to finding Queen Anne and her entourage. And if they have entered our territory..."

The emperor scratched his cheek again, pondering the matter.

"Your Majesty?" Don Estuban said.

Gustav Adolf lowered his hand and made a short, firm gesture with it. "Take them under my personal protection. I will not have it said that I do not protect women and children in my realm."

Cambrai

France was full of toll-gates. Every bridge, every sorry excuse for a turnpike, every branching of the road seemed to have some stout peasant with a half-rusted halberd or pike left over from his grandfather's time waiting for passers-by, intending to demand a few *sous* to let a carriage and horsemen pass. In many cases, Jacques-de-Péage would see a few well-armed riders and a well-built carriage and decide to raise the little gate and just let them pass—but others were resolute, full of bluff and vigor, claiming ancient right and royal leave to operate their business. *Honored Monsieur, it is upon my honor to earn daily bread for my family.*

Vendôme would have run them down with a firm charge, but Mazarin was usually willing to pay the small fee and pass. It was better to go unnoticed than to attract more attention.

In the midst of a summer thunderstorm, the queen's

entourage crossed the border between France and the Low Countries. The scenery, such as it was, did not change any more than the weather. Within the carriage, the little king slept and his mother dozed, while Katie and the duchess of Chevreuse took turns alert, in case either of their charges needed assistance.

Mazarin drove the carriage, sheltered under a heavy cape, while Achille rode with the duc de Vendôme and his sons on horseback. It was no understatement to say that they did not trust the nobleman's change of heart. Mazarin would have preferred that the knight of Malta be the driver; he was still hobbled from the wound he had received at Amiens. But he praised the medical attentions of Katie Matewski and dismissed Mazarin's fears.

"On horseback I don't need to walk," he had said, "and even with one leg I'm twice the swordsman and three times as good a shot as you are."

Even if he thought that Achille would bend to suggestion, he wasn't disposed to argue.

When they stopped to rest and water the horses, Mazarin made sure to position himself between the carriage door and where Vendôme and Achille stood, out of the rain, rubbing down their mounts. He made no attempt to conceal it, and finally the duke looked at him and said, "You don't trust me, Monseigneur Mazarin."

"I will not deny it."

"Your queen has made up her mind. I would have thought that was good enough for you."

"I don't intend to defend myself to her based on your insinuations, my lord. You will forgive me for being suspicious: you are a soldier, and an experienced one."

"Meaning?"

"A raw recruit is easy to read, I should think. If you meant harm to the queen, you would have taken some action already. But as an experienced campaigner, you could be playing the long game."

"I have declared upon my honor that I am her man. She has accepted me."

"Yes," Mazarin answered. "She has. I have registered my objections, and she has noted them."

"And ignored them."

"Regrettably. I hope she does not rue her decision, or worse yet, find it a fatal mistake."

"Are you trying to provoke me? Because if I were... less of an experienced campaigner, as you say, I might feel that you impugn my honor."

"I do not think we should be discussing your *honor*, Your Grace. Your honor was unaffected when you killed the king of France."

"That was a mistake, as I explained. And it pains me greatly."

"Forgive me for being skeptical."

"Are you going to make an issue of this on a continuing basis, Monseigneur?"

"No," Mazarin answered. "But as the queen's life is in my care, I intend to make sure to whatever extent I am able that you have no opportunity to do her harm. It may not be your goal; but I will not take the chance that you are deceiving her. And us."

Vendôme did not answer right away; he focused on his horse's tack. Finally he turned around to look at Mazarin directly.

"I will do as I have promised," he said at last. "And there will be a reckoning for you, Monseigneur.

Not here, and not now; not until after the queen has been escorted to a place of safety. But there will be a reckoning.

"I hope that, under the cloak of sanctity that accompanies your priestly vows, you are still a man."

With their arrival in the Spanish Netherlands, there had been some discussion regarding secrecy—whether the queen should travel openly, revealing that she had been pursued by the agents of a usurper king. Vendôme had been in favor of the idea: he argued that they were now beyond Gaston's reach, and that conducting themselves as fugitives was undignified at best and suspicious at worst. Both Mazarin and Achille believed the opposite. Gaston might well be in league with the Spanish; certainly his mother had always favored warm relations with the Hapsburgs. If the duc de Vendôme wanted to travel openly, Mazarin was more than happy to be a part of his entourage rather than the queen's. Due to his services across the continent after his exile from France, he was well-known, or feared, or both.

So they came to Cambrai, a fortified town. They entered through the Porte Saint-Denis on the south side, with the rain still falling but reduced to a depressing drizzle; in the lee of a covered archway near the church of St. Géry, Mazarin climbed down from the driver's seat and into the carriage to consult with his queen.

"We should try to find a hostel, Majesty," he said. "It'll be dark soon."

Anne had pulled the carriage curtain aside, admitting a wan, gray light into the passenger compartment.

The air outside was damp and muggy and stank of city; inside it was hot and still and smelled of nursery. The king was sleeping peacefully in the arms of the duchess of Chevreuse, who looked sweaty and tired.

"I am very tired, Jules," Anne said.

"I can imagine. The road—"

"No. You misunderstand." She folded her hands in her lap. "I am tired of running and hiding. I am tired of looking over my shoulder for the next agent of my brother-in-law. I think that it is time we changed tactics."

"We discussed this."

"We did. And I agreed with you at the time, believing that . . . the other opinion was wrong." She had not quite brought herself to mention César de Vendôme by name, or address him directly since she had taken his oath. She would sometimes spare a look or a word for one of his sons, but she kept the father at a distance.

"Has something changed, my Queen?"

"I have tried to comfort myself with prayer, seeking reassurance that my aunt will receive and protect us. Now that we are in the Low Countries and coming closer, I am unsure."

"There aren't very many choices."

"No. That is absolutely true. We are . . . I feel as if we are at the edge of a precipice, Jules. Behind us are advancing enemies, beyond is a yawning gulf. Nothing is certain."

"That he is king is certain," Mazarin said, gesturing toward the sleeping child. "All of what we do, and much of what we have become, depends on that. I assume that you are firm in that belief."

"From what we are told," she answered, carefully

omitting any reference to Vendôme, "the people of France rejoiced when Gaston received the crown and was proclaimed king. They regard him as in many ways the sort of king that France needs: energetic, assertive, clever, devoted to his queen and... fertile. In short, everything Louis was not. Whether that perception is correct or incorrect may be beside the point. To throw the realm into conflict now might simply be irresponsible."

The gray light from outside etched Anne's face in light and shadow. She was not presentable as queen regent: her hair was wrapped in a tignon, she wore little jewelry—but she was still regal for all that. Yet at this moment, on this afternoon in this place, it seemed to Mazarin that the defiance had somehow drained from her, to be replaced by nothing more than acute sadness—she was advancing the very argument she had so angrily rejected just a few days earlier at Rumigny.

"He has attributes that his brother did not possess, Majesty," Mazarin said. He reached out to her, and she took his hand in her two, letting a handkerchief fall into her lap. Her hands were damp, and he could see that she had given in to tears. "But he is *far* from the king your husband was. Louis was just, he was noble; he cared about France much more than Gaston will ever do. You say that he cares about his wife; but in the end, Gaston cares most about *himself*."

"There are times in the last twenty years, Jules, that the same could be said about my husband."

"I will not speak ill of the dead, my lady."

"No." She let go of Mazarin's hands and picked up her handkerchief. "No, you're right. But I want to approach my aunt Isabella more carefully. Throwing ourselves into her arms is not a position of strength. She would not hand us over to Gaston, but she might convey us to my brother the King of Spain. In either case, my son's fate would be in someone else's hands."

"Then what would you like me to do? You know that I am at your service in all things."

"The archbishop of Cambrai is a Jesuit, a man from Utrecht named Van der Burch. He was confirmed in his see in Ghent, and then here by my uncle Albert when he was governor of the Netherlands before the war. I have never met him, but I believe he could be a trustworthy intermediary between myself and my aunt Isabella."

"So you wish to put us under the protection of an archbishop you've never met who is a protégé of a deceased uncle who surely considered himself an enemy of France, in a city you've never visited."

"He is a Jesuit," Anne said. "A logical thinker. It would hardly behoove someone in his position to conduct himself in any improper manner. He would receive me as a queen. Not looking like *this*," she added, allowing herself a small smile. "And at my request would convey a letter to my aunt on my behalf."

"He is indeed a Jesuit," Mazarin said. "They are schooled to conceal their feelings and shroud their intentions. That is something to fear, Majesty, and I would hesitate to trust him. But . . ."

"But?"

"But if you believe that this is what we should do, then you have my unqualified support. If you wish to be presented to the archbishop of Cambrai as the queen mother and king of France, then I shall compose a letter on your behalf and deliver it in person."

"You're not going to try to convince me otherwise?"

"All of the arguments I have presented have already been made, madame. All of the evidence has been considered. If this is your decision, I will abide by it and do everything I can to carry it out. Because... in the end, I am as tired as you are."

Chapter 40

Paris

The marquis de Mirabel and his staff were already absent from the city by the time King Gaston emerged for his *lever* and summoned him. There was a diplomatically phrased note sealed with the arms of His Most Catholic Majesty, conveying—with respect—the regret that Spain contemplated a state of war between itself and France.

The duc d'Épernon and comte de Chavigny were next sent for, to meet with the king in the *Conseil* room. The general and chancellor arrived at the same time, and paused for just a moment before entering, as if they were evaluating each other.

The curtains were still drawn, except for one that had been pulled slightly apart near where the king stood, looking out across the gardens. The room was only scantily lit.

Gaston did not turn around when they entered, but said, "Apparently Olivares has an up-timer radio."

"Sire?" Chavigny asked from near the door. He and Épernon exchanged glances again.

"Come in," Gaston said. "Close the door."

Épernon closed the door behind him. The two councilors approached the king and waited.

"You have seen the note from the marquis de Mirabel."

"It was placed in my hands, Sire," Chavigny said. "I do not understand how this came about."

"Treason." Gaston turned to face his councilors, his face suffused with fury. "A marshal of France, and apparently *another* marshal of France who had the honor to serve me on the *Conseil du Roi*, have attacked Spanish troops in direct defiance of my orders."

"Marshal Bassompierre—" Épernon began, but Gaston cut him off with a gesture.

"He was *ordered*," Gaston said, "to take command of the force of 'Marshal' Turenne, and march it north. Apparently he has been suborned. I should never have sent him: he is old and weakly willed. And now—and now we may be in a state of war with Spain."

"Where did this battle take place, Majesty?" Épernon asked.

"In Béarn, Monsieur le duc."

"Spanish troops were on French soil?"

"*Yes*," Gaston said. "Yes. They were to travel to the Netherlands with my consent."

"I . . ." Épernon was at a loss for words. "Sire, I do not recall any direction in the *Conseil* that we would permit—"

"*I* permitted!" Gaston interrupted angrily. "I directed that it be done. The Spanish are our *allies*, Jean-Louis, our co-religionists. We should not be attacking them.

And yet—somehow—we have done so. And now we are at *war*."

"Is there anything remaining of the force, Sire?" Chavigny asked. "The Spaniards—"

Gaston laughed, an angry, bitter sound. "I know what you are thinking, Léon. *What stands in the way of the mighty tercios?* Never fear. Apparently, according to Mirabel—who hears from his master Olivares—who received a report from the Spanish commander—the French were utterly victorious. There *are* no Spanish troops rampaging across the countryside, neither cavalry nor infantry.

"I would rejoice more greatly in the superiority of French arms if I did not take note that our country is *surrounded* by Hapsburg territories in Italy, in the Low Countries, and across the Pyrenees. When word of this spreads, there will be tercios on every border. It is a disaster, and I am waiting to hear what advice you will offer."

"We...defeated the Spanish," Épernon said.

"We did."

"If I may ask, Your Majesty," he said, "what possible reason would you have for permitting Spanish tercios on French soil? I appreciate your sentiments regarding *rapprochement* with Spain...but the idea is fraught with danger. Once here, they might never leave."

"I was assured that they would."

"I am hesitant to put any confidence in that assurance, Majesty."

"You are suggesting that the Spanish ambassador is a liar?"

"In a word," Épernon said, "yes." As Gaston's face

grew even more angry, he hurried on. "For decades, the Spanish have wanted to place military force on French soil. I am unable to think of any possible reward that would be worth the danger."

"The marquis de Mirabel informed me of the location of our errant traitor Queen Anne," Gaston said. "In return—"

"Why does that matter?" Épernon interrupted. The impropriety of interrupting the king was so surprising that it stopped Gaston in his tracks. "Sire, you are the king. Anne is the wife of your late brother, and of no consequence. You would trade . . ."

"You do not approve? I do not need your approval."

"Are you dismissing me from your service, Sire?"

"Do you have no interest in serving me?"

"If you do not require my advice before such a decision, and if you cannot tolerate my disapproval after the fact, my King, then I must answer that I do not."

"This is a good day for it, then. Go. You are dismissed, and you should thank me for my indulgence that I do not punish you for your insolence."

Épernon appeared to be ready to reply, but instead kept silent. He bowed and withdrew, passing through the door and closing it behind him, leaving the king and his chancellor alone.

"Sire," Chavigny said. "If I may ask."

"You too?"

"I am your loyal servant, Majesty. But I am desirous of knowing as well. Queen Anne—what makes her important?"

"It is not the dowager queen," Gaston said. "It is her son. If he remains at liberty instead of coming to Paris, he will be a magnet for disaffection. If he falls into foreign hands, especially Hapsburg hands..."

"If I am not mistaken," Chavigny said, "you directed the duc de Vendôme to secure them."

"Days ago, and I have heard no reply. To be honest, my friend," Gaston answered, "I have no idea where they are—or where he is either."

Pau

Don José Garcia Salcedo was the image of a perfect *hidalgo*. Turenne had given him and his most senior officers parole within the boundaries of the chateau, where they had returned after the conclusive battle at St. Jean.

He had communicated with the count-duke of Olivares by radio—which came somewhat as a surprise to the comte de Brassac, but was completely in harmony with what Turenne would have expected from the Spanish minister. The cardinal always found Olivares a more than competent rival. Even though the Spanish court had publicly and pointedly rejected up-time technology as the work of the Devil, Olivares had ever been practical.

So. Olivares knew of the disaster that had befallen his forces; that Turenne had refused to comply with Gaston's direction, and why. When Olivares' order to Don José to return at once was declined due to his detention by his French opponent, Don José had tried and failed to conceal his relief. Still, it did not alter his swagger or his hauteur.

The communication between the defeated Spaniard

and his minister was not, of course, the most important exchange that had happened in the past few days.

"It was clear that the duc d'Orleans expected a different outcome," Servien said. He and Turenne stood on the wall of the Chateau overlooking the town. The weather was warm and dry, and the *intendant* had found it necessary to adopt a rather disreputable-looking floppy hat to keep the sun from his eyes.

"I should say so. But this amounts to raising the flag of rebellion."

"What, by telling him that you did not recognize him as king?"

"Yes, that."

"Marshal," Servien said, "when you refused to surrender your command to Marshal Bassompierre at Albi, you had essentially done so. Soldiers follow orders: they do not conduct policy. In our minds we are remaining loyal to the true monarchy of France: but in Gaston's, we are a treasonous, criminal conspiracy. His orders were for your force to stand down. You did not. Accordingly—" He made a chopping gesture with his hand against his neck.

"He would have my head for refusing to let Spanish troops occupy French soil? *They* attacked *us*."

"You should consider yourself lucky, my lord," Servien said. "*My* fate would be far worse." He gave the universal sign for hanging: arm up, pantomiming a rope, his head turned sideways and tongue stuck slightly out. "And that would likely be the *coup de grâce* after several episodes of colorful entertainment."

"I don't think it matters too much how one is executed. It's like dying on the battlefield—a rifle and a dagger can both kill. I'd prefer not to be dead."

"Choirs of angels—"

"Oh, spare me," Turenne said, but smiled. "So. What is done is done. The man who styles himself king of France now knows that we do not hold him in such high esteem. And our friend and host the comte de Brassac has consulted with his friends of the Blessed Sacrament; it seems that the Spanish ambassador has taken his leave after informing Monsieur that Spain is contemplating a state of war with France."

"Minus three tercios. Tell me, Marshal: do you expect further incursions by Spanish troops crossing the Pyrenees?"

"No, not as long as we remain here. The danger might be greater from the forces in the Low Countries."

"I would not be so sure of that," Servien said. "Cardinal Richelieu had begun to speculate that the 'King in the Low Countries' was not at all in alignment with Spanish Hapsburg aims, and might be seeking his own way."

"I assume he did not rely on that."

"No, nor did he in any wise consider Fernando a potential ally. It merely meant that there would be three Hapsburgs in Europe instead of two, or one. Even if Philip of Spain cannot count on his cousins in Austria and the Netherlands, it does not make them any more likely to be friends of France."

"So what do you suggest, *Monsieur l'Intendant*? Shall we remain here and settle down to till the good earth?"

"I think we will have to wait until we receive direction."

"From the Company of the Blessed Sacrament?"

"Or someone."

"Meaning..."

Servien did not answer, but turned away, shading his eyes with his hand from the sun, since the disreputable hat did not completely serve the purpose. After a few moments of silence, Turenne turned and walked away.

Chapter 41

Cambrai

It was almost too difficult to undertake: shifting the entire focus of their situation from one of concealment and flight to one of display and presence. The weeks of travel, of constantly changing settings and makeshift sleeping arrangements, had taken their toll.

But for all that, Mazarin reflected, *she is still every inch a queen.*

The most resplendent dress in Anne's luggage had been brought out—it was the one that she had intended to wear when she and her husband returned from Beville-le-Comte after the baby was born. It was cream-colored and richly decorated with pearls, with a matching headpiece that held her hair in place and framed her face—on her entry into Paris she would have been radiant like the sun, but here she would be reserved and regal, a proud and defiant widow.

He and Achille d'Étampes de Valençay had outfitted themselves as well as they could. He wore his best soutane and cape, and Achille had the decorations and equipage of a knight of Malta. César de Vendôme had produced a clean doublet and silk blouse, and he and his sons proudly wore the arms and symbols of their house.

The king of France had been swaddled against any possible chill—it had rained in the morning and now was merely damp and almost unseasonably cool. The duchesse de Chevreuse carried His Royal Highness, and Kate Matewski followed close behind; Madame de Chevreuse had made sure to find her a suitable gown to replace her up-timer clothing.

A brief correspondence with the archbishop assured them that they would be received. Accordingly they left their lodgings near the priory of St. Agnes and made their way in procession past the church of St. Aubert, named for the patron of bakers, and into the great plaza before the church of Saint-Sulpice. A crowd of onlookers had gathered in the square—apprentices absent from their masters' work, religious men and women pausing in their devotions, vendors closing their stalls there and in the Grande Place a few hundred yards away to see the commotion.

François Van der Burch, archbishop of Cambrai, had donned his full episcopal attire, including miter and cope, and held his bishop's crook in one hand and a rosary in the other; he stood at the top of the stairs at the entrance to his cathedral, with others arrayed to his left and right. Van der Burch was nearly seventy; he had come to his see in 1619 after serving as bishop of Ghent. It might be said that, like Cambrai, the archbishop's best days were behind him—but he also knew that by choosing to publicly receive Queen Anne, he was making a statement, one he hoped would be appreciated by his patroness, Isabella Clara Eugenia, archduchess of the Low Countries, widow of his late patron Albert of Austria and aunt to the queen of France, the woman whose procession now approached the steps of his church.

It would not have been his desire to turn her away in any case. He had heard the rumors, read the proclamations, and perceived the real danger in which she found herself. Her entourage—a few loyal servants, now recently joined by the duc de Vendôme, bastard son of King Henry IV and brother to both the dead and presently enthroned kings of France—would not be enough to fend off any determined attempt to seize her and return her, against her will, to Paris (or wherever King Gaston wanted to hold her, for whatever reason). It simply could not be that hard.

For her to have avoided such a fate suggested either incompetence, or the protection of someone, or someones, unseen. Archbishop Van der Burch had wondered if it was either—or both. Vendôme, he was told, had ridden into Paris in the company of Gaston and had stood by him when he was crowned and enthroned at Reims a few weeks later; why was he here now?

The archbishop had sent a trusted messenger on a fast horse to Brussels, to present the tidings to the king in the Lowlands and the Infanta Isabella. He certainly *might* have waited for their Majesties' reply before acting, but time was fleeting away—and he didn't want a body of armed men to arrive at the Porte Saint-Denis (or for that matter any other gate of his city) demanding the queen's person and menacing dire consequences for failure to comply. If it was to be his problem, he was going to embrace it—and then hand it to someone else as soon as might be possible.

Brussels

The messenger from Cambrai arrived as Archduchess Isabella of the Low Countries had just sat down to her evening meal, a blanket tucked across her lap and a shawl draped over her shoulders. It was usually warm at this time of year, but even the younger folk in the Coudenberg complained about the draftiness of the palace. For her it was just another indication of her advancing age.

As if I need to be reminded, the archduchess thought to herself, looking down at the bowl of soup set before her.

But even before she could apply her spoon, a gentleman-in-waiting entered, bowing and apologizing for the intrusion. If anything, it was welcome: she had let her thoughts chase themselves around in her mind and needed the interruption. No need to let him know that, of course.

"Can I not be left even to *eat* in peace?"

The young man cringed very slightly, but, undeterred, walked to her dining table, bowed, and offered a sealed envelope in one gloved hand, then stepped back and waited.

"Well?" she said, picking up the envelope and

examining it. The seal bore the impression of the double-headed eagle, claws extended, with the escutcheon in its center...

"The messenger awaits your reply, Your Grace."

"Young monsieur," she said, laying her spoon carefully on the table and fixing him with her gaze—said to frighten lesser men; to his credit he did not look away. *Good*, she thought. *Duty before fear.* "If this is a matter of importance, I shall certainly compose a reply at once. When I do," she continued, gesturing toward the little bell in close reach, "I shall ring for you. In the meantime you have leave to go."

Shoo, she almost added, but did not. He looked almost relieved to be dismissed; he bowed again and withdrew.

She had been looking at correspondence before being settled for dinner, so a letter-opener was conveniently in reach. She took it up and carefully slit open the envelope.

Before she had read half of the letter, she had rung for the young man and asked for her nephew, the king in the Low Countries, to attend her.

"No," Isabella insisted. "It is far more than that. We are making a *statement*, Fernando, and it is a statement that cannot be unmade."

"Giving refuge to my royal sister and her child is a statement? Aunt, we have given refuge to Queen Marie, to Monsieur Gaston himself—this is only the latest instance of French royalty seeking a place to stay due to a dispute in our neighbor's realm."

"You are overlooking the obvious."

Fernando leaned back in his chair and crossed his

arms. "Very well, madame: what *obvious* part of this business am I missing?"

"You have read the pronouncements from Monsieur Gaston, I trust. He considers Anne an outlaw, a traitor and possibly complicit in the death of her husband. Yes, yes, I know it's unlikely, especially the last part," she said, waving her hand before Fernando could reply. "But Gaston has made overtures of peace to my nephew in Madrid. Who is also your brother. An affront to Gaston might be seen as an affront to Spain."

"I did not realize that we were now concerned with affronts to my royal cousin, Aunt. As I see it, we are simply exercising Christian charity."

"Oh, for the love of God!" Isabella snapped. "Whether you think so or not, whether Lady Anne thinks so or not, we will be *taking sides*. And when we choose a side, we make ourselves friends with some and enemies of others. It represents a final, definite break with Madrid. You wanted the Netherlands to be separate? We will be. We will be a third Hapsburg principality—not Spanish, not Austrian."

Fernando thought about it for a moment, then said, "It means work for our diplomats, for certain. Assuming we decide to offer refuge to Queen Anne."

"That is already done." She picked up the letter, as if weighing it, and laid it back on the table. "Archbishop Van der Burch has—"

Fernando held up his hand. "We have not offered anything to the queen, Aunt. The *archbishop* has given refuge to Queen Anne. We must properly respond to His Grace's inquiry regarding our intentions, but even if you think this is the river Rubicon for us, we have not crossed it yet. We need more information."

"How do you intend to obtain it?"

"We'll send our friend Pieter Paul Rubens," Fernando said, smiling. "He'll enjoy admiring his own work in Saint-Sulpice, and he'll find out what's *really* going on."

Paris

When they came for him, it was the middle of the night.

It was an inconvenience of perhaps an hour; Tremblay had accustomed himself long since to rising at the Matins bells from Notre Dame: one would ring, bringing him out of deep sleep, and then a few seconds later the others would join. It was a testament to the unwelcome creep of old age that he was annoyed when he was awoken early.

"Jean," he said, not opening his eyes, "I shall thank you to let an old man sleep."

"Not Jean," said an unfamiliar voice. "Wake now, old man, or be dragged from your bed."

He opened one eye and saw little other than a bright lantern and a gloved hand on his arm. He could not make out any details of the man who disturbed him, nor place the voice that had spoken.

"I would ask the meaning of this intrusion, but I suspect that I would receive no courteous answer. Where is my manservant?"

"I am not directed to answer any questions. You are to accompany me, at once."

Tremblay reached slowly over and removed the hand from the sleeve of his nightshirt. "Then you will step aside for a few moments and permit me to rise and dress."

The man evidently thought this either desirable or prudent, or perhaps both. He retreated from the bedside toward the doorway, and in the glow of the lantern and the light of the shrouded moon Tremblay could make out three or four indistinct shapes; a welcome party had apparently come to fetch him.

He decided at once that he had no intention of being intimidated. He swung his legs onto the floor, and began the process of getting dressed. Once his sandals were on and he was ready to leave, he made sure to arrange the pectoral cross so that it hung properly.

He thought about feeding the cat, but it was nowhere to be found. *Too bad,* he thought. *There seem to be rats about.*

"Since no questions will be answered, I will not ask if I may make use of the chamber pot. Very well, I am ready to go wherever you wish to take me."

"I expected more resistance," the man said, holding the lantern so that his face was visible. Tremblay recognized him, but could not recall a name—a former member of the Cardinal's Guard, a recent addition he thought.

"Yes, I imagine that would have given you no end of entertainment. Now how would it look if you brought me—wherever you propose to bring me—and delivered me in damaged condition?"

"It would look as if I were diligent and fastidious."

"I suspect that you flatter yourself, monsieur. Since you haven't chosen to murder me in my bed, I think that whoever summons me cares even less about your skill than about my condition. Now take me to him—or is it *her*?"

The man flinched very slightly when Tremblay said *her*, which confirmed his suspicions at once. This midnight intrusion was not an arrest—it was an abduction.

He reached into a pocket, which immediately made two of the other men reach for their swords; he very slowly withdrew a well-worn wooden rosary.

"You wouldn't deny me the right to pray, I assume?" Tremblay said, allowing himself a tight smile. "Oh, forgive me. You do not answer any questions."

His three captors were all former Cardinal's Guard, all inducted in the last year; no doubt one or more had been placed by someone—an agent of Gaston, or of one of the many other plotters against Richelieu, or even the king himself—*the king*, he thought: *Louis, of fond memory, the last king we have had; not his brother who falsely claims crown and throne.*

Does he know that his mother is taking this action? Did he command it—or will he find out about it after the fact?

There was the obligatory closed carriage, intended—he supposed—to conceal their destination. That was utter folly. He could have been hooded like a criminal headed for the gallows and he would have been able to tell them where he was at almost every turn. Some of the journey was intended to confuse him, he thought; he sat serenely, fingering his rosary, but he knew this was unlikely to be pleasant.

When the carriage finally arrived at its destination, one of the former Guardsmen drew out a hood, but Tremblay held up his hand.

"We are at the Grand Châtelet," he said. "If this little exercise was intended to conceal that fact from me, then I think we can dispense with it."

"Our orders were—"

"Oh, very well. If your mistress wishes to subject me to further indignity, have at it."

They pulled the hood over his head and pulled him roughly to his feet and out of the carriage, then once his feet were on the cobblestones, they pulled his hands behind his back and bound them securely. He kept hold of his rosary, clutching it tightly, but said nothing; if there was any chance to speak, it would come later, and not be addressed to these ruffians.

The Grand Châtelet was an old structure, imposing and ramshackle, dating as far back as the ninth century. The stink of blood from the slaughterhouses only deepened the sense of dread for those who were brought to it, something the *prévôt de Paris* found appropriate; the law courts met there, so that the business of criminal prosecution could be conducted conveniently for the accusing authorities.

Tremblay was led in through some side door and down a flight of circular stairs; they gripped his arms tightly and made sure that he did not trip, clearly under instruction to bring him whole. They led him along an underground corridor, where he could hear the steady drip of water, coming at last to a room where he was seated upon a stool. His hood was removed, and he found himself facing a small table holding pen, ink and parchment, a beeswax candle that gave the only light in the room, behind which sat Marie de Medici, dowager queen of France. The door was drawn shut, leaving only the two of them.

He affected as much diffidence as he could summon, and was not surprised at all; it seemed to annoy her.

"Ah. *Cardinal*. So good you could join us."

"It is my pleasure, madame. Though it could have been effected in a far more comfortable manner."

"*Your Majesty*, if you please."

"*Your Eminence*, if *you* please," Tremblay said. "If we are going to insist on titles, Highness."

Marie did not seem happy with the repartee, but answered, "Oh, very well, *Your Eminence*. I am sure that you would have come to my *Palais* by invitation, but I preferred to have this little chat in private."

"And the Sieur de Saint-Brisson was more than willing to offer accommodation. Very well, Your Majesty. You have . . . summoned . . . me, and I am here. Of what shall we *chat*?"

"My son is in need of some very specific answers to some very difficult questions, and I intend to obtain them. It is clear to me that you have been at the center of intrigues against him from the moment he returned to France, so you will be able to oblige me."

"You flatter me, Your Majesty," he answered.

"No," she said, "I do not. In fact, I would be happy to drop you into the Seine. But I also do not underestimate you."

Tremblay did not respond.

"You do not seem afraid."

"You do not frighten me, as I have told you. And death does not frighten me either."

"Have I mentioned death?"

"You mentioned dropping me into the Seine. Even if I could swim, the effluence of thousands of chamber pots would probably kill me."

"You try my patience with your badinage. Very well, answer me this: where is Cardinal Richelieu, whose creature you are?"

"At the right hand of the Father, I trust."

"So he is dead."

"As far as I know. Since you have suborned former members of the Cardinal's Guard, it seems foolish to conceal that a funeral mass was held in Luçon for him some time ago, which many of the former Guardsmen attended."

"Was there a body?"

"It would have been an unpleasant sight: the cardinal was mortally wounded—along with your son the king—in April. The body is long since buried."

"If he is truly dead."

"I have no reason to believe otherwise," Tremblay said. "But I do not know. I was not there when he died—or when he was attacked. With your son the king."

Marie leaned forward, staring at him. "You are very fixed on that moment, Your Eminence."

"Should I not be? All of our lives were changed by that base attack. Yours—mine—the queen's—"

"Marguerite?"

"Anne."

"She is no longer queen," Marie said. "She is a traitor, and likely a harlot—the baby she carries with her is not by Louis. It cannot be. He is—he was—"

Tremblay waited for her to complete the sentence. If he was not in discomfort—from the ropes, from the stool, from the need to use a chamber pot—he might have waited all night.

"He was the Most Christian King of France, Your

Majesty. He was your son, and she was his wife, and he is most certainly dead by the hand of a brutal assassin."

Marie de Medici was a hard woman, Tremblay knew. She had come to France thirty-five years ago and had witnessed the murder of her husband, suffered indignities when she was removed as regent, lost a struggle of wills with Richelieu, and been forced into exile . . . and now, at last, having seen her estranged son murdered and her favored one brought to the throne, was being reminded what that meant.

Tremblay knew the assassin who had killed Louis: his own half-brother, son of Henry IV but not of Marie. He wondered if she had been complicit—or if not, if she even realized who had done the deed. If so, she was frighteningly ruthless; if not, he could even find some sympathy for her after all this time, after all she had done.

"I do not need to be instructed on that subject," she said at last.

"The cardinal, even if alive, has fallen, Your Majesty. I do not follow his orders any longer. Those that fear that he has engineered some great and dangerous plot are afraid of their own shadow. It seems to me that France has greater threats than the ghost of Cardinal Richelieu."

She stood up and smoothed her skirts, then walked around the table to stand before him. "Do you know where the harlot queen is, your Eminence?"

"I know that she was in Amiens," he said. There was no point in dissembling.

"She is in Cambrai," Marie said. "She has been received with all due ceremony by the archbishop, in the company of—among others—the duc de Vendôme, my—stepson."

Tremblay could not keep surprise from his face. "Vendôme? But he is—"

"Yes? He is *what*, exactly?"

He killed your son, Tremblay thought. *And my master.* "He was . . . in attendance on King Gaston."

"Apparently he has chosen another side. He was never to be trusted, just as you are not to be trusted."

"Meaning—"

"Meaning, *Your Eminence*"—and this time she coated the title with particular scorn when she spoke it—"that you can be assumed to be telling lies at every turn. But don't worry; there are ways of extracting the truth."

"You would not dare harm a prince of the church. Hauling me here, even binding my hands, is a matter of indignity—but physical harm to a priest seems beyond you. *Your Majesty*," he added, trying to match the scorn he had heard.

"I rather suspect you're right," she said. "But I don't think it will come to that. Guard," she said, raising her voice slightly, "bring in the other prisoner."

The door swung open and two of the former Guardsmen manhandled another man into the room. Tremblay swiveled himself around on the stool to see.

Between two of his captors was the bound figure of Jean d'Aubisson, who had not been treated as gently as Tremblay himself.

From over his shoulder, he heard Marie de Medici say, "I'm sure this fine young man will tell us everything he knows. Or *you* will, to save him."

Chapter 42

Cambrai

When he arrived in Cambrai, Pieter Paul Rubens was not completely sure what to expect.

It had been some time since he had been in this part of the Low Countries. The infanta had impressed upon him the gravity of the mission—what mission recently had *not* been pregnant with significance?—but this was interesting enough, if only because he could view his own work in the church of Saint-Géry. It was twenty years since he had painted "La Mise au Tombeau" under the patronage of Albert, with his dear departed wife Isabella Brant as the model for Mary Magdalene. The course of his life and career had not brought him back to the city since.

He came through the gate without fanfare or reception. As with painting, so with diplomacy: it was important to study the subject, to see the setting and judge the light, before beginning to prepare the palette. Cambrai itself was not revelatory—it was a walled city like any number of other walled cities: full of churches, smells, thieves, and alleys with light and dark—a framework for memories and a breeding ground of new ideas. Without official recognition as the emissary of the archduchess, Pieter Paul Rubens was a face in the crowd, far more an observer than an object of observation.

Three hours after his entry into Cambrai he went into the archiepiscopal palace to present his credentials. The archbishop's clerk was standoffish until he looked at the name on his warrant, then advanced through surprise to eventually achieve obsequiousness. He was taken at once to the private apartments and was presented to the cleric Jules Mazarin, who was the personal representative of Isabella's niece, the French queen Anne.

"Mynheer Rubens," Mazarin said. "My mistress is very pleased to hear that you are in Cambrai."

They had taken seats on a bench in an atrium within the grounds of the archiepiscopal residence attached to Saint-Sulpice. The last few days had been typical late-spring weather in the Low Countries, but today it was fine and clear; the carefully tended trees provided pleasant shade, there was a gentle breeze, and the sounds and stink of Cambrai were muted and distant.

"Not pleased enough to greet me personally."

"If you feel slighted," Mazarin answered, "please accept my apologies. It was thought best that I receive you first."

"It takes more than that to slight *me*," Rubens said.

"I am gratified to hear it."

"Would you prefer to conduct this interview in French?" The cleric nodded; his Dutch might be good, but this was a diplomatic negotiation, and Rubens was equally comfortable in that language. "May one be so bold to ask what position you occupy in Her Highness's household?"

"We have not advanced to the point of having titles, Mynheer—Monsieur—Rubens. We are all at the *lever* and the *coucher*."

"I appreciate that the queen has a...smaller entourage. I am merely curious to know how you come to be a part of it."

"I don't know why it's important."

"It is a detail. Details matter."

"I assume that Her Grace provided you with a list of questions. It would be helpful if I was aware of what she would like to know."

"The archduchess charged me with some general instructions, not any list. I am trusted to develop my own questions."

"Regarding my role in the queen's household."

"There have been rumors..."

"Eh, *oui*? What sort of rumors?"

"Monseigneur Mazarin. You may bear a clerical collar but you, like myself, are a man of the world. Suddenly, their Majesties are blessed with the gift of a child—just as the king is murdered and the queen flees the country."

"I sense that there is some accusation at the end of your analysis."

"No—not truly. It is merely a sketch, not a full portrait. I just find it all suspicious. So indeed does Archduchess Isabella, and His Majesty the king in the Lowlands. I realize—they realize—that blood ties are a matter of responsibility and of honor, but welcoming your mistress at the court in Brussels is a *political* statement. There is an enthroned and crowned king in Paris, and while he accords no status to your mistress—"

"To the queen. You seem very hesitant to use that expression, Monsieur Rubens. Is that not how Her Majesty is called at the court in Brussels? I remind you that she is an infanta of Spain as well."

Rubens looked away at the gardens, a bucolic refuge for the archbishop and his guests. Somewhere, behind some wall, was Anne of Austria, the widow of King Louis XIII of France. If all that he had heard was true, she was truly an aggrieved party: neglected, denigrated, denied what queens most desired: status, honor... *children* ... and at the moment that she would have had all of the first two because of the blessing of the third, a cruel and violent act took her husband away.

What should she have done? She had been in seclusion awaiting the birth of the royal child. She could have traveled to Paris, played the part of the widow, garnered sympathy and found protection. Surely there was one strong voice to speak on her behalf.

Except...

The archduchess—an infanta herself—had made something very clear to Rubens before sending him on his way. *Anne claims that Gaston is a usurper,* she had told him. *She bases this claim on the assertion that her son is the legitimate heir of Louis. That means that this infant is the king of France, not the schemer who sits on its throne.*

Before we acknowledge that as truth, we must be very sure of the ground we stand on. Very sure. She had fixed him with her fierce, flinty gaze. _Do you understand, Pieter?_

He understood.

"If the lady's child is true issue," he said, "then Her Grace will ask an uncomfortable question—when was it conceived? When did the king lay with his wife?"

"You're really asking that question."

"Yes. I really am."

"I cannot say for sure."

"That's not really good enough, Monseigneur—"

"I cannot say _for sure_," Mazarin repeated, interrupting Rubens. "But to the best of my knowledge, the king shared the queen's bed on the night of August the twenty-fifth, the Feast of Saint Louis at the Château de Saluce during their progress to Fontainebleau."

Mazarin looked directly at him, the assurance of truth animating his personality and features. It was a piece of information that Rubens had not possessed, and that Archduchess Isabella had also not known.

"She will swear to this, I presume."

"On any copy of Scripture or holy relic you choose, monsieur. She will attest to it on her honor as a mother, as a queen, and as a scion of the House of Hapsburg. She will assert it today and tomorrow and as long as she draws breath. Her Grace the archduchess of the Low Countries may choose to ignore it, dismiss it, or set it aside for the sake of political expediency, but it will not make it less true. Will that be sufficient for your mistress to do the right and proper thing—or must we seek succor elsewhere?"

Pau

"I still think this is unnecessary," Brassac said to Turenne.

"I understand your confidence in your personal honor, monsieur," the marshal answered. "But you and Monsieur Servien will be much safer in the company of Colonel Maddox and her Rangers. They have served their purpose here, as my advance guard and scouts. I think deploying them as an escort for you now is a good use of their particular talents."

"Surely you still need advance guards and scouts."

"Not as much as you need them."

"And again, I disagree as to the need."

"Monsieur le Comte." Turenne rubbed his forehead. "Your informant in Paris says that the cardinal de Tremblay has gone missing—in the *city*, where your Company is strongest. There is some chance that Monsieur Gaston is on the lookout for the Company's superior. I feel obligated to protect you the best I am able."

"In the countryside?"

"*Especially* in the countryside. Maybe not within a day's ride of Pau, but certainly beyond that. Everyone with anything to gain or lose will be choosing sides, and if anyone believes that you have chosen a side opposing theirs, monsieur, they will not hesitate to do violence to you." Turenne held up his hand as Brassac began to reply. "They will not respect your rank or your pedigree, nor will they take the time to make further inquiry."

"You think civil war is imminent?"

"No," Turenne said. "I think it is already here."

Chapter 43

Madrid

In the hazy predawn of summer, Gaspar de Guzmán,
count-duke of Olivares, knelt on the hassock in his
usual place in the nave of San Jerónimo el Real, hands
folded, his eyes cast downward. Above him, where he
did not look, the crucified Savior gazed down—the
Man of Sorrows who oversaw his own sorrows as he
passed through his own vale of tears. His master the
king was likely awake as well, listening to the Mass
from his royal bedroom above the presbytery.

The count-duke's mind was not on his devotions as
it should be. That was not the fault of his own piety.
Since the death of his daughter María ten years ago,
he had turned ever more to the solace of faith and
worship. But the earthly matters that concerned him
crowded that solace away. This morning in particular
the holy office had seemed no more than rote. It
provided no serenity and conferred no peace.

When at last the officiating priest spoke the words
Ite, missa est, he scarcely heard himself speak the *Deo*

gratias response; without noticing how he had gone from his hassock to the west end of the nave he was away and gone out of the church, not even offering his customary personal thanks.

He emerged from the long gallery into the bright morning sunlight and walked slowly into the manicured garden, nodding to the servants who gave him respectful bows as he passed. Ahead, at the fountain, he could see someone waiting for him.

"Good morning, Cousin."

"Diego," Olivares said, embracing his cousin, the Marquis of Leganés. As usual, Diego Mexía Felipez de Guzmán y Dávila was dressed all in black, only relieved by the chain and cross of the Order of Calatrava on his breast. His carefully trimmed hair and beard and freshly laundered formal attire made him a striking figure—suitable for impressing a king.

"If I am not far from the mark, Gaspar, I should say that you have no good news."

"Walk with me," Olivares said, and the two men began to stroll leisurely along the carefully tended path. Leganés was nearly ten years older and a foot taller than the *valido real*, but he made his stride correspond with the pace set by his younger cousin—to whose influence he owed much of his rank and authority. He had many questions, but waited for Olivares to begin.

"I would like to say that I had good tidings, Diego," he began at last. "But to do so would require me to dissemble. I thought matters were well in hand. After years of effort all that we desired had nearly been placed in our hands. And then..."

"And then," Leganés said, "things took a turn. I have read Mirabel's letter."

"Gaston is a snake," Olivares said, disgust in his voice.

"Surely you knew that."

"The identification and handling of snakes is a part of my brief as *valido* to His Most Catholic Majesty," Olivares answered. *"Ecce dedi vobis potestatem calcandi supra serpentes et scorpiones,* after all."

Leganés had spent more hours commanding troops from the saddle than studying his breviary, but he knew it must be a Biblical verse; he piously crossed himself, and his cousin did so as well.

"'Behold, I have given you power to tread upon serpents and scorpions,'" Olivares obligingly translated. "The Gospel according to Luke. Yes, of course I knew he was a snake. But he was *our* snake: we bought him, we paid for him. And he either betrayed us or he has lost control of his own kingdom."

"If so, then there is an opportunity. France at war with itself cannot but help Spain."

Olivares stopped walking, squinting at his elder cousin in the bright early-morning sunlight. "Truly? What do you suppose we should do, Diego? We've already chosen sides."

"I think you know what my answer would be, Gaspar. There are some problems that can only be solved by the sword."

"This is not one of them."

"Our tercios—"

"The rifles of the devil-spawned up-timers destroyed three of our tercios in Béarn three weeks ago, Diego, suffering few casualties in the process. Our swords, cousin, and our muskets and our pikes and all the rest, are stacked in an impressive, impotent pile in the camp of the army deployed just across the Pyrenees.

Instead of *solving* problems by the sword, we have shown just how impotent our swords can be."

Leganés took his time before answering. This was new information; he had known that his cousin had ordered troops to be deployed across the mountains, in accordance with the ongoing plan to "support" the new king of France. Their fate was clearly part of his cousin's ill tidings.

"Destroyed."

"Utterly. Along with elite cavalry, whose commander thought it prudent to charge massed rifles that could hit his troops with ten concentrated volleys before his men could fire a single aimed shot."

"Are there any of these riflemen on the northeast frontier with the Low Countries?"

"No, but—"

"Then we attack from that direction, Gaspar. If I leave today I could be there in a matter of weeks."

"*No*," Olivares said. "No, cousin. That is not an option. His Most Catholic Majesty's aunt and his younger brother Ferdinand have decided to choose sides as well—and not Gaston's side. My informants tell me that they are sheltering, or very soon will shelter, His Majesty's sister Anne and her infant son, whom they acknowledge to be rightful king of France."

"What does . . . his Most Catholic Majesty think of this turn of events?"

"He does not yet know."

"Surely he has informants as well."

"Not with the same means as mine. This decision was taken only a few days ago."

"Then how do you . . ."

The marquis of Leganés was not schooled in the

study of Latin, and though he was punctilious in his conduct in the highly formalized court of Madrid, he lacked much of the refinement of a courtier. But he was no one's fool, and it took scarcely more than a few seconds for him to deduce the obvious.

"And is his Most Catholic Majesty aware that you possess an up-timer device to communicate with your *well-equipped* informants? And what of His Grace Cardinal Monti—is he, too, aware of this transgression of the royal command?"

"Of course not." Monti was the papal nuncio and a consultant to the Holy Inquisition. "In either case. Monti might suspect, but I believe that a time will come when he might be glad of the facility. There's a reason he hasn't returned to his see in Milan, Diego: our Cardinal Borja doubts his loyalty and not without reason. As for the king..."

"Now we come to it, don't we?"

Olivares looked away from his cousin, back at the buildings of the *Buen Retiro*. Somewhere within the complex centered on San Jerónimo el Real, his Most Catholic Majesty, King Philip IV, was likely rising to greet the day, serene and isolated within his *cordón sanitario*, as the more cynical courtiers called it.

He knew what they thought of his royal master, and what the up-timer books said of him: that he was weak and unduly pious, prone to indecision, even brutish and stupid. In Olivares' experience he was none of those things: royal, but not autocratic; pious, but in a monarch—especially a Catholic monarch—this could only be counted a virtue; decisive when he was presented with clear and honest information, which was always Olivares' intent; and though he could be arbitrary, he was keenly intelligent, with good command of French and Italian and surprisingly skillful at Latin as well.

It was not Olivares' place to seek to correct any of his master's faults, any more than it was his desire to correct any of Philip's subjects' misconceptions about him.

"You misspeak, Cousin," Olivares said. "Now *I* come to it."

"And what would you have *me* do?"

"At this moment I cannot venture to say—it depends on how His Majesty takes the news I am about to impart to him. If he permits me to keep my head and my freedom, Diego, then I shall have a great deal for you to do."

He turned back to his cousin once more. "And in the meanwhile, I can only ask you to pray for me."

Paris

He had quickly learned the streets and courts of the city when he first came to serve here, and Jean d'Aubisson knew them like no one else; the others in the Guard had always sent him on errands they could not be troubled to do themselves. There were places in Paris that the other, more experienced, more *indolent* ones had never been interested in visiting.

But his time in Paris had been different: and now it stood him in good stead.

The Châtelet had been built in the time of Philip Augustus, but had fallen into great disrepair since: the mortar was set, the iron posts placed in the windows and across the entrances to the cells centuries earlier. Trust—or fear—or simple indolence had made the guards in the Châtelet confident that that cement and those posts were plenty good enough to hold the likes of an aged priest and a young former Cardinal's Guardsman as long as necessary, particularly when they had been given a good healthy beating and tossed into cells.

But if there was one thing that youngest brothers from the countryside knew how to do it was to survive and overcome a good healthy beating.

After matins bells rang and all was quiet in the Châtelet, Jean d'Aubisson began to work on the bars that secured a small window on his cell where the plaster was loose and broken. He assumed that it would take some time, perhaps several nights—but to his surprise one and then another bar came free.

He couldn't believe his luck.

The Châtelet stood at the head of the Pont du Change, and the window to his cell overlooked the Plâce du Châtelet. Once he squeezed himself through it and climbed down to the pavement, he was able to creep onto the bridge and in a matter of a few minutes he was across the Seine and into the narrow streets and dark alleys beyond.

Not all streets were narrow. Under the moonlit sky he emerged onto the Rue du Condé. He straightened his clothing as best as he could manage and approached the entrance to the Hôtel de Condé, which was guarded by two men wearing the prince's livery.

"I need to speak with His Grace," d'Aubisson said.

The guards didn't seem impressed. One chuckled, and the other lowered his pike at him and wasn't amused at all.

"And why," the angry one said, "would my lord of Condé want to speak with the likes of you? I'm thinking I should give you another beating like the one you've obviously just gotten."

"He will see me."

"He will have us whipped for wasting his time, you insolent lout. Now off with you, before—"

D'Aubisson reached inside his doublet and drew out a strip of cloth bearing a heart surrounded by rays of light. It had not been of any interest to his captors or those who took out their anger on him. He extended it toward the smiling guard, moving it slowly around the point of the other's pike.

"And what is this?"

"He will see me," d'Aubisson repeated. "I know it is late, and I know it is impertinence, but show him this. When he sees it, I will be admitted."

"And if he decides to have us whipped instead?"

"Then I will take two blows of the knout for every one delivered to you."

Smiling guard looked at menacing guard, who shrugged. Smiler reached behind him and knocked on the gate without turning around. Another guard, pike in hand, opened the gate from the inside and took the scapular from his comrade's hand and closed the gate.

"I really don't want to be whipped," Angry said.

"You won't be," d'Aubisson said. "You'll be rewarded once monsieur le prince hears what I have to say."

"And what might that be?"

"It is for the prince's ears alone," he answered. "He may impart it to you afterward, but I must do my duty first."

Angry thought about this reply, and then said,

"Duty," and spat on the cobblestones a foot from d'Aubisson's right boot.

A few minutes later there was another rap on the gate. The guard behind it opened it and beckoned to d'Aubisson.

"Well," Smiley said. "Looks like there's to be no whipping after all."

Condé reclined on a couch in his dressing-gown and cap. He had been summoned from bed, but seemed more intent than discomfited. D'Aubisson bowed respectfully and waited for him to speak.

"You look as if you've had a rough time, young Guardsman."

"Just a little knocking about, Your Grace," d'Aubisson said. "Nothing that can't be set right by a good night's rest."

"To be young again." Condé fingered the scapular that he held in his hands. "What brings you to my door?"

"I have lately been a guest of Monsieur le Prevôt in the Châtelet," d'Aubisson said. "He had the charge of myself and His Eminence the cardinal de Tremblay."

"Tremblay? In the Châtelet? Is he still there?"

"If he still lives, Your Grace. I . . . escaped on my own. There was no chance to try and rescue him. I thought perhaps you—"

"How did you come to be imprisoned?"

"It was . . . on order of the queen mother."

"Marguerite?"

"No, Your Grace."

"God's mercy—Queen Anne?"

"No. I beg Your Grace's pardon—there are too

many queens and too many queen mothers. I meant to name Her Majesty Queen Marie."

"She—she imprisoned you in the Châtelet? She has no right and no authority."

"Apparently the prevost does not care to gainsay Her Majesty. At her order we were taken prisoner and . . ." D'Aubisson spread his hands.

Condé went from reclining to standing up in one smooth motion; remarkable, d'Aubisson thought, for a man his age.

"I will have words with King Gaston about this, young man. In the meanwhile, you will consider yourself under my, and my house's, personal protection." He gestured to a servant. "See that this gentleman is fed and given comfortable accommodations, and that his injuries are treated by Monsieur Chrétien. Monsieur d'Aubisson," he added, turning back to his visitor, "you shall want for nothing while under my roof; and if you require a position, you are welcome in my household."

"Your Grace is extremely kind. I . . . would like to compliment the men who guard your gate, Sire, for their diligence and attention—and also for their sensible honesty for conveying the token of my adherence to the cause of His Eminence and yourself."

"Ah." Condé reached into a pocket of his gown and held the scapular out to d'Aubisson. "I shall make sure they are suitably rewarded."

"I thank Your Grace," d'Aubisson said, bowing. And he truly was thankful: whatever Marie de Medici had in mind for him and for the cardinal de Tremblay, he was certain that he was well clear of it now.

As so often happens, however, he was completely wrong.

Chapter 44

Brussels

Sometimes, Isabella thought to herself as she sat in the most comfortable chair in her apartments in the Coudenberg, *there is nothing to be done but to bow to the inevitable*.

In these uncertain times—and that was a kind assessment of what the world had been since the up-timers' Ring of Fire had changed it!—it had been necessary to adjust one's worldview and expectations to the realities of the current situation. Fernando had learned to adjust, though there were certainly times that she had found it necessary to prod (or, even less delicately, *shove*) him in the right direction.

Philip had not. Truly it was unclear whether he ever would. His Most Catholic Majesty was in the thrall of that creature Olivares, just as he had been ensorcelled by Olivares' predecessor, the duke of Lerma. Once Isabella had merely relegated Olivares to the status of *annoying little man*, but it had become abundantly clear that he was no mere annoyance, but a living, scheming threat. He knew that the Low Countries were likely lost to Spain's direct control; Philip, in his *cordón sanitario*, serene and unconcerned with the petty affairs of the world, most likely did not.

It is as if Charles the Fifth still stood astride the world, she thought. *As if the Hapsburgs were all one great, happy family. Those days are gone—and will likely never return.*

She glanced at her most trusted lady-in-waiting, who sat as close to the fire as she could manage without actually being closer than her mistress. The woman was drowsing, doing her best imitation of a servant interested in Isabella's well-being and comfort: letting her eyes dart this way and that, busying herself with a bit of embroidery, checking from the corner of her eye that Isabella was not looking. When she suddenly realized that Isabella was looking her way, she set the embroidery aside.

"Yes, Your Highness?"

"I should like to know," she said, "how long I am to be kept waiting to bow to the inevitable."

"Your pardon, my lady?"

"Oh, nothing," she said, waving a hand. "I am impatient."

"Yes, my lady."

"Are you saying that you disapprove of my impatience?"

"No, my lady—I mean, yes—no, I mean—"

"Never mind. You don't know how to answer, and I don't really care about your response in any case. Go find out what's keeping our guests waiting."

The lady-in-waiting stood up and arranged her

skirts and sleeves, as if anyone was actually going to take notice of her appearance, and went to the door of Isabella's sitting room. She opened it, only to find the artist Pieter Paul Rubens standing there, his hand raised as if to knock.

"Mynheer Rubens to see you, Highness," the lady said, turning and curtseying.

"Let him in," Isabella said. "And go find out what's keeping them."

The lady-in-waiting hesitated between leaving her archduchess unattended and following her orders. The orders won, and she went out the door without even a _by your leave_. Rubens closed the door behind her, and came to stand before Isabella, his hands folded in front of him, a rather more demure expression on his face.

"My niece is aware that I am old and getting older," Isabella snapped at him, but then sighed. "Is it me, Pieter, or do things simply take longer than they did when I was young?"

"I suspect not, Your Highness," Rubens answered. "Even though it might seem that way. Louis XIII's widow merely wants to make a good impression. And the little prince—"

"The little prince is scarcely two months old," Isabella said. "He cannot be expected to hold his water in the presence of royalty, nor conform to a schedule. So tell me—now that you have met her and traveled with her, what do you make of Queen Anne?"

"She is much different from what I expected," Rubens answered. "We had heard much about how beaten down she was, how meek and retiring. But she is fierce, my lady. She reminds me of someone."

"Really? Who?"

"You," Rubens said. "She is a true Hapsburg."

"I trust you mean that in a complimentary way."

"Madame. What other way could I mean it? Your Highness knows that I am your most ardent admirer— as the up-timers might say, I am your *greatest fan*."

"Once again, a compliment."

"To be sure."

"She faces difficult odds. Perhaps impossible ones. A young child—no husband—"

"But faith in God and His Son." He paused, as if considering further words, but did not add any. *You mean*, Isabella thought, *for what that is worth*.

"And is she truly the queen of France?"

"You desire to say, as opposed to merely the widow of the king of France? Oh, she's that all right, and devoted to her adopted country. I rather think that it is her brother-in-law who is devoted to the Spanish crown. Though the count-duke is none too happy with King Gaston at this moment."

"And how would you know that?"

"The Spanish lack much skill with the use of codes. Radio is still a mystery to them, and they don't realize that a broadcast from one transmitter can be received by anyone in range."

"What has Gaston done to annoy them?"

"Apparently there's been some sort of battle. Spanish troops have been defeated on French soil."

"Philip *invaded France*?"

"Not exactly . . . they did not expect any opposition. They were opposed, and handily defeated by up-timer weapons. Mirabel has left Paris; France and Spain may be at war. Which puts us—"

"As soon as we receive Queen Anne, it puts us at war with France as well. If we refuse to receive her, we turn away family. I can't see as there is any choice."

"My lady," Rubens said. "Did you not tell me that there is *always* a choice, if only we can determine what it is."

"I find a number of things annoying in my advanced age, Pieter, but ranking high among them is having my own words parroted back at me as if by some dutiful school child."

"But you admit the truth of it. She has not put us in this position; it was circumstance, and the schemes of a duplicitous prince. We are reacting to the situation. I received quite a tongue-lashing from the priest Mazarin on the subject. He asserted Queen Anne's claims for her son, and then asked me if it would be sufficient for your Highness 'to do the right and proper thing'—and I decided that it would. You told me I should make that determination and be very sure. Were you to have second thoughts at this juncture—"

"What makes you think I'm having second thoughts?"

"Your Highness is never happy when you feel that there is 'no choice,'" Rubens answered. "But as we react, we mold the situation to our own desires."

"That is a rosy face to put upon it. My grandmother used to say, 'put a silken doublet on him, and yet he is still Mynheer Pig.'"

"It sounds better in the German, I trust, Highness."

"Yes. Yes, I suppose it does. All right then—I have sent that foolish girl in search of my niece. Perhaps you could expedite matters yourself. I am ready to meet this queen of France."

✧　　✧　　✧

"No," Anne said. "Explain it to me again, if you please."

She had been pacing up and down in the anteroom for several minutes, waiting for the footman to return. A polished mirror over an ornate mantelpiece showed her image pacing as well; to Mazarin it seemed like the precise movements of a pair of royal guards at the Louvre Palace, keeping in exact step.

"It is the Archduchess's choice to proceed as she sees fit, my lady. It seems clear that she is favorably disposed toward you, but..."

"But. But she does not think my son is the king of France."

"She is very cautious."

"I would characterize her response as *cowardly*."

"To her face?"

Anne stopped her pacing and stared at Mazarin, the withering glance that she had begun to use so readily.

"Do you think I would not?"

"No," Mazarin said. He sighed and folded his hands in his lap and looked at them for a long time. "No. I think you would not. The archduchess Isabella is a formidable woman, the ruler of this land, and *your aunt*. Surely you were trained to be more courteous than that, even if the court of Paris and recent experience has made you more forthright. You need her to acknowledge you and respect you, but you need her support and protection even more. You will gain nothing by antagonizing her."

"She could keep me waiting forever."

"She could," Mazarin agreed. "Except that she does not have forever. She has had more time than the up-timer histories gave her; up-timer science has granted her that. But she hears life's clock ticking more loudly than we do. She has a political situation that needs to be considered while she is still around to affect it."

"So she hides behind politics."

Mazarin admired Anne's strength of character, but he could readily see that her patience was strained, as evidenced by her fraying temper.

"My lady, *everyone* with power and authority hides behind politics. It is impossible to avoid. If you would have her support, you must follow her direction."

Anne tried to maintain the steely glare a little longer, then she looked aside, as if her emotions were trying to overtake her and she was incapable of pushing them away. She came over and sat beside Mazarin.

"I can hear the clock ticking as well," she said.

"I know you can, my Queen. So can I." He reached over and took her hand, an intimacy she might not have permitted if they were in public—even if they were only in the presence of Anne's entourage. "But when you do at last meet with Archduchess Isabella, you will be presenting yourself as the queen mother, and Louis Dieudonné as the rightful king. You will know who you are, and whose cause you represent. She will know that as well. It will only remain for her to choose the time and the way to declare it."

"If at all."

"Oh, she *will*. I have it on good authority that though she offered a safe haven to Monsieur Gaston for a time during his exile—and to his mother as well—there is very little love between them. But unless she is ready to formally break with her nephew, His Most Catholic Majesty—Gaston's erstwhile ally—she will take no inflammatory steps."

✧   ✧   ✧

Anne was aware that her aunt had entered the Franciscan order some years earlier, and generally adopted the austere and spare habit of that sisterhood when she appeared in public: but somehow Isabella seemed far from a humble sister from some nunnery when she got her first look at the archduchess.

The clothes of the sisterhood were set off with a golden chain of office that befitted her rank. The actual ducal authority had devolved upon her nephew Fernando, king in the Low Countries, but she still seemed to affect the trappings of that power; she sat upon a chair that had been placed upon a slightly raised dais that dominated the far end of a small, ornate receiving room. The setting was far less magnificent than the audience hall, at which Anne had been afforded a brief glance; but it was certainly more private.

Only Isabella was present, along with a lady-in-waiting who seemed to be busying herself with some sort of embroidery. There was no sign of Fernando or his queen. Nonetheless, the Hapsburg arms were prominently displayed, as well as a draped portrait of Albert, Isabella's long-deceased husband.

For her part, it was not the formal presentation that Anne would have wanted, but it was not casual or intimate either—she would have to walk the length of the hall to reach the place where the archduchess sat, immobile and unsmiling. When the doors were opened and she and her son were announced—*Her Royal Highness Anne of Hapsburg and Bourbon, Dowager of France, and son*—she hesitated for several moments, looking at Achille and Mazarin, at the duchess of Chevreuse who held the sleeping child in her arms, and the other members of her entourage who would not be announced—and nearly turned to walk away.

From somewhere she gathered her will and her resolve, and began to walk forward toward her stern, aged aunt who might hold France's and her own personal fate in her hands.

You will know who you are.

Aña Maria Mauricia, daughter of Margaret of Austria and His Most Catholic Majesty Philip III of Spain. Sister of His Most Catholic Majesty Philip IV. Wife of the late Louis of Bourbon, Most Christian Monarch of France.

Mother of Louis, styled Dieudonné, Blessed of God, to be designated the fourteenth of his name, the true and rightful king of France. He is the king.

The King.

With each step she took toward her aunt, she felt her doubts drop away, that will and resolve strengthen. She walked uprightly and with slow, deliberate dignity as she had always been taught and as she knew—*knew!*—befit the queen mother, dowager or otherwise.

When she came to a point a dozen feet away she stopped and offered a polite curtsey, not as a subject to a monarch, but as an honor due to a distinguished elder. The others stopped farther back, as per arrangement with the court's master of ceremonies.

There were several seconds of silence during which Isabella moved her head only slightly as her eyes seemed to survey the scene—queen mother, entourage and all—and Anne did not look away.

"You seem rather fierce, child," Isabella said at

last, letting her stern expression soften into something more pleasant. "You may keep the fire well banked, but I can see it reflected in your eyes."

She greets me with metaphor? Anne thought. "I will not deny my anger, Your Highness," she said. "When one's husband is murdered, it is difficult to put such anger aside."

"So you have anger for the one who committed the deed. That is a relief, I daresay: I thought you were angry with *me*."

"I am angry with the one who directed the murder, Your Highness," Anne answered. She felt as if Vendôme, standing twenty feet away, was staring directly at her, but she did not look away. "As for yourself: is there a reason for me to be angry with you?"

If the question angered Isabella, she concealed it admirably.

"I have known you from afar since the day you were born," Isabella said, relaxing herself into the chair and folding her hands in her lap. "I favored the match with the young king; I saw Marie de Medici for what she truly was—what she truly *is*—a political creature, fierce as . . . you now seem to be; but she wanted what was best for France."

"It seems an attribute of queen mothers."

"I had not finished, child."

Anne felt a moment of anger, but pushed it aside and did not reply.

"As I say," Isabella continued, "I was asked about the matter, and concluded that the marriage would be for the best. When there is doubt we often palliate ourselves with foolish platitudes such as, *he will grow into the crown*. We hoped...we all hoped... that Louis would learn the roles of king and husband."

Anne did not reply until Isabella made a slight gesture. "He did, madam. I dispute any assertion to the contrary."

"Yes. Yes, he did. Of course. But he is gone now, child, and we must all deal with the consequences. It seems that his brother has made different choices: and it seems that he has little use for you or your son."

"The rightful king."

Isabella tensed, and Anne thought that she would receive another reproof; but instead Isabella looked down at her hands folded in her lap, as if there was an answer there.

"I know what you want from me," she said at last. "My dear, please do not think otherwise. You desire formal recognition of your infant son's claim as rightful king of France. I will be honest: it is not possible to extend that recognition at this time. It is not out of malice or spite. A daughter of the House of Hapsburg has been grievously tried by a ruthless scoundrel who claims what he may not properly deserve: but it does not mean that there are not perils for the Lowlands if I choose to oppose him."

Anne waited for Isabella to continue.

"For the moment, child," she said, "I counsel patience. You could go elsewhere, of course. Perhaps you could throw yourself upon the up-timers, with whom France has formerly been at war. You could journey to Denmark or Sweden, I suppose, or to your mother's family in Vienna. But *all* of those journeys, and *all* of those places, are more dangerous than remaining here in our court. Vienna especially: it is in peril from the Turks, who are an enemy even more dangerous than your brother-in-law.

"Instead, however, should you accept my advice and wait and settle here with us, your safety could be assured. Gaston is not so foolish as to take up arms against the Netherlands: he has more than enough trouble as it is. But he *is* foolish enough to misstep in some way. In the meanwhile, we will prepare a proper royal welcome for your child, one that will be acceptable and suitable to the other crowned heads of Europe."

"You want me to wait."

"Yes."

"Until Gaston makes some mistake."

"That's right, child," Isabella said. "And he will: it is abundantly clear that he is a far better schemer than monarch, and while one can be both, when one chooses the latter role, the former should recede into the background. That will *never* happen.

"What is more—and I realize this is trite, and requires even further trust on your part—there are things taking place beyond this palace, beyond this city, of which you are not aware. Our course is jeopardized, and so is yours, unless we are prudent and patient.

"Whatever recognition the infant deserves, you already possess a dignity and honor that no scheming can remove," Isabella continued. "Your son is a Bourbon prince—and a Hapsburg one as well."

For the first time in the interview, Isabella smiled. She looked directly and beckoned at the duchess of Chevreuse, who held the still-sleeping baby, dressed in a fine little gown with a golden circlet on his head. "Let me see the boy."

She walked forward; Isabella extended her arms to receive him. When the child was placed in her arms, his eyes opened and he looked up at the archduchess.

"*Dieudonné*," she said. "A gift of God. And what a world you are born into, little one; duplicitous uncles and a Ring of Fire. Yet if God is generous, then your sun shall rise."

The baby gazed up beatifically at his great aunt, waving his right arm, partially held in place by the swaddling; he freed it, and reached up toward Isabella's nose.

And then, as so frequently happens, he began to cry.

Chapter 45

Paris

The day had begun sultry and hot, the buildings in Paris baking and then spreading the heat to the cobblestoned and paved streets. Terrye Jo had known hot summers in Grantville, especially before the Ring of Fire; there were days that it was almost too hot to move, even toward the end of the school year—when Ms. Maddox would get them out on the track or in the field to sweat their asses off running or playing soccer or baseball; but there were plenty of places to cool down too, down by Buffalo Creek and elsewhere, and a few places with air conditioning or big fans that blew the air around at least.

In Paris, down-time, there was no escape. No air conditioning, no portable fans, and flies for all the usual reasons—especially down by the Seine.

The rooms that Monsieur—now King—Gaston had set aside for her had a sort of covered patio that gave a pretty good view of the Rue Saint-Antoine without the smells and the flies. There was usually a breeze, and she'd arranged for a little trestle table to be put out there.

Artemisio and Georges had both been a little surprised by the idea, and her manservant Daniel had been shocked almost to the point of making her want to dismiss him. By the end of the first week it was where they usually met and did a lot of their work that didn't involve direct operation of the equipment. It was *score one for the up-timer*.

All morning she had been working on a design for an improved receiver, one that might pick up audio as well as telegraph signals. There were a half-dozen books spread out along with a block of cheap paper and a half-dozen pencils, rulers and protractors and all the rest, and a nice bottle of wine and three glasses: one half-full that she'd used and two empty ones turned upside down. She was working her way through a badly written description from a nineteenth-century telegraphy book when she heard Daniel clear his throat. She was dimly aware that he may have done it a few times before she noticed.

"Mademoiselle," he said when she turned to look at him. "There is a gentleman to see you."

It was their agreed-upon code. A *gentleman* wasn't the king, the queen, their daughter—who actually turned up all the time to see the wondrous up-time wizardry—or King Gaston's agent, the count of Soissons. It was someone important, but no one from the palace.

"Anyone we know?"

"His Excellency the ambassador from the USE."

"Colonel Hand is here—to see me?"

"He said that it was somewhat urgent, mademoiselle. If you are busy I can—"

"No, no. Send him up at once. You didn't...already make him wait a while before telling me, did you?" Daniel did that sometimes, telling her that it was a common strategy in gentle households when the visitor had no appointment, in order to make sure he understood the importance of the host's time.

"Not His Excellency the ambassador, mademoiselle. He...I should not think he would be much pleased with such behavior."

Daniel's reaction showed more than a touch of fear. He did not continue, but also didn't show any sign of leaving.

"Well?"

Just then he seemed to realize that he'd already been given instructions. "Yes, mademoiselle," he said, backing away from the door to the patio. "Right away, mademoiselle."

Terrye Jo hadn't been expecting visitors: she was in work pants and a blouse with the sleeves pinned back—no cravat, no doublet, no jacket and a pair of slippers instead of her usual boots.

It'll have to do, she thought.

After a moment Colonel Erik Haakonson Hand appeared by the door. Daniel, still looking a bit intimidated, said, "Mademoiselle. His Excellency Colonel Hand."

"Very good, Daniel. You may go."

The servant seemed quite pleased with the idea of going and quickly left the two of them alone on the patio.

"Colonel Hand," Terrye Jo said, standing and

extending a hand, which the Swede took. "Great to see you. What brings you here to Spacely Sprockets?"

"Eh?" he answered, his brows furrowed. It was an up-timer expression—*another* up-timer expression—and he thought he knew what she meant but couldn't be sure. "I . . . Miss Tillman. Have you had any other visitors this morning?"

"No. Nobody. I mean, the crew has been around; I sent Georges Cordonnier to Les Halles for a few items, but no real visitors."

"Good. I . . . Miss Tillman, I think you should gather your things together and come to the embassy at once."

"Why?"

"Questions, questions. You are in danger, and it is my charge to make sure you are not harmed."

"I'm in *danger*? Why? I'm just a telegraph operator. A damn good one, I'll admit, but that's it."

"No," Hand said. "That is *not* 'it.' You are a telegraph operator, that is true—one who has sent and received a number of sensitive messages while in the employ of Gaston of Orléans. I have heard a rumor to the effect that someone at the Louvre, perhaps Gaston himself, has ordered your arrest."

"Why would he do that? I haven't—I mean, I don't talk out of school—"

"Desperate men do desperate things, Miss Tillman. I cannot compel you to come with me, but I really must insist. The reason he would do it is not because of what you might have done, but about what you might yet do. Gaston—"

"The king knows I don't—"

Hand stepped close to her and said quietly, "that's the nub of it, Miss Tillman. He is, or might not be,

the king. There is a broadsheet that is circulating
through Paris just slightly faster than Gaston's servants can take it down. The Lady Anne, the queen
dowager, has issued a statement supporting the claim
of her baby son to the throne, and accuses Gaston
of being the motive force behind the actions of her
husband's murderer."

"And does she say who that might be?"

"César de Vendôme, Gaston's half-brother."

"So why doesn't—"

"Why doesn't Gaston simply arrest Vendôme? He
can't. Apparently that prince is in the company of
Anne herself."

"She has her husband's murderer *with her*, wherever
she is? That's pretty damn weird."

"She is in Brussels, a guest of the dowager archduchess Isabella," Hand said. "And yes, it is very strange.
Accusations and counter-accusations are erupting all
over the city."

Terrye Jo turned away and looked out across the
Rue Saint-Antoine, as if somehow she could see those
accusations running down the sunbaked streets.

"You think I am personally in danger."

"Miss Tillman, at least a week ago Cardinal de
Tremblay, one of Cardinal Richelieu's closest advisors, disappeared. It is rumored that he was taken to
the Châtelet. He is a public figure, a prince of the
Church; people know his name. What do you think
would happen if you ... disappeared?"

"You make this sound like Soviet Russia."

"An up-time reference I don't understand. Does
that mean you realize your danger or you are ignoring my warnings?"

"I got it," she said. "What about my people?"

"I don't think Gaston cares about them. Only about you. In fact, as I understand it, he has indicated that he mistrusts *all* up-timers." When Terrye Jo hesitated, Hand continued, "Miss Tillman, there may have been a time when his view of you was as a servant or an employee, but now he clearly perceives you as a threat. None of your subordinates have been privy to the communications that you witnessed.

"I have a carriage waiting outside, and I urge you to accompany me."

"And if this turns out to be nothing—"

"In the unlikely event that I am wrong, then I shall escort you back."

Terrye Jo Tillman had known fear before. Her short stint in the military, even though it wasn't front line duty, convinced her that this century was even more dangerous than the one she'd grown up in. Less than five years after the Ring of Fire the USE had monuments to those who had died in its service, because of the dangers that the seventeenth century presented.

But she had not been afraid since she'd begun to work for the duke of Savoy and Monsieur—now King—Gaston. It always seemed as if she was a prized commodity, an up-timer with a valuable skill, someone who would be protected and never threatened. Now, riding in a curtained, closed carriage through the streets of Paris from the Rue Saint-Antoine to the USE embassy across the river, she wondered whether she could actually be made to "disappear."

It's not too far to the embassy, she thought as they rode slowly along. Colonel Hand had told her not to open the curtains: if she could see out, someone could see in. She knew the city well enough after just a few months, though: she could hear the sounds of Les Halles and smell the stink of the Seine.

He sat opposite her in the carriage; he seemed relaxed, but she could see that he had his sidearms easily in reach.

Expecting trouble.

Then it came: the sounds of horsemen and a shout to halt the carriage in the name of the king. She began getting to her feet as the carriage lurched to a halt: but the colonel held up his good hand toward her and moved to the door, opening it and quickly closing it.

"What seems to be the trouble, monsieur?" she heard him say.

"Stand aside," came the answer. "We will inspect your carriage. There is a fugitive from justice wanted by His Majesty."

"We carry no fugitives," Hand answered. "In any case, this is a diplomatic vehicle belonging to the United States of Europe. We are not subject to your inspection."

"This is not the United States of Europe," the other said. "It will not go well with you to defy the orders of the king."

"And he is not my king," Hand answered.

Terrye Jo leaned forward and very carefully drew aside the curtain so that she could obtain a distant glimpse of the encounter. There were several mounted men, wearing the livery of gentlemen-in-waiting: this was not the Paris constabulary. Colonel Erik Haakonson Hand stood beside one of the harnessed horses, his back turned to the carriage; she could see that he had his coat drawn back and his hands were loose, though not resting either on his scabbarded sword or a holstered pistol.

"There are six of us, up-timer, and only one of you. Are you certain that you want to engage in this dance?"

"I am not an up-timer, monsieur," Hand answered levelly. "I am Colonel Erik Hand, ambassador from the court of the Emperor of the United States of Europe. I have at my belt an excellent firearm. If you don't recognize it; it is a reproduction of an up-time pistol, one of the finest weapons on the continent. With six of you, I shall have exactly enough bullets to make all of your mistresses weep at your graves. With due respect to your king, do *you* really want to engage in this dance?"

As Terrye Jo watched, Hand very slowly moved his hand toward his pistol. It was a hand-crafted repro of a Colt .45, beautifully made and no doubt in perfect working order.

If they knew what it could do, they'd think twice before taking him on. If they didn't, they'd be in for a rude surprise. Meanwhile she was sitting—hiding!—in the carriage, watching a man she already knew to be brave showing exactly what he was made of.

"Our master will be informed of your defiance."

"Present His Majesty with my compliments as well," Hand said, his tone never changing. "May we pass?"

After a few moments she saw them turn and gallop away. She let the curtain drop into place and leaned back in her seat; presently the door opened and Hand climbed back up into the carriage. He rapped on the ceiling and it began to move slowly out onto the bridge.

"That was a hell of a bluff," she said.

"You were watching."

There was no point in denying it. "And listening. Do you really think you could have taken them all?"

"I am an excellent shot, Miss Tillman. But to be honest—no, I expect that I would not. That's not the point, though, as I'm sure you realize. It was about whether they thought I could, and whether any of them as an individual was willing to take that chance."

"That's a huge risk."

"Not really. Since I've come to Paris, I have been observing the men in Gaston's royal guard. A number of them are recently promoted—many of those who served King Louis left or were dismissed. I have seen very few that seem like the type that would willingly risk life and limb for this king. But what would you have me do? Either they respect diplomatic immunity or they don't. It was up to them to decide what the consequences might be, and they decided it was better to complain about my actions than to risk their lives. Happens all the time on the battlefield."

"This wasn't exactly a battlefield, of course."

Hand half-smiled. "I disagree. Of course it was—just not the same kind. I think we've just chosen sides, and it'll be up to Gustav and the council to decide if I've done the right thing. But I was ordered to get you to safety, and I'll be damned if some puffed-up French gentlemen were going to keep me from doing it."

Six months earlier, Sherrilyn had still been wondering how she'd ever get used to extended travel on horseback. But after the amount of time she'd spent in the saddle over the last few months, she realized that she actually *had* gotten used to it. The other rangers didn't even smirk as she dismounted, still feeling every mile in her bad knee.

It had taken them six days riding at speed, sleeping too little and pushing their mounts too hard, to cover the distance from Pau to Paris. In the end she'd left one squad of Rangers behind with Turenne—six sharp-shooters and six loaders—leaving her with thirty-six men to escort the comte de Brassac, Monsieur Servien and Brassac's three manservants along the route.

Brassac had a nobleman's experience and endur-ance, though Sherrilyn had had her doubts at the outset. For his part, Servien was very resilient for a man who looked as if he'd spent most of his life behind a desk. The servants—especially the footman and the clerk—had a rough time of it, and even the gentleman-usher, or whatever he was, didn't seem up to the task.

She wasn't terribly sympathetic, and neither were her troops. The comte decided that he needed to get to Paris in a hell of a hurry, and that was what they were going to do. No one seemed interested in get-ting in the way of forty-odd riders anyway.

They reached the city by night, in a steady warm drizzle that seemed to seep in everywhere. The rangers were a fairly steady lot, not really given to complaining—but after a long day's ride, mud and sweat made everyone irritable. The lead squad commander, an old veteran named Jeannin, rode up to Sherrilyn after they passed through the Porte Saint-Jacques and said, "I thought we were going to the comte's townhouse."

"He has other plans."

"Oh, *oui*? Maybe you'd like to let us know, Colonel?"

"We're going to the Hôtel du Condé. It's the home of one of the comte's friends in this secret company."

"Condé?" Jeannin cocked his head, and a stream of rain ran off it onto his buff coat. "The prince?"

"I guess so."

"Well then," the man said. "At least we'll eat well."

The Hôtel du Condé was an impressive structure, more a sort of little fortress than what Sherrilyn would have called a townhouse. She hadn't been to Paris before, and it was remarkable that there could be a private stronghold like that covering a few city blocks in the midst of shops and tenements; but it was plenty big enough for the troop to ride in through a gate into a wide courtyard. Grooms were ready to take their horses, and Brassac, his gentleman, Servien and Sherrilyn were escorted under an archway and into a mud room where they could clean off their boots and arrange themselves to meet with the prince.

They weren't kept waiting very long. Instead of being brought to an audience chamber, they were taken to a small private drawing room on the first floor, just above where they'd entered; it was decorated with hunting trophies and shields bearing the Condé arms: a blue shield with *fleurs-de-lys* crossed by a red diagonal bar. After admitting them, a servant bowed himself out and left the visitors with a middle-aged man—Prince Condé himself—who was pouring wine at a sideboard.

"*Vieux* Louis," Condé said, turning to face them. He was a striking man in middle age, trim and lean, with a carefully trimmed beard and broad moustaches. He walked across the room and embraced Brassac, who was faintly smiling. "You are too old to be riding so far in the rain."

"I am young enough," Brassac said. "May I present Monsieur Étienne Servien, who I believe you know, and Colonel Sherrilyn Maddox, who I believe you do not. His Highness insists on calling me *vieux Louis*—I have the honor to be seven years older." The comte did not introduce his gentleman, who took up a position at the sideboard, ready to pour.

"Servien," Condé said. "I understand you have some tales to tell."

"When Your Highness is disposed to hear them," Servien said.

"And Colonel Maddox." Condé looked Sherrilyn up and down. "An up-timer. You have been in the service of Marshal Turenne, as I understand."

"He found something for me to do, Sire."

"Good. But I forget my manners. Please be seated," Condé said. "I can have a fire built up for you," he said to Brassac, his stern expression betraying the slightest grin.

"I'm sweating like a pig as it is," Brassac said, taking a comfortable armchair at the prince's gesture. "But I could do with a cup of that wine."

When they were seated, Condé leaned forward, elbows on knees. "You've heard about Joseph."

"Still no word?"

"Nothing definitive. I know more than I did: he and the young guardsman d'Aubisson were taken to the Châtelet on the orders of Queen Marie, who seemed insistent on knowing whether your master is still alive." Condé nodded toward Servien.

"Is d'Aubisson—" Servien began.

"He is under the protection of this house," Condé said. "He escaped and came here to tell me what had happened. Unfortunately, he was also forced to give up certain other information."

"Such as?"

"The location of our sanctuary," Condé answered. "D'Angoumois, the prior, was none too happy to have Gaston's guards stomping around, but they seemed to have no compunction about threatening him."

"Do they know the identity of all of the Company now?"

"Regrettably, yes. But neither that information nor any other revelations by our young friend gave them the answer they really wanted—*is Cardinal Richelieu still alive?*"

"Well," Brassac said, cradling his wine-cup in his hands, "*is* he?"

"Servien?" Condé said.

"I only know that when I left his side, I did not expect to see him again in this life, Highness," Servien answered. "He was gravely wounded. I saw it happen, and I know who delivered the blow."

"So do I," Condé said. "And as I understand it, the culprit is now in the company of Queen Anne—in Brussels."

Servien's usually calm expression was broken in an instant. "Does she know?"

Sherrilyn wasn't sure she followed the exchange. "What—"

"Apparently she does," Condé said. "She knows, Colonel Maddox, that Monsieur le duc is the man who killed her husband. Of course, everyone knows it now: Gaston has caused the identity of the regicide to be declaimed from every street-corner in Paris. César de Vendôme—my cousin—is called traitor by royal decree."

"Oh," Sherrilyn said. *Well, girl, you sound pretty stupid*, she thought. *Maybe I should go hang out with the grooms.*

"Regarding Joseph. The cardinal de Tremblay," Brassac said. "Is there no information? What did d'Aubisson say?"

"He did not see him except once—when he was brought into the cell where Tremblay had been placed. He was then taken away and...questioned."

"Violently, no doubt," Brassac said.

"Nothing that a young man can't survive. Tremblay, however, is not a young man. But I still wonder at the audacity."

"We speak of Queen Marie."

"We do," Condé agreed. "And I fear the worst: that he was questioned in a way that an older man could not survive. Gaston will answer for this, *vieux Louis*, and all the rest. You have my word on it."

"Have you confronted him?"

"No, not yet. I thought to wait until you arrived. Between Vendôme's defection, the fiasco with the tercios down in Béarn, and Anne's escape to Brussels, I would think that our self-styled king should be about at the breaking point."

"He won't break," Servien said. "Sire, if you think that Monsieur Gaston will back down because of circumstance, I regret to say that you underestimate his stubbornness. He is dangerous—especially when cornered. And as long as he occupies the throne and wears the crown, he continues to enjoy power."

"There is one other thing," Condé said, looking at Sherrilyn. "Gaston has decided that up-timers are, in general, suspect. An up-timer nurse was at the birth of his nephew—the rightful king of France; Marshal Turenne employs them; and he has issued a warrant for the arrest of the up-timer whom he employed for radio transmissions."

"Who's that?"

Condé thought for a moment, then said, "I do not know the woman's full name; I saw her in passing at the coronation in Reims. Tillman, perhaps? Mademoiselle Tillman?"

"Terrye Jo Tillman?" Sherrilyn said.

"I believe that is correct. I am informed she was working in an office in the Rue Saint-Antoine."

"Damn."

"Colonel?" Brassac asked. "Do you know this person?"

Sherrilyn smiled. "In my former career I was a teacher. I taught Phys. Ed.—I had Terrye Jo in a class. She was always a slacker—she didn't want to try hard. I always had to send her off to run extra as punishment. She hated me."

"I daresay that is all in the past now," Brassac said. "Or the future. You up-timers have made simple phrases complicated."

"I don't know. That's the sort of grudge that lasts a lifetime, even if you get thrown back into the past. So—is Terrye Jo in prison now?"

"Perhaps."

"We're going to have to break her out," Sherrilyn said. "Whether she still hates me or not, no American is going to rot in a French prison because some king sees her as an enemy."

"Break her . . . Colonel," Condé said, "are you suggesting that we *attack a prison* to rescue one person?"

"Yes," Sherrilyn answered at once. The others in

the room did not respond; there was a sort of stunned silence. "What?"

"Colonel," Brassac said, "consider that I am a peer of the realm; his Highness our host is a prince of the blood; and Monsieur Servien was, until recently, an *intendant* in service with the head of the *Conseil du Roi*. We are not inclined toward—"

"Prison breaks."

"Just so."

"So you're telling me that I'm going to have to do it myself."

"No," Condé said. "We are telling you that whatever activities you found ready to hand as a member of the ... Wrecking Crew? ... are things not done by ..."

"Regular employees."

"You seem dubious," Condé said. "But yes: it is not a course of action we can pursue, and it would not reflect well upon you to act alone. Or on us."

"Fine. I get it. But what *are* we going to do?"

"*We* will do nothing. The matter is in the hands of the ambassador from the USE. If you have concerns, you should express them to him directly," Condé answered. "You will repair to the embassy at once. You may be in great danger."

"I can take care of myself."

"No, mademoiselle," Condé said, "you can not. Not against royal troops. In almost every scenario, you wind up dead or imprisoned."

"So you want me to just ... run and hide at the USE embassy."

Brassac and Condé exchanged a meaningful look.

"Yes," Condé said at last. "At least for now. I am sure that soon the ground will have shifted again."

Chapter 46

Paris

The council room was empty now; Gaston had even argued with Marguerite, who had come to console him. She did not take kindly to his harsh words, for which he would have to apologize later. He had not meant to be hurtful, but it was easier to lash out than to contain himself, even with the one person in whom he could completely place his trust.

He had ordered the heavy curtains parted so he could look out across Paris, but after a short while he had caused them to be closed again. There was nothing there to see.

"Everyone has turned against the king," he said to no one in particular. "Everyone has turned against me."

"Not everyone."

He turned to see his mother, who had come into the council chamber; behind, two of his gentlemen-ushers stood helplessly, as if to indicate that there was nothing they could have done to prevent this force of nature from sweeping past them and into the room where the king stood, despite strict orders that he was not to be disturbed.

"I would prefer to be alone," he said.

"We both know that's not true," Marie de Medici said. She stood with her hands folded in front of her, her expression demure. He recognized the stance and the expression—it was what she used when she wanted to be persuasive.

He was unmoved. "Madame, I believe that I am the best judge of my moods, and as I am your king—"

"*Cher* Gaston—"

"I think that 'Your Majesty' is a more appropriate address," he interrupted.

She looked down at her hands, which she had unfolded and she now held at her sides, her hands forming fists.

"As you wish, Sire. But I would counsel you at this time. I have not turned against you, and I never would do so."

"Of course you would not. And neither would the queen, and neither would my sweet daughter. But I am betrayed by many others, and I must consider what is best for France. I think that is best done alone."

"You are the best judge of that...Your Majesty," she said, looking up at him again. Her hands had folded again. "I would remind you, though, that there are few situations that have no precedent. Your father and brother both dealt with internal strife and wars abroad."

"And both were murdered for their trouble: one by a lunatic and the other by a traitor."

"I know," Marie said. "I was there for the act of the first, and I am painfully familiar with the character of the second—no spawn of my loins, I will remind

Your Highness. He was not to be trusted. He was *never* to be trusted."

"So it seems."

"I have heard a rumor that he has pledged his loyalty to Anne and the bastard whelp," Marie said. "The foolish child, to let such a man be at all close to her."

"It's true." Gaston rubbed his eyes and the bridge of his nose. "My brother's murderer and my brother's treasonous wife have made common cause with each other, and sit at table with the archduchess Isabella. It would not be so bad, but we have stumbled into a war with Spain.

"I must find a way out of this labyrinth, Mother."

"I can help—"

"I must find my way alone."

"That is not the path a wise king chooses, Gaston. Sire," she added, almost as an afterthought. "Councilors and advisors—"

"Have all *betrayed me*," Gaston said savagely. Marie stepped back almost as if struck. With anger in his voice he continued, "It is as if a foul poison has crept into the very air of Paris and infested the stones of the palace. It is as if the coming of the Ring of Fire is the manifestation of the Devil Himself come to Earth, and all of his evil works are being spread through the accursed up-timers.

"Some people think this is a new age of wonders, a golden age of creation and invention and discovery. But it is all deviltry, just as my Spanish cousin Philip believes. It is like a banquet turned to ashes in my mouth. An up-timer attended Anne's birth. Up-timers serve with the rebel Marshal Turenne. They conspire with enemies of France around every corner, under every rock, in every valley and atop every hill. I will *drive them from my realm*. Do you hear me, Mother? I will cleanse this land of all of its contagions: traitors, up-timers, heretics, and those who are unfaithful to the realm. To *my* realm.

"Are you listening to me?" he finished angrily, his finger pointing directly at his mother.

She hesitated, not sure what to say, and he took another step forward, making her step backward again, almost stumbling.

"If you love and serve me as you say, answer me now!" he shouted, his face suffused with anger.

"I . . . listen and hear, Sire," she said, stepping backward again, and then without a further word she offered the slightest of curtseys and hurried out of the room, passing between the gentlemen-ushers, who still stood at the doorway, unsure whether to stay or go.

For his part, Gaston stood stiffly in place, his finger still pointing at the spot where his mother had been standing. He wanted to shout, to pound the table, to pick up something and hurl it—but he did none of those things as he took deep breaths, trying to leash his anger.

This is what it means to be king, he thought. *This. To be mastered by events and to be betrayed by everyone who claims to serve you.*

This is what you have wanted all of your life—what was denied you by accident of birth, what was withheld from you by a devil in a red soutane. This—crown and scepter, throne and court and title.

"Begone," he said at last to the gentlemen-ushers. "And if you admit any person save my wife or daughter, I will have you drawn and quartered."

❖   ❖   ❖

The last instructions Colonel Hand gave to Terrye Jo before leaving for the palace was: "Do not, under any circumstances, leave the embassy."

She didn't have to ask why. The embassy was, or was supposed to be, sovereign territory of the USE; invading the place was like declaring war. But a troop of royal guards, thirty or more, had assembled on the street outside the main entrance. They hadn't tried to pass the gates or come into the courtyard, but they'd formed a cordon along the street. Hand had given orders for all of the other entrances to be locked and barred—no tradesmen would be arriving today, no servants would be leaving.

They were, effectively, under siege.

The USE's ambassador had received a summons that morning from a delegation led by a priest. He had seemed very haughty, greeting Colonel Hand with the most minimal politeness in the foyer of the embassy. Terrye Jo had been upstairs on the balcony watching the exchange; the priest had glanced up and caught her eye and his frown had turned into a sort of cruel smile, the sort that teenage boys used to get when they had a trapped animal, a fox or raccoon, and there was no one around to tell them not to mistreat it.

She didn't like being the trapped animal, so she returned the gaze with her best infantrywoman stare, imagining that she had a rifle trained on his forehead. It wasn't much, but it was enough to make him look away.

"You were supposed to remain in your chambers," Hand told her when he came up the stairs, parchment in hand.

"Yeah, well. Curious."

"I think you unnerved him."

"Good."

"I believe I agree with you. But it doesn't matter." He held up the document. "Whatever the case, I have been summoned to the Louvre and an audience with His Highness. I was told that it would go much easier for everyone if I surrendered you."

"I hope you told him to go to hell."

"I did not," Hand said. He smiled. "Not in so many words. Not because I did not wish to say so, but it was inappropriate to address a man of the cloth thus—especially one of royal blood."

"That was a *prince*?"

"Gaston Henri de Bourbon, Bishop of Metz. We have previously made each other's acquaintance. He is half-brother to the king—a legitimized bastard."

"I didn't like how he looked at me."

"You are not the only one to express that emotion, Miss Tillman. He was in obscurity until Gaston took the throne and summoned him to the *Conseil du Roi*; I believe that he wishes to be made a cardinal."

"So he asked you to hand me over and you told him no. Is that why you're being called to the palace?"

"To be honest I'm not sure that is the extent of it. The summons demands that I provide an account of the activities of *all* up-timers in the realm—an obviously impossible task—and explain why all citizens of the USE should not be expelled."

"This is because I worked for—"

"No, no, Miss Tillman. This is only partially about you, as I say. There is some greater thing at work here."

"That's diplomatically vague."

"Miss Tillman." He stood straight and clicked his heels. "I am, after all, a diplomat."

Chapter 47

Paris

Erik Hand did not go to the Louvre with great confidence about the outcome. His previous—indeed, his only—interaction with King Gaston had been peremptory. *Rude, actually,* he noted: Gaston had insisted that the USE was harboring a fugitive queen whom he had characterized as a traitor to the crown.

What he had believed—but could not be certain of—was that the USE knew nothing of Queen Anne's whereabouts. He had told Gaston exactly that, but he'd as much as been called a liar to his face. The emperor, Hand's cousin, had been enraged by the king's imputations and Hand did not doubt that Gustav would have been willing to send his cavalry on a punitive raid into French territory to avenge the insult.

In the instance, cooler heads had prevailed—that would have been everyone else in the room—and no raid had materialized.

And, of course, Hand had been right. Anne was in

Brussels with the Eternal Archduchess. Clearly Gaston would not be interested in revisiting that battlefield—there was nothing there for him but acrimony and embarrassment.

The king of France had something else in mind: whatever had made him want to arrest the young woman who was now sheltered in the USE embassy.

He'd known that he had done the right thing when he had refused to turn her over to soldiers of the king. Whatever she had done—and he expected that it truly was nothing at all—he wasn't going to subject her to any species of royal justice coming from the Louvre. If that meant that there would be consequences for the USE, then so be it. His cousin Gustav II Adolf had told him to seize the high ground and hold it.

And by God, he would do so.

"His Excellency, the ambassador for the United States of Europe."

Colonel Hand walked slowly through the open doors and into the great audience hall. Dozens of people—perhaps a few hundred—were in attendance, more than he'd ever seen at a royal levee. At the far end of the room Gaston sat on an elevated throne; the queen's seat was empty, and the place usually occupied by the duc de Vendôme was also vacant—no one had taken his place.

Hand made his way slowly toward the king. The others in the chamber stepped to the side as he approached, like the parting of a wave. The room became more and more quiet.

"Ambassador Hand," Gaston said at last when Hand stood before him.

"Your Majesty."

"We appreciate your prompt attention to our summons. Do you know why you are here?"

"I am here at your command, Your Majesty."

"And why, of all people in Paris, would we choose so to command? We are obliged to call upon you as a representative of your people, well-known for their keen insight."

There was a slight titter of amusement. Hand did not turn around, but said, "I think Your Majesty makes sport of me."

"Colonel Hand," Gaston answered, "We do not require your services for the purpose of entertainment. There are many"—he gestured to the crowd in the room—"who are much more amusing than you."

Hand said nothing. He knew that Gaston would get to it eventually.

"You do not wish to oblige us," Gaston said. "Very well, Colonel Hand: we will tell *you*.

"You are now the *deputed* representative of the United States of Europe, sir, a country that did not exist five years ago prior to the event called the Ring of Fire. This country, which has spread and grown in every direction, has done more than simply upset the comity and balance of the nations of the world. It has introduced technologies and knowledge and . . . *ideas* that have never before been known.

"And at every turn, Colonel, these people—these *up-timers*—have proved themselves enemies of this country. Even now, your embassy shelters an up-timer who has betrayed our trust."

The statement made the room even more silent, if that could be possible. Still, Colonel Hand saw no reason to respond; he waited for Gaston to ask him a direct question.

He did not have to wait long.

"Do you deny this, Colonel? These are not your people—you are a subject of the Swedish crown, not an—intruder—into our world. Are *you* going to defend them?"

"Yes," Hand said after a moment. "Yes, Your Majesty, I will defend them. I am honored to represent my nation, and I am honor bound to hurl aside the calumnies that you choose to pronounce against it. What is more, the up-timer that so offends you has served you well and honorably for months, never betraying your trust—even though you have made her question that trust."

Gaston was visibly angry but did not answer.

"I do not understand what has brought about this acrimony, Your Majesty," Hand said. "It is impossible to deny that your nation and mine have come to blows as enemies, and that many brave men have died in these conflicts. But that time is *past*. We do not consider France an enemy. We have no desire to interfere in its internal affairs.

"If up-timers have found employment or involvement in the society of this great kingdom, it is with the blessing and the encouragement of the government of the USE—but no permission has been required. They have come to France on their own, not as agents of our government."

"You dissemble with us, Colonel."

"You call me a liar," Hand said.

"Not a liar," he answered. "Misinformed at the best, and badly directed at the worst."

"A distinction without a difference," Hand responded. "And one further thing, Your Majesty. If *ideas* are crossing the border, there is nothing that you, or anyone, can do about it. If that is what truly angers you, there is nothing that *I* can do about it.

"And there is nothing *you* can do about it either."

He bowed and turned away, walking slowly and deliberately out of the audience hall. He waited for something to happen, or for Gaston—or anyone else—to say a word. But nothing ever came.

The King's Guardsmen at the entrance to the USE embassy had been instructed how to deal with anyone seeking to depart, and were particularly on the lookout for Terrye Jo Tillman—they even had a sketch of her face and a description. They were not so sure what to do when a group approached with the intention of *entering* the embassy—particularly a well-armed group.

Thus, when Maddox's Rangers—not identified as such: merely a well-armed few dozen soldiers moving at a steady pace down the street—approached the gate to the embassy, the commander of the royal troops consulted with his two subalterns and then withdrew from their path. The rangers never stopped moving until they came to the gate; after a short discussion which the commander did not overhear, they were admitted, the gate closing behind them.

Terrye Jo was standing on the balcony when the soldiers entered the embassy. She had not heard any fighting or gunfire outside, so it was apparent that they had not attacked: they were admitted as friends. It was quickly apparent why.

"Ms. Maddox?" she said, and the leader of the soldiers looked up from the foyer to see her standing above.

"Miss Tillman," Sherrilyn said. She couldn't help but smile. "Terrye Jo. I'd heard you were in Paris."

"And I heard you were working for some French marshal."

There was a long, awkward silence, during which the servant that admitted them had a worried look on his face—as if, somehow, allowing armed up-timers into the embassy hadn't been such a good idea after all.

Then Sherrilyn Maddox smiled and began climbing the stairs. Terrye Jo walked down and they met a bit below halfway; she offered her hand to her old teacher, who took it warmly.

"You don't hold any old grudges, I hope."

"Nah," Terrye Jo said. "That was hundreds of years from now. You look good, Ms. Maddox."

"Sherrilyn."

"I'll have to get used to that. But after the other stuff I've had to get used to, that should be easy. What brings you to Paris—and to the embassy?"

"Orders. I've been told that it's not safe for up-timers in Paris at the moment, and that I should come and hide in the embassy."

"I was told the same thing. I think I believe it."

"I'm glad to see you," Sherrilyn said, glancing back at her troop, which was watching the scene closely. "I was told that I wouldn't be allowed to break you out of prison."

"I wasn't in—"

"Well, I didn't know that. When I said that I was going to do it, I got all of the excuses you can imagine why I shouldn't. So now I don't have to disobey orders, or cause a diplomatic incident, or anything like that."

"You'd have done that for me?"

"I'd have done that for anyone from Grantville. From what I've heard about prisons in this century—"

"I saw one." Terrye Jo looked away, thinking for a moment about Miolans. "No thanks. I guess I'm stuck here as long as King Gaston is angry at me. The problem is—I didn't do anything wrong. I'm just a radio operator."

"As I told you," Erik Hand said, entering the foyer and looking around at the Rangers standing on all sides, "this was not about you, Miss Tillman."

He removed his hat and stripped off his gloves, tossing them to the servant. "It is about arrogance and fear and a dangerous view of the world."

"Ms. Ma— Sherrilyn. Let me introduce Colonel Erik Haakonson Hand, our ambassador to France. He's the guy who brought me here and told me to stay put."

"I see you have obeyed me," Hand said. He walked to the foot of the stair; the two up-timers descended to stand on the level with him.

"I didn't really have much choice."

"In the last few years," Hand said, "I have been surprised to see how often up-timers do things even when they 'have no choice.' If we want to talk about something unavoidable, let us discuss *my* orders from my cousin the Emperor. He told me to 'seize the high ground and hold it.'"

"Meaning?" Terrye Jo asked.

"Meaning, Miss Tillman, that when Gaston d'Orleans, king of France—"

"So he says," Sherrilyn interrupted, and a number

of the Rangers murmured agreement. Hand turned around and looked; evidently his glance was enough to silence them.

"Gaston d'Orleans," he repeated, "king of France, saw fit to accuse up-timers of being enemies of his country. Not just you, Miss Tillman, or even you, Colonel Maddox, but *every* up-timer. As for those of us who make common cause..." he placed his hand on his breast and gave a slight bow. "We are complicit as well."

"What did you tell him?"

Hand smiled. "I expressed my surprise at this position, I rejected his accusations, and I turned my back and walked out."

Sherrilyn whistled through her teeth. "That must've gone over like a lead balloon."

Hand paused for a moment, considering the phrase, and then said, "I did not stay to hear the king's reaction. But no one stopped me from leaving the audience hall, or the Louvre. I was not forced to defend my person with my ceremonial sword or my one good arm."

"So what happens next?" Terrye Jo asked.

"You leave the country," Hand answered. "I was not sure how we would be able to guarantee your safety, but I think a solution has presented itself. Colonel Maddox, your government prevails upon you for a favor—to escort Miss Tillman back to the USE."

"Wait—" Terrye Jo said. "Wait. You're *sending me home*?"

"I am trying to protect you from conflict which is surely coming," Hand said. "At any time, King Gaston may decide to attack this embassy and provoke war with the United States of Europe. There is no way your safety can be guaranteed."

"I didn't ask for a guarantee, Colonel. And I can take care of myself."

"I tried to use that line too," Sherrilyn said. "They sent me here."

"I'm not running home," Terrye Jo said. She put her hands on her hips and stared defiantly at Colonel Hand and Sherrilyn Maddox.

"You are being foolhardy and headstrong," Hand said. "I would not tolerate such insolence from you if you were my daughter."

"Then it's a damn good thing you're not my father," she snapped back. "My father is Joe Tillman, and he taught me how to use a rifle. He also taught me that when things got hairy it was time to stand up, not time to run."

"Brave words."

"I'm an *American*," Terrye Jo said. "Gaston doesn't scare me, and neither do the people working for him."

Hand sighed. "I cannot force you to leave."

"You're damn right you can't. I guess you'd better think of something else."

Gaston could not readily refuse an interview with a prince of the blood, even after the public rebuff from the Swede. He did not particularly want to converse with the prince de Condé: the older man had never especially favored him.

He was determined to make the interview short, and decided to have him present himself in the garden. The day had been sultry and humid; no one would want to spend more than a few minutes there. He waited in an arbor, where at least they would be out of direct sunlight.

"Your Majesty," Condé said when he was announced. He bowed, and Gaston nodded distantly, as if it was no more than a tiring formality.

"Cousin. To what do I owe the honor of your visit?"

"I need the answer to a particular question, Sire."

"Please ask."

"Where is Cardinal de Tremblay?"

Gaston frowned. He had been expecting some comment on his exchange with the irritating Colonel Hand, or an inquiry about the announcement by Archduchess Isabella regarding the traitor queen, or something to do with César.

"I have not seen that villain since the coronation, Henri. Why would he possibly interest you?"

"He is missing."

"As far as I know, he vacated the palace, apparently along with much of the devil cardinal's effects, and has scarcely been heard of since. My mother complains no end about it. I think she simply didn't like finding cat hair everywhere."

"I rather think it is more than that, Sire. He was taken to the Grand Châtelet."

"How do you know that?"

"My source is impeccable. He was treated most roughly, and has not emerged. I wish to know what has been done with him, and if he is still alive."

"The Grand Châtelet, you say."

"Yes, Sire," Condé said patiently. "In the dark of night."

"And you know this because..."

"A young man in his service, formerly a Cardinal's

Guard, was taken with him. The young man escaped and came to my hôtel and told me the story."

Gaston frowned. "I have no love for the members of that regiment," he said, "but I have given no such orders. I did not know that there were any of them left in the city."

"You did not order Tremblay's arrest, then."

"I believe I just said that, Henri. Is it necessary that I repeat things in a loud voice so you can hear it?"

Condé bit back a reply, and tried to determine whether Gaston was telling the truth, or simply dismissing the inquiry and turning it back with a lie.

"No, Sire," he said. "I heard you. I can therefore assume that your lady mother was acting on her own volition."

Gaston's frown deepened. "My...lady mother arrested Père Joseph? And had him placed in the Châtelet?"

"Some days past. Nothing has been heard from him since."

"She has not spoken to me of this," Gaston said. He looked around the arbor, then back at Condé. "I care little for this old monk, whether the refugee Holy Father gave him his biretta or not. But I am *not* pleased to hear that she takes such matters into her own hands without consulting me."

"I am gratified to hear that answer, Your Majesty."

"And, Henri...why do *you* care about him?"

"We are long acquainted, my king. It is as you say—unless by your royal command, no one should be unjustly imprisoned. I would ask that you inquire of Queen Marie what she has done with him."

Gaston walked past Condé toward the gate that led out of the garden and back into the palace corridor.

Then he turned and faced his cousin. "Oh, yes, cousin. I will ask her about that, and—I suspect—far more besides."

Without another word he passed between two servants, ignoring their bows, and disappeared back into the Louvre.

Even under siege, the embassy was reasonably well provisioned—though the presence of more than twenty of Sherrilyn Maddox's command strained the USE's hospitality. Still, it was better fare than Terrye Jo had been accustomed to, even with a serving staff.

After dinner, they sat in the library, looking at the broadsheets and proclamations. The royal pronouncement on the treason of the duc de Vendôme, for the murder of King Louis, was still prominent, as were accounts of the action of Archduchess Isabella of the Netherlands, standing as godmother to the late king's son—though there were comments doubting the parentage of the baby.

"That cannot stand the light of day," Colonel Hand said. "The little prince's parentage can't be questioned at this point."

"Why not?" Terrye Jo asked. "That would take away any threat."

"True," Hand said, laying the paper down on a table beside his armchair. "But then the question must be asked: why did he raise no objection months ago, when it was announced that Her Majesty Queen Anne was with child? They rang the bells. All of the churches all over France rang their bells. They would not ring them for a *bastard*."

"Well," Sherrilyn said, "if they didn't know—"

"Insofar as anyone is concerned," Hand interrupted, "the child is the issue of King Louis and Queen Anne. That was not challenged in the winter or the spring—it is too late to challenge it now. What remains is whether King Gaston is heir to his brother's throne, or a usurper sitting in place of a child now in exile in Brussels.

"But I have another question for you, Colonel Maddox. I suspect it is related to this entire question, but I'm really not sure."

"Ask away."

"What is an 'elvis'?"

Sherrilyn looked at Terrye Jo, and the two women laughed at once. "That's an interesting question," she said after a moment. Hand looked offended, then just baffled.

"I informed President Piazza of the—encounter—at the Louvre, and about King Gaston's general mood. He said—" Hand reached into a note-case and drew out a telegraph blank. "Let me quote. 'King is worried because CR'—by which he means Cardinal Richelieu—'may be pulling an elvis.' Do you have any idea what an elvis may be? And what he means by that expression?"

They laughed again, making Hand frown again. "Did I say something amusing?"

"Elvis is not a thing," Terrye Jo managed after a moment. "It's a person. A—a singer. An entertainer. Elvis Presley. He died before I was born, except that for a long time after, people reported seeing him."

"Singing and . . . entertaining?"

"No. In all kinds of places doing all kinds of things. Except he was already dead. There was a big museum and everything—"

"Graceland," Sherrilyn said.

"Graceland?" Hand said.

"Graceland," Terrye Jo continued. "People came from all over to his house, to walk through the museum and see all of his records and awards and everything. But there were always rumors that he hadn't actually died. Even at the Ring of Fire people believed that Elvis was still alive somewhere."

"Miss Tillman," Hand said. "That is by any description the most *ridiculous* thing I have ever heard. But I suppose I should be accustomed to such things by now.

"So—let me see. To the original message—Mr. Piazza is suggesting that His Eminence Richelieu is . . . Elvis? He's dead, but people believe he is alive?"

"I think that's what he's trying to say," Terrye Jo said. "But he really is dead, isn't he?"

"Perhaps. But his body has not been found: I have learned from a reliable source that there was a memorial mass at his home church of Luçon, attended by the remaining members of the Cardinal's Guard. There was no body there either."

"Elvis," Sherrilyn said. "Maybe Elvis is still alive. Still in the building."

"*Still in the building*," Hand said. "Yes. Indeed. I think it is possible that the cardinal is, as you say, still in the building—still alive, despite everything. And it worries King Gaston. More than that, Richelieu was friendly with up-timers resident in France; that explains, at least in part, why he has become so hostile to them.

"In fact," he continued, "it explains a great deal. But the question remains—is Richelieu alive? Is he?"

"No one knows," Sherrilyn said. "Does your 'reliable source' know, do you think?"

Hand shrugged.

"I wish we knew. Fighting a battle without proper information is dangerous."

"This is not a battle," Terrye Jo said.

"Oh, yes it is," Sherrilyn said. "It's the first battle of a civil war, and it might bring the USE into it. The Spanish and the Netherlands and—what, Savoy—and who else, England?

"And Elvis is out there somewhere."

Epilogue

On a road outside Soissons

As Simon Cordonnier made his way along the path that ran next to the small river, he spotted something floating in the water. Curious—the day's journey had been easy enough but uneventful to the point of boredom—he bent down and reached out with his walking-stick to try and catch whatever it was. For a moment, he came close to losing his footing in the mud, but he managed to snag the parcel and bring it to shore.

The parcel was large and wrapped in brown cloth, tied together with string. It was soaked, of course. Cordonnier could see that the string had gotten torn, probably on a sharp rock. He thought there might have been a weight attached to the parcel by the string, at one point. When it broke, the submerged parcel could have been brought to the surface by the current.

Now more curious than ever, he carried the parcel across the field to a stump, where he could sit down and examine it closely. It was the work of less than a minute to untie what was left of the string and open the cloth. Within . . .

He was quite astonished. The parcel contained very fine garments, dyed red and made of watered silk, though they had seen better days: they were torn and soiled in places. A robe of some kind and an odd-looking hat—a four-peaked cap with a sort of tuft or ball at the top. He turned the hat over and over in his hands. It looked very much like a biretta, the headwear of a cardinal of the Universal Church.

Or so it appeared, at least. He'd never been close enough to a cardinal to really examine his clothing. But it certainly looked like a biretta.

But if so, who would have thrown away such well-made and valuable garments? And why?

Whatever the reasons might be, however, they were certainly none of his concern. Probably some political matter, or something involving high affairs of the Church—and a serious one. Either way, not for the likes of a humble shoemaker to question. Perhaps, if Georges was able to come home in the summer, he could ask him about it.

He thought of wrapping the parcel up and throwing it back in the river. But . . .

They really were very fine garments. Whoever had discarded them certainly wouldn't be looking for them any longer, after all, and what was damaged could be repaired by his wife, who was a fine seamstress. The parcel wasn't too heavy to carry easily if he tied it onto the end of his walking stick. That way come sundown it would have dried and become even lighter.

Two minutes later he was back on the road, heading for home.

Cast of Characters

Adret, Seth ben—Jewish businessman in Marseilles.

Amelia, Sister—Nun of the Order of St. Victor, resident at La Garde in Marseilles. Friend of Sherrilyn Maddox.

Angennes, Charles II de, Marquis de Rambouillet—A royal officer and soldier, the husband of the salonnière Madame de Rambouillet.

Angoumois, Phillippe d'—Abbot of the Capuchins in Paris, one of the founders of the Company of the Blessed Sacrament.

Aubisson, Jean d'—A member of the Cardinal's Guard.

Baldaccio, Umberto—"Dottore"; alchemist and scholar in service to Duke Victor Amadeus.

Bassompiere, François de—Courtier and Marshal of France. Involved in the plot against Richelieu on the "Day of Dupes"; arrested and imprisoned.

Beringhien, Henri de—Squire and valet to the King.

Borja y Velasco, Gaspar de—Cardinal, Spain's ambassador to the Holy See; currently leading a revolt against Papal authority.

Bourbon, Christine Marie de—Louis XIII's sister, Duchess of Savoy, married to Victor Amadeus.

Bourbon, Gaston Henri de—Illegitimate son of Henry IV, bishop of Metz.

Bourbon, Gaston Jean-Baptiste de, Duc d'Orleans—"Monsieur." Younger brother of Louis XIII, heir to the French throne.

Bourbon, Louis de—King Louis XIII of France.

Brassac et de Béarn, Louis de Galard de—Seigneur de Semoussac. The Superior of the Company of the Blessed Sacrament.

Brassac, Alexandre de—Baron de la Rochebeaucourt, de Salles et de Genté. Son of Louis de Brassac.

Bullion, Claude de—Minister of Finance under Louis XIII.

Caussin, Nicolas—Jesuit confessor to Louis XIII.

Chavigny, Léon Bouthillier, Comte de—Diplomat and Secretary of State; originally attached to Richelieu. Later chancellor to Gaston d'Orleans and an intermediary between the two men.

Condé, Prince of, Henri de Bourbon—A prince of the blood, second cousin to Louis XIII. Married to Charlotte Marguerite de Montmorency.

Cordonnier, Georges—Telegrapher in Paris; "GJBF."

Cordonnier, Simon—Shoemaker in Soissons. Georges Cordonnier's father.

Corneille, Pierre—Poet and playwright. Spy for Richelieu.

Crussol, François, Duke de Uzès—Gentleman in ordinary to Queen Anne.

De la Mothe-Houdancourt, Phillippe de, Comte— Cavalry commander in service to Turenne.

Du Lude, Gaspard de Daillon—Bishop, later Archbishop of Albi.

Durant, Henri—Radio operator at Castello del Valentino, Turin.

Durant, Sylvie—Radio operator at Castello del Valentino, Turin.

Épernon, Jean Louis, Duc de Nogaret de Valette d'— Soldier, participated in the persecution of the Huguenots in Guienne under la Louis XIII.

Étampes de Valençay, Achille de—Soldier; Knight of Malta, captain of Light Horse; brother of Bishop Léonore and of Jacques, Lord of Valençay, Governor of Calais and Knight of the Holy Spirit.

Étampes de Valençay, Léonore de—Bishop of Chartres.

Gaisson, Colonel Jean de—Turenne's commander of infantry.

Glauber, Johann Rudolf—Alchemist and chemist, in service with Turenne. Inventor of advanced and safe, non-poisonous percussion caps for Turenne's weapons.

Gondi, Jean-François—Archbishop of Paris.

Hand, Erik Haakonson, Colonel—Veteran soldier; cousin of Gustav II Adolf, new ambassador at the court of France.

Hapsburg, Doña Ana Maria Mauricia—"Anne of Austria," Queen of France.

Hapsburg, Fernando—Cardinal-Infante, Governor and later King in the Spanish Netherlands; married to his cousin Maria Anna of Austria.

Hapsburg, Isabella Clara Eugenia—Archduchess of the Low Countries.

Hapsburg, Philip IV—King of Spain.

Jeannin, Alois—Squad commander in Maddox's Rangers.

La Tour d'Auvergne, Frédéric Maurice, Duc de Bouillon—Prince of Sedan, older brother of Turenne.

LeBarre, Jean-Baptiste—Warden of the prison in Château de Miolans in St. Pierre d'Albigny in Savoy.

Logiani, Artemisio—Turin resident, handyman and trained radio operator and technician at Castello del Valentino.

Lorraine, Marguerite de, Duchesse d'Orleans—Sister of Duke Charles of Lorraine and second wife of Gaston d'Orleans, Prince of France.

Maddox, Sherrilyn—Former physical education teacher at Grantville High, later member of Harry Lefferts' "Wrecking Crew."

Maillé-Brézé, Urbain de—Marshal of France. Brother-in-law of Richelieu.

Matewski, Katie—Part of the "Steam Engine" people; employed as a nurse for Anne of Austria.

Mazarini, Giulio Raimondo, Cardinal—In France, "Jules Mazarin." Diplomat and soldier, protégé of Richelieu and partner-by-arrangement to Anne.

Medici, Marie de—Queen-Mother, widow of Henri IV, mother of Louis XIII and Gaston.

Mirabel, Don Antonio de Zuñiga y Davila, Marquis de—Spanish ambassador in Paris.

Miro, Estuban—Spymaster for Ed Piazza.

Montausier, Charles de Sainte-Maure, Marquis de—Huguenot soldier in French service.

Noyers, François Sublet de—Intendant and later secretary of war; superintendent of the Bâtiments du Roi (the king's architectural projects).

Olivares, Gaspar de Guzmán, Count-Duke of—Chief Minister of Philip IV of Spain.

Orléans, Anne Marie Louise de, Duchesse de Montpensier—Gaston's daughter by his first wife. "La Petite Madamoiselle."

Piazza, Ed—President of the State of Thuringia-Franconia. "The Principal."

Richelieu, Armand-Jean du Plessis—Cardinal-Duke, chief minister of France.

Rohan, Marie-Aimée de, Duchesse de Chevreuse—Principal lady-in-waiting to Queen Anne.

Rubens, Pieter Paul—Painter, who also served as a diplomat both for Marie de Medici and, more recently, the Infanta Isabella.

Savoy, Victor Amadeus, Duc de—Duke of Savoy; brother-in-law of Gaston and Louis XIII; hired Grantville team to build a radio in Turin. Married to Christina Maria, daughter of Henry IV of France.

Servien, Étienne—Servant and intendant to Richelieu.

Soissons, Louis de (Bourbon)—Count of Soissons, and cousin of Louis XIII. Créature of Gaston d'Orleans.

Tillman, Terrye Jo—Radio operator; currently in the employ of Victor Amadeus, Duke of Savoy.

Tremblay, Joseph Francis LeClerc, Cardinal de (Père Joseph)—Capuchin monk, friend of Richelieu; recently made Cardinal in pectore by Pope Urban VIII.

Valbelle, Cosme II de—Seigneur de Brunelles. Head of a Marseilles noble and mercantile family.

Vasa, Gustav II Adolf—King of Sweden, Emperor of the USE, High King of the Union of Kalmar.

Vendôme, César de (Bourbon)—Louis XIII's oldest brother, légitimé de France, son of Henry IV by Gabrielle d'Estrées.

Vendôme, François de (Bourbon)—Duc de Beaufort. Louis XIII's nephew, son of César de Vendôme.

Vendôme, Louis de (Bourbon)—Duc de Mercoeur. Louis XIII's nephew, younger son of César de Vendôme.